JARADEE'S LEGACY

ALSO BY S.K. RANDOLPH

VARTERELS' UNIVERSE™

(as paperbacks)

Part I - UnFolding

1. DiMensioner's Revenge

5. ConDra's Fire

8. MasTer's Reach

10. Jaradee's Legacy

Agothany 1 (Companion Shorts 2, 3, 4, 6, 7, and 9)

Part II - CoaleScence

11. Incirrata Secret

13. Corps Stones

16. Mocendi's Gambit

19. Queen's Quest

Agothany 2 (Companion Shorts 12, 14, 15, 17, 18, and 20)

Part III - Quickening

(a work in process)

Told with words and art,

contained in novels and companion shorts,

available in print and eBooks.

JARADEE'S LEGACY

ILLUSTRATED BY THE AUTHOR

VARTERELS' UNIVERSE™
BOOK TEN

S.K. RANDOLPH

Cover & Illlustrations by
S.K. RANDOLPH

CheeTrann Creations LLC

Jaradee's Legacy: Illustrated by the Author (VarTerels' Universe™ Book 10)

Copyright © 2017-2026 by S.K. Randolph
Cover design and art copyright © 2024-2026 by S.K. Randolph
Edited by L.S. Lane
Illustrated by S.K. Randolph
Book design by T. Krantz

ISBN
Paperback 978-1-962777-18-6
eBook 978-1-962777-33-9

Self Published by S.K. Randolph
CheeTrann Creations LLC
Suite 316-160
1410 Valley View Drive
Delta, CO 81416

Web Site: www.skrandolph.com
Substack: skrandolph.substack.com
Facebook: http://facebook.com/S.K.Randolph11

Revised 2026

VU-128-J VU10-JL 260717-0551 | 231129 PIbtA VUPt-1 | 231129 PIbtA VUPt-1 | 6X9X.75X.5-336

*To Debbie Stilson, a steadfast
member of my editing team and
one of the bravest women I know*

*Thank you for your loving and being a
part of the VarTerels' Universe*

VarTereis' Universe ™
SCIENCE FANTASY

JARADEE'S LEGACY

El Stroma
Isle of Osullini
Eilean Motu
Mer a Chi Strait
NorcenMyca Mts
Thornland
Gruseeno Mts.
SianEly Forest
* Neseer
Charnland
Dir
Treden
El QuilTran

Irpa
Amte
Cliffs of Cimondeli
Cimondeli Mts.
Lake Scarla
Plains of Los Ateed
*Tic Calag
Chaporicas Mts
*Chunarrie
Port Saticch *
Seerdrum Wood
*Tahellive
Cupress-Cone Forest
Sea
YarSal
N
W E
S
El SyrTundi

Part 1
Birth

Born in a land divided by strife,
Two birthed from one offered new life.
Carried and hidden to protect for their race
Until it was time to reclaim their true place.

Prologue

Borne over land through dimension and space;
Carried and hidden to protect for the race.
Disparate directions depending on worth,
Immediately followed seclusion and birth.

Jaradee scanned the flatness of Los Ateed el Rida. Nothing stirred on El Stroma's vast, dry plains but tundi sage, quivering in the early evening breeze. Despite the heat radiating from the sun-parched ground, a chill crept up her spine. The Klutarse had not given up. The thought of the Romper's trained assassins turned the chill into a shiver. They would never stop searching for the birth-mates she had carried in her womb until three moon cycles earlier, the infants the Rompeer's general had sent them to exterminate. The future depended on the survival of those babies. They were the only hope separating her people, the Eleo Preda, from certain annihilation.

A slight tremor that set particles of sandy dirt skittering over the ground confirmed her fears. Yanking her face covering into place, she scrambled onto a rickety wooden ladder, lowered the heavy trap cover, and descended to a cavern, where three cloaked figures gathered around a small, smokeless fire.

A masked woman in her medial cycles rose and offered her seat. "What did you discover?"

"Our enemies travel this way." Jaradee sank onto a folded sleeping mat and accepted a battered mug of tepid water.

No one else acknowledged her arrival. Her protectors dared not look her way, nor did they know her name or the names of her children. This did not mean they devalued her or the service she and the children provided. Were they caught, their minds must not hold names or images amongst their memories. She understood.

Overhead, pounding hooves raised small dusty clouds around the trap cover. Her protectors exchanged glances. Neither looked her way.

Jaradee gathered her cloak tighter. "You don't have to stay. Our danger is not yours."

A young woman, her faced hidden beneath a white mask, stared at the fire. "We pledged to follow where you lead. You and yours are the future of the Eleo Preda. Only death can remove us from your side."

Jaradee climbed to her feet. "I am honored. Sleep in peace."

She followed Floree, her birther and friend, along a low passage to a small cave. In nested blankets, two babies slept, their arms wrapped around each other. Jaradee knelt and touched a rosy cheek, brushed a dark curl from a pale forehead, and sat back. "You are so beautiful."

After making sure everything was ready should escape be necessary, she stretched out on a tattered mat.

Floree curled up beside her. "Tomorrow the real journey begins. Try to sleep." Soft snores soon fluttered through the cave.

Jaradee squeezed her eyes shut and calmed her breathing. Illusive sleep, dancing just out of reach, left her staring into darkness. Her thoughts focused on how she had arrived in a cave beneath Los Ateed el Rida.

1

Grateful for the night's dark mantle, Jaradee crept along a dingy back alley on the outskirts of Tahellive and ducked into a recessed door opposite her Uncle Kamer's dilapidated, two-story hovel. Upstairs, a solitary lamp glowed a tremulous welcome. A soldier's shout prompted a quick sprint to the back door. Dodging inside, she jogged up the rickety steps, and slipped into the narrow hallway outside the attic rooms she and her siblings shared with their mother.

A sob choked her. *Oh, Momee.* She inhaled a ragged breath, used her shirt sleeve to scrub away her tears, and tiptoed into the room. Turning, she pressed an ear against the closed door and listened intently. *No one follows.* Relief almost buckled her knees.

Boots pounding down the main street and a soft feminine gasp propelled her to the front window, where her younger brother, Daar, and sister, Katareen, huddled, riveted to the scene below.

Jaradee peered between their dark heads. Rompeerial soldiers marched two by two. Shouldered weapons gleamed in the cool blue light of the descending moon, Dyad. Horses snorted, clanked, and blew smoke from their nostrils. A purple and black clad rider swiveled in his saddle. Klutarse-sharp eyes searched the darkness.

Jaradee pushed her siblings into the shadows and reached for the open curtain.

Daar grabbed her wrist. "If it moves, *he'll* see and know someone is here." He nudged her and Kat away from the window.

"Where will this all end?" Katareen's voice quivered. "Do the Rompeer and his council not care what becomes of El Stroma?"

Daar snorted. "Rumor has it genocide is the goal. Soon, the Eleo Preda will cease to exist and the continent of El QuilTran will belong to the Rompeer."

Katareen stifled a sob. "Why us? We have done nothing to harm him or the Pheet Adole."

Jaradee put an arm around her sister. "Our differences, our longevity, and our mystic talents make them afraid. As long as the Eleo Preda live, we are a threat to the Rompeer's empire. We must leave Tahellive or our lives will become fodder for the Pheet Adole."

Daar scowled. "And what of Uncle Kamer and Momee?"

Jaradee swallowed a lump in her throat. "They won't be returning."

Her brother's gray-blue eyes narrowed. "Where are they?"

Jaradee's gaze telegraphed a message she hoped he could read. "Their spirits are with the ancestors."

Katareen stifled a cry of dismay and sagged. Jaradee steadied her.

Her brother glared, fists clenched at his sides. "You mean they're dead."

The flatness in his voice frightened her almost more than his anger. "Yes."

"When?"

"Today at Market."

Katareen's hand flew to her heart. "What happened?" The whispered words held a sob.

Jaradee set her jaw. "Two soldiers caught Momee. Uncle Kamer tried to save her." She kept her voice steady, refusing to cry or to fan Daar's anger into a blaze.

"You were there? You saw?" Katareen's voice trembled.

Jaradee gave her a gentle push. "Go. Pack what you need. Time is short."

Daar waited until she was out of hearing. "Momee?"

"They took her away. I didn't want Katareen to hope or to imagine the worst."

Cold fury bared Daar's teeth. "The soldier's...they're hunting you, right?"

She nodded. With an angry snarl, he turned and strode from the room.

Jaradee moved to the shadowed side of the window. Alkina, El Stroma's second moon, would rise soon. Capable during its fruitful phase of shining with the dawn's brightness, it could provide the enemy with its victims, but not tonight. Tonight, it would rise in its barren phase. The perfect time to escape.

Jaradee abandoned her long skirt and top for a clay splattered shirt and a pair of her uncle's work pants. After cinching the waist tight with a piece of braided hemp, she pulled on heavy socks and a pair of his boots and turned to find Katareen, red-eyed and frightened, in the doorway.

"I'm scared, Jaradee. What if they know we're Eleo Preda? What if they catch us? I don't want to die or to be a host mother or..." She sniffed.

Jaradee hugged her and held her at arm's length. At thirteen sun cycles, porcelain skin, large, honey-colored eyes, and blue-black hair shouted her lineage like a barker at the Pheet Adolan slave market. "Let's do a little camouflaging. Turn around."

Working quickly, Jaradee braided the long, black hair and wound it into a tight coil. Deft fingers secured it with pins and covered it with a tan bandora. Turning Katareen to face her, she studied the effect. Even with the hat's wide brim casting a shadow, her paleness screamed. By their uncle's potter's wheel, brown clay the consistency of thick cream caught her attention. Dipping her fingers, she smeared it on her sister's cheeks, chin, and forehead. Next, she wound a scarf around her pale neck. The overall effect made her nod. "Alright, Kat, you do my face. Where's Daar?"

"Here." He stepped into the dim light. Shoe black camouflaged the fair skin of his face, neck, and shaved head.

Katareen gaped. "What did you do to your hair?"

Defiance overflowing with hatred, Daar growled, "As soon as you're safe, I'm joining the rebels." He tossed her a pair of pants and a shirt. "Change, and hurry."

Lips pressed together, Jaradee swallowed a sharp retort. Seventeen and strong-willed, Daar knew how to take care of himself. After the murder of their father, his quick thinking and skill had saved them then and gotten them and their mother to Uncle Kamer's home on the continent of El SyrTundi. She hoped his luck would continue to hold.

The clattering of hooves and a muffled shout in the street galvanized the three into action. Katareen tucked in her shirt and fastened the breeches. Jaradee led them down the stairs. Silent as mice on the run, they clustered by the back door. Fists pounding on the front entrance reverberated through the house.

"Gotta move, Jar." Daar elbowed his way to the door and opened it a crack. "I'll go first and create a diversion. The minute they spot me, head for the waterfront. Uncle Kam's friend Mylos will help you. Ready?"

Katareen whimpered. "What about you?"

"Forget you know me." He hit the alley running, sent a stack of wooden boxes crashing to the ground, and dodged between tightly packed buildings.

A shout sounded the alarm. Booted feet hammered after him. Jaradee peered up and down the alley, grabbed Katareen's wrist, and pulled her into the murky darkness.

The empty back streets of Tahellive smelled of squalor and fear. When the patrols roamed the streets, Pheet Adole and Eleo Preda alike hid behind locked doors. Rompeerial soldiers cared little for ethnic origin in this part of town. The impoverished were vermin to be exterminated.

Male voices at the end of the narrow alley sent the girls darting into the darkness between two derelict buildings. Footsteps marched their way. Hand lights threw dim circles from one side of the alley to the other.

Katareen's hands clutched at Jaradee's arm. "Now what?"

Jaradee pulled her sister lower and sheltered her from sight. "Don't move. Don't speak. Don't think." Heart pounding, she fought to suppress the adrenaline rush urging her to run.

Two soldiers stopped, their feet only an arm's length away.

A booted foot kicked a fallen box aside. "To da'am bad the kid gotta away. He woulda squealed plenty when we enjoyed his sisters right under his nose."

The second man searched one end of the alley and then the other. "Don't have the sisters. Better find 'em or you and me'll be doin' the squealin'."

Jaradee waited until their footsteps faded into the square, crept through the opening, and hauled Katareen to her feet. "We have to reach the harbor. If we get separated, go straight to Mylos' boat."

"What if he's not there?"

"Climb aboard and hide. I'll be there if I can."

Katareen gripped her arm. "Please don't leave me."

"Only if there's no other way. Stay close." Jaradee gave her sister a quick hug and took the lead.

Furtive as phantoms in the night, they the way traversed the alleyway and made their way down one back street after the other.

Bordered by the sea on one side, Tahellive had a fish cannery, a foundry, and a lumber mill scattered along the shoreline. It was a workingman's town with a working man's flavor. At the central square, farmers and merchants sold their wares in the Tahe Market. Lining the streets surrounding it to the South, a town hall and courthouse, a steepled temple to the Pheet Adolan gods, and a gallery of shops serviced the needs of the Lord of Tahellive's household and the landholders under his purview. To the North, Throsswel, a warren of winding streets and dilapidated hovels backing a pub, a brothel, and a card house, swarmed up the hill to clear-cut fields that had once been an ancient forest.

On the rare nights when Alkina rose barren and lightless, Jaradee had explored Throsswel, skulking from shadow to darkened doorway until she knew every alley and lane, every place to hide or to avoid. Within a short span, she had ferreted out the best escape routes to the waterfront and to the forest and rolling hills beyond the factories.

Drawing on her unerring directional sense and her gathered knowledge, she led Katareen on a circuitous route from one alley to the next. They met no one, heard nothing, and arrived at their destination undetected.

2

Crouched behind a row of bushes, Jaradee frowned. Undisturbed silence triggered an inner alarm. *Where are the soldiers who patrol the docks and boatyard?* She sat back on her heels and glanced up at the dome. *Thank goodness for Alkina's dimmed light.* A warning-filled gaze locked on Katareen. She motioned her to follow.

Tiptoeing along the side of a single story warehouse, she peered around the corner. A yard full of boats on the hard lay between them and their goal—a yard that felt like a trap ready to spring. She bit her lip. "I'll go first, Kat. If I get caught, hide."

Her whispered instructions left her sister shaking her head. "Don't leave me. I won't know where to go. I..."

Jaradee put a finger to her lips. "If they catch me, hide in the warehouse until it's clear. Mylos docks his boat on the far side of the yard, third from the end."

Not giving her sister time to argue, she darted across a wide-open space and crouched under the nearest boat. When nothing but the muffled noise of machinery from the fish cannery disturbed the quiet, she gave the signal. Kat raced to her side. Jaradee pointed to a row of boats in various stages of repair. Kat nodded. Gathering her courage, Jaradee sprinted over the rubble-strewn ground, squatted between two fishing boats, and shot a glance over her shoulder.

She choked down a warning shout and dropped flat on the ground. The night-muted shape of a man hugged Katareen against his chest, a hand covering her mouth. Her initial struggle ceased. She shook her head and pointed. He half pulled, half carried her into the trees bordering the yard.

Jaradee started to rise. The full weight of a man's hard body pressed her to the ground.

"Daar sent me. Don't make a sound. Follow my lead."

Her brother's name and the familiar tenor of the voice calmed her fear. Soldiers flooding the yard whipped it back into being.

The weight of her attacker lifted, and he crawled under a tarp draping the side of a large, flat-bottomed boat. Scooching after, she rested her head on her forearms and listened. Shouts and running feet conveyed a clear image of the hunt. Booted feet strode past their hiding place and paced back the way they had come. Horses whinnied and snorted. The rhythmic sound of hooves retreating left the dockyard in silence.

Jaradee lifted her head.

A hand gripped her arm. The man whispered, "Not yet."

Again, booted feet paced between the boats and stopped next to their hiding place. Sweat dribbled down Jaradee's forehead. She ignored it and held her breath. The soldier shuffled to the bow of the boat and stopped. After what seemed like forever, the soft crunch of his boots faded into the night. Quiet returned.

Still, they remained in hiding. A ruru bird hooted once, then again. The hand on her arm relaxed.

"Stay."

The man crawled from under the boat and squatted. Another bird called. He lifted the tarp, put a finger to his lips, and beckoned. Once in the trees, he led her along a faint trail ending at the far edge of the woods. A short distance ahead, a freight wagon waited on a rough track facing away from town.

Safe within the trees, she watched him circle the wagon and come to a standstill in front of her.

The rugged face with its crooked nose and full beard sent a wave of relief rushing through her. "Mylos! I wasn't sure if it was you. Katareen?"

Mylos lifted her into the back of the wagon. "Safe. We need to go. Crawl behind the boxes near the front and cover up with the blanket. If we're stopped, don't make a sound." When she was settled, he flipped a cover over the bed and fastened it in place.

The freight wagon shifted under his weight as he climbed into the cab box. A low roar shook the vehicle and eased into a rhythmic pulsing. The release of the brake squeaked, and the wagon rumbled and grumbled its way along the track.

Jaradee allowed herself to relax. *Katareen is safe. Wish I knew Daar was.* She stifled a yawn. *I can't remember when I slept last.*

The jerk of the wagon rolling to a stop and the break engaging woke her from fitful dreams.

A voice barked. "Climb down and bring your travel pass."

Jaradee forced herself to remain still and listen.

Mylos landed with a thump next to the wagon. "Here you go." Pheet Adolan words spoken by a friend sounded strange to Jaradee's ear.

"What's your cargo?"

"Supplies for the mill. I have the manifest if you need to check it."

Jaradee admired the ease in Mylos' voice.

"Got any fruit in there?"

Mylos flipping the tarp back, the creak and sigh of the wagon bed, and the snap of a lid being pried off a box left Jaradee tensed and ready for flight.

"Catch."

In her mind, she saw the fruit arc.

"Thanks." The soldier's tone sounded less brusque. "Have a pleasant trip. Keep your eye out for a couple of Eleo girls. You see any, you let me know."

"Will do." The wagon groaned under Mylos' return to the cab. The break released. Once again, it rumbled along the rough track.

The unbroken rhythm of the journey erased Jaradee's fear, but not her exhaustion. Unable to fight her fatigue, she slipped into restless dreams.

A hand shook her. Bolting upright, she came face to face with Mylos, brushed tangled hair back from her face, and demanded, "Where are we? Did we make it?"

Mylos moved to one side.

Katareen's face appeared at the back of the wagon. "Jaradee!"

Scrabbling on hands and knees, Jaradee crawled to the tailgate, jumped to the ground, and threw her arms around her sister. "I'm so glad you're safe."

The crunch of boots preceded a teasing laugh. "Aren't you glad *I'm* safe, Jara?"

Jaradee swung around, flung her arms around Daar's neck, and planted a kiss on his cheek. "How?"

He shot her a saucy smile. "I'm smart, that's how."

"I believe I get some of the credit." A tall, well-built man walked around the wagon. Sparkling amber eyes gleamed in an ebony face so beautiful it took Jaradee's breath away. He smiled at her. "I'm Kuparak. It is good you are safe, Jaradee Myrlinduh. I imagine you are hungry." He gave Daar an indulgent smile. "You may finish your reunion while we eat. Then we have work to do."

Arm in arm with her siblings, Jaradee followed Mylos and Kuparak into a cabin beside a small lake, where several others gathered around a long table.

Kuparak waved a hand. "These are my companions. We will share names when our bellies are full. Let us give thanks.

Gratitude and love abound
For animals, plants, and fertile ground.
We give thanks for life and health,
Abundant gifts; El Stroma's wealth."

Jaradee glanced around the table as she ate from a plate heaped with more food than she had seen in several cycles of the moons. Fifteen people chatted about everyday things, laughed at one another's jokes, and seemed to enjoy their time together. Kuparak glanced up and smiled. A rush of heat to her tan cheeks made her lower her gaze and concentrate on eating.

After the meal and cleanup, everyone but Jaradee, her siblings, and Mylos departed in Kuparak's wake.

Katareen curled up in a much-used chair. "I'm so full. I don't remember the last time I ate that much." Her eyelids drooped. She yawned and squirmed into a more comfortable position. "Thanks for rescuing me, Daar." Her lids closed, and she slept.

Mylos pointed toward the back door. Once outside, he plopped onto a rickety step. His sympathetic expression almost brought her to tears. "I'm sorry about your Uncle Kamer. He was a good man. I'll miss him. Daar tells me your mother's alive."

She sniffed. "The last time I saw her, she was. I'm afraid her age will make her dispensable."

Mylos shook his head. "She's not that old, and she's strong. I imagine they'll use her as a slave. I've already put the word out to watch for her. Once we know where she is, we can attempt a rescue."

Daar jumped from the porch and sat at her feet. Impatience and the need to know bristled around her brother like the quills on a porcudillo.

Ignoring his obvious desire to ask questions, Mylos said, "What would you like to know, Jaradee?"

She pulled the pins from her hair and combed her fingers through its thick waves. "Who is Kuparak?"

"He's—" The subject of her inquiry rounded the corner of the cabin. Mylos nodded a welcome. "I'll let him answer for himself."

Kuparak sat on the ground and leaned against a stump. "I am the son of the spiritual leaders of the Giroblania, the tribe of your mother's origin. I am in El SyrTundi to help bring peace." He shrugged. "Or, if peace is not possible, to save El QuilTran by whatever means necessary."

Daar couldn't contain himself. "How do I join you? I want to fight for our people. How do I learn—"

Kuparak raised a hand. "Patience. Perhaps if you let me speak, I can answer your questions and your sister's."

Daar hung his head. "Sorry."

The big man gave him an indulgent smile. "You did well today, Daar Myrlinduh. You stood by your word. Do not let your youth stop you from knowing the truth when you hear it. Tomorrow, you will begin your training to be a Vasrosi." Laughter reshaped his handsome features. "If our cause intrigues you, that is."

Surprise kept Daar motionless, and then he grinned and jumped to his feet. "I would be honored, Kuparak. I—"

"Sit and listen. You have much to learn."

Daar, fair skin flushed with excitement, settled against the porch, his gray-blue eyes fixed on the Vasrosi leader.

Kuparak rubbed a smudge of dust from his immaculate breeches, adjusted his back against the stump, and fixed his attention on Jaradee.

"We knew of your situation because Daar, without giving himself away, reached Mylos' boat. Mylos brought him to me. I had received word that Rompeerial soldiers hunted two Eleo Predan women. Our plans developed from there." He looked at Daar. "It seemed an excellent opportunity to test your courage and your resolve and to help your sisters."

White teeth glinted. "We are, Jaradee, an alliance of Eleo Predans from Thornland and Charnland, who work to save our cultures and our homeland. Vasrosi, the word for protector in my ancestral tongue, is the name we fight under. Our preference is to bring this cultural clash to a peaceful conclusion. We are, however, prepared to battle to the death.

"Daar informed me that your father and uncle are dead. I offer you my condolences and our protection until you decide what is best for you and Katareen. If you choose to remain here, you may not, under any circumstances, use the mystic gifts you carry. The Pheet Adole have developed a type of techno sorcery, which they call SorTechery. It will bring them right to our door. Do you have questions I have not addressed?"

Jaradee saw nothing dishonest in his face. His words carried the weight of truth. Had they been in their country, she would have done a subtle mind probe. Since arriving in El SyrTundi, she had learned to use instinct alone. "What does the Rompeer know of your alliance?"

"Lusktar Rados knows we exist, but not who we are. Since our goal is not to shed another's blood, we have not left a trail of death. Our activities have centered on rescuing those who have come to his notice and collecting information for our leaders back home. I believe he considers us a nuisance rather than a threat."

Jaradee fought to keep herself awake. Sleep-heavy lids fluttered. Her head dropped forward.

Kuparak's hand on her knee woke her with a jolt. "You need rest, Jara. Mylos will show you where the women sleep. We will talk more tomorrow."

He stood. "Daar, let's go for a walk."

Jaradee touched the place where his hand had been and watched him leave with a sigh of regret.

A knowing smile tugged at Mylos' full lips. "Interesting, isn't he?" He teased. "Come on. I'll show you where to bed down."

In the small bedroom, mattresses lined the walls. Four had personal belongings piled on top; one had a pillow and blankest stacked in the middle.

"That one appears to be yours, Jara. I suggest you sleep in your clothes and keep your boots on. Just in case—"

"Wait. Where's Katareen?"

"Stop worryin', girl. She's makin' friends. Get some rest." He stifled a yawn. "See you in the mornin'."

Jaradee watched him go with a slight qualm, scrunched up her pillow, stuffed it under her head, and prepared to lie awake until her sister returned. In moments, slumber claimed her.

3

Jaradee's eyes flew open. The barren moon's inky night darkness enshrouded her. A soft shhhh stifled her gasp of confusion.

"Stay low and alert." The whispered words held a warning. A hand gripped her wrist and guided her between piles of bedding. Another pair of hands helped her climb through the window. Muffled sounds, the window sliding shut, a gentle nudge, and they were running. Behind them, an explosion illuminated the clearing. She glanced around, searching for Katareen. The light flickered and went out.

"Don't gawk, girl. Run!" The woman beside her shoved her into the trees.

Jaradee stumbled, caught herself, and concentrated on keeping track of the faint sounds of running feet.

When at last she and her companion stopped, dawn sent faint, iridescent shafts through the twisted branches overhead. Jaradee gripped her knees and inhaled a controlled breath. Her erratic heartbeat steadied. Wiping the blood from a scrape on her palm, she silently thanked Mylos. *It's a good thing I slept in my boots.*

Her companion, a woman several sun cycles her senior, sat on the ground massaging her calf. "I'm Floree."

Jaradee hunched her shoulders, rolled them back, and listened to the bones in her neck crack. "Jaradee. Thanks for your help. What happened?"

Floree yanked tousled dirty blonde hair into a ponytail and secured it with a thin strip of leather. "Soldiers found the cabin. Musta followed your trail. Question is: how'd they slip by the tukoolo?"

The lack of accusation in the clipped reply did little to ease Jaradee's stab of guilt. "What do we do now?"

"We head for a designated place to regroup." She rummaged through a pouch at her waist and offered a handful of dried fruit. "Eat and then we go. Won't do to get caught now."

Jaradee accepted the food. "I need to find my sister and brother."

Floree climbed to her feet and brushed the dust and debris from her pants. "Let's get going then." Gazing domeward, she adjusted her direction to parallel the rising sun. "The Vasrosi are the only ones who know about the place we're going. You must promise never to reveal its whereabouts. To do so would jeopardize many lives."

"I promise." She retied her boot and straightened. "I've been thinking I'd like to join you—to help our people."

Floree's matter-a-fact smile warmed her. "Kuparak is the one to talk to if —" A faint snap somewhere behind them erased the smile. "Come on. We have a long distance to travel."

Under different circumstances, Jaradee would have loved the hike through the ancient forest. But her uncle's boots rubbed and blisters turned her long stride to a hobble. Her low back burned. Sweat soaking her shirt left her too warm one moment and too cool the next. Ahead of her, Floree never flagged and never seemed to tire. The turning's light had faded, when she stopped behind a tall elder-leaf and put a finger to her lips. She picked up a small round pebble, took aim, and tossed it down a rugged slope ending in a rocky ravine.

An unusual bird, its mismatched wings cutting a silent path up the incline, landed on Floree's arm. Jaradee studied its curious structure with interest. One side of its body looked normal; the other appeared to be made from a glass-like material. Similar to a collapsible telescope, the eye on its glass side focused in her direction. A gentle mind touch tingled and withdrew. The bird lifted into the air and swooped back the way it had come.

Jaradee tracked it until it vanished. "What happened to it?"

"The Rompeer's researchers experiment on animals and birds. When they're done, they toss them on a trash heap. Kuparak can tell you how they survive to become tukoolo."

"It left a message in my mind." Jaradee felt a touch of wonder.

Floree appeared unfazed. "What was the message?"

"It is safe for us to venture into the Cupress-Cone Forest."

"Good." The woman wiped her hands on her pants. "Let's get you to safety."

Sidestepping to the bottom of the slope, she hiked a diagonal path up the ravine, threaded her way between slender silver-trunked trees, and half ran, half skated down a steep bank to a small creek. Wading into the middle, she followed its course upstream before dodging into a grouping of cupress-cone pines and along a faint track into a clearing.

Mylos and Daar, dwarfed by the giant trees, hurried toward them. Jaradee's panicked gaze searched the area and focused on her brother. His expression confirmed her worst fear. "Where's Katareen?"

Daar grimaced. "She's not here."

Jaradee grabbed his arm. "Where is she?"

Floree joined them. "They captured her during the raid. I didn't tell you because I knew you would go back to find her. We would have lost you both."

Jaradee swung around. "How dare you make that decision for me?" Anger and fear turned her back the other way. "Where's Kuparak, Daar? I want to see him right now."

Her brother glared. "He's tracking the soldiers."

"He's an excellent tracker, one of the best." Floree's calm washed over her. "I understand your anger, Jaradee, but Kuparak told me to get you to safety."

Jaradee turned her back and pressed her hands against the rough bark of a stately cupress. Her forehead resting on her hands, she imagined her anger abating. Peace flowed through her, peace and the knowledge that Katareen was as yet unharmed. Thanking the ancient tree in the ways of the Eleo Preda, she rejoined her friends.

"Tell me what happened, Mylos."

"Kat wasn't the only one taken, Jara. They grabbed four others at the same time." Amber-flecked blue eyes narrowed. "Tealin and Camilyn were making their final patrol of the evening. Kat and Solee asked to tag along. Somehow, soldiers slipped by the tukoolo. One girl screamed. The next thing we knew, soldiers flooded the clearing. That any of us got away is a miracle. I hope—"

Two boys stepped from the shelter of the trees. A blood-soaked sling and a pronounced limp spoke volumes. Everyone sprang into action. Daar and Jaradee assisted the boy with the injured leg.

Mylos steadied the boy with the sling. "Easy, Umbba." He pulled the boy's uninjured arm around his shoulder and put an arm around his back.

Floree led the way through a labyrinth of towering cupress-cones to the base of a humongous tree. Mylos helped Umbba through a narrow opening the height of a tall man. Daar and Watuli followed. Jaradee could not hold back a gasp of astonishment.

The hollow interior of the massive tree housed a small camp. Ten two-man tents pitched around the perimeter surrounded a smokeless cook fire. Torches stuck into the walls cast light and shadow across the moss-strew ground. Jaradee stared, confounded, from the tents to the fire to Floree busily working to clean Umbba's wounds.

Daar grinned. "Incredible, huh?"

Mylos spoke briefly with Floree and hurried toward them. "Daar, come with me. We need to cover any tracks we might have left. Jara, Watuli could use your help and then see what Floree needs."

Grateful for her training in the healing arts, Jaradee examined Watuli's ankle, wrapped it with a compression bandage she found in a med case by Floree's side and gave him a dose of anti-inflammatory herbs. After covering him with a blanket, she left him to rest and joined Floree.

"How's Umbba?"

Floree tossed bloodied rags into a beat-up metal bowl. "He's lost a lot of blood. How he made it here is a mystery. The boys are checking to make sure he didn't leave a trail." She finished applying a bandage and sat back on her heels. "I stitched up the gash in his arm. He's young and strong. Let's hope that speeds his healing." After tucking a well-worn blanket under his chin, she indicated Jaradee's feet. "Let's have a look."

Jaradee pulled off her uncle's boots and grimaced. Floree peeled off her bloody socks. Blisters lined her toes; a nasty one adorned her heel. Floree cleaned, anointed, and bandaged them with deft professionalism and then helped her to a seat by the fire.

"How about a mug of tea?" Floree set a pot of water on a grill covering one end of the pit.

The homey sound of mugs clanking, the rustle of paper, and the occasional hiss and pop of the fire did little to help subdue Jaradee's concern. *Has Kup rescued Kat?* Accepting a mug of tea, she inhaled the aroma of wild mamochelli and forced herself to sip it. Each swallow of the hot liquid slid down a throat tight with unspoken fear. The building pressure boiled over. "Where is Kuparak?" Setting her mug on the ground, she hugged her knees. "Why isn't he here? What if he can't find Kat?" She started to rise, flinched, and stayed put. "I can't remain here when she may be hurt and frightened." She squeezed back unshed tears. "What if she's—"

Floree's arms closed around her. "She's not dead, Jara. They don't kill Eleo Predan women who are of childbearing age. Katareen is young and healthy. They'll use her as a host mother. That gives us time to find and rescue her."

Jaradee pulled away. "Lusktar Rados finds her type of beauty fascinating. What if he sees her and makes her one of his courtesans? I promised Momee I'd take care of her, Floree. I have to go back." A glimpse of her bandaged toes stopped her tirade. She shook her head. The tears came. Sobs shuddered through her. When her tears slowed and she could breathe a steady breath, Floree handed her a clean cloth.

"Thanks." Jaradee hiccuped, wiped her face, and blew her nose. "Sorry. Guess I needed to do that."

A deep voice startled her. "Women's tears cleanse the heart."

Floree smiled and kept her from jumping to her feet. "It is good to see you, Kuparak. Jaradee has been asking for you." The smile widened into a delighted grin.

The next instant, Katareen hugged her, planted a kiss on her damp cheek, and sat back. "No more tears. I'm here. Kuparak and his men saved us." The light faded from her eyes. "All of us accept Solee. She's..." Katareen's dark hair, loosened from its braid, hid her face.

No one spoke. The fire snapped. Camilyn knelt beside her. "Let's find something to eat. I'm starving."

Floree rose. "I'll help you." She guided them to a hamper on the far side of the fire pit.

Kuparak sat down by the fire. "She'll be fine, Jaradee. The death of her friend bruises her heart, but she is strong and determined." He glanced at her feet. "Looks to me like she fared better than you in the foot department." His beautiful smile warmed her.

4

S upper had been an upbeat meal with an undercurrent of sadness. Daar and Mylos had returned. They had obliterated all evidence of travel to and from the cupress camp. The tukoolo reported no signs of Rompeerial soldiers, but remained on guard and alert. An abundance of food had appeared as if by magic. Watuli had awakened hungry and glad to have a sprain and not a break. Umbba slept the deep sleep of one whose body fought to replenish itself. Rest, Floree had stated, would be his best healer.

Kuparak ordered the torches turned low. Everyone except Jaradee, Floree, Kuparak, and Zarrin settled for the night. They sat around the fire, sipping Eleo Predan brandy from tin mugs.

A relaxed silence settled over the group. Jaradee watched Kuparak from beneath her lashes, trying to understand his effect on her. Beside him, Zarrin, a short, squat man with a shaved head and muscular body, observed Floree with a hunger that Jaradee realized with a flash of insight she understood. A final sip of brandy, and she set her mug aside.

"Tell us what happened, or I won't sleep." She kept her gaze on Zarrin, who shook himself free of personal thoughts and looked at his leader.

Kuparak cupped his mug and studied its contents. "We caught up with the soldiers on this side of Tahellive." His gaze met Jaradee's. "They did not expect trouble. Katareen and the others were in a military truck with a driver and one guard. A motored-cycle escort rode in the front and behind. Zarrin and another man created a diversion. The erupting chaos gave us an opening to rescue Katareen, Camilyn, and Tealin. Solee attempted to keep up, but her injuries slowed her down." He took a long draw from his mug. "A motored cycle came out of nowhere. The rider shot her in the back. There was nothing we could do." He held out his mug.

Zarrin filled it. "She was dead before she hit the ground." He took a swig from the bottle. "And so was the rider." Wiping his mouth with the back of his hand, he muttered something under his breath and sighed. "I'm to bed. Tomorrow's goin' to be long." Not bothering to stand, Zarrin crawled the short distance to his tent and ducked inside.

Jaradee looked at Kuparak. "Tomorrow?"

"The longer Katareen remains in El SyrTundi, the more dangerous it will become for her and for us. She is beautiful and young and has not been with a man—exactly what Lusktar Rados desires for his concubines. His men have seen her and will continue to hunt her. The one who presents her to the Rompeer will win his favor and his thanks. Tomorrow Zarrin begins the journey to take her home, where she will go into hiding with the women and children in the Gruseeno Mountains."

Jaradee frowned. "And me? Will you be sending *me* home, too?" Disapproval laced the query.

Kuparak glanced at Floree. "No. You and Floree will stay with me. Mylos, Umbba, and Watuli will remain with us. Daar will accompany Katareen and return here with Zarrin. Since the Rompeer's men have seen Tealin and Camilyn, they will make the journey, too. Time away will keep them safe and allow their images to slip from memory. By the time they return, they'll have been forgotten."

A cloud of worry darkened Kuparak's expression. "Zarrin's actions have changed Vasrosi from a nuisance to a danger. Let's hope we can repair the damage by staying undercover." He twirled a stick between his long fingers. "I suggest we get some sleep."

Floree stood up and stretched. "See you in the morning."

Jaradee smothered a yawn. "Aren't you posting guards tonight, Kuparak?"

His winsome smile flashed. "The tukoolos will warn us if we have company."

"Floree said you'd tell me about these tukoolos."

With his forearms on his knees, he gazed into the fire. "Floree has suggested you are interested in joining Vasrosi." He regarded her with interest. "Is she correct?"

"Daar tells me the Pheet Adole intend to kill us all and make El QuilTran their own. I want to help our people. So, yes, I would like to join the Vasrosi."

Kuparak stirred the fire. Sparks flickered and died. He stoked the coals under the cooking grate and arranged tinder and a small log at the opposite end. Flames licking the dry edges hissed softly as the wood caught fire.

Jaradee observed his elegant features shift in the light. *Why am I so attracted to you?*

A final adjustment to the log and he tossed the stick on the fire. "I believe, Jara, you have much to offer the Vasrosi. We will talk more after the others leave. You asked about the tukoolo." He interlaced his fingers. "The Rompeer's researchers experiment on animals of all sorts but, in particular, birds. When they're done, they toss their victims on the trash heap. Once the sun sets, members of Vasrosi rescued and delivered those still living to a Pheet Adolan glass blower and adornment designer named Tazio and his Eleo Predan wife, Nioka. Nioka is a shameena and mender. She heals the animals and, in the case of the birds, builds the armatures to replace their injured wings. Tazio rebuilds the damaged parts with spun quartz crystal and a type of blown glass that is tougher than most metals."

"But how do they move the wings? The whistler hawk we saw today flew with no obvious problem."

"A tiny power cell stimulates silica transmitters attached to the brain stem and produces impulses throughout the bird's body. Nioka models the contour feathers, wing, and tail feathers for each bird. They are flexible and light. This process works for other animals, too, but our tukoolo are predominately birds."

Jaradee fingered a black curl. "How do they communicate?"

"Once the tukoolo forms a connection to a Human it can use telepathy."

"I am still fighting to understand the variety of technologies used by the

Pheet Adole. El QuilTran is a much simpler place." She stifled a yawn. "I believe it's time I slept. Thank you for explaining tukoolo. When will Zarrin and Katareen leave?"

"Early. Floree will wake you. Sleep well." Kuparak banked the fire and disappeared through the opening in the trunk.

Jaradee remained by the fire for some time, attempting to herd her thoughts into some kind of order. How would Katareen, Daar, and the others reach El QuilTran? How could she serve the Vasrosi? And, why did the Rompeer hate her people? Question after question collided and splintered into more. Yawning, she opted for bed.

After relieving herself where Floree had directed her earlier, she crawled into the tent next to Katareen and lay down. Murmuring voices caught her at the edge of sleep. Pushing the tent flap aside, she peered around the dim space.

Kuparak, Mylos, and Zarrin huddled by the fire. Mylos ran a hand through tangled hair and persisted. "I'm telling you, I felt the burn of SorTechory."

Zarrin folded his arms and scowled. "The tukoolos have not alerted us."

"Not the time to argue." Authority weighted Kuparak's response. "The tukoolos didn't warn us at the cabin either. Do you think the soldiers have developed a way to bypass them? Wake the others. Cover the fire. Camouflage the tents. Hurry."

Jaradee placed a gentle hand over Katareen's mouth and whispered next to her ear. "Wake up. No noise. Put on your boots." She scrambled from the tent and held the tent flap aside. Katareen scooted out and stood up.

Mylos hurried toward them, put a finger to his lips, and pointed. Kneeling, he pulled a narrow rope. The tent collapsed. He motioned Jaradee to the back edge, indicated a stake at her feet, and gripped an identical one at his. She grabbed hers, and at a nod from him, followed his lead. A quick jerk pulled a blanket of moss and bark forward to camouflage the tent underneath.

He led the way to a rope ladder anchored in the trunk. "This leads to a hollow branch. When you reach it, crawl in and pull the ladder in after you. *Don't* come out until one of us gives you the all clear."

Kat gripped a rung and began to climb. Jaradee followed. Katareen reached the opening and crawled inside. Vertigo pressed Jaradee against the trunk. Controlling the desire to vomit, she crawled after Kat. Taking a moment to steady her nerves and her stomach, she pulled the ladder rung by rung until the end slid over the lip of the opening.

Groping her way to Katareen's side, she pulled her close and rested a cheek against her hair. Silent as a raven's wing, darkness enveloped them.

5

Jaradee strained to hear anything that would tell her whether the Pheet Adole had discovered the camp. Nothing stirred but Katareen's soft inhale and exhale. Jaradee struggled to keep sleep-heavy lids open. Even a light doze would dull her senses, something she could not afford.

Time crept by. The quiet scrape and slap of a ladder descending caught her on the verge of succumbing. Disentangling herself from her sister's sleeping form, Jaradee wormed her way around the piled ladder. Far below, the faint glow of embers in the uncovered pit illuminated a man's figure. Two more walked into the fire's glow. Ebony skin gleamed as Kuparak turned to greet Zarrin and Mylos. After a brief discussion, Zarrin hurried to the narrow entrance and slipped out. Mylos followed soon after.

The sluggish passage of time nudged Jaradee to act. Mylos' reappearance stopped her. Quick discourse with Kuparak brought a nod from the Vasrosi leader. Torches sprang to light. A low whistle signaled all clear. Ladders dropped from openings around the cupress trunk and cascaded down the walls. Mylos and Kuparak secured the ends to stakes in the ground and Vasrosi members began the descent to the ground.

Jaradee crawled back to Katareen. A gentle shake woke her. After pushing the ladder over the edge, Jaradee led the descent. Near the bottom, firm hands gripped her waist and guided her down the last few rungs. Kuparak smiled at her obvious confusion before he turned to assist Katareen.

Zarrin entered the camp with a skittish whistler hawk perched on his arm. "It wouldn't tell me anything. Just that it has a message."

A gleam of satiny color from its prosthetic wing accompanied the bird's transfer to Kuparak's arm. Its nervousness vanished.

A tingled telepathic message startled Jaradee. "It wants to communicate."

Kuparak's thoughtful gaze traveled from the whistler to her. "Mind talk is one of your gifts?"

She nodded and drew Katareen to her side. "Kat uses it a little, but her—"

Katareen shot her a quelling look and pulled her away from the men. "Is it safe to share with them? Uncle Kamer told us to tell no one. I trust Mylos and Kuparak. They wear their truth like a badge of honor. Not Zarrin." She looked back at the group by the fire. "He is not what he seems."

Jaradee frowned. "Stay here. I'll bring Kuparak." She walked back to the men. "Kuparak, Katareen has a private question for you."

Mylos controlled his reaction as his leader passed him the small hawk. Zarrin pursed his lips and kicked a small twig into the pit. Kuparak followed her and placed himself between Katareen and the men.

Jaradee felt a subtle protective curtain enclose them. She clasped her sister's hand.

The Vasrosi leader gave Kat his full attention. "You have a question, Katareen?"

"Uncle Kamer told us we should not let others know if we carry the talents of an Eleo Predan shameena. One of my gifts is assessing the honesty in others. I share this with you, Kuparak, because I feel your truth." Her intent gaze did not waver. "I do not feel this in Zarrin."

Kuparak's jaw tightened. Katareen gripped Jaradee's hand tighter.

The protective ward faded. Kuparak spoke in a normal tone. "I understand. Jaradee will take you to Floree. Perhaps she will have something to help."

Jaradee felt him follow their progress as they made their way to where

Floree knelt by Umbba. When Jaradee looked his direction again, Kuparak stood chatting with Mylos, and Zarrin waited by the entrance. Mylos listened, nodded, and knelt to build up the fire. Kuparak slipped out of the opening behind his lieutenant.

The muffled sounds of tents being raised and camp being restored to its functional norm drifted around the hollowed interior of the cupress. Katareen fidgeted. "What's taking them so long?"

Floree patted the blanket. "I need your help, Kat. Jaradee, Mylos will show you where the food's stored. I imagine everyone's hungry."

Mylos led her between two tents and lifted round lids covered with moss and leaves. Beneath them, he exposed watertight hampers containing carefully packed food: prepared rations, root vegetables, fruits, and a variety of dried meats.

Jaradee shook her head. "I'm so impressed by the Vasrosi's ingenuity. This camp contains everything we need *and* it can disappear in moments."

Mylos nodded. "When a bunch of people fighting to stay alive get together, miracles happen."

Jaradee's thoughts skipped from breakfast to Kuparak's willingness to believe Kat. *I wonder...*

Mylos cleared his throat. "You mind helping me with these?" He held out a bag of fruit, a jug of harvest honey, and a small pouch of dried cinnamon chips.

"Sorry. I was dream turning." She took the bag of fruit.

He grinned. "I bet I can guess the star of *your* dream." Keeping his back to the space, he said, "But I'd rather know what Katareen told Kuparak. Why she didn't want to share her gifts with us?"

Jaradee drew in a breath and expelled it with a soft sigh. "You should ask Kuparak when he returns. You already know our gifts and we yours."

Understanding dawned. The nostrils in a nose broken in a brawl with Rompeerial soldiers flared. A scar-bisected eyebrow raised. His lips parted in a sneer, showing a chipped tooth. "I see." A calloused hand stroked the whistler's feathered side. "Kuparak wants you to find out what the bird knows."

Jaradee gave a soft whistle. The hawk flew to her shoulder and nuzzled satiny glass against her cheek. "The soldiers are closer than we think and waiting for a signal, so they can catch us by surprise." She sucked in a breath. "Zarrin is a spy."

"Food can wait." Mylos returned the food to the hampers and shut the lids. "I'll see if Kup needs any backup." He ran a finger over the bird's back, turned on his heels, and with the stealth of a feline predator, crept out of the opening.

Jaradee touched the side of her wrist to the hawk's crystal breast. It stepped on to her forearm, and she lowered it to eye level. Opening her mind to the small raptor brought a flood of images. When they ceased, it bobbed its head, expressed its intent to find Kuparak, and soared out the opening.

Jaradee hurried to Floree. "Trouble heads our way. Soldiers hide on the far side of the ravine. The plan is to catch us unawares."

The healer finished tying a bandage and climbed to her feet. "Katareen shared her concerns. I gather the whistler hawk confirmed it?"

"Yes."

Floree motioned Camilyn, Tealin, and Daar to join them. After a quick but vague explanation, she said, "Tealin, I'm leaving you in charge. Daar, you are Tealin's back up. Kat and Camilyn will help you. Be prepared to strike camp and hide if we give the signal. In fact, strike the tents and cover them."

Daar groaned. "We just put them up, Floree."

Tealin elbowed him in the side. "Stop being a crybaby and get a move on." He nudged him toward a tent. "Don't worry, Floree."

Katareen hugged Jaradee and hurried to help.

Floree tucked a loop of stout rope in her waistband and motioned Jaradee to stay close. As silent as shadows, they stepped into the faint dawn light, ducked behind a bush, and listened. Voice murmuring led them between trees to a clearing, where Kuparak and Zarrin stood engrossed in conversation.

Kuparak's easy stance and relaxed countenance contrasted with the tense anger holding Zarrin rigid. The shorter man swore under his breath and turned to walk from the small clearing.

Mylos blocked his path. "I don't believe Kuparak has finished, Zar."

Zarrin slipped a hand in his pocket and lurched to one side. Sinewy and quick, Mylos diverted him back the way he had come.

Mylos grabbed the traitor's wrist and it yank free of the pocket. A small black box flew across the clearing.

His bullish head swung one way and then the other. Fists raised fists, Zarrin lumbered forward.

Kuparak's muscles rippled into action. A panther's grace carried him through the air. The impact flung Zarrin to the ground and ended with Kuparak standing unperturbed, staring at him.

"I would never have expected you of all people to turn traitor. What have they offered you for the lives of your friends and your people, Zar?"

The man scowled and started to rise. "You're fightin' a battle you can never win, Kup. Go home; prepare your families to serve the Rompeer or die. I intend to survive."

A minatory heave brought him to standing. His fist flew. Kuparak blocked the punch, brought his fist up under Zarrin's chin, and sent him stumbling into Mylos' waiting arms. Floree stepped into the clearing and tossed Kuparak the rope. Jaradee waited in the shadows, her senses alert and searching. The whistler landed on her shoulder. Tiny sparks flashed in its glass protected brain, forming a connection between them. Its telie-eye focused on the men in the clearing.

Zarrin struggled to keep Kuparak from tying his hands behind his back. "You can't hope to keep me prisoner, Kuparak. I'll get away. Then I'll..."

Kuparak touched a finger to his lips and whispered a quiet word.

Zarrin's mouth clamped shut around a garble of muffled sound. Two older men materialized and stationed themselves on either side of him. A contorted sneer laced with wariness replaced his bravado.

Kuparak stepped away. "Take him to the Conclave Arcana."

Terror and chagrin whipped Zarrin's scowl into pleading. His escorts each took an arm. The three men vanished.

Mylos wiped sweat from his brow. "Won't that call the soldiers to us?"

Jaradee joined Floree. "The hawk offered his mind as a conduit for a protective shield. Kuparak signaled, and I set it only long enough for them to teleport Zarrin."

Mylos studied her. "You're good, Jara." He switched his attention to Kuparak. "Who were his escorts? And what will happen to him?"

Kuparak massaged his earlobe. "How long have you lived amongst the Pheet Adole, Mylos?"

"Father brought me to El SyrTundi when my mother died. His sister lived in Tahellive, where her Pheet Adolan companion ran a business in Throsswel. I was maybe fourteen sun cycles."

"And how did you meet Jaradee's uncle?"

"Kamer and I were friends in Thornland and kept in touch. When Father died, I contacted him to ask if he'd like to go into the fishing business with me. Why?"

"I have a proposition for you. Jaradee and Floree will stand as my witnesses."

Mylos raised his brows and waited.

"I need a deputy whom I can trust." The Vasrosi leader extended his left palm. "Would you be interested?"

After a pensive silence, Mylos rested his on top and touched the center of his forehead. "I am honored, Kuparak."

The radiance of Kuparak's smile seemed to warm the entire clearing. Jaradee caught herself smiling and noted Floree doing the same.

"The two men, Mylos, were Arcana Journeymen. Their job is to protect those working for the Conclave Arcana. Zarrin is now facing the leaders of his district council."

Mylos frowned. "And the soldiers who are awaiting his signal? What of them?"

Kuparak's expression grew implacable. "We let them wait. The tukoolo will keep us informed." He motioned Mylos to lead the way. "I believe morning meal is long past due."

Jaradee fell in behind Mylos, her thoughts in turmoil. *And what of Katareen? Do we still take her to safety?*

6

At Kuparak's insistence, casual conversation accompanied the morning meal. Afterward, everyone helped clean up, and then gathered around the fire pit.

Kuparak took Katareen aside and engaged her in a quiet discussion.

Daar elbowed Jaradee in the ribs. "What's that about?"

She gave him an annoyed stare and massaged her side. "I believe we are about to find out."

Katareen dropped to the ground beside her. Kuparak sat on a log. His astute gaze traveled from one member of his team to the next. "Before we take Kat, Tealin, and Camilyn home, if indeed that is their destiny, I have a job that must be done. Kat and Jaradee, I will need you to accompany Mylos and me. Floree, you will be in charge here. Camilyn will help you with the injured. Questions?"

Daar spoke up. "What about the soldiers?"

A hint of levity softened Kuparak's sober expression. "We'll need a distraction to cover our departure. I am certain you and Tealin will find a means to lead them away from the Cupress-Pine Forest."

The boys' eager nods made their leader's smile flash, then cool. "Do not get caught. They will harvest everything you know, and like the tukoolo, leave you for dead. We cannot help you. Do I make myself clear?"

Tealin, the older of the two, answered. "We understand, Kup. Daar and I will not get caught."

"Make sure you don't." Kuparak gave a low whistle. A tukoolo flew into camp and perched on the log next to him. He rubbed its feathered back and grew even more serious. "This is a smoky galee—smoky because of its black and gray feathers. As you can see, it is the size of a large hawk, and the Pheet Adole have experimented on it." The galee stepped onto his arm. Kuparak angled it to show the satiny sheen of the head, wing, and tail on its right side. "For our new members, his reconstructed side has a mirror-like glaze. In shadow, it absorbs the darkness. In the light, it reflects the world around it. When the tukoolo is with someone it trusts, the blown crystal is clear and you can see the heartbeat and the synapses in its brain spark. I call this one Toa, which means warrior in the language of my ancestors. Toa reports directly to me. Each Vasrosi has a tukoolo. The name of your tukoolo is a sacred pact between you. Do not share it with anyone you do not trust." He whispered to Toa.

The bird soared from camp and, within moments, a smaller bird flew through the entrance and came to rest on Kuparak's arm. He held it aloft. "This is an El Storman harrier. Tealin has his tukoolo, Daar. I have asked this one to consider you as its compeer or partner. Bird and man must bond. Please come here."

Daar walked forward, shining eyes fixed on the beautiful hawk. For a long moment, bird and boy studied each other. Then Daar raised his arm and whistled a soft note. The bird fluttered to a gentle landing. Firelight glowed on the spun crystal chest and tail. The eye piece swiveled, and, like a telescope, lengthened and retracted. Daar did not move. Jaradee wondered if he even breathed.

The hawk unfurled its wings and stretched to its full height. Its majesty brought a gasp of admiration from Daar. Wafted air from its wings folding rustled his hair. His laugh of delight filled the camp.

Kuparak rested one hand on the boy's shoulder and the other on the bird's cinnamon and gold back. "It has accepted you as its compeer. If you sense the connection, I will create the psychic bond."

Daar, for once at a loss for words, nodded.

"Rethet Ceerus." Kuparak lifted his hands and stepped back.

Jaradee watched her brother's chest fill with air, saw the wonder in his face, and smiled. "It is beautiful, Daar. What will you call it?"

"It is a male. I will call him Rangi after the air spirit of El Quil'Tran." He faced Kuparak. "Thank you for your trust, and for this unbelievable gift."

"We are not done, Daar. Shape shifting is not a shameen gift you have refined. As a Vasrosi, you will need to access this ability to save yourself and others. You must learn to tether your thoughts to Rangi's and to take the shape of a harrier hawk. Tealin will work with you. When you're ready, come back to me."

Tealin led the way. Daar, with Rangi on his shoulder, walked carefully after him.

Kuparak turned his attention to Katareen. "You also require a tukoolo." The flutter of wings announced a small, brown and white raptor and ceased as it landed on his arm.

"This is a berigora falcon. She is smart and quick and has already expressed the desire to be your compeer."

Wonder and excitement enhanced Katareen's natural beauty. "But aren't you sending me home?"

"Even if our final decision is to send you to El Quil'Tran, you will require the aid of a tukoolo." His brows arched. "Unless, of course, you don't want one."

"Please, Kuparak, I want her." Gulping a breath, she offered her forearm. The berigora stepped on. Katareen tensed and gave a soft laugh. "You are heavier than I imagined." Eyes shining, she examined the falcon. One side glistened with the sheen of blown quartz. Half of its creamy breast reflected the light of the fire. She stroked its wing and sighed. "I love her."

Kuparak laid a hand on her head and one on the bird's back. "Rethet Ceerus." He stepped away. "What have you named her?"

Tears streamed down Katareen's face. "I asked what she wanted to be called. She loves the moon and the stars. I will call her Tupuni."

"Tupuni rejoices in your choice. She is ready to fly with you. You know how to shift shape, but only do so when tethered to Tupuni. If you forget and use your own talent, the Pheet Adole will find you with SorTechery. Am I clear?"

"I understand." She gasped. "I sense her in my mind. We are one. I—."

Jaradee's hands flew to her mouth as her sister flashed into the form of a berigora and flew a circle with Tupuni. Kat landed in human form, the falcon perched on her shoulder. "Thank you, Kuparak. Does this mean I am a Vasrosi?"

His eyes sparked with a touch of laughter. "It does. Go. Get acquainted, but stay in camp." He placed a hand on Jaradee's shoulder. "I believe you have already chosen your compeer and she you."

A high whistle preceded the whistler hawk through the narrow entrance. It flew straight to Jaradee and perched on her outstretched arm. Kuparak looked from bird to girl. "Are you ready, or do you need time?"

The hawk side-stepped to her shoulder and nuzzled her cheek. Jaradee smiled. "We're ready."

Kuparak spoke the words of tethering. A connection so strong it threw her head back and her arms wide, caught her off guard. The whistler lifted into flight. Tingling energy shot through her body. Her heart beat quickened. Her eyesight sharpened. The next instant, the body of a whistle hawk encased her. Soaring upward until she could go no further, she began a slow, descending spiral, joining her compeer in a duet of interwoven patterns. Her raptor sight searched the dimly lit camp, picked out each member of the Vasrosi, each tent, each twig, piece of moss, speck of dirt. A slight tug in her mind brought her back to the ground in human form. Her delighted laugh soared after her compeer, where it circled once more, dropped to her shoulder, and nibbled her ear.

Kuparak's gorgeous smile warmed her like the sun after a long rain. "You are well-matched. What will you christen her?"

"She is Kariahe, Heaven's Star. I will call her Karia. Thank you for connecting us."

He shook his head. "I did nothing. You connected the first time you were together, but Rethet Ceerus strengthens the tethering. Now, I must help your brother. Then you and I must talk."

Daar strode toward them, Rangi on his shoulder. His expression told Jaradee how much he loved the hawk. "I haven't seen him happy in a while. Not since they killed Pa."

Kuparak acknowledged her statement and her brother's arrival with a nod. "Have you ever shifted shape, Daar?"

"Never. I am so excited." He grinned.

"Calm your emotions. I need your complete attention. Shape shifting is dangerous for the scattered mind."

Rubbing a hand over his shaved head, Daar steadied his breathing. "I'm ready."

"Until you feel secure, Rangi will be the judge of when to shift. He will create the tether. Feel it?"

Blood rushed to Daar's cheeks. "He is in my mind."

"Good. He will show you how it is to be a hawk."

Daar closed his eyes. Jaradee sensed Rangi taking him step by step through the process and admired the bird's patience with her younger brother. When Daar opened his eyes, reverence and uncertainty flashed as he looked from Rangi to Kuparak. "I felt its heartbeat, the air moving in and out of its lungs, and the quickness of its thoughts. Are you sure I can do this?"

"I am certain." Kuparak paused, his demeanor confident. "What counts, however, is whether *you* are sure. Don't attempt a change if you're not."

Daar pressed a hand to his chest and stood motionless for some time. A long sigh left him relaxed and smiling. "I am ready. And I am sure."

The next instant, Rangi lifted into flight. Daar shifted and flew after his compeer. One circle, two, the third ended with him facing Kuparak, elation brightening his smile and his arm raised to receive Rangi.

As hawk talons wrapped around it, Jaradee observed the tether release and Daar return to himself. Stunned silence held him motionless, and then his excitement overflowed. "I shifted! He jumped back and grinned after throwing an arm around Kuparak. "I did it. No..." He stroked Rangi's chest. "We did it."

Kuparak smiled. "Well done, Daar. You already understand the power of partnership."

Jaradee glanced up at Kuparak, wondering if he realized the gift he had given her brother.

—

7

Jaradee leaned against the trunk of a huge pine and squinted in the forest dimness. The tethering of tukoolo to their compeers had taken most of the morning. Preparing a meal and eating had used up another chunk of time. Too late to do much else, Kuparak had sent Tealin, Daar, and their tukoolo on a reconnaissance flight.

Glad to be outside after two turnings within the cupress hollow, she inhaled forest smells and savored the fresh air in her lungs. The Vasrosi camp provided safety and cover, but the perpetual darkness left her struggling to keep her emotions in check.

Kuparak emerged from the trees with Toa on his shoulder. The handsome pair, black man and black raptor, emitted a combined power that snatched Jaradee's breath away. White teeth flashed as Kuparak scratched the broad breast of his compeer and murmured, "Go." A soft screech accompanied the galee's launch into flight.

The Vasrosi leader strode to her side. "We must talk." He led her through the trees to another clearing where six large, dark green stones formed a circle beneath the towering pines. "This is an Elysian Round, a rare occurrence on El SyrTundi. We have them at home in Thornland in the SianEly Forest and along the Charnlandian border. The round is sacred and promotes balance, peace, and wisdom. Let us sit and talk."

Jaradee hesitated. Each stone, she realized, had its own essence. Walking the circle, she examined them one by one until a spark of recognition stopped her. She pressed her palm against a smooth stone, felt a tingling up her arm, and sat down.

Kuparak picked his seat and faced her. "You never cease to surprise me, Jaradee. Mylos told me you and Katareen had much to offer, but..." He smiled. "Do you realize the strength of your gifts?"

Jaradee experience a stab of sorrow. She touched a leather thong around her neck and withdrew a fiery gemstone. "From a young age, I have been training as a shameena. My grandmameen taught me much before the soldiers took her away. She gave me this as a reminder to use my knowledge with discernment." Savoring the smoothness of the blue stone, she admired its inner fire. "What did you want to talk about?"

Kuparak rested his forearms on his knees. "What do you know of Protariflee?"

Jaradee searched her memory. "Uncle Kamer mentioned it once. He told me the Rompeer ordered the development of Protariflee to keep the wealthy families of El SyrTundi from constant war with one another. He didn't explain what it is...just that it's done."

Kuparak straightened. "Lusktar Rados ordered the research and ultimate use of Protariflee for two reasons: to ensure the family lines of the wealthy continued and, as your uncle noted, to keep wealthy households from engaging in wars against one another. When the young of the wealthy reach puberty, they harvest eggs and sperm and handpick samples to freeze for a later time. The Rompeer's men capture Eleo Predan women, who are then impregnated with fertilized eggs, one male and one female, from different family lines."

Jaradee furrowed her brow. "Why Eleo Predan women? Why not use Pheet Adole hosts?"

"They hope the Eleo Preda gene for a long life will pass to the birth-mates, and thus into the genes of the Pheet Adole."

"What happens when the babies are born?"

"They place each child in the care of a nurser and reintroduce it into its family of origin. The premise for this appears to be the belief that gestating in the same womb will create a closeness between the babies, not unlike twins, that will last throughout their lifetimes."

Jaradee tucked her grandmameen's stone beneath her shirt. "I'm guessing they reintroduce the birth-mates when they attain marriageable age, and thus two families form an alliance. How long has this been in effect?"

"I would think about seven or eight sun cycles."

"And what has this got to do with me?"

"The Vasrosi has infiltrated the Protariflee Center. Four of our members are now certified to extract and implant eggs. We also have a small cryogenics storage unit off the premises where we can store the eggs and sperm of important Eleo Predans. One of our certified Protariflee Agents spent time in El QuilTran and came back with samples from leaders and shameenu. We plan to gather as many as we can. If it becomes necessary, we will get them to safety off planet."

Jaradee raised her eyebrows and waited.

Kuparak's candid gaze remained steady. "I would like you and Katareen to give samples. Your bloodline reaches back to the beginnings of human life on El Stroma. Your genes carry the memories of other generations and other places."

She studied her folded hands. Forest-calm embraced her. A bird's chirped song accompanied the ebb and flow of her thoughts. At last, she looked up.

"Of course, we will donate samples. What of Daar? Will you also have him do it?"

"When the boys report back from their reconnaissance, we will decide on what diversion tactics will work best. They will carry out the plan and lead the soldiers away. Once they're safe, Tealin will take Daar to the Center on the outskirts of Chunarrie."

"I have never been to the capital. Uncle Kamer had promised us a trip when things settled. I'm sure he realized they never would. Tell me of El QuilTran. I have been gone almost a sun cycle. The warring was in its beginnings."

Sadness and anger changed light to shadow in the man's extraordinary eyes. "Rompeerial soldiers invade and conquer one small village at a time. We don't know how long we can hold out against the technical warfare waged by the Pheet Adole. They…"

Daar and Tealin materialized at the circle's center, their tukoolo perched above them in the trees. Karia landed on Jaradee's shoulder. Toa alighted on a thick tree branch above his compeer's head.

Tealin spoke urgently. "The soldiers are restless. They performing a sweep of the area on the far side of the creek. We must move now, or they *will* find us."

Kuparak frowned. "Do you have a plan, Tealin?"

The young man shook his head. "No, but Daar does."

"What's your plan?" Kuparak's intent gaze rested on her brother.

In his concise and methodical fashion, Daar explained. Jaradee glanced Kuparak's direction and smiled. Like any boy of seventeen, Daar could be impetuous, but their granddee had taught him well.

"The camp is empty but for two soldiers who guard the perimeter. Eight others search between the elder-leaf marker tree and the stream bank. There's a campfire on the opposite side of their camp." Daar pulled a fisted hand from his pocket and held it out. Uncurling his fingers, he revealed six ammunition rounds on his palm. "Tealin and I can wait until it's clear and drop these in the fire. The noise should bring the others back to camp. We met four Vasrosi from the cabin headed this way and told them to stay hidden. The explosions will be their cue to scatter through the woods and lead the soldiers back toward Tahellive. We'll catch up and create diversions when necessary to keep the soldiers moving in that direction. If we haven't lost them by the time we reach Throsswel, we'll lose them there. When we're safe, Rangi will let Toa know."

A slow smile and a nod affirmed Kuparak's acceptance of the plan. "Who are the other Vasrosi?"

Tealin listed four men. We left two women in camp to help Floree."

Kuparak looked pleased. "Good. That accounts for those who were at the cabin. Get a move on. I'll take care of the women and see you in Chunarrie."

The boys shifted and took flight. At a sign from Kuparak, Toa followed.

Disquiet radiated from the man beside her. Her thoughts raced as she waited for him to make the next move. A series of muffled whistles raced through the woods. The circle of stones faded, leaving the forest floor covered with pine needles and mulch. Kuparak grabbed her arm, pulled her into the trees, and pressed her behind him. A Rompeerial soldier strode into the canopy-filtered light and spoke over his shoulder. "I'm telling you I heard voices."

A second soldier, half-hidden behind a massive trunk, scowled. "You've been hearing stuff all day. We've found nothing on this side of the stream. Better get back to..."

The distant sound of shots fired cut him short. Both men froze, exchanged harried glances, and sprinted back toward the soldier's camp.

Kuparak pulled Jaradee to her feet. "He headed back to the hollow pine. After giving a low whistle, he listened intently. A repeated, throaty cackle answered.

"It's safe. Tell Katareen to get ready to leave." He touched her shoulder. "Tell no one where we are going. In fact, don't tell Kat anything except to be ready."

She crept around the trunk and into the narrow entrance. Muted darkness engulfed her. A hand covered her mouth. An arm circled her waist and half lifted, half carried her deeper into the hollow. Hot breath brushed her cheek. Strong fingers tightened around her neck. The last thing she remembered—agonizing pain in lungs fighting for air.

8

Jaradee came back to herself in slow motion. The feel of the ground registered first, followed by a dull pain in her temple. Hands tied in front of her; ankles trussed with rough rope; a mouth full of tasteless cloth tied in place ignited the kindling of despair, stoking her fear. No light and the smell cupress wood added fuel to the fire. *Where's Kat? Floree? The others?*

Silence weighted by not knowing intensified. A torch wavered, steadied, and moved toward her. Light pooling around a uniformed soldier emphasized her danger. A boot toe nudged her. "I know there is a camp nearby. Where is it, and the rest of the accursed Vasrosi?"

Feigning unconsciousness, Jaradee lay unmoving. An image in her mind gave her hope. Karia was close.

A hand gripped the front of her shirt and yanked her to sitting. "Don't play games with me, Eleo Predan filth. Where's the real camp and how many trashers like you are there?"

The muffled wha, wha of wings, the startled shout of the soldier, the torch flying from his grasp, and total black gave Jaradee the opportunity to wiggle away from the enemy. Hands gripped her armpits from behind and hoisted her to standing. Ropes at her hands and feet fell away. The gag loosened. She yanked it off and spit out the wad of cloth. The next instant, she stood outside in the twilight shadows. The tether with her whistler hawk snapped into place. She shifted and flew to a high branch, raptor senses trained on the hollow cupress.

The soft sounds of shuffling feet floated up to her perch. Kuparak and Mylos dragged the dead weight of the soldier between huge cupress trunks and disappeared. Katareen peered around the edge of the entrance, stepped into the open, and stared up at the branch where Jaradee perched close to Karia.

Jaradee landed beside her and assumed her human form. Katareen threw arms around her and clung to her as she feared Jaradee would vanish if she let go.

"I was so afraid for you, Jara. There was no way to warn you. If it weren't for Tupuni, we wouldn't have hidden in time ourselves." She stepped away, honey-gold eyes feasting on Jaradee's face. "You're alright, aren't you?"

"I'm fine...just frustrated that I let them catch me. Where are the others?"

Floree joined them. "They're breaking camp. Too many close calls to stay here. We have a haven in the foothill near Port Saticch. It's harder to get to, but all the safer for it."

Kuparak stepped into the clearing, his expression grim. "It's done. Mylos is taking care of the body. I would have preferred to leave the Pheet Adole alive, but—" A stern frown stretched his full-lips into a firm line. "Never forget the sanctity of life." He turned his attention to the group emerging from the hollow.

Two women Jaradee remembered from the cottage by the lake preceded Umbba, who inhaled deeply and moved to one side. Though still pale, a touch of color highlighted his cheekbones, and his eyes had lost their injury induced dullness. Camilyn appeared next, supporting Watuli with an arm around his waist; she helped him to a moss-covered stump.

"Everything is in order, Kup. We secured the ladders in their hollow branches, stowed the tents, and lowered and covered the fire pit. Nature will take its course, at least until we get back."

Kuparak nodded. "Good. You know the plan. Mylos will accompany you to the edge of the forest. From there, JoJana will lead the way to the Chaporticas Mountains near Port Saticch." He provided a rolled map and a small El Stroman compass. "Watuli knows the safest places to camp. Since you will be on foot most of the way, I suggest you travel at night. Once Watuli and Umbba are fully healed, you can fly."

JoJana, a fair-skinned Thornlandian with short brown hair and irises the deep green of the stones in the Elysian Round, accepted both items and tucked them in her pack. "How long before you join us?"

"It depends on what we discover in Chunarrie and what I hear and see along the way." He touched a fisted hand to his heart. "Travel in safety."

With a nod, Mylos led his charges through the gigantic Cupress-Cone Forest.

Katareen moved closer to Jaradee. Kuparak gave a low whistle. Toa, Karia, and Tupuni dropped from the trees and flew to their respective compeers.

"We leave with just each other and our tukoolo and fly north of Tahellive. By dawn, we should reach a safe house. It is rare for hawks to fly in large groups. Toa and I will lead the way. Tupuni and Katareen will follow, keeping east of us but within sight. Jaradee, you and Karia will be our rear guard. Stay to my left and behind Katareen. Keep your tethers strong. Your tukoolo will know when to land. If you sense trouble or need help, let your tukoolo send the message."

Jaradee felt the subtle snap of her tethered joining to Karia. Waiting until her leader and her sister were airborne, she shifted and soared upward. Above the forest canopy, cool air caressed her body and supported her wings. The scattered sparkle of other worlds and other times bedecked the night dome. Dyad's quarter phase, straight above, cast its cold blue light on the landscape below. Topping the eastern horizon, the curve of Alkina, El Stroma's pale rose moon, hung free of its usual topaz haze, a rare and marvelous occurrence. Intoxicated by flight and beauty, Jaradee almost lost sight of her sister's berigora shape. A warning whispered through her mind. Karia banked to the east. Jaradee followed. Katareen and Tupuni, graceful silhouettes against shimmering rose, dropped lower, skimmed a stand of elder-leafs and sallow weepers bordering a rushing stream, and vanished.

Jaradee's heart clutched. A dark shape shot after them and landed on the bank of the stream. Remaining hidden, she swooped into the trees and shifted behind an elder-leaf. Karia perched several trees away, her telie-eye searching.

Her desire to act barely contained, Jaradee forced her thoughts into stillness. An image flashed and melted away. Katareen hid in the branches of a weeper on the opposite side of the stream. Over head, Toa spiraled downward. Kuparak was nowhere to be seen.

The shadowy figure loosed a vacant, windy cry. A shaft of moonlight trapped it and highlighted the churning of dim-gray clouds comprising it. A zigzag of white careened a diagonal path from one side to the other, cutting the figure and the clouds in two. The rumbled rejoining vibrated through the night.

Kuparak materialized, facing the creature. Another flash of lightning... Another rumble of cloud against cloud...Billowing fog formed and shaped a mouth-like orifice.

Kuparak called. Jaradee swooped to the ground, shifted, and released the tethered connection to her tukoolo. A berigora landed beside her. Katareen appeared. Together, they walked from the trees and made their way to Kuparak's side.

Jaradee, mesmerized by the strange creature, studied it with a touch of wonder. Not as tall as Kuparak, its amorphous body absorbed the moon's light one moment and faded into the night shadows the next. Vision orbs that morphed from gray to blue, from blue to gray, regarded them with the innocence of a child. The coolness of the rain misting around it dampened her skin. She glanced at Kuparak.

He put one arm around her and the other around Katareen. "This is a maelstrom. It formed at the top of the Gruseeno Mountains on El QuilTran and brings a message from Conclave Arcana. Zarrin has escaped. The Conclave fears he will board one of the Rompeerial ships anchored off the coast of Neseer. Journeymen track him, but if he makes it to El SyrTundi, he will have the advantage."

Jaradee reached a hand toward the maelstrom. Moist softness caressed her fingers. "Does it have a name?"

The creature's body roiled and steadied. Intense azure orbs gleamed. "I am Squal." The clouds forming its body mass churned. It spun upwards, hovered, and returned to land. "Danger closes the gap. Leave. I will obscure your departure. May the storms of El Stroma protect you."

Kuparak hurried them beneath a weeper tree. Squal billowed into a massive thunder cloud and floated above the stream bed. Torrential rain pounded the ground. Wind whipped the treetops and created a frothy foam on the water's surface. The cloud tripled in size, obscuring the night dome and blotting out the light of El Storma's moons.

Jaradee's tether to Karia snapped into place. Lightning ripped the clouds in two. A crack of thunder followed. Katareen and Kuparak shifted and flew through the stand of trees. Jaradee shaped a whistler hawk and raced to catch up.

Silent flight carried them away from the raging storm and put distance between them and an enemy they did not know.

9

Kuparak led the way, his galee form untiring. Dyad completed its journey across the night dome. Alkina's pale rose sphere slipped along the far curve of its arc. Behind them, the maelstrom had vanished and the sun's soft dawn light announced the start of another turning.

"Land now!" Tupuni's cry filled Jaradee's mind.

Kuparak's black galee swooped into a thicket of berry bushes. Kat and Tupuni flew after him. Jaradee glided downward and landed on a stout branch to find her sister sitting cross-legged on the ground, her head in her hands. Kuparak, attention riveted to the morning dome, stood nearby. Allowing the tether to Karia to dissolve, Jaradee fluttered to the ground and materialized.

"Are we still being followed?"

"Toa is off to find out. He can fly higher than the rest of us. Hopefully, no one will notice him." With great care, he cupped a large leaf filled with dew and offered it to Katareen. "Drink this, Kat. Then pick some berries. We only have a short distance to go, but I prefer not to lead the enemy to our benefactors."

Kat lifted her head, blinked back a tear, and accepted the leaf. "Thank you." She sipped the sweet liquid and climbed to her feet. Plucking a red berry, she popped it into her mouth. A smile blossomed. "I feel better already."

Jaradee followed her example. Soon the emptiness cramping her belly eased, and she felt her energy returning. "Potent berries." She smiled with her mouth full.

Kuparak grinned. "They are used to make a drink for the Rompeer's athletes." The grin faded. Total concentration took its place. "Toa returns. Make sure you have eaten enough."

A black dot appeared high above their hiding place. Gradually, Jaradee made out the shape of a body and wings stretched wide to catch the currents. With leisurely grace, the galee spiraled downward, landed at the top of a tall tree some distance away, and pecked at the feathers on its breast. Its cackled song echoed through the morning. Launching into the air, it flew well beyond the berry thicket and dropped from sight.

Kuparak gathered the girls to him. "Company not far behind. Shift shape and remain hidden here. Don't panic. Toa feels certain our enemies will pass us by." He shaped a galee and lifted into flight.

Jaradee pulled Katareen down beside her, changed to a hawk, and allowed the thick leafy bush to camouflage her existence. The berigora appeared and nestled close. Karia and Tupuni were nowhere to be seen.

Overhead, a huge, winged form blocked the sun. Another shot past it, circled, and made an awkward landing some distance from the thicket. A man with huge, gawky wings tipped his head to watch his companion alight. Two men are talking. The first nodded; the second bird-man slipped his arms free and set about adjusting something on his friend's back. He stepped away, said something, and watched. Wing-shaped appendages opened, wafted back and forth, then lowered. Another adjustment and the first man pumped his wings and lifted with a total lack of grace into the air, trailing a stream of gray smoke behind him. Waiting long enough to assure that his companion would remain airborne, the second slid his arms into place, experimented with the ailerons, and fiddled with something on his chest. A squinted gaze toward his comrade and the powerful thrust of his huge wings launched himself upward in a billowing cloud of white. Soon, they were both out of sight.

The sun, now high overhead, warmed Jaradee's feathered back. Still, Kuparak and Toa remained absent. Katareen ran a long wing feather through her beak, fluffed up her neck feathers, and seemed to hunch lower.

Again, a shadow blocked the sun. A black galee landed and Kuparak materialized. "Don't shift. We'll talk when we get to the haven." He returned to his galee form and soared into the afternoon light. Whistler hawk and berigora falcon followed.

The short flight ended in the alley of a dilapidated barn. A cow mooed a welcome. Jaradee shifted and smiled at the ginger cat rubbing against her leg.

Katareen appeared, knelt, and murmured, "Hello, Tag." She scratched the white diamond under its chin and stood. Kuparak put a finger to his lips and peered through a crack between the weathered boards.

Moments later, a short, stocky man strolled into the barn. "Good to see ya, Kup. Wasn't sure you'd make it when I saw them broticos. Thought they might be followin' ya." He pushed a batter hat back and sized up the girls.

Kuparak smiled. "Good to see you, Harie. Gotta place where we can rest?"

"Best stay here. Soldiers have been turnin' up at odd times. Also, a couple of Klutarse in their fancy scarlet and black uniforms rode in yesterday. Doubt they'll be back, but..." He glanced upward. "You'll find a basket of food, water, and some blankets in the loft. I'll come back for a chat after dark." He pulled his hat low on his brow, grabbed a bucket, and whistling strode from the barn.

When they had settled in the loft, Kuparak glanced at Katareen. "Did you sense anything wrong?"

She shook her head and opened the food hamper. "No. Just honesty and curiosity. I'm starved."

The basket contained thick slices of meat and cheese between slabs of freshly baked bread, a jug of water and four mugs, and a variety of fruits. Kat handed out sandwiches. A bite left her nodding in appreciation. She licked crumbs from her lips. "Delicious."

Jaradee nibbled at hers. "I didn't know the Rompeer's soldiers could fly. Is that why they've been experimenting with birds?"

Kuparak took a deep drink of water. "I heard they'd recently gotten a man airborne. I would guess what we saw were prototypes being tested."

Katareen paled. "We don't stand a chance against soldiers who fly."

Jaradee gave her a quick hug. "Sure we do. We have tukoolo to help us. Which reminds me...does Zarrin still have a tukoolo?"

"No. I reprogrammed his to guard Cupress-Cone Forest. It reports directly to Toa." Kuparak grimaced. "Unfortunately, Zarrin knows how to create his own tukoolo. And he knows about ours."

"What if the Journeymen don't catch him?" Kat fingered the crust on her bread.

Kuparak's tone hardened. "I have men in Tahellive. If he boards one of the Rompeer's ships, they'll be waiting for him." A yawn brought him to his feet. "Eat. We don't know when our next meal will be. And I suggest a nap." He grabbed a blanket and spread it on the hay. Sleep caught him almost before his head came to rest on his arm.

Jaradee deposited a blanket next to Katareen and made herself comfortable. "Finish your meal and join me." From beneath half-closed lids, she watched her sister chew her last bite and then sit in silence for some time, her brow furrowed in thought. With a sigh of frustration, she snuggled next to Jaradee, wiggled one way and then the other, rolled onto her side, and slept.

The sound of a door opening invaded Jaradee's dream. A wooden rung creaked. She rolled onto her side. Kuparak's eyes, fixed on the top of the ladder, glowed in the dim light from the loft doors.

Mylos' head appeared above the floor. "Got some news. Not good, I'm afraid." He climbed up and plopped down in the hay next to Kuparak. "I detoured on the way here. There's been a raid in Chunarrie. The hidding place for the cryogenics canisters burned to the ground."

Kuparak rubbed his chin. "Did they save anything?"

"The last batches are hidden at the Protariflee Center. Our people aren't under suspicion. At least, not yet."

Katareen stretched and sat up. "What made you take a detour?" Her gaze searched his face, her tone held an edge Jaradee rarely heard.

Mylos returned her gaze with an open, straightforward expression. "The two broticos landed back there by the berry thicket." He whistled a low trill of notes. A hawk landed on his shoulder. "This is ReRe. He told me you where to find you. When the broticos took off, I followed. They landed in a compound on this side of Chunarrie. I decided since I was close, I'd do a little reconnaissance in the city. The haven, nothing but charred beams, still smoked."

Kuparak cleared his throat. "Anyone hurt?"

Mylos' brows bridged his crooked nose. "They trapped one man in the fire. The rest escaped. Denee answered ReRe's call. That's how I learned about the canisters." He looked back at Katareen. "Satisfied?"

She knee-walked to his side and planted a kiss on his cheek. "Thanks, Mylos, for your patience. I'm not sure what I felt when you arrived, but..." She shrugged.

He shook his head. "You're good, Kat. Zarrin was in the compound. He might have recognized my energy signature, Kup."

Kuparak opened the food basket and passed Mylos bread, meat, and cheese. "Eat. It seems we need to get moving. I prefer not to put Harie and his family in more danger than they already are." He turned to Kat. "When Mylos has eaten, he's going to take you to meet Floree and the others."

Katareen straightened and folded her arms. "And Jaradee?"

"She's coming with me to Chunarrie, Kat. I'd take you, too, but your Eleo Predan appearance would put us and you at risk. They've already seen you and..." He pulled out a folded piece of paper and handed it to her. "Harie gave me this."

Jaradee peered over her sister's shoulder. Her heart lurched in dismay. The artist who had done the sketch captured a likeness of Katareen that took her breath away. The sizable reward for her capture printed across the top increased her alarm.

"What do they want me for?" Kat's voice shook.

"Lusktar Rados wants you for his women's household."

Her fair skin turned pink. "You mean he wants me to be a courtesan?" Stubbornness wiped fear from her face. "He does not get to have me. I will go with Mylos, Kuparak, but you must promise to keep Jaradee safe."

"I will do my best, Kat. Please tell Floree what has occurred here. We will join you when we can." He swung his leg over the top of the ladder and began his descent.

Mylos washed his meal down with a mug of water and climbed after him.

Jaradee stood and helped her sister to her feet. Pulling her into her arms, she inhaled the smell of her hair and forced her tears to remain unshed. "I'll come to you as soon as I can. Trust only those your inner knowing affirms as true." She held her at arm's length, memorizing the pale face, the silky black hair, the eyes the color of honey straight from the hive. "Be safe, Katareen."

Kat hugged her one last time and disappeared down the ladder.

—

10

Jaradee stood to one side of the loft doors. Night crept away, inviting the new morning to begin. In the distance, two black shapes imprinted against the gold and salmon dome grew smaller and smaller. That Mylos would give his life for her sister did not ease the tightening in her throat nor dry the tears refusing to remain unshed.

The ladder creaking announced Kuparak's return to the loft. Soon, they would leave for Chunarrie. She turned to find him repacking the food basket.

Grabbing a blanket, she folded it. "Will we see Harie again?"

"No. I've told him to keep his family clear until we're gone. I don't want them to have memories of you. What they don't know may keep them alive." He pitchforked the hay to cover all traces of their presence.

Toa swooped through the loft doors, circled overhead, and swept once again into the morning sky. Kuparak waited for her to shift and together they soared after him, the sun rising at their backs.

Wings pressing the air, the rapid beat of her whistler heart, the sense of time unending accompanied the long flight. Farmland transitioned to forest transitioned to an arid sun-soaked land, stretching in all directions. Still, the ebony galee pressed forward. Fatigue threatening to drag Jaradee from the heavens gave way to astonished delight. Cresting the horizon, a land of scattered plateaus grew more beautiful with each wing stroke.

Raptor-enhanced vision picked out a trio of table-topped mesas rising side by side. Lush, green forests covered the valleys in between and crept midway up the steep bronze sides of the plateaus. A river cut one valley in two; a lake, longer than it was wide, divided the other. Atop the central plateau, the residential mansion of the Rompeer held center stage. Ivory stone towers topped with burnished copper turrets tossed the sunlight domeward. Manicured parks and gardens formed splashes of color around it. High ivory walls divided the grounds from the city proper at one end and the citadel at the other.

As they flew closer, Jaradee picked out large rotaveles strategically placed along the sides of the three plateaus, their cars, pulleys, and counterweights exposed to the elements; their shafts ending in cleared acreage below. Four suspension bridges, two on either side of the middle mesa, connected it to its neighbors. The city, composed of buildings of various heights and shapes, covered the back third of the plateau and, she discovered, was reachable by a steep, graded road constructed at the end furthest from the palace.

Toa and Kuparak banked left, swooped into a valley beyond the trio of tabletops, and landed amongst leafy, deciduous trees. A dark-skinned woman stood by a tall fagus beech, waiting for them to shift. Without a word, she led the way along a barely discernible track to a door blending so well with its surroundings Jaradee didn't see it until their guide opened it and stepped through.

Inside the cabin, the woman, hands on hips, flashed a white-toothed smile at Kuparak. "About time you came to visit."

He scooped her into a warm embraced and winked at Jaradee over her luxurious black curls. With one arm still around the woman's shoulders, he maneuvered her to his side. "Jaradee, this is my sister-sibling, Talarah Whalend. Talarah, meet Jaradee Myrlinduh, offspring of Kier Myrlinduh and Necee Walerain."

Talarah's mouth formed a round of surprise that became a welcoming smile. "The seed of your family goes back to before the first settler arrived on El Stroma. I am honored to meet you."

An unexpected flood of fatigue drained Jaradee's energy reserve. "I'm g-glad to—" The room tipped. Her knees buckled. The last thing she remembered—Kuparak catching her.

The odors of burning wood and food chased gentle dreams into a full-bodied yawn. She stared at a rough-hewn ceiling. *Where am I?* Sitting on the edge of a narrow cot, she combed her fingers through tangled hair. An image—*Kuparak and...*Her brow wrinkled with the effort to remember. *Ah yes. Talarah.*

Tiptoeing to the half-closed door, she listened with a touch of wistfulness to the banter between sister and brother. *Is Kat safe? Daar?*

Peering around the door, she discovered Kuparak and Talarah sitting at a table beside a small fireplace, their dark faces glowing, their amber eyes alive with laughter. She paused, uncertain of her welcome.

Talarah glanced her way and smiled. "You're awake. Good." Jumping to her feet, she pulled a third chair to the table. "Come, Jaradee. We have been remembering our childhood...a happier time, a time prior to the Rompeer's reign." Her beautiful face, so like her brother's and yet so feminine, invited her to be a part of their joy.

Jaradee joined them and accepted a mug of water so cool and crisp it took her breath away. "This is delicious." She took a deep swig.

Kuparak grinned. "There is a spring out back." He looked at Talarah. "How about some food, sibling of mine? Decisions are easier to make on a full stomach."

Jaradee started to rise. "I'll help."

Talarah shook her head. "Sit. Everything is ready to serve. I know you have questions for Kuparak. Ask now while you have time."

"Thank you, Talarah."

"My friends call me Tala. Kup is one of the few to use my full name." She crossed to a small stove and began to fill bowls with something so deliciously aromatic Jaradee's mouth watered.

Jaradee forced her thoughts away from food and pictured the tabletop mesas. "As we flew in, I saw buildings on all three plateaus. Where is the Protariflee Center?"

"It is on the mesa closest to us, along with institutes of learning, medical centers, and research facilities. They reserved the far mesa for industry and manufacturing. The three plateaus are laid out in a grid. Of course, this Rompeer did not design Chunarrie."

Talarah placed steaming bowls of vegetable stew in front of them and sat down. "I continue to marvel at the technology the Pheet Adole have developed." She dipped her spoon. "But my musings do not answer your questions, Jaradee."

Sipping a taste of the steaming stew, Jaradee licked her lips. "This is wonderful, Tala." She savored another mouthful and swallowed. "Why are you collecting sperm and eggs from our leaders?"

Kuparak stirred his stew, then sat back. "If the Rompeer's plan to annihilate the Eleo Preda and claim El QuilTran succeeds, we want to have a plan in place to ensure the survival of our people and our history."

"If he succeeds, how do you plan to keep the samples safe?"

"Friends at the travel port in VenTra have promised to transport the samples to safety in the Far Universe."

"Since someone destroyed the building in Chunarrie, where will you store the samples now?"

Worry clouded Kuparak's expression. "Today, I will go to assess the damage. You will remain with Tala."

Jaradee placed her spoon on the table and folded her arms. "I'm going with you."

Tala's eyes gleamed. "You're not leaving me behind."

"And if there's trouble?" Kuparak looked from one to the other.

Tala pushed her chair back and began to clear the table. "We'll cross that valley when and if we get there. Help me clean up, and we can be on our way."

Together, they made quick work of the table and the small work area. Tala made a final circuit of the cabin, securing the windows and doors, and turned to her brother. "Tell us what you need."

"Since you insist on coming..." His smile flashed. "And since I could use the help, stay close and alert. You know the area, Talarah. Jaradee does not. If we encounter trouble, take her to safety."

Talarah rested her hands on her hips. "And your plan?"

"I want to see the damage first and then see if we can sneak into the Center. Neither is without risk. Mylos shared that both are being closely watched. I wish he were here. I expect the Rompeer's men to be suspicious and edgy. We could use another pair of eyes."

The door swung wide; Mylos strode into the cramped room. "Your wish, Kup, is my command. Hey, Tala." He put an arm around Jaradee's shoulder. "Kat is safe with Floree. I also received a message from the boys via my tukoolo. They have led the soldiers back to Tahellive. As soon as the soldiers give up the search, Tealin and Daar will head for Chunarrie."

Kuparak shared his plans with Mylos and led the way outside. Jaradee called Karia to tether. The link snapped into place. She shifted and lifted into the air, taking her assigned place next to Tala's shifted form, also a whistler hawk.

In a loose formation, they soared high above the valley toward the mesa housing the Center. Their tukoolo shot ahead and vanished into manicured trees at the rim of the tabletop. Within a short time, Kuparak's smoky galee swooped into a copse of trees. Soon, Jaradee stood once more on solid ground. Her flesh prickled a warning. Mylos materialized and pulled her behind a thick bush. Tala perched above them in hawk form. The sound of voices drawing near kept the small group noiseless and stationary.

"You're certain we are unexpected?" The undertone held a distinct note of aggression.

A voice responded. "We'll catch them this time and destroy every Eleo Predan sample they're hiding."

"You're certain you know who *they* are?"

A pause, pregnant with uncertainty, preceded the second man's answer. "I don't, but they *will* give themselves away. I'm sure of it."

The soldiers strode into the open.

Toa swooped to Kuparak's shoulder, his right side reflecting the leafy trees. Jaradee sensed the exchange of information between the man and his tukoolo. The galee's telie-eye extend and snapped into place. With a soft gurgle, it soared over the expanse of green between the trees and the Center.

Kuparak motioned his team into a huddle. "A surprise inspection is underway. Mylos and I will do a reconnaissance flight. Talarah, you and Jaradee stay here." He gave them both a no nonsense stare. "Don't improvise unless it becomes necessary. Understood."

The dewy-eyed innocence in Tala's face made Jaradee smile and Kuparak put his hands on her shoulders and study her with a brother's concern. "I mean it, Talarah. Keep yourselves safe." Without another word, he shifted.

Mylos' hawk flashed after the smoky galee.

Tala stared after them. "At least, they don't treat us like the women in the Rompeer's household who are pampered, educated, dressed up like dolls, and married off to serve their husband, to have his children, and to remain hidden from sight for the rest of their lives." Scowling, she lowered to the ground and rested her back on a tree. "*And* to put up with their mate having as many consorts as he chooses."

Jaradee studied her friend's face. "When your culture hides you away from society, you know nothing different. It would be harder for us. We've experienced freedom."

Talarah folded her hands in her lap and gazed at the dome. "Sure am glad I'm me."

"And I am happy to be me." Jaradee settled next to her and let her mind search for Karia. The whistler hawk explored the far side of the Protariflee Center Park. The image of several military vehicles arriving in the parking lot filled her mind.

Tala's hand on her arm kept her still. Their eyes met. Talarah mouthed, "Don't make a sound."

11

Soldiers in dark khaki rounded the end of the Center, their red and silver insignias gleaming in the late morning sun. A signal from the leader sent three men sprinting toward the trees. A man wearing the black and purple of a SorTech lowered a large pack from his shoulder to the ground and knelt beside it. Opening a flap, he withdrew a sizable rectangular box.

Tala turned a grim face to Jaradee and whispered, "SorTechory. Tether and change now. Put distance between you and the SorTech. Go."

The snap of Karia's tether sent Jaradee into shifted form. Her raptor instincts in charge, she swooped along a path through the trees, shot upward, and landed at the top of a tall, leafy sycama. Somewhere near, Tala's bird form perched camouflaged by leaves, her tukoolo close at hand. Below them, the three soldiers spread out, searching with furtive silence. The SorTech affixed a patch to his temple and regarded the black box.

A slight tingle penetrated Jaradee's thoughts. In a tree across the way,

Karia's telie-eye lengthened, focused, and retracted. Reigning in her fear, Jaradee flew further from the SorTech and closer to the Center's entrance. Soldiers marched workers into a plaza, checked identification bracelets, and ran a small handheld box over each one. When they finished checking the last woman, they gave the order to return to the building. As the workers filed inside, the soldiers, except the three exploring the woods, gathered on the lawn. Keen hawk ears picked up the frustration in the leader's voice when he dismissed his troops with the admonition to stay alert.

After a brief conversation with the leader, the SorTech packed up his gear, ambled along a path into the woods, and knelt behind a tree. Reassembling his equipment, he began a second search. Jaradee silenced all thought. The last military vehicle braked to a stop in front of the building. Three soldiers jogged from the trees and climbed aboard. The SorTech packed up and trotted across the open area. He stowed his equipment and climbed into the front seat.

As the truck turned from the drive onto the main road, Karia landed beside her. High above the Center, a smoky galee circled, began a spiraled descent, caught an updraft, and glided into the trees. Kuparak materialized. Talarah appeared next to him. Toa and Tala's tukoolo settled in a tree at the edge of the lawn. Jaradee released her tether to Karia, glided to the ground, and changed.

Kuparak drew them further into the trees and faced her. "You have a question, Jaradee?"

She bit her lip. "What is SorTechory? I felt a current run through my mind. How does it discover an untethered shift or telepathic thought or—" Lifting her hands in a questioning gesture, she shrugged.

Kuparak stroked his beardless chin. "I don't know the workings of The Box. It is that combined with the power of sorcery which creates SorTechory."

"Is the SorTech a practitioner of mystical arts?"

Talarah entered the discussion with a shake of her head. "Pheet Adolean sorcerers can only access a few feats accomplished by our shameenu. The Box allows them to detect mystical powers, but only when they are in use."

Kuparak grinned. "Now, you know what we know. It is rather mysterious, is it not?"

Mylos heard the soft sound of wings. "Kup, the Center is clear, but you will not appreciate what else I learned."

The Vasrosi leader raised a single brow. "Well, do not keep us in suspense."

"They only saved one cryo container." Mylos tugged his beard. "If a Pheet Adolan technician finds it, we lose everything."

"Host mothers have already selected, right?" Talarah looked from one man to another. "Why can't the remaining embryos be implanted in them?"

Kuparak frown in frustration. "We've hidden the host mothers are hidden up the coast. "

Jaradee glanced at Talarah. "You have two women right here."

His frown deepened. "I can't let you put yourselves into such a dangerous position."

Talarah gripped Jaradee's hand. "It is our decision to make, Kup, not yours."

A challenge flashed between the siblings. Mylos started to speak. Kuparak shut him up with a look. "You may not be the right match, Talarah."

"We won't know that unless we're tested." His sister's response, spoken with utmost calm, seemed to diffuse his anger.

He sighed. "Then I suggest we find out if it's safe to run them." A glance in Mylos' direction brought a nod. A moment later, he shifted and ascended into the fading light.

Jaradee walked to a stump enshrouded in shadow and sat down. Dusk's coolness chased a shiver of anticipation over her bare arms. *What if...*Shaking her wavy, dark hair free along with her uncertainty, she pondered whether she might soon become the host of embryos created from the eggs and sperm of Eleo Predan leaders? Thoughts of her mother, a powerful shameena, brought tears to her eyes. She blinked them away and smoothed her hair into a queue at the nape of her neck, wound its leather thong around it, and secured it.

Unlike Katareen, she had not inherited the pale beauty of the Thornlandian Eleo Preda. Her mother, half Thornlandian and half Giroblania from Charnland, had given her the deep tanned skin and dark eyes of her mixed mating. She glanced at Kuparak and Tala, members of her mother's tribal family. Periodically, the tribes arranged mix-matings to enhance emotional ties between cultures. Jaradee felt privileged to have been birthed as a result of this most honored tradition.

Mylos materializing beside Kuparak ended her musings. Talarah's beautiful smile flashed. Jaradee's anticipation quickened. Her ambiguous feelings stifled, she joined her friends.

"Our contact told me Lusktar Rados has given orders to remove all military personnel from the premises. He does not want the specimens damaged. It's the perfect time to test." Mylos frowned. "But we have one problem. A contingent of men has been ordered to remain around the perimeter."

Kuparak addressed his sister. "I suggest we wait until dark. Mylos, what is the best approach to the building? Can we all go together?"

Mylos rubbed his scarred brow. "Four is too noticeable. I'll take Jaradee, then come back. You, Tala, and I will make the second trip. He put an arm around Jaradee. "Are you sure you want to volunteer, Jara? If it works and the Rompeer finds out, his men will hunt you like an animal."

"How can I not do this? Saving our lineage and our history must come before personal safety, Mylos. Besides, we will have you and Kuparak to guard us."

The Vasrosi leader grew solemn. "I cannot promise to stay with you, but I can promise you will be well protected." His gaze sought his sister. "And you, Talarah? Are you sure?"

Her beautiful face softened and then grew stern. "Like Jaradee, it is my duty and my personal desire to serve."

"I will honor your decision, sibling of mine, but you must swear to be prudent."

She smiled. "I swear, Kup. Let's get this done."

Long shadows lengthened and crept up the side of the Center. A personnel rotation kept Jaradee and her companions within the trees. Workers and technicians moved in and out of the building.

Once it grew quiet again, Mylos moved away from Jaradee. "Fly to the opposite side of the woods, circle back, and land by the annex on the other side of the grounds. If we get separated, don't fly straight back here. Make sure anyone watching will not suspect you are more than you appear."

Before she could reply, his hawk form lifted to a low branch where Karia waited. Jaradee opened to her tukoolo's tether. Staying within the trees, Mylos led her to the furthest edge of the woods. Once in the open, he swooped below the lip of the mesa and soared over the tree-covered valley. A wide circle brought them back to the tabletop. A long, low glide ended by a square building. After shifting to Human, Mylos waited only long enough for her to materialize and then led her inside.

Rakes, hoes, hoses, and planters lined three walls. Mylos reached through the center of a hanging coiled hose, withdrew a wad of black fabric, and handed it to her.

"This is a mask. Everyone you meet today will wear one, Jara. We must obscure our identities so that if the Rompeer's men capture us, they cannot cull information from our memories."

Jaradee pulled a bag with holes for eyes and a nose over her head. Mylos withdrew a second mask, covered his head and face, and rapped on the wall. A door opened and a uniformed technician, his face hidden, beckoned them into an elevator.

Lights glowed in a panel next to the door. Ignoring them, the technician inserted a card into a reader on the left. A small door opened, exposing a panel of electrical wiring. A quick jerk disconnected a yellow wire. The technician lifted the panel and flipped a switch. The elevator jerked to a start, descended, and stopped.

Beyond the doors, a woman greeted them. She nodded to Mylos. "You can go. By the time you return, I will be ready for our second host." Her attention focused on Jaradee. "No names and no information that could tell me who you are or you who I am. Other than that, do you have questions?"

Mylos stepped into the elevator, and the doors slid shut, blocking him from view.

Jaradee experienced a moment of misgiving, swallowed, and steadied her resolve. "How many tests, and how long for the results?"

"First, we'll draw blood and examine your womb and ovaries. Further studies will be based on the results. I believe your friend told you we have one container of specimens. This container holds six cryogenics canisters, one of which is damaged. With your permission, we will harvest eggs from you to be fertilized by sperm from a Thornlandian leader. If we are lucky, we will obtain an embryo for implantation in you and more to be frozen." She paused. "It's a lot, isn't it?"

Jaradee appreciated the understanding. "It is. I suggest we get started." Her own sounded much calmer than she felt.

—

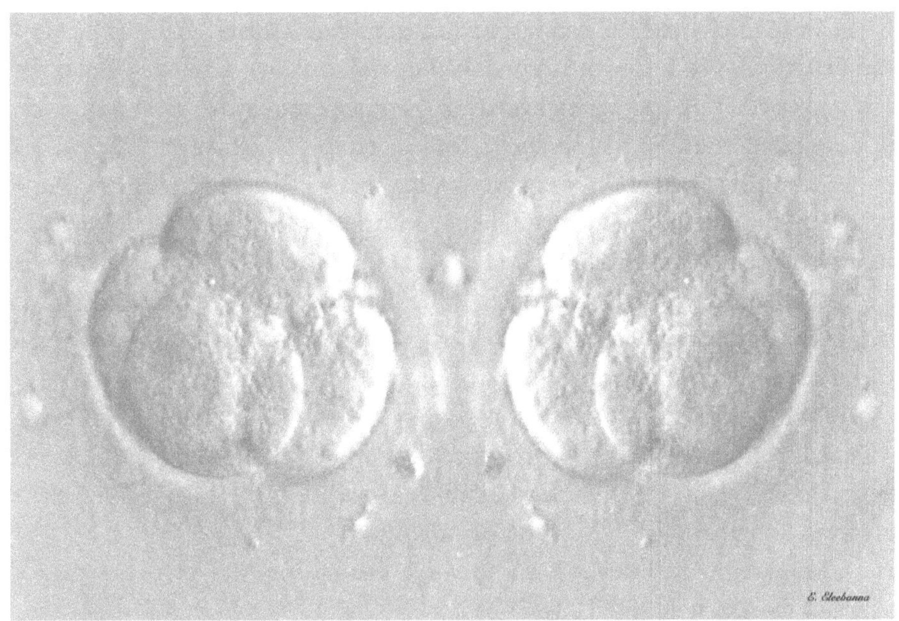

12

Jaradee woke up confused, disoriented, and smothered by something covering her head. Her first instinct—to pull it off—was arrested by a gentle hand on her arm. A face in a half mask filled her vision.

"Do you remember where you are?"

"No." She touched her belly. Memories, some vivid, some vague, flooded the present with a series of impressions. Confusion faded. "I'm in the Protariflee Center. Is it done?"

"It is. You now carry the future of our people within your womb."

"And Ta—"

The woman shook her head. "No names. She's recovering,"

A warm hand rested on Jaradee's forehead. Sleep tugged her lids shut.

When she woke for the second time, she lay staring dazedly at the white ceiling. *How long have I been sleeping?* Thirst pawing her throat suggested a long time. She pushed herself to sitting and reached for the glass by the bed. Savoring the first sip, she swished it around her mouth, and swallowed.

A woman entered the room, checked her vitals, asked if she was hungry, and departed. A second woman marched in and took her for a walk along the hall and back. The next several turnings passed in much the same way. Each turning Jaradee walked further, exercised longer, and felt stronger. The nausea she had been warned about remained mild, hitting in the morning and gone by afternoon. She had not seen Talarah, and no one had shared information about her friend's condition.

Just when she thought the tempo of her life would never change, a masked face peeked around the edge of the door. A woman entered, closed it, drew a curtain over the observation window, and pulled off the mask.

Talarah's smile brightened the room. "We made it, Jara!" The smile widened. "It won't be long before we can leave the Center. Mylos has gone to fetch Floree. They'll meet us at the cabin." She sat on the edge of the bed, a protective hand on her belly. "How do you feel."

Jaradee removed her mask and made a mental inventory. "Other than a touch of nausea, I feel good. You?"

Talarah tipped her head. "I feel..." Her head tilted the other way. "Good. Nervous. Excited. Scared. I almost lost one of the babies." She stared into space and chewed on her lip. "They had to bring in a Pheet Adolean physician. He saved it."

Jaradee felt a rush of alarm. "Does he know who you are? Will he give you away?"

"He thinks I'm a host mother for a wealthy family." Her brows furrowed. "What concerns me is that he saw my face."

"That's not good, Tala. Does Kuparak know?"

The Vasrosi leader strode into the room and set a large bag on the bed. "I do know. That's why we're leaving the Center tonight." He indicated the bag. "You'll find clothes and necessities for the journey in there. I'll be back for you at dusk. Don't leave this room. Keep your masks handy and rest. We have a long trek ahead of us."

Before either woman could speak, he pulled the door shut behind him. A short time later, a soft knock and a feminine voice asking to come in sent them hurrying to don their masks.

Jaradee motioned Talarah behind her. "Come in."

Her attendant entered the room and waited for the door to close. "You are safe for the moment, but the longer you stay here, the more danger we will all be in. I'll help you dress."

She rummaged in the bag and pulled out the full-legged pants and tunics worn by slaves in the Rompeer's household. Matching shoes and long scarves appeared next. The attendant looked up. "Don't just stand there. We have little time."

Jaradee scrambled from her clinic gown into a pair of rust-colored pants and a dark brown tunic. She crammed her feet into shoes a good size too small and winced.

Talarah held out her shoes. "I think these will fit you better. Give me yours."

While they finished dressing, the attendant shoved their few personal belongings into the bag and set it by the door. Next, she showed them how to fashion the scarves to hide their hair and faces.

"Crack the door open when you're ready, and I'll make sure you're presentable." Clutching the bag, she left.

Talarah blew out a breath and pulled off her mask. "I think she's scared."

"Wouldn't you be if you were harboring fugitives right under the nose of the enemy?" Jaradee walked to the mirror in the small personal space, grimaced, and tugged at her failed attempt to tie the scarf. "Can you help me with this?" She handed it to her friend. "By the way, thanks for trading shoes. I could almost feel new blisters forming."

Talarah took the long piece of cloth and shook it out. "Glad they fit." With deft movements, she wound and tucked until a look of satisfaction suggested success.

Facing the mirror, Jaradee smiled. "Looks great. Let me help you."

Talarah studied her reflection. "I think we're ready."

Jaradee opened the door and ushered the waiting attendant into the room. A quick inspection brought an affirming nod.

"No one will know you are not what you seem. Remember to keep your eyes lowered when you are being addressed. Always bow when a conversation is finished. And never turn your back on a Pheet Adolean male, no matter his station. Your escort waits for you. This way."

She led them through a maze of corridors to the elevator in which they had arrived almost a moon cycle ago. "I wish you the best of luck. Stay safe. And please protect what you carry." Pivoting, she hurried away.

The elevator doors whispered opened. Kuparak, wearing head gear that obscured his face and the uniform of a Rompeerial house slave, motioned them inside. A masked attendant pushed a button. The elevator shot upward. The doors opened. With a slight bow, Kuparak ushered them into the annex.

Jaradee glanced at a wall of coiled hoses, shovels, and spades. They were no longer in their safe haven. A vague mental tug told her Karia waited close by. Beside her, Tala's tension hit her in waves. Kuparak, removed the cloth covering his face, put a finger to his lips and preceded them into the coolness of the El Stroman night.

The garden path ended in the lot where a motor carriage waited. Kuparak helped them into the enclosed cab and took his place on the exterior bench seat beside the driver. The engine rumbled; the vehicle rolled along the drive to the road. After a short wait, the carriage merged into the chaos of early evening traffic.

Jaradee wished she knew what had been planned, where they were going, how they would be able to reach the cabin when they could not shift shape. A whistle in her head made her gasp. Talarah gripped her hand and lowered her head. A military vehicle lumbered by. The motor carriage turned a corner and stopped. Kuparak yanked open the door.

"Gotta move. Stay close to me." He jogged down the dreary lane.

Grabbing Talarah's hand, Jaradee matched his pace. The lane ended opposite a rotavele station at the lip of the mesa. A dim light illuminated the enclosed platform. A one-person guard house stood off to the side.

A shout boomed. Running feet pounded their direction. Kuparak nudged the women ahead of him into a small eateria smelling of dirty Humans and frying fat. They found a corner table near the kitchen. Kuparak took a shadowed seat, providing him with a view of the eatery door. Jaradee and Talarah sat with their backs to the room

A Pheet Adolean boy about Daar's age tossed a single sheet of grimy paper on the table. "Ya need anything to drink?"

Kuparak kept his head lowered over the menu and spoke in Pheet Adolean. "We will order drinks with our meal."

The boy shrugged and shuffled back to a bar.

Talarah's gaze flitted from her brother's face to the door. "What if they search in here?"

Her worried undertone brought only a minute shake of Kuparak's head.

A tingled warning shot up Jaradee's spine. She gripped the edge of the table and mouthed the word SorTechory.

He nodded, placed the menu face down on the table, and fastened his gaze on the almost illegible scrawl.

Jaradee squinted. "Help is close. Stay put."

Talarah angled it to see better. "Do we trust it?"

Crumpling the paper into a ball, Kuparak shoved it into a pocket, waved the boy over, and ordered the night special for all of them. At the bar, a man guffawed. Another threw a punch. The eateria erupted in a brawl. Kuparak launched to his feet, grabbed Talarah, and pushed her ahead of him through the exit. A hand on Jaradee's shoulder kept her in her seat. A quick glance gave her a glimpse of a scar-bisected brow above a blue eye.

Mylos sat beside her. "I'll tell you when to go. Leave by the kitchen exit. Don't look back. Don't stop. If we get separated, hide in the alley."

He blocked an airborne chair and sent it crashing to the ground. A man followed, landed in the midst of broken pieces, and lay still. A siren screamed its approach.

Pulling Jaradee to her feet, Mylos shoved her toward the kitchen. Inside, a chaos of bodies and spilled food pulled her up short. A hand on her elbow guided her through the mayhem and out the back exit into a spider web of alleys and narrow streets lined with commercial buildings. When at last they came to a stop, she wrapped her arms around herself, gulped in air, and prayed she had not put her pregnancy at risk.

As her breathing normalized, she took stock of her surroundings. A slight wind rustled through bushes and trees. Clouds roiled overhead. The waning moon made periodic appearances, highlighting a second rotavele station. Several Rompeerial soldiers clustered near the guardhouse. A single guard joined the group, seemed to listen, shook his head, nodded, and returned to his station. Soldiers spread out and began a search of the area.

Sheltered in a dingy, unlit doorway, Jaradee peered over Mylos' shoulder. When nothing was discovered, the soldiers reassembled and marched toward town. She started to move. Mylos shook his head and continued to observe the guard house.

A man detached himself from a shadowed portico a short distance away and sprinted to a patch of bushes near the rotavele. The clouds parted. Moonlight illuminated the night. The guard, framed in the arched opening, scanned the deserted platform, stepped into the open, and made his way along the walkway bordering the rim of the mesa.

The moon dodged behind a cloud. Darkness enclosed the world. A muffled cry cut short by silence echoed in Jaradee's mind.

Mylos came to attention and gripped her shoulder. A rush of adrenaline left her shaking. Her heart slammed her breast bone. Every nerve in her body screamed run. Jaradee glanced at Mylos. He shook his head. Digging her nails into her palms, she held herself motionless.

13

Agust stirred the bushes, expelling the lone figure of a man. The cry of a galee dispersed on the wind. A gray-black bird landed on the man's upraised arm. The lithe figure of a woman joined them.

Mylos released his grip on Jaradee's shoulder. "Let's go." He trotted toward the guardhouse.

Gathering her flagging energy, she jogged after him. By the time she fell in step beside Talarah, they were halfway to the platform. Mylos motioned them ahead. The sound of armored horses racing along the road propelled them faster. Kuparak helped them onto the rotavele platform.

Overhead, pewter-colored clouds churned. Large rain drops pelted the metal roof. Kuparak pulled Mylos aboard, slid the accordianed metal door shut, and pushed several buttons on the control panel. A band of horsemen rode into the open lot and reined to a halt. The rotavele lurched and dropped. Thunder rumbled. Armor clattered. A bolt of lightning ripped the clouds in two. Torrents of rain plummeted, drenching everything in sight.

Jaradee huddled with Talarah in the shelter of the cage, her attention riveted upward. Mylos peered through the metal gating at the valley below.

Kuparak shot him a quick glance. "Did Floree make it?"

"By now she's at the cabin." Mylos kept his attention fixed on the valley floor. "Toa alerted my tukoolo you were in danger. Floree knew the way to the cabin, so we split up and I came here." His spine tensed. "I don't see anything moving below, but that doesn't mean we won't have company. What's the plan?"

"Toa tells me the area is deserted, but three riders are closing in. You take the women. Toa and I will create a distraction if needed. We'll meet up at the cabin. Stick to the creek-bed if you can. Wade upstream to the broken pine before you angle inland."

The rotavele rattled to a stop. In the distance, the muffled pounding of horses hooves announced their eminent arrival. Mylos hustled Jaradee and Talarah into the trees and gave them a moment to adjust to the darkness. A quick over-the-shoulder glance showed Jaradee the muted shapes of two galees lifting into flight.

Mylos grabbed her elbow and hurried her into the creek's gurgling center. Cold water sloshed around her ankles and soaked her full-legged pants up to her calves. Shivering, she yanked her scarf from her head, wrapped it around her shoulders for warmth, and slogged after Mylos. Not far behind, a blue-lipped Talarah struggled to keep up. Jaradee stopped, fashioned her friend's scarf into a shawl, and put an arm around her waist. Guiding her around big rocks and away from low hanging branches, she kept her upright. Blood coloring the water crimson brought them to a standstill.

Karia landed on Jara's shoulder and gave a sharp whistle. Mylos splashed back to their side. "We can't stop." He scooped Talarah up and trudged onward. Karia launched domeward. Mental images formed in Jaradee's mind. The soldiers had left their horses on the bank and now closed the gap, one long stride at a time.

Jaradee pushed herself faster. Images blurred and steadied. The last soldier in line dropped from sight. Kuparak took his place. The point man rounded a bend. Kup dragged the second soldier soundlessly into the forest. The leader paused to look back. Cursing under his breath, he retraced his steps. A shadowy shape lunged from the trees, hit him on the back of his head, and watched him fall face first in the creek. The figure knelt by his unconscious body and pushed his head under the water.

Jaradee shook the image from her head. For the first time, she realized that Kuparak was what her people called an Animilero, a man trained to protect and to kill. Their deep love of all things living did not distract from the fact that, when necessary, the Animilero would take a life, animal or Human, without a moment's hesitation.

A misstep landed her on one knee in the watery coldness. Soaked and frustrated, she heaved herself to standing. A strong, black hand steadied her.

The Vasrosi leader regarded her from a face devoid of expression. "Climb onto my back. I will carry you." He knelt. She wrapped her arms around his neck and straddled his waist. Traversing the stream to the far side, he plodded after Mylos' dim figure.

The warmth of Kuparak's body seeping into her chest provided Jaradee with a respite from the cold. Weather in this part of El SyrTundi, arid and hot during the turning, cooled rapidly when the sun set. The approach of dawn brought with it the turning's coldest temperatures. The dome overhead had begun to lose its austere darkness. A hint of morning formed a circular horizon line of pale salmon and gold.

Untiring, Kuparak waded upstream. Mylos climbed the bank and carried Talarah into the trees. By the time Jaradee and Kuparak arrived, Tala lay pale and silent on the forest floor.

Her brother knelt beside her and placed a hand on her forehead. His worried gaze scrutinized the blood-soaked pants. "Tala, open your eyes."

Dark lashes fluttered. A tongue slid along dried lips. Tears leaked from over-bright eyes. "I lost the babies."

Kuparak kissed his sister's cheek. "We'll get you to the cabin. Floree is there. She'll know what to do." He picked her up and cradled her next to his chest. "Don't give up, Tala." Making his way between stocky-trunked tundi pines and angular perjunis, he forged ahead.

Jaradee stumbled after, hands pressed over her belly. Dread clouded her excitement about her babies. *Floree will know what to do.*

Mylos appeared at her side. "Almost there. Can you make it, or do you need a lift?" A smile softened his rugged features.

"How far is 'almost there'?"

"As the tukoolo flies not far. Dodging trees will add a bit."

"I'll be fine." Rolling her shoulders back and stretching her neck one way and then the other, she forced herself to relax and continue. Her goal, to make it with both embryos still in utero, seemed almost within reach.

The sun sent shafts of light between trees, highlighting patches of moss, glowing through lacy witch hair lichen, and scattering shade into sharp-edged pieces that reassembled in the shifting light. Kuparak had disappeared up the faint animal trail with Talarah. Mylos had shifted to his hawk form and flown domeward with ReRe at his side. Jaradee placed one foot in front of the other, yearning for rest and for water. She licked the salt of dried sweat from her lips and stepped around the mangled limbs of a perjunis conifer. Kuparak strode to meet her, lifted her in strong-muscled arms, and carried her the last stretch to the cabin. Once inside, he lowered her onto a chair by the table and placed a mug of spring water at her elbow.

Jaradee stared at the mug, too tired to reach for it. Kuparak picked it up and pressed it into her hand. Of their own accord, her fingers gripped it and raised it to her lips. The first sip slapped her tongue with a fresh coolness that left her gasping. She swished a second mouthful over her gums and teeth and swallowed, washing the dryness of the journey away with her fatigue. She sighed and placed the mug on the table.

"That certainly helped to wake me up. How is Talarah?"

Kuparak frowned. "Floree examines her now. We will know soon whether she has lost the babies. And you, Jaradee Myrlinduh, how do you feel?"

"Other than exhausted, I'm fine."

Floree slipped into the room and hurried to her side. "Any cramping or nausea?"

Jaradee shook her head. "Talarah? Is she alright?"

The older woman turned to Kuparak. "May I speak freely?"

"Tell *us* what you have learned. Did Tala lose the babies?"

Floree poured herself some water and sank onto a chair. "She lost the female. But the male fetus is strong. She needs to be where she can receive proper care, Kup. She is more fragile than she appears."

Kuparak studied her with a hint of worry. "What do you suggest?"

Floree sipped her water. "You must take her and Jaradee back to El QuilTran."

His hand clenched. "Jaradee and Tala must not remain together. If we are caught, all would be lost. They must travel separately. How much time does Tala need to recover her strength?"

The healer drained her mug. "Even if she rests for several turnings, she will not have the stamina to travel on foot, Kuparak. You must take her in a wagon, motor or horse drawn, and then by boat."

Mylos materialized next to the table. "We've got trouble, Kup. Zarrin is in Chunarrie at the Rompeer's estates."

Kuparak launched to his feet, an expression on his face Jaradee hoped would never appear in connection to her name. "How did you find him?"

"ReRe and I were doing a quick reconnaissance flight over the city and the Protariflee Center grounds to make sure everything had returned to normal. A motor vehicle pulled up to a bungalow on the north side of the Rompeerial estates. Zarrin, accompanied by two men, climbed out. He was escorted into the bungalow. My guess is that he's about to be interrogated."

Kuparak paced to the stove, swung around, scowled. "He knows our plans for using Protariflee."

Mylos nodded. "He knows what Talarah and Jaradee look like...What all of us look like. What if he shows them the secret area at the Center?"

"Zarrin does not know about it, nor about this cabin. He does know about the Cliffs of Cimondeli and might guess Katareen is hidden there. The fact is...Zarrin knows far too much." Kuparak turned to Floree. "Mylos and I have some business in Chunarrie. Take care of Jaradee and Talarah. You'll be safe here for a short time. If we do not return within three turnings, leave. Toa will communicate through Karia and..." He paused.

Floree smiled at Mylos and then Jaradee. "My tukoolo is Puna for the freshness of Spring. I trust you to honor my sharing." She gazed up at Kuparak. "Be careful, Kup." She left to check on Talarah.

Kuparak moved to the door. "Stay alert, Jara." He flashed into the shape of a galee and winged his way through dusk-shadowed trees in the wake of his tukoolo.

Mylos followed, shape shifted, and soared upward.

Jaradee stared after them for some time before shutting the door and leaning against it. *Kuparak is an Animilero. Zarrin may not live to tell too many tales.*

14

Jaradee stretched out on a narrow cot. Next to her, Talarah slept the exhausted sleep of one whose physical and emotional bodies had suffered much. Although fatigue nudged Jaradee to follow her friend's example, sleep refused to come. Closing her eyes, she followed her breath in and out and in and out. Vague images formed and melted away. Sleep crept closer. She yawned, resettled her fatigued body, and began to feel drowsy.

A new image kept her at the edge of wakefulness. Spiraling clouds swirled in the lapis blue of the night dome, slowed, and focused. The Chunarrian central mesa, bathed in Dyad's icy light, spread below her. Aware of her body resting on the cot and Tala's soft, intermittent snores, her conscious mind fought to understand. The scene below zoomed out, then in. *I'm tethered to Karia's mind.*

The whistler hawk swept over the Rompeer's garden and landed on a low branch opposite a bungalow window. Globe lamps illuminated a main room, where Zarrin occupied a chair opposite a Rompeerial soldier, his expression wary.

Karia's acute hearing picked up bits of conversation.

The soldier tapped an unfolded map. "Show us where the Vasrosi shelters are located." The gruff voice held the hint of a threat. "And, Zarrin..." Eyes, mere slits in the man's determined face, glared. "Don't waste my time."

The ex-Vasrosi bent over the map, angled it one way, then the other. A shrug lifted a shoulder. "Nothing on this one."

The soldier whipped it aside. "Then look at another one."

Zarrin pointed out two spots. "There's one here in the Cupress-Cone Forest and one by Lake Tedra." He pushed the map toward the soldier and sat back, blank-faced and tense.

A black and purple clad Klutarse walked from the shadows, leaned across the table, and calmly straightened the map. "*We* already found those, and *you* know it. Tell this man what he needs to know, or he'll leave you in *my* hands."

"We've been at this for hours. I need a break." Zarrin sounded like a peevish child. "I've told you everything I know."

A fist slammed the table. "You've told us nothing." The soldier slapped a piece of paper and a writing tool in front of him. "I want the name and description of every lookout bird for every Vasrosi. I even want to know your lookout."

Zarrin scowled. "I don't have one. Mine was destroyed."

The Klutarse loomed over him. "But you know how to create one, correct? And you know where the birds come from, how they work, and how they are assigned. Start writing."

Zarrin squirmed in his chair but said nothing. A knife flashed into view. The Klutarse grabbed the front of his shirt and kicked the chair from under him. "Tell me—"

An explosion ripped through the night. The bungalow shook on its foundation. The Klutarse staggered backward. Zarrin yanked free and stumbled to one side. The bungalow went black.

Jaradee gasped and jerked to sitting, blinking as though blinded from a flash of light.

Floree hurried to her side, fingers searching for a pulse. "What just happened?"

"I was tethered to Karia. She's outside the window at the bungalow where Zarrin is under guard at the Rompeer's estates. A loud roar...an explosion...I think." She felt a moment of panic. "Our bond broke. Do you think Karia is hurt?"

"You'd know if she was. Give her some time. I'm betting the blast stunned her. Or she could be protecting you."

Talarah moaned. Floree moved to her side, brushed tangled hair from her face, and checked her vitals. "Go back to sleep, dear one. Rest is the best medicine for you and your child."

Talarah blinked and clutched her hand. "I didn't lose them both?"

Floree kissed her forehead. "You carry the boy, your brother and Dyani's child."

"But I lost *my* daughter." She turned her face to the wall.

Floree motioned Jaradee from the room and followed. "You need sleep, Jaradee Myrlinduh. Your babies need you rested for travel."

Jaradee sank onto a chair. "I won't sleep until I know what has happened to Karia."

Hands on her hips, Floree adopted her healers sternest tone. "I'll help you find your tukoolo, but only if you promise to rest afterward."

"I promise, Floree. What do I need to do?"

"I'll tether to Puna. She will do a search. Once I know what the situation is, I'll tell you. Then we can then decide what course to follow."

Jaradee fussed with a speck of dirt on her tunic. "I need to see. Can we both tether to Puna?"

Floree pulled a chair closer and sat down. "Not without her permission." The birther closed her eyes. When she opened them, worry creased her brow. "Puna would prefer to find Karia and report back. I'll make tea."

Not even the homey sound of a kettle coming to a boil assuaged Jaradee's nagging concern. When Floree handed her a steaming mug of tea, Jaradee balanced it on the arm of the chair without taking a sip.

"Drink the tea, Jara. Puna won't be much longer."

"She's in touch with you?"

Floree's soft laugh spoke volumes. "We, like you and Karia, are rarely out of touch. In fact..." She took the mug from Jaradee. "It seems your compeer was dazed by the explosion. See if you can tether to her now."

Jaradee leaned back and closed her eyes. A slight tingle and a tentative tether formed, melted away, and reformed. For an agonizing moment, nothing happened. Then Karia's touch throbbed stronger. Images flooded Jaradee's mind.

No lights could be seen anywhere on the Rompeer's estates. The din of confused shouts and running feet floated through the night. A smoky galee landed in the tree next to Karia. With darkness as a cloak, a man materialized, skulked to the bungalow's back entrance, and disappeared inside.

Karia soared upward. Jaradee's mind filled with the night dome. El Stroma's second moon, Alkina, hovered above the horizon, its fruitful phase brightening the world in a semblance of dawn. The hawk swooped over the Protariflee Center and dropped below the tabletop to the valley. The tethered connection to Karia broke.

Jaradee's eyes flew open. "She's gone. What happen..."

A soft whistle shrilled at the cabin window. Floree opened it wide. Puna and Karia fluttered to their respective compeers.

Almost crying with relief, Jaradee stroked the feathered half of her tukoolo's breast. "I'm so glad you're safe, Kariahe."

An imaged flashed and faded. Jaradee started to speak.

Floree stood. "I got the message, too. Kuparak and Mylos return soon. We are to blow out the lamps in case they are followed."

Darkness and forest quiet descended on the cabin. An occasional flicker of light from the small fireplace splattered tiny patches of yellow-orange over the worn wooden floor. The quiet creak of the porch step and a hawk's soft whistle did nothing to ease Jaradee's anxiety. She strained to hear. Only the whisper of branches in the night breeze drifted in the open window.

When she thought she would burst from anticipation, Kuparak pushed the door ajar and stepped inside. A finger to his lips stopped questions. Silence permeated the room. Again, apprehension built in the cabin.

Jaradee dozed, jerked awake, and dozed. Someone lifted her and carried her to her cot. The world slipped away as she tumbled into dreaming.

Light woke her to a turning overflowing with questions. A glance at

Talarah's unoccupied cot added to her growing list. Throwing back her blanket, she slid her feet into shoes and shuffled into the empty living space. Easing the door open, she peered outside. The sharp sound of an axe blade splitting wood led her to the back of the cabin.

Mylos leaned the axe against a tree and mopped his brow. "Awake at last." He smiled. "You're looking rested."

"Where is everyone?"

The smile lost its light. "Gone. It's just you and me until Floree returns. She said to make you eat and rest."

Jaradee ran fingers through tangled hair and flinched. "Where did Floree go?"

"With Kuparak, Talarah, and…" His brows bridged his nose. Nostrils flared in frustration. "Zarrin went with them."

Jaradee gaped. "Zarrin. I thought…"

Mylos kicked a split log to one side. "So did I. Kuparak is tight-lipped most of the time, but last night he refused to discuss anything regarding Zar's presence. This morning, he did say he planned to take Zarrin to someone who would know if he lied or told the truth."

"I bet he's taking him to Katareen. He didn't tell the men anything they didn't already know, Mylos. Perhaps Kuparak wants to give him a second chance." She tucked a wavy tendril of hair behind her ear. "When will Floree be back?"

"She'll be back with women to guard you on your journey."

"And Talarah?"

Mylos balanced a log on its end, picked up the axe, and swung it hard. The log split in two; the axe blade wedged in the stump. "Kup is taking Tala to El Quil'Tran. I will act as Vasrosi leader until he comes back. Floree will escort you home when she returns." He stacked split logs in a neat pile. "Let's find some breakfast."

Jaradee rummaged around the pantry and found the makings of a small meal. Mylos slouched in a chair, nibbling a crust of dried brown bread, his demeanor downcast. A heavy sigh blew crumbs from his mustached upper lip. He sat up and glared across the table.

"I know you want to know what else happened in Chunarrie, Jara. Why don't you just ask?"

"Because you're acting like a caged animal. I don't want to get my head bitten off."

He tore a piece of bread in two and slathered it with berry jam. "You've guessed that Kuparak is a trained Animilero. In accordance with his training, he has a high regard for life but knows how to end one with efficiency that would astound you. The guards are dead. No struggle. No sound. He blessed them in the language of their gods, and we escaped with Zarrin."

"And you are upset because of the deaths or Zarrin?" Jaradee rubbed a spot on the table.

Mylos stroked his curly black beard. "Some of us are born leaders. Me...I perform best in a secondary role. I'm a good follower, especially when it comes to war. My experience in battle is almost nonexistent."

"You've captained your own boat and run your own fishing business."

"That's different, Jara. I grew up with a grandfather and father who taught me the how to do both. But war..." He frowned. "War is about making life and death decisions. If it were just my life..." The fine lines around his eyes deepened. "But it's about the lives of others, people I care about, people who have families...mothers, fathers, children, friends who care." He stood up and began to clear the table. "I just hope Kup comes back fast."

Jaradee pushed her chair back. "I've avoided thinking of the conflict with the Pheet Adole as war. But it is, isn't it?" She pressed her hands against her belly. "These babies are vital to the outcome. These babies must live."

Mylos slipped an arm around her waist. For a time, they stood immersed in thought, their blanket of safety thinning one thread at a time.

15

With the rise of the sun on the third morning, Floree and two female Vasrosi warriors arrived at the cabin. A message delivered to Floree via her tukoolo warned them not to travel to El QuilTran. Lusktar Rados had been informed that two rebel women had been artificially impregnated at the Protariflee Center. His men guarded all ports and searched all ships, coming and going. Jaradee would be safest in El SyrTundi, at least for a time.

Over the course of the next seven cycles of El Stroma's moons, Jaradee and the three women journeyed from one sheltered haven to the next. Sometimes they traveled on foot; sometimes on horseback. They stayed in a shelter only long enough for Jaradee to rest, then they moved on.

Today would be the last travel day. The birthing drew near and Jaradee fatigued faster. She and Floree had made the decision to stop until after the babies were born.

While Floree and her two protectors packed and policed their camp, Jaradee sat on a stump, her hands resting on her large belly. She marveled that two lives existed inside her womb. *Two babies...a boy and a girl...Rethdun and Rayn...named after El QuilTran's storm deities.* The quick jab of a tiny foot startled a soft laugh from her throat. Lifting a hand, she kissed the palm, pressed it to the spot, and remembered the first time the babies had moved. The turning they flipped heads down, she had thought fish swam in her belly. Each movement, no matter how big or how small, melted her heart.

Floree smiled at her. "Carrying a child in your womb is a miracle of surprising moments. Carrying the saviors of your people...She grew serious...I can't even imagine how that must feel."

Jaradee hugged herself. "If I think about it in those terms, I feel unworthy and overwhelmed. I simply love them." She patted her belly. "How much longer?"

"We'll be at the Cliffs of Cimondeli by late afternoon. Puna and Karia have gone ahead to scout the area. The route I've chosen will take us a bit longer, but it's much safer and unexpected. Don't overtax yourself. We can rest as often as you need.

Jaradee leveraged herself to standing and rubbed her low back. "If my belly grows much bigger, I won't be able to get up at all."

Her birther grinned. "You carry healthy babies, Jara. Be glad."

"I am glad. And I will be happy to be in one place for a time." Jaradee inhaled morning air. "You're sure Katareen will be at Cliff Haven?"

"She's there and can hardly wait to see you."

Jara's bright mood dimmed. "And Daar? Have you heard anything?"

Floree squeezed her arm. "All I know is that he is with Mylos."

"And Kuparak?"

"Nothing, Jara. I'll tell you if I hear. It's time to go."

With Floree leading and her protectors behind, they hiked a meandering route. Karia greeted them at the cliffs with a whistle of welcome and landed on the low branch nearby.

Jaradee shielded her eyes and surveyed the weather-worn formations stacked in a random pattern from the forest floor to the upper plateau. Varying shades of burnt sienna, bronze, and brown glowed in the light. Plant life flourishing in the cracks and crevices between them added vibrant splashes of greens and yellows. "What an interesting formation. How was it formed?"

Floree smiled. "A long time ago, planetary changes pushed the cliffs up from the ocean floor. As the water receded, mud, silt and sand solidified. Water erosion formed a labyrinth of passages and caves. Ancient cliff dwellers made Cimondeli their home until a series of flash floods drove them inland. A Charnlandian shameena told us where to look for it."

Gazing at the massive cliff face, Jaradee wrapped her arms around her tummy. "How will I make it *up there*?"

"A way has been invented to bring elders to Cliff Haven." Floree pointed to the near end of the cliff face. "See the ropes hanging over there?"

"Yes."

"Come. We will get you to safety."

Floree led her to the foot of the cliffs. A stretcher-like apparatus, lifted by a rope and pulley system carried her to a shelter hidden midway up the face.

Eager hands helped her from the stretcher. Katareen hugged her, stepped back, and laughed through her tears. "My goodness, you are..." Her mouth rounded in astonishment. "Huge! I am so glad you're finally here. I thought I might never see you again." She planted a kiss on Jaradee's cheek. "You look wonderful." She laughed. "We have so much to share."

Linking elbows, Katareen guided her to a beat up, old sofa and plopped down beside her. "Tell me everything, Jaradee."

"First, Kat, tell me if you've seen Kuparak."

Her sister's eagerness flattened. "He brought Zarrin to see me. Not here at Cliff Haven, of course. He took me to a rendezvous point near Harie's farm. We met him there."

"Did Zarrin tell the truth about his time with the Pheet Adole?

Katareen pursed her lip and tipped her head. "My inner knowing says yes he did. I gather he realized the Pheet Adole planned to use him and dispose of him. Not a great thing to discover when you've forsaken your people, is it? Enough of Zarrin. Kup told me he would travel with Talarah to El QuilTran and come back to continue the fight." Her gazed grew distant.

Jaradee knew that look meant more to come. "And?"

"Jara, Kup lied. I'm not sure what about. I just know he didn't tell me the truth. Can we talk about you now? What's it like to be pregnant?"

. . .

everal turnings later, labour began. Floree and two female healers had set up a private space, which included a birthing chair stolen from the Protariflee Center's warehouse. When the babies began their descent into the birth canal, the center of the seat would be removed for them to drop through into Floree's waiting hands.

As the pain increased and the contractions came closer and closer together, Katareen and Floree settled Jaradee in the reclining chair. Grateful for the exercises that she and Floree had practiced to help during the birthing process, she focused on the birther's soft instructions and reminders. Katareen remained at her side, wiped sweat from her brow, and whispered encouraging words in her ear. Her sister's love and Floree's unruffled presence kept Jaradee calm, even as spasms wracked her body.

Floree looked up from where she sat on a low stool in front of the chair. "Take a deep breath and push."

Jaradee let out an agonized cry as the first head crowned.

"Another breath, Jara, and push...harder this time."

Womb wrenching contractions ripped through her. A child cried out. Jaradee's eyes, bleary with pain, sought Floree's.

"It is your son, Jara. He was in hurry to meet you." She handed him to a healer who placed him on his mother's bare chest and covered him with a small blanket.

Jaradee touched the waxy substance coating his cheek. "Welcome to the world, Rethdun Torin Vilandree."

Another contraction knifed through her. The healer picked up the baby and moved aside.

Floree gasped as Rayn dropped into her waiting hands. "I almost missed you, little one." She gave her a gentle swat on the bottom.

Panting, Jaradee propped herself higher on the arm of the chair and listened for a cry. None came. Floree laid the child on Jaradee's belly and tickled her feet. A rebellious intake of breath and a cry shook the small body. Hard cramping dropped Jaradee back in the chair. Two placentas slid, one after the other, from the birth canal into a waiting bowl. Floree set them aside for use in the birthing ceremony the haven residents, male and female, would do to celebrate the birth-mates and their mother and to express gratitude for the abundance of new life represented.

Exhausted but triumphant, Jaradee cuddled her clean, rosy babies, one in each arm. "Rayn Jaradee Palmira, you are so beautiful." She looked at Floree's tired face. "Do you think they know each other?"

A smile washed the fatigue away. "I do. Watch." Floree placed the birth-mates side by side in a cradle made by one of the Vasrosi. Before she had finished tucking a blanket around them, they had snuggled together. Rayn sucked her tiny thumb, her other hand resting on Rethdun's chest. Rethdun curled around her, stretched his arm over her, and slept.

Jaradee studied them with a touch of wonder. Rethdun, longer and huskier, had the fair skin and dark black hair of a Thornlandian. Rayn had her mother's curly hair and soft brown skin. Although smaller than her birth-mate, she had the long, slender limbs of her father's clan.

Katareen touched Rethdun's small fist. "They are so beautiful, Jara. Are you happy?"

"I'm tired, Kat. Tired *and* happy."

When Katareen's and Floree's responsibilties in the safe haven took them away from her side, Jaradee would take the babies to visit Awinta, the Serveero of Cimondeli. A woman early in her fiftieth cycle, she greeted her visitors with a big smile of welcome. Her dark skin and amber eyes reminded Jaradee of Kuparak and Talarah. She felt a deep kinship, one that Awinta seemed to return.

During their visits, Rethdun and Rayn would sleep curled together on a woven blanket and Jaradee would watch Awinta weave on her big loom. To the sound of the treadle and the whisper of the shuttle, Jaradee learned that the Serveero belonged to the Giroblania, Kuparak's tribe. She also learned about Cimondeli. The biggest safe haven, it housed the women and children related to Vasrosi warriors in El SyrTundi. Education, a large part of what occurred in the haven, encompassed everything from how to read and write, to the geography of El Stroma, to the culture practices of both the Eleo Preda and the Pheet Adole, to classes in martial arts. Those who lived in the cliffs shared the responsiblities of keeping it running. Tasks were assigned based on a resident's skills. Visitors were also given things to do. Jaradee looked forward to the time when she would be able to contribute.

Life settled into a comfortable routine. Rayn and Rethdun thrived.

Jaradee and Katareen took classes together in EriaCapo, a form of martial arts practiced to music. And Jaradee spent time with Floree learning more about the healing arts.

Three full moon cycles had passed when Daar arrived at Cimondeli. Katareen, the first to see him, yelped in delight and sprinted to his side. "Daar! We have been so worried. How are you? Where were you? Is Kup here, too?"

Jaradee handed Rethdun, replete on mother's milk, to Floree and hurried to join them. "We have missed you, Daar." She noted the strain and fatigue at war on his face. "You are worried?"

"Mylos sent me to tell you to leave Cliff Haven. It's time to take the birth-mates and try to reach El Quil'Tran. If you can make it to Tahellive, his boat will be ready. If it's not safe to go there, go where you will be safe." He glanced toward the babies. "May I see them?"

Jaradee hugged him. "Of course. You are their uncle after all." She led him across the nursery area and picked up her daughter. "This is Rayn. Why don't you sit and hold her?"

Daar hesitated. Katareen pulled him down on the old sofa beside her. "She won't bite, Daar."

He grinned and perched his niece on his knees. "She is beautiful. She looks like you, Jara."

Jaradee sat with Rethdun in her lap. "What have you heard from Kuparak?"

Daar bounced Rayn on his knee. "Mylos discovered Kup took his sister to the transport center near VenTra. A shuttle from an inter-universal vessel had landed for supplies. It departed about that time and shortly thereafter the ship left orbit, headed for the Inner Universe. No one has heard from or seen either Kup or Talarah since, so we're pretty sure they boarded the spacecraft. Who can say where they are now?"

Katareen pressed for more information. "What happened to Zarrin, Daar?"

He shrugged. "He's disappeared. Mylos thinks he might have escaped. Other Vasrosi think he went with Kup."

"Then Mylos is still the Vasrosi leader?" Floree's satisfied tone made Jaradee smile.

Daar nodded. "He is, and he's doing great. Speaking of Mylos, I gotta get back. He said to tell you Karia and ReRe are always in communication. If things get rough, he'll find you." He passed Rayn to Katareen, tickled Rethdun under the chin, and stood up. "Tell Awinta what's up. And leave as soon as you can, Jara." He flashed from sight, leaving his sisters astonished at how much he had changed.

Jaradee laid Rethdun on a blanket. "Please watch them, Kat. Floree and I need to confer with Awinta and tell her we're leaving."

Kat's chin jutted forward in the way Jaradee recognized as trouble. "I'm going with you, Jara. You need me to help with the babies."

"You and I don't get to make that decision. Let's see what Awinta says. She may need you here."

Floree snuggled Rayn. "Why don't you go with Jaradee, Kat. I'll watch the babies."

Awinta stood at her loom, eyes following the progress of the shuttle. Removing her foot from the treadle, she turned. "ReRe let my tukoolo know Daar brought a message that will affect us all. Your brother has become a man since he left to join Mylos. You should be proud."

Kat remained in the entryway, her expression defiant.

Jaradee crossed to the loom and studied the pattern in the fabric. "I am, Awinta, but I worry his anger will get him into trouble."

The older woman smiled. "If that is how he must learn control, I am sure it will".

Jaka, a man in his middle years, hurried into the space. Jaradee shared Daar's message. Jaka left to organize the Vasrosi and their tukoolo's to stand guard. Awinta pulled two woven scarves from a basket next to her.

"I made these carriers for the birth-mates. Let's join Floree and I will show you how they work."

Katareen, stubbornness churning around her, trailed after them, but said nothing.

Awinta wrapped and strapped Rethdun securely to Floree. Jaradee soon snuggled Rayn in her new carrier.

"Look, she's already asleep. I hope she stays that way."

Awinta made a final adjustment. "I suggest you sleep with the scarves wrapped and ready. If there's trouble, you can slip the birth-mates into place and go." She turned to Katareen. "I know you want to go with your sister, but I need you here, Kat. You will stay with me, Kat. If possible, you can join Jardee and Floree later."

Katareen started to speak, seemed to think better of it, and sighed. Stubbornness misted into acceptance.

Awinta hugged her. "Thank you, Kat. You and I are a good team." She addressed Floree. "I suggest you leave by the exit to the upper cliffs. Karia and Puna await you there." Hugging her, she stepped back. "Gather your things and go. Kat, come with me. We must create an illusion without alerting a SorTech."

Katareen hugged Jaradee. "Take care of each other and the birth-mates. Be in touch when you can." With tears brightening her eyes, she hurried after Awinta."

Jaradee stuffed a knapsack with diaper clothes and extra clothing for Rayn. Floree gathered Rethdun's and added packets of dried food. She tossed several packets on the sofa. "Put some in yours too, Jara. We'll need to eat so we don't starve the babies."

"We're lucky the herbs you took while I was pregnant worked, Floree. With both of us able to nurse, travel will be much more efficient.

Floree kissed the top of Rethdun's head. "And if necessary, we can separate and join up later."

A commotion at the foot of the cliffs brought Katareen running back.

"Brotico's search the cliff face. Awinta says to hurry."

Kat's warning and the tingle of SorTechory propelled the women toward the exit at the top of Cimondeli Cliffs. Jaradee glance back. A wave of sadness surprised her. *This has been a good home. I wonder if I will ever see it again?*

16

A tremor overhead and sudden activity in the cavern down the short tunnel snatched Jaradee from her reverie into the reality of now.

Floree bent over her, a cautioning finger to her lips. The deep resonance of male voices, out of place in her world of women, sent a thrill of fear up Jaradee's spine. *The Klutarse have found us.*

Scrambling to her feet, she adjusted the woven carrier. Floree, with Rethdun already snuggled and sleeping, slid Rayn into it, shoved a knapsack in her hand, and hurried her away from the main cavern. At the foot of a steep incline, a labyrinth of tunnels opened in front of them. Somewhere within their midst a second exit existed.

Floree flipped on a small hand torch and swept it from one gaping entrance to the next. "We take the third on the left, then another left, and then—"

The distant sound of leather on stone propelled them with quiet stealth Through the first tunnel. Not far along on the left, a large, low-ceilinged cavern gaped like a swamp gator's maw. The shaft of light from the torch flashed over the sandy floor and picked out a tunnel opening on the opposite side. Ducking low, they skirted the perimeter of the cavern.

A smothered cough, much too close, sounded an alarm. Floree grabbed Jaradee's hand and dowsed the light. Feeling her way in the pitch black, she led the way up, around a corner, and then straight. Her pace quickened as the floor began a steep ascent. She paused to whisper instructions. "Hold onto the strap on my knapsack. Follow me. The tunnel is about to become quite narrow."

Jaradee touched Rayn in her carrier. "Not too narrow, I hope."

"We're about to find out."

Wrapping an arm around Rayn, Jaradee tightened her grip on the strap and inched forward. The soft scrape of Floree's boots ceased. The arm protecting Rayn bumped her pack. Jaradee stopped.

Floree's hand found her shoulder. "Can you hear anyone tracking us?"

Jaradee concentrated her attention back the way they had come. "I don't hear anything, but..."

Turning on the torch, Floree allowed a small shaft of light to leak between her fingers. A short distance ahead, a ladder leaned against the wall at the end of the tunnel. In the rough ceiling, the dim light etched out the square shape of a trap door.

Hurriedly relocating the ladder, Floree grabbed the side rail. "Let's hope the trap door is quiet." Encumbered by the carrier and the sleeping baby, she climbed midway, leveraged the door open a crack, and peered out.

Jaradee kept her attention riveted to the dark tunnel behind them. Neither her hearing nor her intuition sensed the Klutarse closing in.

Floree pushed the door wider. Sunlight flooded the space. Shielding Rethdun from the light, she heaved her knapsack out and crawled awkwardly over the edge.

Jaradee climbed the ladder, tossed her pack ahead of her, and squinted against the mid-turning brightness. Covering Rayn's head with a corner of the scarf, she clambered over the lip of the opening, gripped the trap door, and helped Floree lower it and cover the edges with dirt and gravel.

Jaradee scanned the landscape. The open Plains of Los Ateed stretched to the horizon one direction and bordered foothills on the other. The trap door had deposited them a good distance away from the gradual rise of the hills toward a mountain range in the distance. Standing where they were announced their position like a beacon.

"Gotta move." Floree shouldered her knapsack, wrapped her arms around Rethdun, and sprinted across a wide expanse of cracked, dried ground toward a swale between two parched hills.

Jaradee hugged Rayn closer and grabbed her pack. A short distance into the shallow vale, creeping vegetation obscured their tracks. Further in, a grove of tall, slender sgàile trees hid them from view.

Wending their way beneath almost translucent white leaves, they trudged into a second grove. Rayn began to whimper and wiggle. Jaradee shushed her with a soft kiss.

Floree dropped her pack. "We'd better nurse these sweet ones, or they'll bring the enemy right to us." She sank to the ground, removed Rethdun from the carrier, and tossed it aside. Undoing her shirt, she settled him at her breast.

Jaradee leaned against a silver-white trunk and helped Rayn's searching mouth to find what it sought. Savoring quiet time with her daughter, she slid a thumb under her small kneading hand. Tiny fingers gripped it. Dark eyes searched her face. A milky smile formed around the nipple and then vanished into rhythmic suckling. Next to her, Rethdun drank his fill and pushed away. Wide awake and alert, he gazed up at Floree, squirmed to look over his shoulder at Jaradee, and kicked his sturdy legs.

Already he and his birth-mate were showing distinct personalities. Although Jaradee and Floree nursed both babies, Rayn preferred to be fed by her mother. Rethdun happily nursed from either. Jaradee marveled at how quickly they grew and changed.

Karia's low warning whistle ended the moment of peace. A quick image flitted through Jaradee's mind: dust clouds obscuring the hooves and legs of fast approaching horses.

With efficient, soundless movements, the babies were returned to their carriers, all signs of their brief stop were eradicated, and Floree led the way deeper into the foothills. Above them Karia and Puna flew, one scouting ahead, the other circling back. A rush of gratitude for Kuparak and the gift of her tukoolo brought her eternal question to mind. *Where are you, Kup?* She glanced around. *More to the point—where are we?*

Jaradee looked at her daughter's dark head and picked up her pace.

Coming abreast of Floree, she mouthed 'time out' and stopped beside a sallow tree.

Floree pushed aside the low-hanging curtain of willowy branches, motioned her beneath them, and let them swish back into place. "Time for a break?"

"Check-in time. Do you know where we are?"

"I believe we're on the eastern side of Chaporticas Mountains, but..." The shake of her head didn't inspire much confidence.

"So you don't know what's up ahead?" Jaradee adjusted her backpack and wrapped the carrier tighter.

Floree produced a small water flask and offered it. "Puna saw an old homestead a bit further on. It looks empty. If it is, it might be a place for us to hide for a time. Has Karia shared any information?"

"No. Wait." Jaradee concentrated. She described a series of images from her tukoolo. "Three horsemen met a Klutarse by the trap door. Just before they arrived, our protectors emerged and headed toward a small valley south of here. Two men followed. The third tied his horse to a tree and searched close to where we fed the babies. He found nothing, mounted his horse, and galloped after his comrades. Our protectors shifted and flew further south, leading them away from here. The men continue their search that direction."

Floree drank from the water flask, wiped her mouth with the back of her hand, and smiled. "The protectors will continue to lead them away from us. With luck, the Klutarse and their men will follow. Let's find the homestead and see what it's like."

The sun had begun a slow dive toward the horizon by the time several weathered gray structures in what had once been a large clearing came into view. From their vantage point on the side of a hill, Jaradee studied it with mixed feelings. Empty and forsaken, a small, weathered house with a pitched roof, a rickety veranda, and a small porch stood to one side. Whoever had lived there raised chickens and other animals and managed a large garden. The clearing, surrounded on three sides by tree-covered hills and backed by tall mountains, could only be seen from where they stood. Their tukoolo would be able to see anyone coming long before the homestead became visible.

Floree let out an extended sigh and began the trek downhill and across a field of wildflowers bordering the overgrown clearing. When at last they reached the house, the babies set up a chorus of wails. Perched on the edge of the porch, Jaradee fed her hungry daughter and watched the sun tint late-turning clouds teal and lavender and splash the darkening dome with magenta. The breathtaking sight made her seriously consider taking up residence.

"It is quite beautiful, Floree. I rather hope we can stay."

The next turning while the babies napped, Jaradee left Floree on guard and explored the clearing behind the house. Nestled in a grouping of trees, she discovered a small structure built of moss-covered field stones. A battered door hanging on one hinge groaned as she pulled it open and looked inside. A wooden bucket sat on the floor next to a hand pump.

Sprinting to the house, she peeked in the front door. Rethdun and Rayn slept on a blanket in a protected corner. "Floree, come and see what I found."

Leaving the door ajar so they could hear the birth-mates if they cried, Jaradee led her to the stone building and motioned her inside.

"Oh, Jara. Does it work?"

Jaradee grinned. "Waited for you. Shall we give it a try?"

Floree grabbed the handle. "You bet." When nothing happened, she stepped away. "You try."

Rubbing her hands together, Jaradee pictured water flowing, grabbed the pump handle, and pumped. A drop fell into the bucket. She kept up a steady rhythm until a gush of murky water spurted from the spout. The longer she pumped the clearer the water became. Floree cupped her hands under the stream and took a sip.

"It's great. I'll pump. You try it."

"Oh, Floree. We are so lucky!" Jaradee laughed and skipped in a circle. "We have a well! Now all we need is a way to feed ourselves."

Floree grabbed her hand. "Let's see what else we can find."

Their inspection of the clearing, both delightful and overwhelming, turned up a chicken coop and a shed with gardening tools, an axe that needed sharpening, and a wooden box of rusty carpentry tools. A second, larger shed appeared to have housed a cow and perhaps a horse. Next to it, they discovered a pigpen.

Jaradee wiped sweat from her hairline and plopped onto the edge of the porch. "I wonder why the owners went away and left so much behind?"

Floree rubbed at a spot of mud on her pants. "We may never know, but..."

Rethdun let out a hungry cry. Floree picked him up. "You're wet. Let's change you, and then you can eat."

Rayn stared up at Jaradee, waved her small fists in the air, and kicked her feet. "Bet you're wet too."

By the time feeding ritual was complete and Jaradee and Floree had shared the last ration packet and a dried apple, the birth-mates had curled up together and fallen asleep.

Jaradee sat on the porch, listening to the quiet sounds of trees and night insects and the swish of tall grass in the soft breeze. "It's so peaceful. I sure hope it lasts. It would be lovely to have a snug little home when the winter snow flys, a home where the birth-mates could grow up, where we could all be safe. "

Tipping her had back, she closed her eyes. *I wish this homestead could be our home. I wish...*

17

Early the next morning, Floree tethered to Puna and flew in search of a farm or village, where she might obtain supplies. Jaradee gazed after her with a touch of envy. Helping Rethdun to sit up, she mused aloud. "I know we have to stay hidden." She remembered the detailed sketch of Katareen on the reward poster and flinched. "I bet the Rompeer has put a price on *our* heads." Rethdun blew a bubble and bounced happily. Rayn cried, demanding attention.

Jaradee laughed. "I'm the lucky one. I'm here with you."

By middle turning, she paced outside to search the bright dome. *Where are you, Floree?* The sun sliding beyond its zenith some time later increased her growing anxiety. Leaving the birth-mates asleep in their corner bed, she stepped onto the porch, shaded her eyes, and scanned the dome again.

Karia alighted in a tree nearby. A message from Floree whispered through Jaradee's mind. *"On the way back. Hide all signs of you and the birth-mates. Not trouble...Caution."*

Jaradee made a quick sweep of the small front room and cooking area, tucked Rayn into the woven carrier, and with Rethdun straddling her hip strode across the clearing and into the trees. She and Floree had discovered a makeshift lean-to far enough away from the house to be a good hiding place should the need arise. When they reached it, she threw Rethdun's carrier on the ground, laid him on it, eased his sleeping sister from her carrier, and placed her beside him. Sitting with her back against a tree, she waited, forcing herself to stay awake.

Shadow and light performing a slow dance on the forest floor hinted at time passing. She nursed the birth-mates, sang them quiet songs, and felt a wave of gratitude when slumber wrapped them in its silent cocoon.

Impatience and concern warred inside her. *Where are you, Floree?*

The faint sound of voices drifting through the trees answered her question. Wary of giving herself away, she ignored her desire to creep closer to the clearing. The wha wha of hawk wings alerted her to Karia's arrival.

"All clear."

Hesitant to wake the babies, she ducked from the shelter, stretched, and peered through the trees. Floree darted into view and jogged toward her.

"You won't believe my day, Jara. We have food and blankets and seeds and..."

Rethdun gave a lusty cry. Rayn's lighter tones soon joined the chorus.

Jaradee picked up her daughter. "Let's get them to the house. I can't wait to hear everything."

Each with a baby straddling a hip, they strolled back through the trees. The crow of a rooster stopped Jaradee in her tracks.

"Chickens? Did you bring back chickens?"

Floree grinned. "Chickens and a nanny goat and two kids and...Oh, Jara, I met the greatest family. Winnoe is Eleo Predan and a Vasrosi. Nodin is Pheet Adole but has joined the rebels. In fact, Mylos had been in touch with them to keep an eye out for us. Puna made contact with Winnoe's tukoolo. That's how I found them." She urged Jaradee around the corner of the house.

Jaradee gasped. "Look at all this stuff." She hurried forward and took a quick mental inventory of enough supplies for a moon cycle or more. Her heart gave a leap.

"You think we'll be safe here. Are we staying?"

"I think it's a great place to raise the children." Floree kissed Rethdun's chubby cheek. "What do you think, Rethdun?"

He flailed his small fists, bounced on her hip, and gurgled.

Jaradee laughed and bent to pet a black and white cat, sitting sedately on the porch step. "It already feels like home. Thank you, Floree."

"Don't thank me. Thank Mylos and Winnoe and Nodin." She climbed the two well-worn steps to the porch. "I suggest we feed the babes." Her happy gaze rested on the pile of supplies. "Then we have work to do." She disappeared inside.

For a moment, Jaradee stood in the late afternoon quiet. She gazed from the house to the trees, savored the scent of wildflowers in the air, and marveled at her good fortune. "I have healthy children, a wonderful friend, and a safe and peaceful place to live."

Karia landed on her shoulder, nibbled her ear, and soared up to a high branch, her telie-eye searching the hills and fields. Jaradee looked up at her compeer. The whistler hawk would warn her of danger—danger that would arrive at their door when they least expected it.

Shrugging away her fears for tomorrow, she turned her attention to enjoying today.

E. Eleebanna

Part 2

Escape

Trapped in the net of their enemy's making.
Separate directions result in hearts breaking.
Escape made essential, protection supplied,
Sending one of the two across the divide.

18

Discovery wrenched two hearts open wide.
One was transported across the divide.
The other remained submerged and well-hidden
Exploring that which had long been forbidden.

Floree sat up in bed, her heart pounding. A quick mental search of the house and gardens netted her nothing out of the ordinary. Puna's distant presence suggested her compeer patrolled over the foothills. *What woke me?*

Unable to shake the feeling that she had awakened for a reason, she pulled on pants and a shirt and tiptoed from the room. Rayn and the birth-mates slept upstairs in peaceful oblivion. She chose not to wake them...at least not yet.

Making her way to the front door, she slipped on her boots and stepped into the night quiet. Her senses searched. The coolness of spring, the scents of wildflowers and rich earth, a breeze rustling the treetops felt normal and comforting. She crept into the overgrown field bordering the clearing and scanned the nearby hills. A chill skitter over her skin.

"Brotico!" Puna's telepathic warning dropped her to her knees, eyes glued to the dome. A large flying figure gliding out of the foothills blotted out the star-studded consistency of night and pressed her lower. Descending circles narrowed its search. It swooped over the field, hovered above the homestead, and soared back the way it had come.

A breath whooshed from her lungs as she crawled between sturdy stocks to the edge of the overgrown clearing. Hidden in the shadow of tall trees, the dilapidated house looked empty and forlorn.

Rethdun and Rayn have thrived here. The past three sun cycles have been good to all of us. Worry creased her brow. She and Jaradee had hoped their peaceful life would last. Tonights invasion, however, proved the truth of their tukoolo's reports. Rompeerial soldiers drew closer.

The screen door squeaked. Jaradee crept onto the porch and slouched against the wall, her gaze darting from Floree to the dome. Floree half rose. Puna streaking above her sent her back to her knees. Karia's whistle sounded from the trees. Jaradee ducked behind a porch chair. A second winged creature banked over the homestead, hovered, and flew out of sight.

Puna's *all clear* in her mind propelled Floree to the house and up the porch steps. "Those were broticos. That means the Klutarse are close by. We have to leave now. I'll get the horse and the wagon. You get the children."

Jaradee slipped through the half- open door. Floree hurried to the small paddock. She glanced up at the darkened moon. *Alkina's barren phase will cover our departure.* Mentally reviewing their route, she hitched the horse Nodin had loaned them to the wagon and led it to the back door.

Jaradee lifted the birth-mates into the wagon bed, scrambled aboard, and crawled in a special compartment built beneath the seat. When the children were nestled beside her, Floree wedged boards across the opening and piled a hamper of supplies, a pile of baskets, and a rolled up tarp in front of them.

Jumping to the ground, she made her way to the front of the wagon. A soft squeak accompanied her climb to the seat. A cool breath of night air calmed her quaking nerves. A gentle slap of the reins sent the horse ambling onto a well-camouflaged track traversing the forest to the mountains beyond.

A final look at the homestead made her heart jump. Above the clearing, four winged figures blocked out the stars. *More broticos!*

Tethered to Puna, she wove a curtain of quiet invisibility around the wagon. Concentrating on what lay ahead not behind, she guided the horse along the track.

The trees had begun to thin at the base of rugged, looming mountains when she tugged on the reins and brought the horse and wagon to a stop. Absorbing the pre-dawn silence, she stared ahead uncertain. Puna had not sounded an alarm and yet...

The figure of a man stepped onto the track. Floree's heart skipped a beat, then settled into a normal rhythm. The curtain of invisibility faded. Mylos strode toward her, ran a hand along the gelding's side, and helped her down from the seat. A second man stepped into the open, amber eyes glowing in an ebony face. As though unsure of his welcome, Kuparak's smile flashed, then vanished.

Floree threw her arms around him. "Kuparak, it is so good to see you!"

A board clattered into the wagon bed. Jaradee's eager face popped up. "Kup? Is it really you?"

Two small figures crowded next to her. Rayn studied him from behind a mask of uncertainty. Rethdun's solemn young face showed no fear, only curiosity.

Kuparak lifted the birth-mates down and knelt. "So *you* are what all the fuss is about." He offered a hand. "I am Kuparak."

Rayn moved closer to Floree. Rethdun shook the hand. "I am Rethdun." He glanced at Jaradee. "Maman knows you."

"Indeed she does." Kuparak grinned.

Mylos climbed aboard the wagon. "We can talk later. ReRe says the soldiers found the track. The broticos are flying this way."

A flurry of activity returned Jaradee and the children to their hiding place. Kuparak shaped a smoky galee and circled upward. Floree joined Mylos. The horse ambled forward, its tail flicking, its ears twitching.

Mylos leaned closer. "Tether up and hide us. I haven't mastered the invisibility charm."

Floree searched for her tukoolo, found no trace, and frowned. "Puna isn't answering." She scanned the beauty of dawn's dome. A hawk swooped from the early morning mist and landed on her shoulder. The shimmer of invisibility veiled them.

Mylos frowned. "What happened?"

"A SorTech journeys with the soldiers and the Klutarse. Puna was too close to respond. We need to find cover. We're a target even with the curtain."

A smoky galee, wings glistening silver in the rising sun, hovered above a series of outcroppings, caught an updraft, and shot domeward. Circling back, it disappeared behind jagged stones piled as though tossed from a careless hand.

Floree slapped the reins, urging the horse into a trot. "Kup found a place to hide." As they rounded the first towering pile of bronze and orange rocks, the galee, perched in a sturdy pine, lifted into flight and soared into the mouth of a narrow gorge. Floree guided horse and wagon beneath the ribbon of blue formed by the high walls and emerged in a tree-covered canyon.

Kuparak materialized at the horse's head and led it between pines and fagus beech to an overhang sheltered on all sides by trees and rocks. He patted the horse's nose and walked to the front of the wagon.

"We should be safe here, at least for the night. Let's set up camp."

Mylos climbed over the seat and removed the boards hiding Jaradee and the birth-mates.

Rayn yawned. "Uncle My." She held out her arms and giggled when he picked her up.

Rethdun followed, his paleness emphasized by dawn's early light. Serious eyes the color of aged amber scanned the world and its occupants. "Are we safe?"

Mylos ruffled his black hair. "We are safe, Rethdun." He placed Rayn beside her birth-mate. "Take care of Rayn while I help make camp."

Rethdun put a protective arm around her, guided her to the back of the wagon bed, and helped her to sit on the tailgate.

Floree swung herself to the ground. "What about the broticos? Are they still searching?"

Kuparak began to unhitch the horse. "They are, but they're searching the woods behind the homestead. If we're lucky, they'll be occupied there for some time. If not, we are well-hidden here."

Jaradee rounded the end of the wagon. "What can I do to help?"

"Stretch a highline between a couple of trees near the back of the overhang. I'll bring the horse. Then pack the supplies in the secret compartment and see what you can do to hide the wagon."

Floree lifted the birth-mates from the tailgate, sat Rayn on her hip and with Rethdun's hand in hers made her way under the protuberance of rock and brush. Mylos greeted her with a smile.

"It's been awhile since I saw the children. They've grown."

Floree kissed the top of Rayn's head. "They are maturing much too fast." She tilted her head. "I have a question or two. How long has Kup been back? Who's the Vasrosi leader...you or Kuparak?"

Kuparak walked up beside her with Jaradee. "I am honored to serve as Mylos' deputy. I have been back less than five El Stroman moon cycles." His gaze grew distant and sad.

Jaradee touched his arm. "And Tala?"

The sadness intensified then faded. "Talarah is on the planet of Thera in the fourth galaxy from the great central suns. She and my son are with Zarrin in the Central Mountains."

Mylos' expressed a touch of surprise. "Zarrin?"

"He accompanied us on our journey. His association with the Klutarse changed him. By the time we reached Thera, he had mastered his temper and his desire for wealth. He will take good care of Tala and Lortin." He sighed. "I miss my sibling sister, but I'm glad she is safe."

Jaradee finished arranging the stones for a fire pit. "How did you discover Thera?"

Kuparak smiled. "Let's make camp and prepare food. I will tell you our tale after mid-morning meal."

Replete on dried fruit and bread and exhausted from their journey, Rayn and Rethdun napped. Floree reclined next to Mylos, her gaze flicking from the fire to the enraptured expression on Jaradee's face. Kuparak, a hand resting on Jara's smaller one, leaned forward to stir the fire with a stout stick. Propping it on a stone, he stared into the flames, then turned to the woman next to him.

"Before I begin my story, I wish to apologize for leaving you and Floree to face the anger of Lusktar Rados alone, Jaradee. Talarah's safety became my primary concern." A quizzical expression creased his brow. "That and the fact that I feared my growing love for you, Jara, inspired my ignoble behavior. It is my hope you will both forgive my actions and understand my concern for my sibling." He squeezed Jaradee's hand. "We will talk more of this later."

Jaradee's shy smile and the flush highlighting her warm brown skin expressed without words her response to his roundabout declaration. Floree nestled closer to Mylos, whose gentle touch made butterflies flutter in *her* stomach.

Demeanor grim, Kuparak began his tale. "It was not my plan to leave El Stroma. It was, rather, to find my sister-sibling the care she required to carry my son full term. When we reached the Cliffs of Cimondeli, it became clear I needed to take her to El QuilTran. Not only was she physically fragile, her mental state was such that I feared for her life." He withdrew his hand from Jaradee's and rubbed the palm against his thigh.

Floree sat up and wrapped her arms around her bent knees. "Losing a child causes emotional upheaval...even when it is an unborn fetus. The girl child implanted in her womb was her biological daughter. Her death left a wound in Talarah's heart."

Kuparak nodded. "Losing the child stole her will to live. Taking her to the shameena of the Giroblania became my goal." He shrugged. "We did not make it to our homeland. Soldiers tracked us. Talarah's weakened state made travel arduous and slow. In desperation, I took her to Tazio and Nioka near Tahellive, hoping their work with injured birds might translate to Humans."

Jaradee studied him. "Did it?"

He sighed. "They helped the physical body to heal but could not break through the melancholia. We stayed too long in the hopes that time might bring about a change. One night, Tazio came home from making a delivery to the Rompeer's estate. Our presence had been detected by a SorTech. Nioka advised us to leave El Stroma. As long as we remained, she said, we would be hunted and a danger to others. We left Tahellive immediately. I took Talarah to VenTra. A friend bought us passage aboard *The Serprentin*, a galactic cruiser headed for the Inner Universe."

Mylos pulled Floree into the crook of his arm. "Did you know where you wanted to go?"

"I had no idea. The ship made several stops along the way. We could have disembarked on Roahymn or RewFaar, but neither felt right. When *The Serprentin* began its orbit of KcernFensia, I joined the crew of the shuttle craft and spent a bit of time at the supply deport. There, I spoke with a man who suggested Thera, a little known planet close to the distant sun. He thought if anyone pursued us, Thera would be the last place they'd look."

Jaradee twisted to see him better. "How long was the trip?"

Kuparak rubbed his chin. "We made several long jumps using vortex portals to cut time. The trip to Thera took almost two sun cycles. Talarah gave birth to Lortin on board the ship.

Coming back, I secured a job on a jumper. It traversed the Clenaba Rolas system in less than a moon cycle. The trip from The Rim to El Stroma was the slowest leg."

Mylos tossed a small log on the fire, watched the shower of sparks settle, and looked at his deputy. "I know why you came back." He smiled at Jaradee. "How did Tala feel about being left behind."

"She wanted to stay on Thera. By the time we arrived, she had begun to regain her sense of self. She loved the Central Mountains and the people we met there. Given Lortin's birth parents, she could not return here, so Zarrin chose to stay with her. I am as indebted to him as he is to me." He glanced beyond the light of the fire and smiled at the two sleep-tousled children standing in the shadows. "You can bring Rayn and join us, Rethdun. I have something for you."

Floree caught a glimpse of silver as he withdrew something from his pocket. A premonition shot through her...a premonition that something auspicious was about to occur.

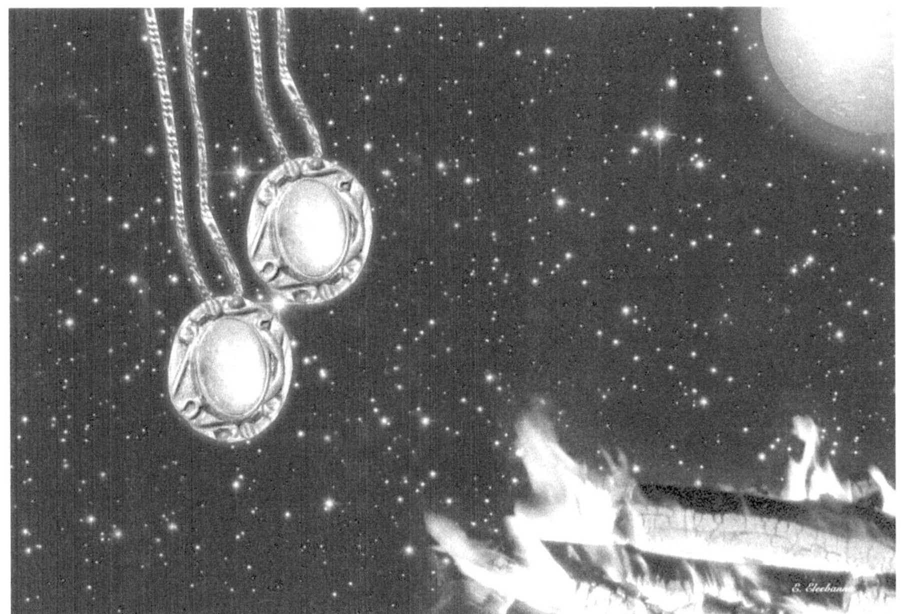

19

Floree beckoned the birth-mates into the flickering firelight. Rethdun urged Rayn ahead of him. She ran to Jaradee and scrambled into her lap. Rethdun moved to stand beside Floree. His steady gaze rested on Kuparak. The air around him sizzled with expectation.

Kuparak contemplated the contents of his hands. "I have a birth gift from Tazio and Nioka for the children. I believe you, Jaradee, and you, Floree, should hold these gifts in trust." Long silver chains spilled between his fingers. Holding a clasp in each hand, he let two identical silver lockets drop and swing in light of the fire. Moonstones surrounded by silver and gold glowed. "Inside you will find portraits of the birth-mates created by Nioka in a shameena's trance. Contained within the moonstone are the spirits of the children's tukoolo. Today, we will call them forth and tether the birth-mates to their compeers." He gave Jaradee a locket with a miniature portrait of Rethdun.

Floree opened Rethdun's and examined Rayn's feminine visage. "Nioka is very good." After showing it to Rethdun, she looped the chain around her neck and tucked the locket beneath her shirt.

"She is indeed." Kuparak beckoned Rayn to his side. "Do you know what a tukoolo is, Rayn?"

Her shy gaze brightened. "Maman has Karia. She watches over us."

He smiled. "I have a lovely falcon who wishes to be *your* tukoolo. Would you like that?"

She bit her lip. "Will it protect me?"

"It will." He observed her closely. "Are you, Rayn Jaradee Palmira, ready to accept your compeer for now and all time?"

Rayn gazed at Kuparak's face, her countenance grave. "I am ready."

A high pitched cry escorted a small falcon under the overhang. It landed on Kuparak's shoulder, its telie-eye scrutinizing its compeer.

Rayn stepped closer. The tukoolo fluttered to her raised arm and nibbled her cheek. A tiny, startled smile became a grin. "This is my friend...Kia."

Kuparak touched her head and the back of the falcon. "*Rethet Ceerus.*"

Color flooded Rayn's tanned complexion. "I love Kia." Petals of understanding unfurled. "I am Kia." She carried her compeer to Jaradee. "Look, Maman. I have my own tukoolo. This is Kia."

Jaradee kissed the rosy cheek. "I am proud to know your compeer, Rayn."

Rethdun walked to Kuparak. "I, too, have a compeer."

"Are you ready to tether, young Rethdun?"

"May I tether to a galee like you?"

Kuparak considered the child's face. "I believe a woodland galee might serve. Does that feel correct?"

Rethdun closed his eyes, calmed his breathing and lifted both arms. "Aquila, come to me."

A galee almost his height landed at his feet. One side of its body reflected the fire. A telie-eye searched the faces of those gathered around the pit. Rethdun knelt. "Aquila." The satisfaction in his voice made Floree smile.

"*Rethet Ceerus.*" Kuparak's hand on Rethdun's head and the back of the galee brought a gasp of delight.

Rethdun stroked the raptor's back. "You are my compeer." He pressed his hand to his heart. "Thank you, Kuparak."

Kuparak bowed his dark head. "You are welcome, ConServator of the Eleo Preda."

Rethdun returned the bow. "When do I fly with Aquila?"

Kuparak laughed. "You know far too much for a boy of three sun cycles. I will teach you to tether to your compeer when your maman says I may."

Rayn's beautiful eyes widened. "I fly, too?"

Jaradee looked from Kuparak to the children. "They are very young to shift, Kup."

Mylos came to his feet. "But they will need to learn soon or be trapped in this canyon. ReRe and Toa return with word of the soldiers." He walked into the open, shaded his eyes, and peered up at the blue of the afternoon dome.

Kuparak stood and brushed off his breeches. "Floree and Jaradee, please work with the children. Teach them to tether to their compeers. Aquila and Kia will help them make the shift." He joined Mylos.

Floree sat with Rethdun and his tukoolo, explaining what it meant to tether and how to form one with Aquila. The child listened with rapt attention, laid a hand on the galee's head, and shifted. Aquila lifted into flight. Rethdun followed and soared with his compeer over the trees. Circling back, he landed and materialized, his face aglow.

"Aunt Floree, I love my tukoolo. I love to fly." His forehead wrinkled. "I must think about this." Aquila strutting next to him, he walked into the sunshine and sank onto a rock near the overhang.

Rayn's gaze followed her birth-mate, looked up at her maman, and back at Rethdun. "I want to fly, too."

Jaradee held up the falcon. "This is a strelke. See its pretty blue wings and speckled breast."

Rayn nodded and ran a finger over Kia's feathered wing. "Why is its head a different color?"

"Akasci, mother of all things, thought brown feathers would look best. This is what you will look like when you fly, Rayn. Now, listen closely and remember everything I say." When she had explained tethering and the importance of doing exactly what her tukoolo asked, she looked from the falcon to the child.

"Tell me what I just said, Rayn."

The small face crinkled in thought. "Tethering is when my mind connects to my Kia's. I must never shift unless we are tethered. Kia will tell me in my head when it is time to be strelke and when it is time to be me again." She flashed a satisfied smile at her maman. "I did right?"

Jaradee laughed. "You did right. Are you ready to shift?"

She shook her head and pointed. "No. Kia says wait."

Floree turned in time to see a smoky galee swoop through the trees and land on a sturdy pine branch. Jumping to her feet, she strode to Mylos' side.

Kia flew to Jaradee's shoulder. Rayn gripped her hand. Rethdun appeared beside them with Aquila at his heels.

Kuparak shifted and with his compeer flew domeward.

Mylos hurriedly joined them. "Broticos are headed this way. With luck they'll pass us by. Jaradee already hid the wagon and supplies. The fire has out gone out. I'll scatter it and make sure we've left nothing behind. Take the children as far back under the overhang as you can. Your tukoolo are on guard. If they contact you, let me know."

Floree gazed at his bearded face. "What about the horse?"

He shot a look its direction. "It's well hidden."

"And what about you?"

"I'll be close." He scattered the fire pit, tossed dirt over the remains, shifted, and flew to the top of a fagus beech.

Rethdun slipped his hand into Floree's. "Please, Auntie, Aquila says we must hide." He led her over the rubble-strewn floor to a mound of rocks spilling down the canyon wall and scrambled over it. Glancing back, he motioned Floree to follow. When she reached the far side, he took her hand and pulled her after him into a crevice concealed behind the spill of loose stones.

"We're right behind you." Jaradee's whisper urged her forward.

The crevice ran under the mountain for some distance. The roar of fast flowing water grew louder the further she went. Cool darkness brought her to a halt. "Rethdun, where are you?"

"Here, Auntie." A soft blue light flared. Holding out his hand, he showed her a small, shimmering ball hovering above his palm.

Jaradee and Rayn crept from the crevice. "I hear water." Jaradee eyed the blue light. "How did you..."

"Aquila taught me. He says we are safe, but not to go further under the mountain. Big drop into a rushing river not far ahead."

Floree shook her head. "We knew they'd be special but..." She ruffled Rethdun's hair and knelt. "What else does Aquila say."

Rethdun put a finger to his lips and clasped Rayn's hand.

Floree mentally reached out to her tukoolo. An image formed. Puna perched in a tree. Her telie-eye followed the progress of two winged men soaring above the canyon. A circled search brought them back to the gorge. One landed in the shade of a dark pine. The other swooped between the high bronze-orange walls. Puna's eye zoomed out. Three broticos glided from the gorge and landed beside their comrade.

The men conferred amongst themselves. Lifting into flight, they fanned out over the canyon. Crisscrossing its length and breadth, they scoured every inch of the terrain. A signal from their leader, brought them to the ground so close to the overhang Floree almost stopped breathing. One man pointed through the trees. The leader shook his head, tightened the strap on his helmet, and launched upward. Two broticos shot after him. The fourth looked in the direction of the overhang, shrugged, and followed.

Floree blew out a breath. "They're leaving. Let's go back."

Rethdun's small ball of light quivered and dimmed. "Not gone."

Exchanging glances with Jaradee, Floree scrutinized the young boy. "Tell me when it is safe."

The roar of water, the only sound in the hollow beneath the mountain, did little to sooth Floree's nerves. Rayn had fallen asleep in Jaradee's lap. Rethdun stood beside his tukoolo, watching the blue light on his palm.

Floree observed the young face with a touch of wonder. *I knew you would be extraordinary, but I had no idea your gifts would appear so soon.*

The boy smiled. "I carry the memories of my grandsire, SaHal Elan Torinhota." He touched Aquila's blown glass side. "We are safe."

Floree followed him from the darkness of the crevice into the dusk-filled space beneath the overhang. A hand on her arm made her jump. Rayn's soft voice called out, "Uncle My."

The Vasrosi leader took the child from Jaradee. "Kuparak and Toa are making a final pass to make sure we are in the clear. When he comes back, I suggest we eat and sleep. At dawn we leave for Tahellive."

Rayn squirmed in Mylos's arms. Her gaze found Kia. "I fly, Maman. Kia says now."

Mylos put her down. "What do you think, Jara?"

"I think it's important for her to try now while things are calmer." She took her daughter's hand. "Remember what I told you, and do what Kia says."

The small falcon fluttered to the ground. Rayn knelt and touched her back. The next instant, two strelkes shot upward.

Rethdun shifted and followed Aquila after her. Galee and falcon flew in formation over the canyon, swooped under the rocky overhang, and landed. The birth-mates materialized hand in hand. Kia fluttered to Rayn's shoulder. Aquila rubbed his head against Rethdun's arm.

Jaradee went to her knees. "Well, Rayn, what do you think about flying."

Her daughter threw her arms wide. "I love it, Maman. And I love my Kia." The joy fled her features. "Trouble."

Floree swung around. Puna landed on her shoulder. Kuparak marched toward them. "The broticos are back; a group of soldiers and Klutarse are not far behind. We must leave, and we can't fly."

Mylos took command. "I'll release the horse. It knows to go home. ReRe says Rethdun found an underground river. It may be our only escape route. I'll meet you there."

Floree grabbed Rethdun's hand. "It's this way."

A flurry of wings brought Karia to Jaradee's shoulder. Kuparak scooped up Rayn and strode after her.

Soon they were gathered in the hollow under the mountain, the roar of water in their ears and damp, cool darkness pressing them into a tight group.

20

Floree peered back the way they had come. *Where are you, Mylos?* Kuparak's grip on her arm kept her from going to find him...that and Rethdun's firm grasp on her hand.

She whispered through the blackness. "He doesn't know where we are."

"ReRe will lead him here." The certainty in Kuparak's voice calmed her panic. He lowered Rayn to the ground. "Stay here. Toa and I will fly the river and see what we can discover." The sound of galee wings melted into the rumbling rush of water.

Jaradee moved into the void left by Kuparak and gripped Rayn's hand. Next to her, Rethdun's small ball of light began to glow. Not daring to wander far, they huddled together, faces tense and alert in the soft blue light.

Rayn turned. "Uncle My."

The soft words, almost lost in the splash and roar of water, left Floree's knees weak with relief.

A hand lamp illuminated the hollowed space. "Where's Kup?"

Floree pointed the direction of the water's roar. "He's exploring."

"Stay here." Illuminating the descending arc of the ceiling, Mylos moved to the drop off, stared down the river, and strode back to the group. "We can't wait much longer for Kup. The soldiers are bound to discover the overhang. Once they do, it's only a matter of time before they find the crevice."

Jaradee edged forward. "Can't we hide it?"

Mylos tugged at this beard. "Only by destabilizing the spillage and that would trap us."

Floree grimaced. "Aren't we trapped anyway?"

"No, we're not." Kuparak walked into the beam of the hand lamp. "The flight down river will be tricky, especially for the children, but we can make it. I suggest we make a run for it."

Mylos passed his light over the crevice. "How about the broticos? Can they follow us?"

Kuparak shook his head. "They're too big. The galee is a tight fit in a couple of spots."

Puna nudged Floree with her beak. "Puna says they're closing in."

Mylos knelt in front of the birth-mates. "You must do exactly what Kup says. Promise?"

A solemn nod from both and Kuparak took his place. "I will lead because I know the way. All of us have raptors as our chosen compeers. That means we have good vision in the dark, but you will need to pay attention. Rethdun, you will follow me with Aquila, then Floree and Puna, then you, Rayn. Kia will be by your side the whole way. Your Maman and Karia will be right behind you." He rose. "Jaradee, stay close to Rayn. Mylos, you and ReRe will come last." His eyes narrowed. "The water is filled with turbulence, protruding rocks, and swirling eddies. Stay as close to the ceiling as you can. The channel gets lower the further we go and narrows prior to widening at the end. Do your best to imitate everything I do. *And* stay close together." He looked at Mylos. "Any other instructions?"

"No. How far?"

"About the distance from overhang to the outer mouth of the gorge. Let's make the shift here so I know everyone is ready. Rayn, you first."

"Jaradee gripped her daughter's hand. "Tether with Kia. When you change, stay close to me."

"I will, Maman." Two falcon alighted on a rock nearby.

ReRe swooped from the crevice and landed.

Mylos shot a glance over his shoulder. "They found the wagon. Let's move."

Kuparak's shift to galee triggered the change for Rethdun. Floree gave Mylos an encouraging smile, shifted, and shot after the woodland galee. Rayn and her tukoolo followed with Jaradee and Karia right behind. Like a mural of raptors, they soared above the raging water.

Floree flew close to the woodland galee. Attention riveted on Rethdun's shifted form, she shot along the subterranean riverbed. Water tumbling and churning far below, inched closer and closer. The ceiling pressed her hawk body toward it. Shimmering droplets showered around her, soaked her, left her shivering from the wet cold and her growing fear. Rock walls, like a fast-closing vice, grabbed at her wing tips. In front of her, Rethdun flew onward, his compeer close behind.

The shrill shriek of a whistler hawk ripped through the water-worn tunnel. A terrifying image——Rayn's falcon form caught in the surging current——flashed through her mind. Spreading her wing tips, she hovered ready to dive. Another horror-filled shriek sliced through the river's roar. The flailing bird bobbed into to view. Floree dove. Roiling water pitched the small falcon beyond her reach. Fighting to avoid the surging current, she arced upward. Below her, a woodland galee swooped, clasped the floundering strelke in its talons, and lifted above the gushing river. Two whistler hawks streaked by, forming a rear guard behind the galee and its precious burden. Floree shot after them.

The riverbed curved, then straightened. Fingers of flickering light highlighted a jagged opening. Ahead, smoky galees tipped to accommodate the narrow exit and glided through, woodland galees in their wake. Two hawks soared after them.

Floree floundered, forced herself to follow, and swooped through the opening into a thunderous roar. Frothing mist and sudden light blinded her. *Rethdun, where are you?* Panic pressed her forward. The world dropped from beneath her. Trapped in the sound and fury of cascading water, she plunged out of control. Mist reached for her fatigue-drained body. Her will to fight fled. A shadow loomed. Awareness dissolved.

Consciousness returned in a flash flood of memories which prompted her return to shift. Magnified human senses flooded her awareness. Puna perched on a branch above her. Hard ground contrasted with the comfort of her head resting in Mylos' lap. Gurgling fluid rolled up her throat. Strong hands helped her to sitting. Water and bile spewed from her mouth. A series of choking coughs shook her. A hiccupped breath and then another eased her rebellious stomach. The magnificent waterfall pounding over the side of a steep cliff tipped her reality back in time.

She fought the desire to vomit. "The waterfall almost…"

Mylos's arms around her eased the panic churning her stomach. "You're safe, Floree."

"Rayn?" Her frantic gaze darted over the landscape.

Jaradee sat crosslegged, cradling a sodden falcon in her hands. Rethdun knelt beside her, kissed Rayn's tiny, bird head, and whispered her name. "Rayn. Rayn, come back to me." The strelke shuddered and blinked. The small body quivered. Rayn materialized, threw her arms around her mother's neck, and sobbed.

Kuparak gave Rethdun a pat on the back. "Good work, Rethdun. She heard your call."

Floree wiped her mouth on a sleeve. "Did you save her, Kup?"

Kuparak grinned. "I did not. Aquila snatched her from the river."

"Did you save me?"

He smiled again and shook his head.

Rethdun planted a kiss on her cheek. "I saved you, Aunt Floree. Aquila told me what to do."

Tears streaming, Floree hugged her young rescuer. "Thank you, dear Rethdun."

He wiggled from her grasp. "I'm hungry."

A surge of normalcy made her smile. She looked at Mylos. "Is it safe to build a fire to dry off and cook?"

He smiled. "It is. ReRe is standing guard. Toa is fishing, so we'll have food soon." He unfastened his shirt and handed it to her. "Here. Get out of your wet things. We'll build a fire."

Soon, a bonfire blazed, the men left to patrol the area, and Floree undressed and slipped on the big shirt. Jaradee, who had somehow managed to remain dry, took off the blouse under her tunic and wrapped it around her daughter. Brushing pine needles into a pile, she arranged witch hair and moss on top, laid down, and nestled Rayn into the warm curve of her body. At the river's edge, Rethdun straddled a rock with an arm around his tukoolo. His gaze made repeated journeys from the top of the plummeting waterfall to the hazy mist created where it crashed into the plunge pool.

Floree arranged wet clothing around the fire and scanned the dome. "Let's hope the clothes dry before the broticos see the blaze."

Kuparak strode from the woods, his bare chest glistening in the sun, his bundled shirt bulging with secrets. "I found tubers and torrac roots to have with our fish." He spread the shirt out on the ground next to Jaradee. "And I collected a few herbs along the way. Nature is good."

Floree gazed again at the cloudless dome. "Where are Mylos and ReRe?" She glanced around. "And Toa?"

"Mylos and his compeer flew back to the canyon to see what has transpired. They return soon. As for Toa..." He pointed. "My tukoolo seems to have caught our meal."

The smoky galee swooped over the river, hovered, and released a large fish into his waiting arms. Kuparak held it up. "Rethdun, look. We have a fish to prepare for cooking."

Aquila flew to a tree branch. The boy scrambled off the rock and ran to examine the fish. "What kind is it? Is good to eat? Can I help clean it?"

Kuparak grinned. "It is a river rockeye. See how big the eyes are? It is very good eating. Yes, I will teach you the art of cleaning a fish and honoring its life."

Boy and man walked to the shore and laid the fish on a flattish rock. After explaining the importance of honoring all those who gave their lives to provide for human life, he taught Rethdun a prayer of gratitude. They stood side by side and repeated it in unison.

> *"I release this life to the great beyond,*
> *Where it came from and all life dawned.*
> *Honor, love, and deep thanksgiving,*
> *I offer now for this gift of living."*

Floree marveled at Kuparak's ease with so young a child. *More than that, I marvel at Rethdun's grasp of difficult concepts. Shifting to a galee is not easy for an adult to manage. He saved my life. I bet the next time he catches a fish, he'll know how to clean it and cook it."*

She scanned the dome. *Where are you Mylos? Are we truly safe?*

While Rethdun and Kuparak cleaned the fish and Jaradee and Rayn napped, Floree busied herself preparing a small fire pit to bake the tubers and torracs. She covered the bottom of the pit with rocks heated in the bonfire and covered them with a layer of dirt. Next, she placed the vegetables on top, scooped in another layer of dirt and placed more rocks. By the time she finished, Kuparak and Rethdun had cleaned the fish and wrapped it and the herbs Kup had gathered in large burdock leaves. Small rocks arranged in rows on the top of the pit created a grid to hold the fish. Leaves and branches piled over it marked the spot and added another layer of insulation. Dinner was in the oven.

Floree washed her hands in the river and again scanned the dome. The sun edged toward the horizon and still no Mylos. *Fretting won't help.* She brushed her hair back from her face and turned to find Kuparak behind her.

"He'll be here soon, Floree." He knelt and drank from cupped hands. "You did a great job with the cook pit."

"My granddah taught me the ways of my ancestors. I didn't realize at the time the importance of his lessons."

"Sometimes we forget to give our elders respect for the knowledge they hold. I, like you, learned at my granddah's knee. He was a great man and a good leader. I miss him." His gaze swept upward. He pointed. "There. See. Two hawks fly this way. Perhaps it would be best to hide the birth-mates…in case."

Jaradee jumped to her feet as Floree hurried toward her. They collected the dry clothes. Each grabbed a child by the hand and dodged between trees into the woods. Jaradee donned her blouse and dressed Rayn while Floree scrambled into her clothes

Rethdun, with Aquila close at hand, peered from behind a tree. He clapped his hands and smiled. "It's Uncle Mylos, Maman. He looks happy."

Floree kissed Rayn. "Stay here with Rethdun and your maman. I'll take Mylos his shirt and make sure it's safe to come out." Skirting the bushes alone the shoreline, she ran forward.

A smiling Mylos accepted the shirt and slipped it on. "Why don't you get Jara and the children. The smell of fish and herbs is making my gut rumble. I'm bettin' it's done. Kup and I will check, and then I'll share what I learned."

Rethdun walked from the trees. "We're safe."

Mylos knelt. "How did you know?"

"Aquila told me. He and ReRe are friends."

Mylos rose and gripped his small hand. "Go on, Floree." He winked at Rethdun. "The men will check the fish."

Grinning at Rethdun's delight, she turned to find Jaradee and Rayn emerging onto the shore. "Please, Maman, can I go to Uncle My? Please?"

Jaradee laughed and released her hand. "Go, but don't get in the way."

The words were lost on the little girl. She ran over the sandy ground straight into the arms of her uncle, who picked her up and spun her around.

A rush of happiness left Floree realizing it had been some time since she had felt anything but fear.

Jaradee shot her an amused look. "Better enjoy it while we can."

Floree linked an arm thru hers. "Were you in my head?"

Jaradee laughed. "No. My heart felt your joy. Come on, dinner smells great, and I want to hear what Mylos learned."

Floree ambled beside her friend, a moment of dread clouding her happiness. "I'm not sure I want to know what he discovered."

"Why not? It can't be all bad, can it?"

Floree swallowed her uneasiness. "I guess not."

first thing they discovered was the wagon." He gave Jaradee an affirming nod. "Not only did Jaradee cover it with branches, she pulled a couple of boards loose, threw witch hair and dried leaves in the bed, and tucked moss into the corners. If nothing else, her quick thinking made them question how long it had been there. A search of the overhang gave the soldiers nothing to make them suspect it had been occupied. When they found the the crevice, they crowded through like curious children. ReRe flew after them and sent me mental images.

"The soldier in charge took one look at the river and made the decision that no one in their right mind would attempt an escape that direction, especially with two small children. When they discovered nothing else of interest in the cavern or the canyon, they remounted and rode back through the gorge. On the other side, they divided into groups and continued their search. When nothing turned up, the broticos were sent to explore along the river on the off chance we'd found a way to navigate it."

Kuparak tossed the remains of a tuber into the fire. "How did they miss us? We were right here in plain sight?"

"ReRe and Puna tethered and created an invisibility curtain."

Jaradee looked surprised. "I didn't realize the tukoolo could do that."

Kuparak picked up a stick and poked the sizzling tuber. "They can do what their compeers can do. Once they experience something, it becomes part of their knowledge base." He tossed the stick in the fire. "What else did you learn, Mylos?"

"A SorTech rides with the Klutarse." ReRe flew close enough to listen to him explaining that The Box has been updated to detect mental activity within a defined radius."

The dawn of understanding left Floree nodding. "That's why Puna didn't respond when Mylos asked me to create a curtain around the wagon. When she knew it was safe, we tethered and it formed. How did she know?"

Kup smiled. "Tazio implanted a small learning chip in each tukoolo's brain. Puna detected the change and understood what she had to do. Speaking of tukoolo, Toa says we need to leave here soon. What's the plan, Mylos?"

"We split up." Again, Mylos caressed his beard. "Kup, you take Jaradee and Rayn to the safe haven near Tahellive. Floree and Rethdun will come with me. We'll meet you there."

Rayn jerked awake, looked at her mother, and whimpered. Her bottom lip quivered. "Please, Maman, don't make me fly."

Jaradee started to speak but stopped as Kia flew from the trees to perch on Kuparak's arm. He held the beautiful strelke in front of Rayn. Fluttering to the birth-mate's shoulder, it examined her with its uninjured eye.

The child blinked, nodded, and wiped a tear from her cheek. "When I fly, Kia will take good care of me." She bit her lip to stop the quivering. "I am afraid." She scrambled from Jaradee's lap. "Kia says I must try."

Her tukoolo lifted into the air. Rayn hesitated.

Rethdun walked to her side. "I will fly with you, Rayn."

Aquila soared upward and hovered.

In unison, the birth-mates shifted and shot over the forest. The larger galees soared off the wing tips of the two smaller falcon. Four silhouettes swept over the trees and swooped above the river. The children landed in human form by the fire; their compeers alighted in a tree nearby.

Rayn clasped Rethdun's hand and gazed at the stars. "Being closer to the night dome is wonderful." She smiled at her birth-mate. "I love flying with you." Determination set her jaw. "We will always fly together."

Unexpected dread sent a chill up Floree's spine. A glance at Mylos told her he had experienced a similar flash of emotion. He stood up and pulled her to her feet.

"Alkina enters her resplendent phase tonight. Her bright light will expose us to detection if we wait too long. Kuparak, you, Jaradee, and Rayn leave first. Stay within the trees for as long as you can."

Stubbornness bloomed in Rayn's expression. Her eye's flashed and her small mouth pressed into a thread-thin line. When Jaradee tried to take her hand, she pulled it away and hid it behind her back. "I fly with Rethdun."

Her mother knelt. "We need to go ahead and make sure everything is safe. You can fly with Rethdun when we meet in Tahellive."

Rayn clung to her birth-mate. "Promise we will fly together again."

Jaradee spoke with conviction. "When we are safe, you will fly together."

Rethdun gently removed his hand from Rayn's. "Go with Maman and keep her safe. I will take care of Aunt Floree."

Rayn, eyes glistening with unshed tears, kissed his cheek, hugged Floree good-bye, and tethered to her tukoolo.

Toa launched upward. Puna and Kia followed.

At a sign from Kuparak, three birds lifted with graceful elegance into the cool light of the moon, soared over the trees for a short distance, and then dropped into forest shadow, fleeting memories slipping away with the night.

Rubbing her arms to chase away goosebumps, Floree turned to Mylos. "How long do we wait?"

Rethdun gripped her hand. "Go now. Aquila says the broticos come."

"Aquila is right." Mylos squeezed his shoulder. "ReRe says the SorTech will soon reach the river." He handed Rethdun a leafy branch. "Use this to help erase our presence."

Rethdun took the branch. Mylos buried the fire and scattered the pine needle bed. Floree clear away the remains of their meal, and then helped Rethdun to sweep away any footprints on the shore. While they worked, their tukoolo flew in opposite directions, gathering information.

Images formed in Floree's mind: shadowy figures lurking near the far side of the falls, broticos launching into the air. She hurried to Mylos's side.

He glanced at the falls. "I saw. We need to go, and we can't fly." He scooped up Rethdun, helped him to settle on his back, and hustled her ahead of him into the velvet dark of the night woods.

Puna shot after them, landed on her shoulder, and sent a series of images flitting: a brotico landing by the river, a second joining him, hand lamps chasing up and down the shore, then darkness; both broticos launching into flight, one searching the course of the river, the other gliding over the trees.

Knowing ReRe had alerted Mylos, Floree pressed onward, her attention glued to Rethdun's small back.

Dyad's cool radiance did little to illuminate the way. Cold blue shadows spattered the ground. The trees, resembling carved obsidian statues, reached toward the moon, their upper branches glistening in the icy light.

Floree stubbed her toe, swore at herself for letting her attention wander, and glued her gaze to the uneven ground. The terrain's gradual ascent, now steeper and rockier, became harder and harder to navigate. Mylos turned, helped her over a sizable rock, and mutter a series of profanities under his breath. Kneeling, he helped Rethdun to the ground and stared back the way they had come.

"We're not moving fast enough. ReRe reports that the broticos are closing the gap."

"Either we find a place to hide or we fly." Floree rubbed her knee. "Dyad sets soon, and Alkina's dazzling light will help us and them." She peered beyond him. "Rethdun, where are you?"

Mylos swung around, squinting through the darkness. "Rethdun?"

"I'm here." Awe infused his whisper.

Hurrying toward the sound, Floree rounded a tree and froze. Mylos stepped around her, sucked in a breath, and gripped her shoulder.

In a fading patch of cool blue, Rethdun stood with Aquila on one side and a silvery-white wolf on the other. "This is Forêst. My grandsire sent him to help us."

ReRe flew to Mylos and perched on his shoulder. Puna alighted near Floree. Mylos put a protective arm around her. "How can Forêst help us, Rethdun?"

Floree felt Aquila and Rethdun tether. Rethdun flashed from view. His name caught in her throat and died. Two wolves, one large, one small, sat on their haunches, eyes glowing. Rethdun materialized in human form. "We can be wolves. Forêst with lead us to safety."

A desire to gather him into her arms impelled her forward. Mylos stayed her with a hand on her arm. "How do we know this is not a SorTech's trick, Rethdun?"

The small boy's serious expression changed to a knowing smile. "SaHal sent him. Forêst belongs to him." He ran a hand over the wolf's silky fur. "My grandsire explained that the SorTech does not know my identity. He only knows a boy has been born who will become the ConServator of the Eleo Preda, and the boy must die. My grandsire does not wish me to join him so soon." Seriousness aged his young features. He looked from one to the other. "We must hurry. Aquila says change now or be caught."

Mylos rose. "Do we tether to our tukoolos?"

Rethdun nodded. "Tether to ReRe first. ReRe will tether to Forêst. Then make the shift." He walked to Floree. "Don't be afraid, Aunt Floree. Being a wolf is..." He laughed. "Wonderful." A frown wiped away his delight. "Hurry." He shifted.

Floree took a breath and tethered to Puna. The change, both subtle and ancient, flooded her with an earthy groundedness so unlike her bird form that it took her a moment to assimilate it. Forest smells bombarded her. The feel of the ground under her four paws radiated power up her legs and along her spine. Surprise left her shaking. Forêst's presence in her mind warned her to remain calm.

A soft growl brought her around to face Mylos in wolf form. Flecks of gold glinted in blue eyes surrounded by grey fur. Wonder flowed from him through her.

Above them, wings wafted the air in a silent warning. Aquila, Puna, and ReRe flew in three directions. Forêst trotted up the mountain, glanced back, called his pack to heel, and continued a soundless climb.

Floree marveled at the sinuous power of her wolf body, its acute hearing, exceptional sight, and agile mind. Giving herself up to its magnificence, she moved through the night unhindered by the terrain. Forêst's scent made him easy to track. Rethdun ran close at his heels. Next to her, Mylos, moved with power and vigor. Above them, Alkina arced across the night dome. In the moon's resplendent light, she followed Forêst on fleet feet through the night shadows.

22

Rethdun reveled in the beauty of wolf. Nothing in his short life, except tethering to Aquila, had brought him so close to his true nature. The ancient wildness coursing through him tempted him to howl at Alkina——the shameena moon——the moon of his ancestors.

Forêst's huge head swung toward him. Silver-blue eyes, their message explicit, silenced him. The head swung back. The powerful wolf leapt effortlessly onto a smooth flat rock. Rethdun jumped, fumbled, and slid backward. Strong jaws fastened on the fur at the nape of his neck, lifted him, and set him down. Floree and Mylos arrived on the rock beside them. Forêst panted a welcome.

For a time, they sat together in the quiet. Overhead Alkina's descent stole the light shadow by shadow from the world below. The night had passed and dawn crept ever closer. Two broticos made a sweep of the trees at the foot of the mountain, circled, and flew back toward the distant sound of falling water.

Predatory vigilance held Forêst motionless, his nose lifted. He jumped to the ground on the far side of their rocky perch, jogged around a smooth-barked tree, and into a hole beneath piled rocks and mountain brush. When everyone had crowded inside, he curled up in the center of the shelter, cautioned his pack against conversation of any kind, suggested rest would be appropriate, and slept.

Maintaining their wolf forms, Floree and Mylos laid side-by-side. Rethdun sat for a time, his ears twitching, his nose sniffing. Restless energy carried him around the enclosure. Forêst raised his head and growled a soft command. Rethdun curled up next to the alpha leader. Slumber soon quieted his busy mind.

He awoke to a stomach hungry for food and tongue thirsting for water. Yawning a wide-mouthed yawn, he stretched his lithe, little body, and clamber to his feet. *Four feet. I am a wolf.* Happiness shook him like a dog with wet fur.

Looking around told him two things: he was alone in the den and the others were close at hand. An urgent need to shift to Human carried him into the open. Floree and Mylos sat in the afternoon sun deep in conversation. Forêst was not present.

Mylos beckoned him. "Change, Rethdun."

The shift left him momentarily confused. Aquila swooping to the ground nearby steadied his nerves and helped him to anchor in his humanness. He stroked his tukoolo's glassy side. "Thank you, Aquila." Tilting his head, he listened to his compeer. "I honor you, too."

"Come and eat." Floree offered a handful of berries. "Forêst will be back soon."

Mylos scanned the dome. "As soon as the sun sets, we'll continue our journey. Forêst suggests we rest in our wolf forms so our human thoughts do not give us away." He yawned. "I believe I will take his advice." He shifted and padded into the den.

Rethdun climbed onto a rock beside Floree and accepted more fruit. "Do they still search?"

She nibbled a dark red storm berry. "Let's just say they haven't given up." Curiosity prodded her. "How do you like shaping a wolf?"

He finished chewing, swallowed, and licked his fingers one by one. "I love it, Aunt Floree. I just wish Rayn were here. Do you think she's safe?"

"As safe as you are——as safe as you will ever be. I'm sorry we had to separate you."

Rethdun studied a blue stain on his thumb. "I believe it was a right choice."

Her soft chuckle made him look up. "How old are you, Rethdun?"

Furrowing his brow, he counted. "One, two, three...almost four. But my grandsire's memories and knowledge are much older than that." He yawned. "I will nap now."

He tethered to Aquila, shaped a young wolf, and loped into the den. Clearing a spot with his front paws, he circled into position and, tucking his tail around himself, slept.

Three turnings passed in a similar fashion. The pack traveled by night, took human form at dawn, and slept and gathered berries during the day. Rethdun learned everything he could from Forêst. He tried raw meat, caught a small rodent and let it go, and grew more comfortable with his wolf body and his grandsire's memories.

The fourth morning of their trek, he woke to a rough tongue licking his cheek. Forêst stood over him, a warning in his gaze. *"Follow. Stay close."*

Rethdun climbed to his feet, shook himself free of sleep, and sought out Mylos and Floree. A question rose in his mind.

"Safe." Forêst's brusque reply ended with a quick nip on the ear and sent Rethdun from the den, his mind blanked of all human thought.

Clouds obscured the night dome and cast a dense darkness over the terrain. Forêst loped along an animal track that meandered higher up the mountain and ended on a ridge traversing the tops of three connected peaks. Avoiding the openness of the ridge, the silver-white wolf skulked over tundra lichen into taller brush and finally into a tree-covered ravine. A zigzagged course took them up the other side and down a slope ending beside a small lake. After quenching his thirst, Forêst lifted his nose to sniff the cool night air.

Rethdun slurped water until his thirst demanded no more and sat with his tail curled around his rump. Mind still and attention focused on his mentor, he waited.

A night bird called. An insect chirped. Water kissed the shore in a rhythmic lap, lap, lap. A sudden breeze chased over the lake's surface, ruffling

Rethdun's fur. Distant thunder rumbled. The scent of Human flared his nostrils.

Forêst growled, waded into the lake, and began to swim. Rethdun touched the water with a tentative paw. Felt a moment of panic and jumped in. Legs pumping, he strove to stay afloat and to keep Forêst's bobbing head in sight. When it seemed he could manage no longer, jaws fastened on his nape and lifted him free of the lake. His mentor waded through shallowing water and released him on solid ground. With a tiny yip, Rethdun shook sparkling droplets from his fur and flopped down on damp leaves and grass.

Forêst again lifted his nose. Nostrils flared, he swung his head one way and then the other. Seeming to be satisfied, he nudged Rethdun to his feet and led him into a brake of trees bordering the lake. When they had traveled some distance, Forêst stopped, snuffled the air once more, and curled around himself and slept.

Rethdun sat and licked a paw. The urge to assume his human shape overwhelmed him. The tether to his tukoolo strained to release. Aquila circled above them and alighted in a nearby tree. Shifting left Rethdun panting and slightly stunned. Gulping a breath, he calmed his thumping heart and inhaled the cool night air.

Mylos walked from the trees and stood looking at him. "It is good to see you, Rethdun Vilandree."

Floree dropped to her knees and hugged him so hard he thought he might smother. Holding him at arm's length, she examined him from head to foot. "Are you alright? I know the shift to wolf is a hard one for you."

Rethdun pondered her statement, then smiled. "It is not the shift to wolf, Aunt Floree. Returning to Human is..." He threw his hands up. "It makes me feel lost."

Forêst rose, stretched his back in a rounded arch, and yawned. He sat on his haunches, his gaze resting on Rethdun. *"You will not lose your wolf shape, young cub. Do not be afraid. It is part of you now as it is part of Aquila."* His ears twitched. His blue gaze darted over the landscape. *"You are close to Tahellive. Mylos and Floree will take you there. Stay safe."* Running into moon-glow and night dark, he faded from view.

The impulse to shape shift, to run after him, to stay with him always left Rethdun panting. He gripped his knees and fought for air. Love for Rayn and Jaradee and Mylos and Floree coursed through him. The desire to know more of Kuparak and to be certain of Rayn's safety kept him stationary. Love of his tukoolo and his galee form warmed him. He turned to find Mylos and his aunt watching him.

Floree offered her hand. "I thought we might loose you."

Rethdun took it. "Let's go find Rayn."

Mylos searched the dome, where rain clouds roiled and churned. "Alkina's return to its direct course is whipping the planet. We're near the safe haven. I suggest we hurry. The storm is about to break. ReRe tells me it is safe to fly. Tether up and let's go. Stay in a tight group."

He shifted and flew to a tree branch. Rethdun felt the tether to Aquila snap into place. He made the change and came to rest on a branch next to his tukoolo. Floree observed him for a long moment, made the shift, and soared domeward with Mylos at her side. Rethdun and Aquila lifted into the air. Delight in the freedom of flight sent him spiraling upward. Aquila streaked past him. Rethdun shot after him, marveling at his good fortune...*Wolf and galee...who could ask for more?*

23

Rethdun raced between Mylos and Floree along the copse of trees and into woodlands bordering the fields west of Tahellive. A small boy's delight in flying, interrupted by Aquila's warning cry, brought his conscious awareness to the storm brewing overhead. Pinning his attention on ReRe and Mylos, he glided deeper into sturdy pines, skimmed along a rushing creek, and landed near a small, rustic cabin tucked at the back of a roughed-out clearing.

Kuparak jumped from the narrow stoop and strode to meet Mylos and Floree.

Unsure what to expect, Rethdun clung to his galee form. Nothing moved in the cabin. Only the fast fading presence of his mother and birth-mate indicated they had ever been there. Controlling his rising panic, he fluttered to the stoop and materialized.

When Kuparak finished his discussion, tears spilled down Floree's cheeks.

Mylos, his expression hard and stricken, embraced her. Reined in emotions propelled Kuparak toward the cabin.

Rethdun studied the ebony features, the amber eyes, the full lips and held his breath.

Sitting on the edge of the narrow porch, Kuparak gazed at him from behind a mask of adult calm. "The soldiers have captured Rayn. We were out numbered, Rethdun. I tried to save her but..."

Rethdun saw the pain and anger, the huge sense of loss. A stab of sorrow clamped tight around his throat. He pushed one word between quivering lips. "Maman?"

The urgent question, ragged with dread, lost itself in a loud clap of thunder. Wind shook the cabin. Clouds dumped their watery burden. Lightning threw a jagged banner across the night dome. Thunder crashed and rumbled, fading into the sounds of wind and rain.

Mylos urged a distraught Floree ahead of him into the cabin. Numb from cold and shock, Rethdun barely felt Kuparak scoop him up.

Musty dimness enclosed them. A rickety table, two chairs, and an upturned box were the only furnishings. Mylos tossed a beat up cushion at Floree's feet and lowered his lean body to ground next to her. Kuparak sat cross-legged. Floree sank onto the cushion and opened her arms. Rethdun walked to her side and rested a hand on her shoulder. She lower her arms and sighed.

Wuthering wind shook the cabin. Tree branches brushing the walls sounded like monsters trying to enter. Rain pounded the roof. No one in the cabin moved.

Kuparak inhaled a rugged breath. His long fingers clenched. He exhaled.

"When we arrived here, Rayn, still angry because Rethdun had been left behind, threw a temper tantrum. When she finally grew quiet, I left with Toa to discover the way of things in Tahellive. I returned to find a frantic Jaradee. Rayn had sworn she would find Rethdun, waited for her mother to fall asleep; and when she did, shifted and flew with Kia to begin her search.

"I told Jaradee to stay hidden." He uncurled his fingers and stared at his palms. "I promised to find her daughter, but she refused to remain behind. We left together, but soon separated to cover more territory. Had I not sent Toa to watch over her, I would not have known she found Rayn or that the

Rompeer's men were in pursuit. By the time I reached them, Jaradee lay in a motionless heap between two soldiers."

A loose shake caught by a gust of wind beat against the roof. Kuparak paused to let out a long emotion-filled breath. "Perhaps, Rethdun, it would be best if you did not hear this."

Rethdun returned his serious gaze. "Maman is dead, isn't she. I must understand how."

Kuparak squeezed the bridge of his nose. "How did you…" He shook his head. "Never mind."

Floree twisted to look at him. "Will you at least sit in my lap, Rethdun?"

He kissed her cheek. "I will stand, but you may hold my hand, Aunt Floree." Intertwining his fingers through hers, he brought his full attention to Kuparak. "I am ready."

A nod from Mylos and Kuparak picked up the thread of his story.

"I dispatched the two soldiers to meet their gods and examined your mother. When I rolled her over, blood soaked her clothing. The superficial wounds to her arm and shoulder would have been easily managed. The knife wounds in her stomach…" He clasped Rethdun's hand. "There was nothing I could do. She knew she was dying, Rethdun. Even so, she tried to hold on. She asked me to guide you to manhood and made me promise to find Rayn and to give her the moonstone locket. And then she begged me to help her die."

A blast of wind threw the door wide. He lumbered to his feet, pushed it shut, and secured the latch. For some time he remained there, his shoulders weighted with sorrow. When he returned, he knelt in front of Rethdun.

"I am what is known by our people as an Animilero, Rethdun. Do you know what that is?"

Rethdun thought to search his grandsire's memories, decided Kuparak must speak, and shook his head.

"Animileros are men and women who are born to protect the leaders of the Eleo Preda. We are taught to value all life. We are also trained in the arts of death. Your mother knew I could help her die with peace and dignity."

Thunder rumbled in the distance. The wind's wailing decreased to a whisper. The rain's pounding patter ceased.

Rethdun placed his free hand on Kuparak's shoulder. "I know you helped her. Tell me how."

Kuparak's unwavering gaze met Rethdun's. "I gathered her into my lap and held her next to my heart. A wave of unbearable pain consumed her. When the pain dimmed, she whispered her love for you, for Rayn, and for me. When it reclaimed her, I sliced through a large artery in her inner thigh. As her blood soaked the ground, she reached up and touched a tear on my cheek. In her final moments, her beautiful face grew still and peaceful. Pain no longer held her in its grip. Death claimed her gently, Rethdun, and escorted her spirit to be with her ancestors. I brought her body here. She is buried out back in an unmarked grave."

Enshrouded in loss, Rethdun could not move. Words gathered but remained unspoken. Tears formed but refused to fall. His heart, like his eyes, felt dry and empty. He squared his shoulders. "Thank you, for your love of Maman, Kuparak. Tell us of Rayn."

Surprise showed momentarily on the man's face before it hardened. "A Klutarse has taken Rayn to the Rompeer in Chunarrie. She is, at this point beyond our reach. The last time I saw her, she was trying to jump off his horse." A tiny smile appeared. "She fought hard to get away." The smile faded. "But she is small to overcome a well-trained man. He did not hurt her; he dare not. I knew I could not save her, Rethdun, so I chose to help your maman."

Needing to be sure...to understand, Rethdun tethered to Aquila and stretched his consciousness outward until he discovered his birth-mate's essence. Satisfied she lived, he squeezed Kuparak's hand. "Show me Maman's grave."

Rethdun stared at the mound of dirt covered with rain-limp leaves and tried to picture his mother lying there. Across from him, Floree's tears fell, soaking the grave with their fluid farewell. Mylos whispered a song of passing. Kuparak waited in silence beside him.

Rethdun gripped his stomach. A sense of urgency roiled into existence. SaHal's presence strengthened. Rethdun looked from one adult to the next. "I *must not* be captured." His grandsire's essence faded. He sighed. "I am very tired. Will you decide what is best to prevent it?"

Floree's arms enclosed him. He sat in her lap, rested his head on her shoulder, and cried. Tears tumbled and sobs quaked. The world seemed dark and forbidding and filled with loss. Aquila landed next to him. Forêst's image filled his mind. Beside the silver wolf, his mother smiled. The image dissolved. He looked up at Kuparak.

"I'm glad you came back to El Stroma." Wiping his tears, he climbed off his aunt's lap, walked into the cabin, pulled a blanket around him, and let sleep mute his sadness.

The murmur of adult voices drifting around him ended his escape into dreaming. Dim light filtering through the open door dispersed over the floor. Yawning, he sat up. *Maman is gone. Rayn is with the Rompeer. I am too small to fight for her.* He climbed to his feet. *I will find you someday, Rayn, and we will fly together again.*

Walking onto the stoop, he surveyed a clearing reclaimed by nature. Mylos and Kuparak talked in subdued tones. Floree, sadness weighting her shoulders, lifted her faced to the morning sun. He sat beside her.

"She isn't gone, Aunt Floree." He touched his heart. "She is right here."

Floree put an arm around him. "How did you ever get so wise?"

He shot her an you-know-why look.

Her soft laugh made him snuggle closer. "What's for breakfast?"

She passed him a piece of fruit. "Do you know what we're doing today?"

He chewed a juicy bite. "Are we leaving?"

Mylos joined them. "Kuparak is going to Chunarrie to watch over Rayn. You and I and Floree are going to VenTra. Do you know where that is?"

Rethdun ignored his memories and shook his head.

"Do you remember Kuparak saying he took his sister-sibling to another planet?"

"Yes." He shoved the last piece of fruit in his mouth.

"I'm going to take you to the transport center and you and Floree———"

Rethdun covered his ears. "Don't tell me any more. That way it will be an adventure, and my memories won't know what others should not discover."

Kuparak walked up. "Better listen to him, Mylos." He offered a hand to Rethdun. "I'm leaving, and I doubt you will be here when I get back. Take good care of Floree."

Rethdun shook the hand. "Take good care of Rayn."

"I'll do my best." He turned to Mylos. "Toa will keep you informed via ReRe." Gathering Floree up in a bear hug, he released her and smiled. "Good knowing you. If you ever get to Thera..."

She grinned. "I'll look up Tala. Take care of yourself."

Two smoky galees soared upward. A lump formed in Rethdun's throat. Aquila fluttered to the ground beside him. Its telie-eye scanned the dome and contracted.

Rethdun knelt and put an arm around his tukoolo. "Thanks for being my compeer, Aquila." The woodland galee nibbled his cheek and flew to a nearby tree.

Mylos stood at the edge of the stoop. "VenTra is a good distance from Tahellive. I'm sure glad Alkina's return to its direct orbit is complete. We should have good weather. I suggest we fly."

SaHal's memories stirred. "Why don't we alternate flying and traveling as wolves? That way we can cover more ground and keep the Pheet Adole guessing."

The strain in Floree's face softened. "Your grandsire speaks?"

A shrug and a smile provide his answer.

"If you are captured, Rethdun, how will you hide your grandsire's memories?"

"I don't know, Aunt Floree. Let's not get caught." He joined her on the stoop. "How soon do we leave?"

Mylos scanned the dome. "Tonight we travel in wolf form and rest during the day. We don't have Forêst to guide us, but I know this side of the Chaporicas Mountains. I suggest we rest until dusk, then we can eat and begin our journey."

Floree climbed to her feet and stretched. "I could use a nap. Come on, Rethdun." She led the way into the dim cabin and arranged a blanket into a bed.

Rethdun curled up beside her and listened to her soft breathing. "I will get away. I have to."

—

24

T hree long turnings had passed with at least four more to go when Rethdun woke with his senses reeling. The night had been colder than usual. He, Mylos, and Floree had assumed their wolf shapes and curled up together close to their small fire. Sometime earlier, he had sensed Mylos' shift to hawk, but dreams had pulled him further into the bottomless depths of his grandsire's knowledge and power.

SaHal, a chieftain leader and master shameenu, had lived a long, full life. He like his grandsire before him bore the stewardship of his family's ancestral memory. Rethdun now shouldered the responsibility. He rose each morning steeped in new learnings and spent the day observing life from his new perspective. On this waking, he looked around, knowing he had changed. Floree sat alone by the fire, an aura of fear surrounding her.

He stood and stretched. "Where's Mylos?"

"Toa alerted ReRe. Kuparak's in trouble. Mylos left to help...if he can. You and I will continue to VenTra." She seemed to shrink. "I'm afraid, Rethdun.

Everyday the threat to your life grows. Mylos has contacts at the transport center who can help us. I don't know anyone." A sigh of hopelessness exited her body like air from a deflating balloon. "How will I ever get you to safety?"

Rethdun's newfound knowledge spun through his mind and then grew still. "Forêst will be here soon. He knows the way." Scrambling into her lap, he snuggled into the crook of her arm. "*We* will be fine, Aunt Floree."

She rested her cheek on his dark hair and sighed. When she released him, he smiled. Her fear had lessened and hope had returned.

"I don't know what you did, Rethdun, but thank you. Let's see what we can scrounge up for a meal. I'm pretty hungry."

Rethdun climbed to his feet, tethered to Aquila, and shifted to a wolf. A soft yip brought a barked response. A short time later, Forêst walked from the trees and deposited breakfast at Floree's feet. She tethered and shape shifted. The three shared fresh meat, and then began their journey.

The sun shimmered close to the horizon when they came to a halt on a narrow lake shore beach. Lapping noisily, Rethdun quenched his thirst and sat back on his hunches. Beyond the lake, stands of sgàile trees scattered over rolling hills. Shimmering white leaves fluttered in the late afternoon breeze. Slender white trunks cast long shadows over the shore. Forêst nudged him to standing, gave a clipped yip, and trotted along the beach. Floree flanked him. Rethdun jogged close behind.

Forêst paused. Intense, silver-blue eyes searched. The scents of horse and Human drifting over the water laid his ears back. A soft warning growl cautioned Rethdun to stay close. The big wolf lengthened his loping stride and led the way between the slender, white trunks. When the copse enclosed them, Forêst shaped an ivory galee and soared upward. Floree made a quick shift. Rethdun felt Aquila urging him to change. A final sniff and galee wings carried him between translucent leaves. An unexpected break in the canopy left him exposed above a narrow glade bordering a much older and less hospitable forest. Aquila hovered, then swooped into mist-dulled light and tall forbidding trees.

An arrow whizzing past sent Rethdun streaking after him. Tundi oak, beech, and Ulmus elm surrounded him. Soaring to the top of an ancient tree, he landed. Green feathers tipped with gold camouflaged his presence. Not far ahead, he sensed Floree's blanked mind.

Twigs snapping and an occasional equine snort announced the arrival of four mounted soldiers. Riding one behind the other, they wound their way between sgàile. Helmet shaded eyes, searched the vale. The leader, a squat, burly man, raised a hand and halted, where open terrain transitioned to primordial forest. He peered into the murkiness, turned, and glared at his men.

"See anything?"

A chorus of no's left him scowling.

The man behind him patted his horse's neck and indicated the oppressive woods. "Is that Seerdrum Wood?"

Dismounting, the leader looped his horse's reins over a low branch. "It is. Bring the SorTech and the girl. We'll wait here." He cast a worried glance at the woods. "And hurry."

The soldier wheeled his horse and trotted back the way they had come. His comrades dismounted.

Rethdun considered flying after the departing man. Knowledge and memory, held him in check. Obscuring his thoughts, he allowed his grandsire's wisdom to be his guide. He did not move nor think. Somewhere close, he could feel Forêst's ivory galee. Aquila circled high above the trees with Puna not far below him.

The soldiers formed an uneasy group. Talking in low tones, they cast furtive glances in the direction of the lake. When the two horses ambled into the vale, they moved closer together. The lead horse carried the SorTech and his black box; the other, the man who had fetched him and a small dark-haired child. At a sign from the leader, the SorTech jumped to the ground, untied the box, and began setting up his equipment.

Curiosity teased Rethdun to fly nearer. Grateful for SaHal's wisdom, he melded with leaves and rough oak bark. Floree's presence faded into elm and beech. Nothing of Forêst's presence remained.

The SorTech peered into the woods. "Are you sure you want me to use this here?"

"Just get it done, so we can leave." The command hissed between barred teeth.

With a shrug, the SorTech donned his patch, removed the lid from the box, and proceeded to twist nobs and press buttons. The horses tossed their heads and snuffled uneasily. A tingling sensation shot up Rethdun's spine.

The child, her chin resting on her chest, dark hair obscuring her face, remained unaffected.

Again, strong memories kept Rethdun still. Much about the child reminded him of Rayn. And yet...

A frenzied howl, rustled the tops of the trees and wailed around the glade. A horse reared. A soldier ducked. Another dodged a horse's frightened sidestep.

The leader yanked the SorTech to his feet. "Did you feel anything?"

A windy gust scattered the yelled words. A second whipped the trees into a writhing dance. The black box trembled and lifted above the ground. As though thrown by an invisible hand, it shot through the air and crashed into a tree. Men ducked flying debris and fought to calm their horses.

Still, the girl-child sat unmoved. Using the chaos to obscure a mind touch, Rethdun reached out. Shock left him stunned.

The SorTech spun around. Bulging eyes scanned the woods, hesitated on Rethdun's tree, and narrowed. "I found some——"

The leader's horse laid its ears back, tuck its tail close, and swung its hind quarters. The SorTech stumbled backward. Grabbing the horse's reins, the burly leader, threw himself into the saddle, and shouted, "Get out of here!"

Another frenetic howl shook the vale. Fighting to gain control of his mount, the man guarding the child lost his grip. Limp limbed, she flopped to one side and toppled to the ground. She lay unmoving, a single spot of stillness in the seething panic around her.

Throwing his arms around the horse's neck, the guard cast a frantic glance at his leader.

"Leave her." Urging his horse forward, the leader, galloped for the lake. His men mounted and raced after him. The SorTech cast a final look in Rethdun's direction and galloped back through the copse of ghost-white trees.

Seerdrum Wood went deathly quiet. Mist wafted through the trees. A suffocating silence crept over the glade. Aquila circled lower. Puna landed near Floree. A silver-gray wolf stepped from behind a tree and walked to the child's side.

Rethdun flew to the ground and took his human form. He knelt and put a small hand on her motionless body. His brow furrowed. Tears blurred his vision.

Floree materialized and knelt. Gentle hands turned the child over and brushed dark hair from the pale face. "She resembles Rayn, but…" The words followed a quivering exhale. "She's empty of any conscious thought or memory. I believe she's what SorTech's call a mimic." She peered closer and took a small wrist between her fingers. "Although faint, she has a pulse."

Rethdun moved to Forêst's side. "She is Eleo Preda. They harvested her memories, stole her will to live, and imprinted Rayn's features over hers." An inquiring look from Floree almost made him smile.

She shook her head. "SaHal. You have absorb much of his knowledge."

"It is my destiny, Aunt Floree." He stared through the sgàiles. "We don't have much time."

She blanched. "We can't just leave her here, Rethdun."

He slipped a hand into hers. "We don't have to. Look."

An aged woman walked toward them. Gray hair brushed hunched shoulders. Eyes the pewter gray of storm clouds gazed at Forêst, moved to Rethdun, and then to Floree. Kneeling, she place a gnarled hand on the child's forehead. The small body quaked. Dulled eyes blinked open. Fear flared.

The woman smiled. "You are safe, child." She turned to Forêst. "You and your pack may traverse Seerdrum Wood. Do not linger and do not look back. The child will join the Callichea." She and the child began to glimmered. "We will protect you within our domain." Like a mirage, they melted away.

Forêst's head swung in the direction of the distant lake. A growl rumbled.

Rethdun waited for his aunt to assume her wolf form, tethered to Aquila and shifted. Four small paws carried him after his grandsire's familiar into the dense shadow of the woods from which few Human's emerged unscathed.

The journey seemed unending. Forêst's non-stop pace carried them across rushing streams and beneath tangling, ancient branches. Soft whispers pursued them, ruffled their mist-damp fur, and left their hackles raised and hearts pounding. When at last Forêst stopped beneath the low-hanging branches of a weeping pine, Rethdun sank to the ground and dropped his head between sore paws. Fatigue tugged his eyelids shut. A warm back next to his gave him permission to slip into sleeping unencumbered by fear.

Dreamless time passed. His interior world gradually awakened. SaHal leaned over him, whispered a complex story, and vanished. Rethdun's pointy ear twitched.

Shafts of early morning light shot between trees. Floree sat on a stump, combing her fingers thru tangled blonde hair. She smiled. "I know you're awake. Shape Human and join me. Forêst returns soon."

A huge yawn ended in the embodiment of his human form. Confusion kept him still. Awareness of his humanness came slowly. A tremor shook him and left him focused and present. "You are less fearful this morning, Aunt Floree."

She smoothed her hair away from her face and secured it. "I have you and Forêst to protect me. We leave the Wood today and will reach VenTra in one turning plus one. I am feeling hopeful." Her brow furrowed. "Tell me what SaHal's memories hold about the Callichea."

Rethdun sat cross-legged and picked up a small round stone. Rolling it between his palms, he waited for his grandsire's knowledge to rise to the surface. "It is said they are the oppugnant spirits of women, both Eleo Preda and Pheet Adole, who escaped the Rompeer's household, and were pursued and murdered. It is unclear how they found their way to Seerdrum Wood. What is clear, however, is that any man foolish enough to enter their domain is most often found mindless and wandering. Had Sorcha not given permission, I would be in as much danger from the Callichea as I am from the Rompeer."

Floree's bows raised. "Sorcha?"

"Sorcha is the High Yennedo. She rules the Callichea and the Seerdrum Wood."

Forêst appeared and joined them. An image formed in Rethdun's mind.

He scrambled to his feet. "Sorcha sends a warning: 'Soldiers search for the child. The Callichea will do their best to distract them. It is time to leave'."

His tether to Aquila transitioned him to wolf. Floree changed and padded after Forêst. Another turning of travel had begun. Rethdun kept his gaze front. *Don't look back. I wonder why? Nothing in Grandsire's memories holds the answer.*

—

25

Muted light changing to shadow, the only indication of time passing, escorted the pack through Seerdrum Wood. The ground trembled. Forêst's ears flattened. Prickles crawled over Rethdun's skin. Resisting the temptation to glance back, he sprinted between the alpha leader and Floree's smaller form. Forêst lengthened his stride. Rethdun double his effort to remain abreast of the adults. Changing terrain beckoned. Sunlight called. Forêst picked up speed again. They raced beyond the border, crossed a rock-strewn expanse, and slowed.

High-pitched whines echoed through the woods. Forêst and Floree dodged behind a hedgerow of wild shrubs and stubby trees. Slinking low, his tail tucked between his legs, Rethdun followed.

Floree materialized. "I believe it's safe to look back now."

A shiver stood Rethdun's fur on end. Edging closer to Floree, he shifted, gripped her hand, and peered toward the murky woods.

Translucent forms, faces contorted with hate, streaked between the trees.

A soldier, unseated by his terrified mount, landed in a jumbled heap amidst howls and cackled laughter.

The horse shrieked, reared, and dashed for the rocky field. Riderless and lathered with sweat, its frenzied gallop carried it past their hiding place and beyond.

A second horse tore through the trees, threw its rider, and trotted into the sunlight. Shaking and sweat-covered, it tossed its head and galloped toward the hedgerow.

Within Seerdrum Wood, more apparitions gathered. Arm in arm, they circled the thrown rider. Struggling to regain his footing, he push up to his knees. Women's mouths gaped wide. Horrifying screams ended in maniacal laughter. The man whimpered and collapsed.

His comrade lurched toward him. Misty shapes enveloped him. A pain-filled yowl vibrated the air. He, too, crumpled. Luminescent forms, mouths spewing wailed laments, hovered over the prone bodies.

Sorcha's haunted eyes, found Rethdun. One word filled his mind.

"Go!"

Forêst's ivory galee shot domeward. Floree's berigora lifted into flight. Rethdun embraced his galee form and flew after Aquila. Open fields flowing below them were soon replaced by a wide river and a sprinkling of small villages. The beautiful ivory galee pressed onward until the distant sparkle of Dyad's light on the ocean appeared in the distance. Swooping into a thicket of young trees, he landed and assumed his wolf shape. Floree alighted at his side, shaping Human as her feet touched the ground. Rethdun perched in a tree, scanning the landscape with a galee's piercing sight.

Forêst's commanding bark brought him to the ground and into his natural shape. He ran a hand over his head, listened to night sounds, and looked at Floree. "I'm hungry."

Her soft laugh made him smile. Forêst left to hunt, while he helped her prepare their camp. Soon a small fire blazed. Dried grass and leaves raked into a flattened pile provided a bed. By the time they'd finished, Forêst reappeared, a pair of rabbits clamped in his jaws. Shaping wolves, they joined him in a meal. Dyad dropped below the horizon. Alkina, glowing warm topaz within its rosy mist, reached its zenith and began its descent. Evening wrapped them in a cool cloak. Curled together, they slept, their wolf fur keeping the night chill at bay.

SaHal's strong presence woke Rethdun to pre-dawn light and Forêst's intense, pale eyes only inches from his. The alpha licked his face, loped through the thicket, and faded into memory.

Rethdun shifted and sat up his gaze fixed on his last memory of the great silver wolf. Floree stirred, rose to her hunches, and changed shape. "He's gone, isn't he?"

Rethdun clasped her hand. "He left only moments ago."

She studied him and looked toward the horizon.

"I know the way to VenTra." He pointed east. "It's a turning's walk that way."

Climbing to her feet, she gazed at him. "Anything else I should know?"

He stood up and looked beyond her. "Only that we have company."

She shoved him behind her and whipped around. Her tension evaporated. He stepped around her and smiled.

"Hi, Uncle My."

Mylos ruffled his hair. "Hi, yourself, Rethdun." He pulled Floree into his arms.

Her happy laugh made Rethdun smile. She stepped back. "Kuparak?"

"He's recovering. Let's fly until time for a mid-morning snack. I know a patch bursting with wild berries. We can eat, and I'll share Kup's story."

The flight carried them over the farmlands between the Chaporticas Mountains and El SyrTundi's eastern seashore. When they finally landed, Rethdun's human legs carried him straight to the berry patch. Hunger growled. Not waiting for the adults to shape shift, he picked a plump yellow berry and savored the rich flavor.

Mylos materialized and walked down the row grinning. "Growing boys think they should eat non-stop."

Rethdun swallowed a mouthful. "How do you know? You've stopped growing."

The man shot him a quirky smile. "Haven't always been this big, ya know."

Heat flooded Rethdun's face. "I know *that*, Uncle My."

They picked and ate in companionable silence until Floree appeared looking much tidier than earlier in the turning. When she had collected a sizable handful of berries, they made themselves comfortable beneath a tree.

Mylos finished his last berry. "I believe you have a question, Rethdun."

Anxiety knotted Rethdun's full stomach. He swallowed a small lump in his throat. "D-did you see Rayn?"

Fingering his curly beard, Mylos frowned. "I did not see her. She is sequestered in the women's quarters at the Rompeer's estates. Kuparak is fairly certain she's safe. Rumors suggest she will be placed in the children's residence until her first bleed of womanhood." He glanced at Floree and raised a brow.

She nodded.

Mylos continued. "She will then be educated and trained in the art of Amorparu.

Rethdun plucked a piece of grass and pressed it between his palms. SaHal's knowledge surfaced and provided an explanation. His shoulders hunched and relaxed. "I understand, Uncle Mylos. Rayn will become a courtesan to Lusktar Rados." He let the grass fall and rubbed his hands together. "Tell us of Kuparak."

"Kuparak tangled with a guard at the Rompeerial compound in Chunarrie. When I arrived, he had been imprisoned awaiting an interview with Lusktar Rados. Daar and a group of Vasrosi helped me to rescue him. He is now recovering at the Cimondeli safe haven with Awinta. Katareen is there, too. She sends her love and wishes you well on your journey."

Floree touched his knee. "And who watches over Rayn?"

"I have appointed Daar head Vasrosi in Chunarrie. He watches and waits. If an opening presents itself, he will snatch her away."

Loss choked Rethdun. He steadied resolve. "I must leave El Stroma. The sooner we reach VenTra the better. The SorTech in the Seerdrum Wood sensed me. He knows my energy signature…" He frowned and wrinkled his brow. "Or at least he thinks he does." An unexpected smile replaced his frown. He stood up and threw his arms wide. "Rayn and I are four sun cycles this turning."

Floree gathered him into an embrace that left him grinning.

Mylos slapped him on the back and withdrew a small, wrapped bundle from his pocket. "Katareen sent you a gift."

Rethdun cradle it in his hands, felt the weight of it, breathed in the scent of it. His heart beat quickened. Sitting next to Floree, he untied the yarn securing it and placed the bundle on the ground. Inside, he discovered three things: a smooth blue stone and two curls, one silky and dark, the other curly and coarse. Tears blurred his vision.

Mylos knelt beside him. "Katareen felt certain you would know the curls belong to you and Rayn."

Rethdun fought to control his emotions. "These must be hidden in the locket behind the picture. No one must know they exist."

Floree withdrew the locket. Taking it off, she pressed a tiny, gold knob. The locket sprung open. Mylos inserted the point of his knife beneath the metal ring securing the picture and pried it loose. Rethdun kiss Rayn's curl and placed it behind her tiny portrait. When his curl rested with it, Floree reassembled the locket and hid it beneath her shirt.

Mylos slipped his knife into its sheath. "Why did you want them hidden?"

Rethdun climbed to his feet. "The curls prove the existence of Eleo Predan birth-mates and their genetic heritage." He turned to Floree. "Promise you will keep the locket safe."

Her gaze unwavering met his. "I promise, Rethdun Torin Vilandree, to guard it with my life."

He kissed her cheek. "Thank you, Aunt Floree."

"What of the stone, young Rethdun?" Mylos placed it on his palm.

Rethdun studied it, felt the stir of memory, and nodded. "It is called a Remembering Stone. When I give it to the correct person, it will absorb my childhood memories. If all goes well, I will receive the stone again as an adult. When I do, I will remember what happened on El Stroma."

Mylos bit his upper lip. "Why do you have to give up your memories?"

"SaHal explained in a dream. I am young to carry the weight of his knowledge and gifts on such a perilous journey. By removing my memories, his knowledge will be concealed and my personal remembrances will not give us...you away."

Floree looked worried. "Will SaHal's wisdom be lost forever?"

"No." Rethdun kissed her cheek. "My grandsire's memories will resurface when I am somewhere safe." He anticipated her next question. "I'll know who should be the bearer of the stone when I meet her."

"Her?" Mylos's quizzical expression got a laugh from Floree.

"You don't think a woman can handle such a responsibility?"

"I...Well..."He grinned, pulled her to her feet, and gathered her into an embrace. "I know *you* could."

Rethdun observed the exchange with a touch of sadness. Shook himself and tugged at Floree's shirt.

Laughter filled eyes looked his way. "Yes, Rethdun?"

He held out the Remembering Stone. "Please keep this for me until I need it."

Disengaging from Mylos' arms, she took the stone. "I promise to keep it safe." She glanced up. "I believe we should go."

Mylos, pulled her to him again and kissed her. Without a word, he shift and shot after ReRe.

"Aunt Floree?" Rethdun stared after them. "He loves you, right?"

She smiled. "Yes, I believe he does. Let's go."

He embraced his galee form with as much love as he had seen in Floree's face. She and Puna shot domeward. Aquila lifted into flight. Rethdun joined the caravan of birds, sadness for Floree and Mylos tucked deep in his heart.

When Rethdun awoke the next morning, Floree sat across from him, her expression sad and distant. Mylos was nowhere to be seen. Scrabbling to his feet, he hurried to her side. "Are you alright, Aunt Floree. Has something happened to Mylos?"

She pulled him onto her lap. "We are close to VenTra. Mylos has gone to complete arrangements for our journey and to borrow a motor carriage." She brush a tendril of hair from his forehead. "You and I have a difficult task to do while he's gone."

"What task, Aunt Floree?"

"Puna and Aquila cannot come with us when we leave El Stroma. We must release them to tether to another Vasrosi."

A pang of sadness so deep his entire body ached left Rethdun gulping air. A glance at Floree told him she hurt, too. Touching her cheek, he managed a shaky smile. "I think we should fly with them one last time." He climbed from her lap.

She blinked back tears. "I think so too."

The strength of Aquila's tether took Rethdun by surprise. The woodland galee alighted beside him, his crystal side reflecting the landscape, his good eye unblinking. Rethdun shifted. Side by side, they lifted into flight and soared beneath the morning dome. Aquila caught an updraft and glided higher. Rethdun streaked after him. The world below ceased to exist. The dome and his tukoolo filled his senses. Aquila spiraled downward. Rethdun hovered. When his tukoolo showed no sign of returning, he dropped to the ground and materialized in human form. Images filled his mind. He knelt and bowed his head. His beautiful galee rubbed his feathered head against his cheek and gave a soft whistle. Wing wind ruffled Rethdun's hair. When he looked up, Aquila flew in the direction of Chunarrie.

Weighted by sorrow, he climbed to his feet. Floree offered her hand.

He took it. "I feel empty."

She sighed. "Me, too. Puna didn't want to leave."

"Neither did Aquila. Where will Puna go?"

She will stay close to ReRe and Mylos, at least for now. Aquila?"

Rethdun gazed toward Chunarrie. "He goes to guard Rayn. He will not take another compeer until she is free."

Floree hugged him. "Oh, Rethdun, I'm so glad. With Aquila and Daar and Kuparak to look after her, we don't have to worry quite so much."

Mylos arriving with a motor carriage ended their conversation. They climbed aboard, the engine rumbled, and the carriage rolled onto the road to VenTra.

Rethdun took a final look the direction Aquila had flown. *I will not fly again, Rayn, until we are together.*

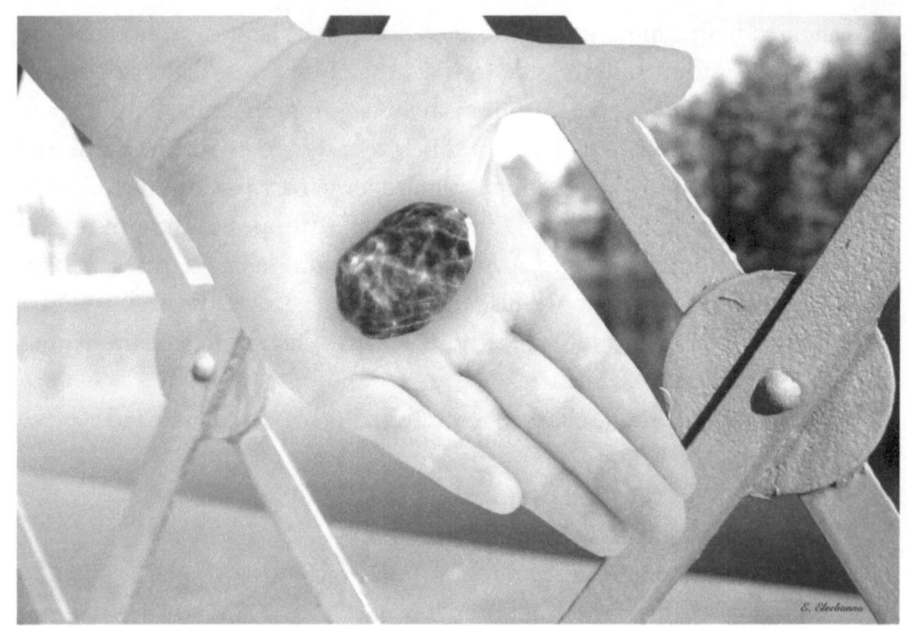

26

They had been in VenTra for several turnings when Rethdun woke to his heart beating a new rhythm. "Today will be *the* turning." He stared at the ceiling, examining his mixed feelings. *What memories will the stone take? What will it leave? Will I feel anything?*

Half expecting SaHal's knowledge to come to his rescue, he searched without success for anything to ease his disquiet. *I need Aunt Floree.* Tiptoeing to her room, he peeked inside.

Floree met his expectant gaze with a sleepy smile, rolled onto her side, and propped her head on her elbow. "Good turning. You look serious. Is something wrong?"

He crossed to the bed. "We will meet *her* today."

She sat up and searched his face. "How do you know?"

A shrug drooped his shoulders. He squared them and forced a tentative smile.

"I can only imagine how frightening it must be to know the memories of everything you've ever known are about to leak from you brain. How are you feeling?"

"I'm afraid I won't know you. I understand I must forget Rayn and Maman and Kup and Mylos but..." His bottom lip quivered. "I must also forget the teachings of SaHal Elan Torinhota." He brightened. "At least, my grandsire's knowledge will only go into hiding. When we are safe, it will reemerge." He fiddled with his sleeping top. "I think I should carry the stone today...in case."

Floree left her bed and opened a small bag. "Keep it safe. I'll stay close. If you need help, call me. Why don't you get dressed and meet me in the living room."

Rethdun stood at the second story window of Raveler's Inn. VenTra, his first urban experience, fascinated him. So many people, all in a hurry, took his breath away. Men in suits and women in long dresses rode and walked along the street at all hours of the turning. Children, garbed as miniature grown ups, marched with adult companions...never alone.

He smoothed his new clothes. Mylos and Floree had taken him to a store. He leaned his forehead against the window. *Stores are almost as interesting as all the people...each one, a paradise of merchandise.* Floree had picked out four outfits for herself and three for him. Mylos had let Rethdun give the clerk silver pecêns in exchange.

The coins had fascinated him. SaHal's memories informed him their importance. How much money one had marked one's station in life. The less you had, the more difficult your life could be.

The smell of sweet soap and perfume wafted across the room. Floree, looking nothing like the woman he had grown up with, joined him by the window. She wore a stylish, blue dress instead of the baggy pants and big shirts she had always worn. Her shiny blonde hair peeked from beneath a bonnet bedecked with ribbons and flowers. He smiled. She had been as giggly as Rayn on a happy day when Mylos purchased it.

"You look pretty, Aunt Floree."

"Thank you, Rethdun. You look quite handsome yourself."

He touched the fine fabric of his jacket. "My new clothes are nice, but they make me feel that I must always be careful."

She rested her hands on his shoulders, her eyes level with his. "Rethdun, I have something important to ask. You and I can no longer be Floree and Rethdun. Do you think you could call me Momee?"

His heart gave a small stab of sorrow. He swallowed. "I can. What will you call me...Momee?"

"What do you think of the name Charid Darine?"

"Charid." I like it. Do you have another name besides Momee?"

"I am Esta Mae Darine. We are from the town of Port Saticch."

Rethdun searched SaHal's memories. "Port Saticch isn't far from here. It's a seaside town a bit smaller than VenTra."

Floree laughed. "You know too much, young Charid."

Rethdun didn't smile. "Not for much longer, Momee."

They spent most of the turning packing the small trunk they had purchased for the trip and preparing for an early departure the next morning. Mylos arrived late afternoon with identification papers, tickets, and medical forms. After dispatching their luggage to the transport center, he escorted them to a small eatery. Following a tasty meal, they strolled to a waterside park.

Rethdun left Mylos and Floree holding hands and talking in quiet, serious voices. Wandering along a bayside walkway, he stared at night's beginning reflected in the water. *Soon, my memories will fade like the dusk into night. Will I know I'm forgetting my whole life?* He glanced at Floree and Mylos. *Will I remember Momee?*

A small, smooth pebble glistened at his feet. Picking it up, he turned it one way and then the other. *How can one small stone hold everything I've ever known?*

The whisper of silk petticoats brought his attentions from the stone to the face of a girl perhaps twelve sun cycles old. Sapphire blue eyes met his gaze with candid interest. "Hello, I'm Fianna Gwynn Palmira. My friends call me Gwynn. What's your name?"

"Ch-charid D-darine."

"I won't bite you, Charid." She took his hand and lead him to a park bench. "You dreamt of me too, didn't you?"

He summoned an affirming nod.

"I know you have something for me to guard and pass on." She withdrew a small, blue-velvet pouch from beneath her top and removed its matching blue ribbon from around her neck. "My grandmaman made this for me. She told me you would give me a stone, The Remembering Stone. She said I would be guarding *your* memories."

Rethdun inhaled. Trepidation cleared and words formed. "I did have a dream about you. You are on your way to the Inner Universe on the *Meti Chalan II,* too. But...I won't remember you, will I?"

She shook her head. "No, but I'll introduce myself when it is safe." Her lovely face grew solemn. "Are you scared."

The hand he placed on his heart trembled. "I'm afraid I will forget Momee and even who I am. I wonder if I'll have a history...a story to call my own. I understand there are things I *must* forget, but..." He shivered. "I wonder if it will hurt or..." Another shiver shook his shoulders.

Gywnne clasped his hand. "Grandmama says the anticipation of something is harder than the actual event. Perhaps you should give me the stone."

Rethdun studied the sea and the moon's path to the shore...how moonlight changed the darkness to light. He slipped a hand in his pocket and curled his fingers around the stone. "Did your grandmaman tell you anything else?"

"She said your memories seeping into the stone will be painless. For a short time, you will feel lost. Then your life...your now moments...will become your story." Her beautiful face grew thoughtful. "Oh yes, she said to tell you SaHal will be with you always. Do you want me to get your maman?"

He shook his head and removed the stone from his pocket, clutched it for an instant longer, and dropped it onto her palm. "What now?"

"We'll hold it together. Put your hand on the stone."

Cool hardness pressed against his palm. Gywnne interlaced her fingers through his. Side by side, their hands resting on a park bench in VenTra, the forgetting began. SaHal's wisdom and knowledge withdrew, leaving Rethdun immersed in his personal recollections. Much too fast, these memories melted like snowflakes on his tongue. At first, the loss of each remembrance——person, place or event——left a tangible tear in his psyche. He cried out in dismay, wishing for just one more moment to savor their significance. Panic crept into lack of awareness. He felt happy...even lighthearted.

A hand squeezed his. A strange voice whispered, "I promise to guard the stone with my life."

The tantalizing words evaporated. He frowned and glanced up. The bayside park, the ocean, the moon seemed familiar. The elderly woman sitting next to him did not. He searched the park. "Where's Momee?"

"I believe we should find her, don't you. My name is Gwynnith Torin. You may call me Tori. What's your name, boy?"

He bit his lip. "Momee told me not to speak to strangers."

She smiled. "You maman is a wise woman, but I'm not a stranger. I knew your grandsire."

Thinking hard, he frowned. "Do I know him?"

"He died before you were born. But I knew him well." She took his hand. "Come along, *Charid*, your maman will worry if we don't find her soon."

Holding tight to her hand, he skipped along the walkway.

A harried woman hurried toward them. "Charid, I've been looking *everywhere* for you."

"Momee!" He pulled his hand free and ran to hug her. "I got lost."

She knelt and held him away from her. "Are you alright."

"Yes, Momee. Tori found me." He looked over her shoulder, wiggled from her grasp, and held up his arms. "Uncle My!"

Mylos snatched him up in his arms. "You scared us, Charid. Who's your friend?"

Gwynnith regarded him with interest. "I am Gwynnith Torin. Please call me Tori."

Mylos bowed. "Thank you for returning Charid to us."

"You are most welcome." She inclined her head and smiled. "Would you mind if I had a private word with Floree?"

Charid squirmed. "Uncle My, I want to see the ocean."

Mylos put him down. "Promise to stay by me?"

"If you can catch me." Giggling, he raced toward the water.

Floree assessed the elderly woman whose candid gaze reminded her of someone...someone she couldn't quite place. "Do I know you?"

Tori moved to her side. "You do, my dear. Let's sit on the bench. We have things to discuss." When they were seated, she placed her elegant handbag between them. "Please take my hand."

Floree clasped it and gasped. A surge of heat ran up her arm. "You were in my dream." She glanced after Mylos and his young charge. "Is it done?"

"It is my dear. Now, we must do a bit of work on you. Your memories contain information harmful to those who serve our people."

Floree rubbed her hand. "You will rearrange my memories, correct?"

"I will. Don't worry. Once you have reached your destination, they will resurface. You understand why this must be done?"

"I do. What about Mylos?"

"He will not remember you and Charid left El Stroma. The rest of his memories must remain in tact for his work as the Vasrosi leader."

Tori clasped her hand. Floree sucked in a breath, blinked, and grew still. Momentary confusion left her dazed. When her mind cleared, she inclined her head to observe the woman sitting next to her. "Do I know you?"

"Only in passing, my dear." She stood. "I believe your friend is ready to escort you to the inn." With a brief nod to Mylos, she joined a young girl waiting by the walkway and, taking her arm, continued her stroll beside the sea.

At the inn, Mylos accompanied them to their suite. Floree tucked Charid in bed and rejoined him in the small parlor. Wondering at her slight feeling of discomfort, she remained standing and folded her arms. "Thank you for all you did tonight, Mylos." She paused. "I seem to be dealing with a touch of confusion. I'm not sure..."

"It's alright, *Esta*." He tugged a curl in his beard and rose. "I understand. Get some sleep. We must be up before dawn. I'll see you then." A quick kiss on the cheek and he was gone.

She touched her face and furrowed her brow. *What was that about...It's alright, Esta. I understand?* Shaking herself, she prepared for bed.

Esta woke to persistent but soft pounding on the door. After a quick peek through the peep hole, she opened the door. Mylos, anxiety screaming around him, marched into the room.

"Get dressed. We have to go."

She made a hasty retreat to her room, dressed, and stuffed a few remaining things in her bag. Shaking Charid awake, she helped him into his clothes, ran a brush though is hair, and hurried him into the living room.

Mylos knelt in front of him. "I need you to do exactly what I ask and no noise."

Charid, eyes as big as the moon, nodded.

Moving to the door, Mylos stepped into the hall. "Stay here. I'll be back."

Charid clutched a fist full of skirt. "Are we in trouble?"

"No, but we must be as quiet as kittens. Esta touched a finger to her lips.

Mylos stuck his head in the room. "Hurry! We don't have much time." His urgent undertone sent them scurrying after him into the hall and down the back stairs. A door at the bottom exited onto the street. Mylos urged them faster. Behind the inn, a darkened motored carriage purred.

Mylos lifted Charid into the back, assisted her, and climbed aboard. The motor hummed. The carriage rolled along the narrow lane.

Running feet rounded the building. "Stop in the name of the Rompeerial Guard."

Esta gripped Charid's hand. Mylos rapped on the wall behind the driver. The carriage lights flared. It leapt forward. A peek out the small, back window gave a glimpse of a Rompeerial motor wagon pulling onto the street. It stopped to pick up the soldier and, engine rumbling, raced after them.

With little time to spare, their carriage rolled through the open gates of the Transport Center. The guard waved them on. They turned one corner, then another, and came to a stop beside a one story building. Mylos jumped to the ground, spoke with the driver, and hurried her and Charid inside.

A uniformed man greeted them with no questions and an impersonal smile. He escorted them to a small, windowless office. Pounding on the front door, changed the smile to a look of grim determination. "Please take a seat. I'll be with you when I can." He hurried into the hall and shut the door behind him.

Mylos waited a heartbeat, then opened it a crack. Angry voices drifted along the hall. A calm response received a barrage of demands. Mylos eased the door shut, whipped out his kerchief, and wiped the sweat from his face and neck.

Esta tried to remain calm. "What's happening? Are we safe here?"

"The Transport Center is owned by the planetary government of Metchalia." Mylos stuffed the kerchief in his pocket. "In accordance with intergalactic law, the center is consider to be Metchalian territory. It is, therefore, governed by Metchalian law. The Rompeer and his soldiers have no authority here, nor do Transport Center officials have to hand over El Stroman citizens…unless they choose to do so."

Stealthful feet filed past the door. Again, Mylos eased it ajar. Angry protests followed by shuffling feet and the muffled roar of an engine fading into the distance suggest the Rompeer's soldiers had lost the battle.

The uniformed man returned and sat at his desk. Mylos handed him their papers. After a cursory glance, he stamped them and handed them back.

"A carriage is here to take you to the ship." He regarded Esta with a stern countenance. "You will be shown to your quarters. I suggest you remain there until *well after* take off."

He ushered them to the back door. Esta paused. "Thank you, sir."

The man executed a stylish bow. "Welcome to Metchalia, Esta Mae Darine. May your journey be a safe one." He withdrew into the building.

Esta stared after him and then at Charid. "We're not in El Stroma anymore."

27

Esta, Charid, and Mylos waited in a room, where floor to ceiling windows provided a spectacular view of the space port. Unlike Charid's obvious excitement, the sight of the *Meti Chala II's* shuttle gleaming in the moonlight stimulated a flood of doubts for Esta...doubts about leaving El Stroma...doubts defined by emotions she could not identify.

Mylos handed her a boarding packet. "You've made the right choice, Esta. Time away is exactly what you need. The death of Charid's father has taken its toll on both of you."

His words, spoken in a loud tone, increased her unease and triggered a deluge of unwanted memories. She pulled a hanky from her crocheted purse and dabbed her eyes. "I know, Mylos. It's just that..."

Charid came bounding up. "Uncle My, look at the shuttle! Momee and I are going on it to the ship. Aren't we lucky?"

Mylos knelt. "You're a lucky boy, Charid. Be good, have grand adventures, and take care of your maman."

"I'll take good care of Momee. I promise. When do we go?"

"You'll board soon."

Charid clapped his hands. "And how long before it takes off?"

"The shuttled lifts off in two time circles. *Meta Chala II* leaves orbit tomorrow mid-morning." Mylos' answer held a note of wistfulness. He gave Charid a quick hug and stood. "I'll see you when you get back."

Esta brushed an invisible speck of dust from her dress and lifted a gaze filled with unasked questions. "Take care of yourself, Mylos."

"You, too, Esta Mae. Don't forget m..." He pressed his lips together. "Have a good time." He pivoted and walked away.

Sadness and an overwhelming sense of loss gripped her. Bewildered, she turned to stare at the reflection of his retreating figure in the window. With each step he took, her heart seemed to grow smaller. Glancing at Charid, she frowned. *You are my son. Your father is dead.* She searched the shimmering glass. Only their future remained.

E sta sensed trouble, even before the tall, slender woman striding toward them stopped in front of her.

"Esta Mae Darine?" The brusque question matched the woman's stern demeanor.

"I am Esta. May I help you?"

She cast a hard look Charid's direction. "Please bring your son and follow me."

Esta remained unmoving. "And you are?"

"Liaison Officer Tademori. I arbitrate disputes between Metchalian and El Stroman officials." Her tone softened. "We must go now."

With a nod, Esta beckoned Charid to join them.

He ran to her side. "Do we get to go on the ship now?"

Tademori didn't answer, but turned on her heels and marched to the door. She guided them to a small office, gave them clipped but clear instructions to stay put, and left.

A man in a suit entered and took a seat at the desk. A second man followed and remained standing behind a black box. After appearing to adjust settings, he pressed a small round pad to his temple, and nodded.

The first man gazed at a folder. "It says here…" His finger traced an invisible line. "…you are Esta Mae Darine and the boy is your son, Charid Wilhan Darine. Your husband died a sun cycle ago in a boating accident off the Port Saticch coast." He glanced up. "I have reason to believe this may not be true."

Esta drew in a startled breath. "I'm sorry? Are you suggesting that Wil is alive?"

"No, Madame Darine, I am suggesting you are not who you say you are.

"I beg your pardon?"

Charid squirmed to look at her. "You look like Momee. You talk like Momee." He scooched off the chair and threw his arms around her. "You are Momee!"

Grateful for a moment to organize her scatter thoughts, she helped him onto her lap. "I don't know who you think I am, but my papers are in order. Wil's death certificate is among them." She smoothed Charid's hair. "Our son was born in the Port Saticch birthing center. You have seen his papers. I don't know who you're looking for, but I do know this office and the Transport Center are *not* El Stroman but Metchalian. Therefore, I am asking for the protection of Metchalia."

Liaison Officer Tademori marched into the room and presented a document to the man in the suit. "I have been ordered to assist Madame Darine and her son through the boarding process. If you have further concerns, please discuss them with my superior." She held the door open.

Charid jumped to the floor. Excitement buzzed around him. He pulled Esta to her feet. "Come on, Momee. It's time!"

Tademori nodded them through. As the door eased shut, the man at the desk barked. "Did you sense anything?"

The second man answered, "No, sir. Not one thing."

While Charid's delight at being aboard the *Meti Chala II* distracted the liaison officer, Esta calmed her rising concern that El Stroman officials would somehow convince the Metchalians to withdraw their protection.

When they reached their small stateroom, Tademori followed them inside.

Taking out a box half the size of her palm, she pressed a switch, watched intently, and slipped it back in her pocket. She smiled. "We can talk. My name is Zyna. I'm Eleo Predan, and I know Mylos. He asked me to help you in any way I can. If you need me, the yellow button on your control console will let me know."

She showed them how to use the control panel, answered a barrage of questions from Charid, and reminded them to stay in their cabin until after take off.

The door slid shut. Esta sank onto a chair. "I need a hug, little man."

Charid obliged and planted a wet kiss on her cheek. "We are on the ship, Momee!"

She studied his eager upturned face. *What is different about you? Shaggy, straight black hair, dark chestnut eyes, fair skin...*She shrugged. "Shall we explore our stateroom."

"Do you think there's something to eat?"

She laughed. "Indeed I do. Let's see what we can find."

They discovered recessed bunks, one above the other, hidden behind sliding panels on the wall. Under the bottom bunk, an inset switch released the catches on four drawers. Further exploration showed them a small room with a cleansing stall and commode area. A communal area with a built in couch and two chairs surrounding a low, round table occupied one corner of the room.

Putting his hands on his hips, Charid surveyed their quarters and walked to a panel on the wall next to a foldable table. "Momee, what about here?"

Esta joined him and examined the panel. The small screen beside it provided instructions and a list of available food. She punched in two codes and pressed the green square. After a brief pause and a soft buzz, the panel slid open.

Charid clapped his hands and laughed. "Oh, Momee look!"

Esta removed a tray bearing gleaming glasses of fruit drink and small bowls of pudding and carried it to the round table. "Won't you join me, Charid Darine?"

He bounced onto the couch and picked up a spoon. "What do you think the pudding tastes like?"

Esta laughed. "Guess we'll have to try it."

Charid took a bite and grinned. "So good, Momee. Taste it."

Scooping up a small spoonful, Esta took a tentative nibble. Smooth sweetness rolled down her throat. "I've never tasted anything like it. What do you think?"

Swallowing a second bite, Charid grew solemn. "I love this moment, right now, Momee."

Somewhat surprised by her small son's wisdom, she raised her juice glass. "A toast...to loving each moment as it comes."

He tapped her glass, took a deep drink, and sighed. "We're finally on the ship."

The first few turnings, filled with exploring and learning the ways of living aboard an inter-universal passenger ship, passed quickly. At first, Esta scrutinized every new person she met, continually looked over her shoulder, and refused to leave Charid alone, even in the Children's Center, where she had to sign him in and out and where several Metchalian aids were always in attendance.

Zyna had told her the trip to the Clenaba Rolas System, the closest solar system of any size on the far side of The Rim, would take almost two sun cycles. The Meti Chala II's first stop would be the planet of RewFaar. Esta had made note of the trip details and decided her best bet lay in living each day as it came.

She and Charid soon established a rhythm to their turnings. He spent most mornings at the Children's Center enjoying organized play and, more important to Esta, learning. She joined a women's' group. Each member who wished to present a workshop about something they enjoyed was encouraged to do so. *Journal Writing, A Healing Art* caught Esta's interest. After the well-scripted presentation, she returned to her quarters in a thoughtful mood. *Someday, I will write a journal about the events in my life. Perhaps it will be as healing as the presenter suggested.*

One morning near the end of the trip, she strolled along the passageway and stopped to chat with a woman whom she had met at the Children's Center. They conversed casually about their similar-aged sons and shared funny stories about their own childhoods. Laughing at a particularly delightful story Esta came to the realizations of two depurate things: she hadn't laughed in a long time and the woman sharing the story was Pheet Adolean.

After she and Charid returned to the stateroom, he turned on the view screen to watch space, time, and stars gliding by. She sat beside him, her thoughts nagging her to pay attention to the lesson which had presented itself for her consideration.

She reviewed the conversation with the Pheet Adolean woman. *I have always distrusted the Pheet Adole.* A search of her memory left her frowning. *Why? Why would I hate the people I grew up with? My papers state that Charid and I are Pheet Adole. Yet I do not feel the truth in the words. Are we truly from El SyrTundi?*

Charid tugged at her arm. "Momee, where did you go?"

"Go? Ohhhhh. I was dream-turning about——" His eager smile stopped her. "Do you need something?"

"I met a really nice girl in the common space. Her grandmaman is interested in meeting you. Can we eat evening meal in the dining hall?" He shot her a sheepish grin. "My tummy is talking."

"Oh, Charid, you do make me giggle. Yes, we can eat in the dining hall. Change your shirt and wash up. Then we'll go."

When they arrived at the entrance, the waiter escorted them to a small private alcove. Esta hesitated. "I think there must be a mistake. This isn't our usual table."

"It's not a mistake, my dear." An elderly woman accompanied by a young woman of perhaps eighteen sun cycles walked up to the table. The elder smiled up at the waiter. "Thank you, Ilan. Please bring a seafood starter and sparkling water."

He bowed and hurried away.

The younger woman assisted her companion to a chair facing the room and took the seat next to her.

While Esta and Charid made themselves comfortable, their hostess adjusted her long skirt and lifted an elegant lorgnette. Magnified violet eyes regarded them, first one and then the other. "I am Gwynnith Viola Torin and this is my granddaughter, Fianna Gwynn Palmira. We are delighted you could join us for evening meal."

—

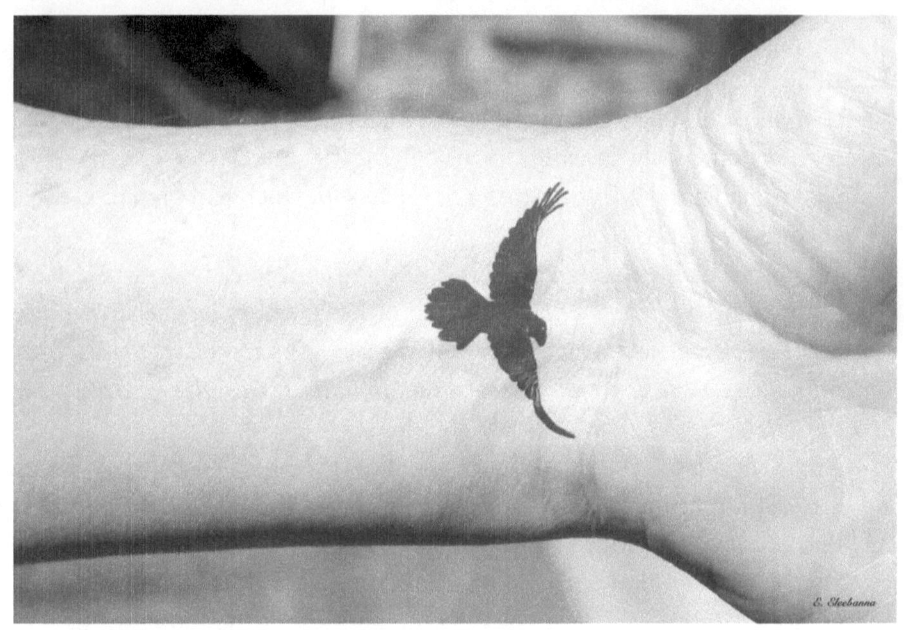

28

Dinner, both the food and conversation, proved to be excellent. When the dessert dishes had been cleared, Tori turned to Gwynn. "Why don't you and Charid go for a walk. Esta and I will meet you in the Observatory." She glanced at Esta. "In a full circle."

Charid jumped to his feet. "I love the Observatory. May I go, Momee."

Esta laughed. "Of course, you may. Please do what Gwynn asks, and have fun." She gave Gwynn a smile of thanks and returned her attention to Tori."

The elderly woman folded her lap cloth and placed it on the table. Her finger's brushed Esta's hand.

A tingling sensation skipped up Esta's spine, pooled at the occipital, and spread like an army of ants over her skull. Memories of another life...her true life...replicated the night dome in her mind. A shooting star streaked across her line of vision, showered her with sparkling light, and extinguished. Her vision cleared. Tori came into focus.

Restraining the impulse to glance over her shoulder, she interlaced her fingers and breathed a sigh of acceptance and gratitude. "Thank you, Tori. Will Charid remember anything from his childhood?

Wrinkled fingers traced the fold in the lap cloth. "He will not. His time on the ship...yes. His birth-mate...no. Once you are safe on your new home planet, SaHal's knowledge will resurface. Time will provide the answers to the puzzle of his personal destiny. The Pheet Adole will not stop searching for him."

Tori placed a gold ring on the table. A purple stone gleamed in a nest of delicate filigree. "This is yours. Mylos had Nioka and Tazio create it for you. If you should return to El Stroma, as I believe you wish to do, it will absorb your memories of Charid and where he resides. Mylos knows how to unlock the information should you require it. Do you have questions for me?"

"Where do you go from here? Will you return to our home planet?"

Sadness etched the lines in her face deeper. "We will never return. It has become a cruel place and will only grow worse. You and I and those on this ship left ahead of the maelstrom. If the Eleo Predan people are to survive, they must leave their home planet and secret their ancestral roots on other worlds. I am taking Gwynn to KcernFensia, where she will marry a good man, a man whose father had the forethought to remove his family at the first hint of Lusktar Rados' plan for genocide." She signaled the waiter. "We arrive in RewFaar tomorrow. The man who will help you is Arien Vallon. He wears the sign of the raven on his left wrist."

The waiter arrived. "You require something, Madame?"

Offing a small pouch, she smiled. "This is for you. Thank you for taking such good care of my granddaughter and me."

As he took it, her finger's brushed his. Confusion flickered and died. He bowed and walked away.

Tori sighed. "He will only a remember an old woman who gave him a gift." She remain seated. "One more thing, Esta. You must maintain your charade until you are safe. Keep your mind centered on the present moment. Do not allow yourself to look back. Our lives, yours, mine, Charid's and Gwynn's, depend on your discretion and control."

"I understand." Glancing toward the entrance, she noted a man talking to the steward. His gaze darted her direction before he walked from the room.

Tori pushed back her chair. "Let's find the young people."

True to her word, Esta kept her thoughts centered on preparing to debark the next morning. The ship, she had been informed, would begin its orbit during the night.

Charid bounced into her line of vision. Excitement made him fidget and fiddle and get underfoot.

"Please, Charid, turn on the view screen. This will be your last opportunity to enjoy it."

"I don't think I can sit still, Momee. Aren't you excited? We have been on the ship for such a long time." He became matter-a-fact. "When we boarded in El Stroma, I was a little child...only four sun cycles. Now, I am six!"

Esta gave him a good natured swat on the bottom. "Go or I will put you to work."

An impish grin, always an indication of mischief, tugged the corner of his mouth. "I can help."

She swept toward him.

He skipped to the view screen, touched the panel, and flopped down on the couch.

She returned to her packing and the occasional random thought demanding her attention. She and Charid had bid Tori and Gwynn good-bye in the Observatory. They would not see them again. Loneliness washed over her. She looked at Charid. *We have been surrounded by people and safe for two sun cycles. Soon, we will be on our own...alone.* The name Arlen Vallon whispered through her thoughts.

When Charid finally wore himself out and fell asleep, she settled on the built in couch. The stateroom, quiet for the first time since their return from dining, had been their home from almost two sun cycles. Their unknown destination, a precaution she agreed with, grew ever closer. *What will we find there? And what of events on El Stroma? Rayn and Kuparak? Mylos?* Thinking about him stirred up a tempest of emotions. Not remembering had been easier.

The yellow light on the console blinked...once, twice. Esta hurried to the panel and touched a green light. The door slid open. Zyna stepped through; the door whooshed shut.

Pulling out the small black box, she pressed a button, rotated, and put it back in her pocket."It's almost time. Charid?"

"Sleeping, but dressed and ready to go."

She lowered her muscular frame onto the couch. "Good. Sit. I have some things to share."

Esta joined her. "Things."

"The shuttle will be leaving for RewFaar in four time circles. Vasrosi supporters will help you to transfer to a jumper craft scheduled to depart as soon as you and Charid are onboard. Be careful and keep your mind centered on Esta Mae until you are at your destination. We're fairly certain we have a Klutarse masquerading as a businessman on *Meti Chala II*. We suspect he brought a SorTech with him. So, please be careful."

Zyna leaned closer. "Mylos asked me to deliver this message: 'Zyna and her team will help you come back to El Stroma if you wish. Take care of yourself. I love you, Floree'."

Controlling the desire to whoop for joy, she focused on her primary concern. "What of Charid?"

"We have found a couple in your new home who would be thrilled to adopt Charid. They're good people. Our contact on the surface, will meet you at the drop site and take you and Charid to meet them. If you are comfortable and like the couple, we will collect you when we swing by to pick up Arlen in about three moon cycles."

"Who is Arien?"

"He's a Vasrosi based on the planet of RewFaar. His assignment is to pave the way for you and Charid and to make sure you're safe in your new home."

Esta regarded Zyna. "His second name is Vallon, correct?"

"It is."

"I had no idea Vasrosi had such a long reach."

Zyna smiled, her first since she walked into the stateroom. "Kuparak didn't waste the trip back to El Stroma after he left Tala on Thera. Every place the return ship stopped, he made contacts. Our people must leave El Stroma or die, and they'll need help to do it." She stretched and stood up. "I have to go. I suggest a quick nap. Be careful and be safe."

Esta stared at the door, her thoughts in a jumble. "Mylos loves me! I can go back to El Stroma." A yawn consumed her. "Put Floree's life away. You are Esta, and Esta needs to nap."

The ship's announcement system, blared. "Passengers disembarking on RewFaar prepare to board the shuttle on level two. RewFaaran passengers..."

The stateroom door slid shut. Charid pranced ahead, bumped into a man standing in the hall, and skidded to a stop.

"I am sorry, sir."

"Quite alright, young man. You seem a bit excited."

Esta joined them and clasped Charid's hand. "Excuse us. We have friends to see off." She hurried down the hall. Once inside the lift, she searched her memory. *Where have I seen him before?*

In the waiting area, she straightened Charid's jacket and smoothed his hair. "Have you ever seen the man you bumped into before?"

He nodded. "He's been watching us play at the Children's Center for the past few turnings. He even asked me my name."

Esta frowned. "Why didn't you tell me?"

Charid shrugged. "You didn't ask."

"Oh, Charid." She hugged him. Her gazed searched the area. The absence of the strange man didn't make her feel any better.

A disembodied voice announced, "Please form a line. Have your papers in hand."

Esta clutched their paperwork. "Hold onto my skirt, Charid. Don't let go no matter what. If you see the man, yank twice."

"Yes, Momee."

The passengers filed onto the shuttle, strapped into their seats, and prepared for take off.

Charid squirmed to look one way, waved at a friend, and then twisted the other way. "I don't see him."

The woman next to them glared.

Esta caught his arm. "Sit still. We'll look when we're on the ground."

Sulky but quiet, he settled in his seat.

The shuttle exited the ship with the smoothness of silk. Charid succumbed to excitement engendered fatigue and napped. Esta forced her busy thoughts into silence and stared at the seat back in front of her.

Cushioned by a blast of air, the shuttled landed. The voice announced directions. People filed down the aisles and into a long tunnel. At the end, a steward directed them to an entry window. A uniformed man shuffled through their papers, applied a stamp, and motioned them toward a door marked *Declarations.*

Esta's calm façade masked her nervousness. *Why is the man here? Why his interest in Charid? Is he the Klutarse?*

The Declarations officer reviewed her list of possessions and handed it back. "Anything else to declare?"

"No, sir."

"I'm afraid we will need to take a closer look." The officer's pleasant demeanor and unwavering gaze did little to ease the knots in her stomach. He beckoned a young man forward. "Please take Madame Darine and her son to room three." He nodded to Esta. "Thank you for your patience." His attention moved to the next person in line.

Esta kept her fear in check and gripped Charid's hand. When they reached room three, a man in a RewFaaran military uniform met them at the door. "This way please." Bypassing the desk, he walked to an exit at the back of the room.

A moment of panic made her hesitate. He reached for the door handle, exposing a raven tattoo on the inside of his wrist. Her gaze flew to his face. He mouthed the words *Arien Vallon*, pushed the door open, and motioned them ahead of him. A military vehicle gleamed in the dim light. A young soldier stood at attention beside it.

"We got word you are being followed." He looked at Charid. "How quiet can you be?"

"Very quiet, sir."

"Good man. Grantese Tyler is going to hide you. Your maman will change her clothes and ride with me. If we are stopped, you pretend you're a mouse."

The Grantese and Charid hurried to the back of the truck.

Speculative brown eyes regarded her. "On RewFaar women are never seen in a military vehicle. Do you think you can impersonated a soldier."

Esta saluted. "Yes, sir. I can, sir."

"Good, you'll find a uniform behind that screen. Hustle."

"What about…"

"Leave your things. They'll be sent with your baggage as soon as you're safe."

When she returned clothed in the private's uniform, her hair tucked beneath a beaked cap, Arien took her to the back of the truck and opened a door. Charid peeked over the edge of a wooden box surround by several others in neat, organized stacks.

Tyler waited while Charid got comfortable, closed the lid, and jumped to the ground beside them. "Anything else, sir?"

"Stay alert. If anyone tries to follow, make sure they don't get far. And don't get caught."

"Yes, sir." He tipped the brim of his cap and strode to a second truck.

Arien threw the latch on the door and moved to help her into front. She shook her head. "I'm fine. Much more at home in pants than a skirt. What about our papers?"

"Climb in and give them to me."

He propped up the seat on his side, exposed the pristine springs underneath, pried them loose, and pulled out a packet wrapped in waterproof paper. Slipping her papers into the gap, he dropped the seat back into place and handed her the packet. "Open it and familiarize yourself with your new identity. When you're done stick 'em in the dash box with mine. I have a couple of things to check, and then we'll leave."

Esta unwrapped the packet and scanned the papers inside. *I am Private Jase Mantroe. I work under Arien. I was born on RewFaar and have lived here all my life. I'm single; my relatives migrated.* She replaced the papers and put them in the box. *Yet another personality. I wonder what's happening on El Stroma. I wonder if he remembers…Get a grip, girl. You are not safe yet.*

—

29

Arien climbed into the truck and slammed the door. "We've got company." He shot her a side ways look. "Remember you're a soldier. Buckle up."

He pushed the dashboard starter and the truck rolled forward. At the double back doors, Tyler strode up to the driver's side. The window slid down.

"Trouble ahead. Thought you might need me here."

"Good man. Get in back and protect Charid. Keep him safe, Tyler. I'll take care of Esta. Go."

A knock on the wall told them Tyler was onboard. Arien flashed the lights. The doors opened. The engine revved and the truck pulled onto a wide, empty expanse between the buildings and the security fence. On the far side, Arien merge onto a well-lit road. Busy evening traffic flowed around them. At the main gate, the sentry waved them through.

Esta glanced in the rearview mirror. Nothing seemed out of place. She looked forward. *How would I know?*

The road widened into four lanes. The truck sped up. She gasped. *RewFaar sure is different than El Stroma.*

Arien kept his speed consistent "A vehicle is pulling up beside us on my side. If I tell you to duck, don't hesitate."

Esta sat stiff-backed, her gaze fixed on the road ahead. She heard a low, accelerating roar.

"Hold on, girl. We have an turnoff coming up."

A vehicle pulled along side. The turnoff came into view. At the last instant, Arien veered left onto an exit ramp. An intersection dumped them onto a two-lane road. A second turn put them on a narrow, dark street. Warehouses lined both sides. Arien eased the truck into an alley. A darkened opening yawned to the right. He turned. A door dropped silently into place behind them.

"Stay put. "Arien jumped to the ground

A man carrying a dim hand light hurried toward him. "They doubled back. Gotta get you outta here. Car's right here. Called ahead. The jumper's ready."

"Tyler's in the back with the boy. Let him know what's up." Arien lifted the seat and removed her papers from their hiding place. "Give me your fake papers."

He crammed the papers in where her's had been and lowered the seat into place. "Get out this side."

Scooching across the seat, she jumped to the ground. Tyler and Charid emerged from the back of the truck. The man with the light hustled them into the waiting car——Tyler, Charid, and Esta in the back; Arien in the front beside the driver. Two men climbed into the truck.

The car inched forward in total darkness. A second door vanished upward. A man motioned them through. Keeping the car's lights off, the driver turned left and drove between square containers stacked in long rows. Esta looked back. The truck turned right and disappeared around the end of the building.

Charid snuggled next to her. His hand crept into hers. "I'm scared."

Esta hugged him. "So am I."

Arien twisted around. "Look at your maman, Charid. Tell me what you see."

Charid considered Esta. "She's wearing a soldier's uniform." His brow wrinkled. "Are you a soldier, Momee?"

Arien answered. "She *is* a soldier. Tyler is a soldier. Our driver, Tanwar Gorda, is a soldier and so am I. Everyone in this car is a soldier. How would you like to be a soldier, too."

Entreaty filled his small face. "Oh, Momee, can I be a soldier?"

She kept her expression solemn. "Yes, Charid, you can."

He looked at Arien. "I would love to be a soldier, sir."

"Excellent. Repeat after me: I, Charid Darine, solemnly swear to be a good soldier, to obey orders, to protect those I love, and to honor the soldier's code."

Charid repeated the words with such earnestness, Esta could not help but smile.

Arien saluted. "Welcome, Private Darine. Your first order is to hold you maman's hand so she won't be afraid."

Charid saluted. "Yes, sir." He clasped her hand. "Don't be afraid, Momee. I'll take care of you."

Tyler turned a chuckle into a cough.

Gorda winked in the rearview mirror.

Arien faced front. "Let's go."

The route Gorda drove to the jumper base took them through the dawn-lit streets of Dabborm, the commercial district to the west of the Telisnoe Shuttle Port. Esta wanted to press her nose to the glass to take in as much as she could of this world, a world so different from her own it left her speechless. Instead, she sat soldier-straight and gazed at sleek cars, unlike anything on El Stroma, almost soundless, streamlined trucks, and more people, even at this early hour, than she had seen in VenTra. A motored cycle whizzed by. The rider leaned into the corner and sped up.

"Did you see that Momee? *I* want to ride one of those when I'm bigger."

Esta hugged him. "Perhaps you will, Charid." A moment of sadness surprised her. She returned her gaze to the outside world. *And I probably won't know.*

The buildings grew fewer and more scattered. Gorda merged onto a road leading away from Dabborm. Arien picked up a pair of field glasses and scanned the landscape ahead.

Charid squirmed. "Are we almost there?"

Putting the glasses in the case beside him, Arien turned. "Private Darine, how brave are you?"

"I'm brave, sir."

"Good, you and Tyler stay alert back there. Remember, you job is take care of you maman."

Arien caught Esta's eye. The message was clear. She gripped Charid's hand.

Arien faced front. "You ready. Gorda?"

"Yes, sir. Hold on everyone."

Two motored cycles roared toward them. Esta glanced over her shoulder at the truck careening after them.

Gorda accelerated, heading straight for the cycles. One dodged to the left, the other to the right. The car shot between them. Bike engines revved. Gorda yanked the steering wheel to the left, shot along a narrow, one lane road, and through an open gate. Armed men, stationed on either side, stood with weapons ready. Shots echoed through the morning.

Tyler touched his ear-mic and listened intently. "Trouble. Unexpected visitors at the jumper craft."

Arien glanced in the rear view mirror. "At least the men following us didn't make it through the gates. Sure glad the RewFaaran soldiers are on our side. Take us to the repair hanger."

Circling the perimeter of the jumper port, Gorda pulled into a huge domed building. A woman rushed forward, her brimmed hat pulled low on her forehead. She opened the back door. "We got the cargo, Arien. You take care of the guests."

Esta climbed out. Charid scrambled after her. The woman grabbed his hand and strode toward the back of the hanger. Once inside, she released him and removed the beaked cap. "Good to see you, Esta."

Esta gasped. "Camilyn! Never expected to see you on RewFaar."

The woman's pleasant expression hardened. "Didn't ever expect to leave El Stroma. Life's changing."

Charid tugged Camilyn's pants. "Do I know you?"

She replaced the cap. "Nope, but I know you, Charid Darine. Never thought to see ya though." She touched the com-mic in her ear and frowned. "Gotta go!"

Hurrying after her, they exited through a side door and climbed into the front seat of a black air-van. The engine hummed as they raced in the direction of a bullet-shaped craft outlined by glowing lights and an occasional burst of vapor.

Camilyn started to slow. "When I stop, get out and up the ramp as fast as you can. Take care of yourselves." The truck braked to a halt.

Esta jumped to the ground and helped Charid. Arien and two armed men surrounded them. Arien hustled her ahead of him, picked up Charid and sprinted up the ramp at her heels. The two men followed. At the top, a man ushered them to a bank of seats by a row of windows. The door closed.

Arien sat next to Charid. "Welcome aboard. Lift-off is about to happen."

Charid, bursting with excitement, could hardly sit still. "Will it hurt? Are we safe? Did you have to fight?"

Arien's eyes sparkled with understanding. "Calm down, soldier. I'll answer your questions once we're airborne." He finished strapping him in. "I suggest you look out the window while you can. Once we lift-off, they'll close until we prepare to land at our first jump port." He checked Esta's seat straps. "You may feel a bit lightheaded, Esta, but it won't last."

Lights flashed. A cloud of steam obscured the outer world. The craft lifted straight up. The steam cleared. On the ground below, two men were being escorted into a car. The jumper port grew smaller and smaller.

Arien glanced at Charid. "Here we go, Private Darine. Hold steady."

Window covers snapped into place. The thrust of the craft through the atmosphere pressed them against their seats. Charid covered his ears and closed his eyes.

When the pressure eased, Esta felt a moment of wooziness, then sighed. "Are we safe?"

Arien unfastened his seat straps. "You two unstrap and relax. I need to check in with the captain, and then we'll talk."

When he returned, he sank onto his seat. "Captain says we'll make one stop and two jumps before we reach our destination."

Charid wrinkled his nose. "What's a jump, sir?"

Arien smiled. "While we're on the jumper, you may call me Arien. I'll let you know if we need to be soldiers again."

"Being a soldier makes me feel a lot braver." Charid squared his shoulders and looked at Esta. "I will always take care of you, Momee. I will be your soldier forever and ever."

Esta ruffled his hair. "I am so lucky, Charid. Thank you. Shall we ask Arien the questions we discussed?"

Charid nodded. "Why is this called a jumper craft?"

Arien relaxed in his seat. "A jumper is a ship built to travel through the Universe using special places in space called portal holes. The 'holes' create a short cut from one destination point to another. The short cut is called a jump. It decreases travel time from sun cycles to moments."

"What happens if you take the wrong portal hole?"

"You end up someplace you didn't expect to be and many not be able to return from. The captain has to pay close attention to the course he selects, so we don't get lost."

Tyler walked up to them. "How about a tour, Private?"

Charid looked at Esta. "May I, Momee?"

"Of course, you may. Thank you, Tyler." She watched them go and sighed. "I'm going to miss him when I return to El Stroma."

"So you've made up you mind?"

"I have, but I need to make sure Charid is safe and well cared for. I know you're headed back soon. Will I have another chance if I stay longer?"

"Let's get you to your new home, and then we can decide what's next."

She ignored her growing fatigue. "I saw bigger jumper crafts at the shuttle port. Is this one special?"

A small dimple near the corner of his mouth deepened. "The RewFaaran government gave *Liberty* to the Vasrosi to help us save our people. It's more compact size allows us to land in places not equipped to handle a big ship. When we reach Persow, your new home, *Liberty* will land in a field in a remote and unpopulated area. We'll slip in and slip out. Only those who have volunteered to help will even know we've been there."

"Persow." Esta liked the sound of it. "Have you been there before?"

"I made the contacts there and found the family who will, with your approval, take on the role of protectors for Charid."

A spark of concern flared. Esta studied the tanned face of the man opposite her. The expression remained relaxed and earnest. "How much do they know about him?"

"They know he is important to our people, but little else. I'll share more about them when we reach Persow. I feel certain you'll like them, Esta."

She squelched her concern. Arien had proved he was trustworthy. "How many planets have you visited?"

He stroked his chin. "Five or six. Those closest to the Décussate."

"Do you have a favorite?"

"Roahymn. It reminds me of home. As soon as I can, I plan to settle there." His expression softened. "I met a woman, an Eleo Predan, who's waiting for me. We plan to marry." He gave her a crooked smile. "Any other questions?"

She considered asking him more about her, but sensed it would be an intrusion. Instead, she returned the focus of the conversation to the present. "What happened after you left us with Camilyn?"

He pressed his lips together and leaned his forearms on his knees. "You know a Klutarse and a SorTech managed to board *Meti Chala II*. When we arrived in RewFaar, they met a group hired by the Rompeer to help them. The Klutarse felt certain Charid was the boy he was after and sent his men to watch for him and for you. They gave chase. What they don't know is if you actually left on the jump craft. The RewFaaran's working with us, made sure it appeared this jumper was leaving on a military mission."

"What if they let the Klutarse and the SorTech go? What then?"

"RewFaaran laws are strict. They forbid magic, sorcery, or mysticism of any kind. The planet is controlled by the military. Their soldiers are the best trained in the Clenaba Rolas Solar System. They don't take kindly to trained killers or what they classify as magicians from other world invading theirs. I don't know what they will do with the Klutarse and his sidekick or the RewFaarans who helped them. The thing I know for sure: the RewFaaran government is supportive of the Vasrosi and our cause. They consider genocide a crime against all humanity."

Esta covered her mouth to hide a yawn. "I'm sorry, Arien. It's been a long time since I slept a full night."

He stood. "I'll show you to your quarters. They're not as luxurious as those on the Meti Chala II, but they do have a bed."

"What about Charid?"

"Don't worry about him. We'll keep him occupied. He's as safe as he's been in quite some time."

After he left her, Esta undressed and crawled into her bunk. *I forgot to ask how long until we reach our destination.* She yawned. *I wonder what Persow is like?*

30

Time on the jumper craft passed quickly. Before she knew it, Esta stood at the top of the ramp looking at yet another new world. Persow, small and undistinguished, resided in a four planet solar system near the Décussate, the boundary between the Inner and Outer Universe. Arien had told her it was primarily agricultural. The village of Scitym was the largest population center on the planet. Persow's ocean provided for a small fishing industry. Villagers and farmers traded back and forth, bartering for what they needed.

Charid joined her. "Arien told me this is Persow. It's our new home. Isn't it beautiful!"

Esta surveyed a landscape composed of pine forests to the one side and farmland to the other. "It reminds me of where I grew up."

He grabbed her hand. "Come on, Momee. I want to see more. Arien is coming with us. We're going to a farm." He urged her down the ramp. At the bottom, he let go of her hand, jumped to the ground, and twirled to face her, his arms wide and his expression brimming with joy. "We are home! We are home!" He inhaled a huge breath and threw his arms around her.

She laughed as he pulled her off the ramp. *How strange to stand on solid ground after so long in a ship.*

Charid ran to where Arien waited with two horses. "Do we get to ride?"

The man laughed. "We do. This is Patch." He patted a horse with large white splotches on its seal brown hide. "And this is Streek."

Charid held out his hand to a chestnut horse with a white streak on one side. The animal sniffed it and snorted.

Esta put an arm around her charge. "I think Streek likes you, Charid."

"I like him, too." He turned to Arien. "Please can I ride Streek?"

Arien shrugged. "Don't see why not." He climbed into the saddle and reached for his hand. "Put your foot in the stirrup. I'll pull you up behind me."

Esta, grateful for the pants and boots she had been given to replace the RewFaaran uniform, spoke to Patch in a soft voice, gripped the reins, and mounted.

Arien grinned. "You ride?"

"Of course. Everyone at home learns to ride when they're younger than Charid. I've missed it since moving to Tahellive."

She looked back at the ship. Tyler stood, framed in the doorway.

Charid waved. "Bye, Tyler. Come visit if you can." He wrapped his arms around Arien. "I'm ready, Arien."

The ride through fields and trees soothed the tension accumulated in Esta's mind and body from sun cycles on the run. Patch proved to be calm and easy to handle. Esta felt a kinship...partnership with her mount...that reminded her of being on El QuilTran before the RomPeer's soldiers invaded.

Mid-turning they trotted onto a narrow track beside a river and slowed to an easy walk. The sounds of rushing water, the occasional bird, and trees rustling in a soft breeze lulled her into memories. *Katareen...Daar...Kuparak... where are you? Mylos? Have you rescued Rayn?*

Arien stopped, dismounted, and helped Charid down.

"Momee, we're almost there." Charid's voice brought her attention back to Persow, to the small boy who thought of her as his maman.

Patch stopped beside Streek and dropped her head to nibble tender green shoots. Esta jumped to the ground.

Charid grabbed her hand, pulled her to the river's bank, and pointed. "Look. See the bridge. After we cross it, we're almost home. Arien says the village nearby is called Geela. I can't wait!" He pranced back to Arien. "Can we go now?"

Arien rummaged through a saddle bag and produced three packets of nuts and dried fruit. "Momee and I need a break. Let's have a snack and rest. Then we'll go meet the Perskee family."

Charid took his packet and wandered to the river bank.

Arien tied the horses to a bush and joined Esta on a fallen log. "You look different."

She crunched a nut. "Different?"

"Younger, less harried. I think Persow is good for you."

She savored a piece of fruit before replying. "I'm not on the run, right?"

He nodded.

"That's what agrees with me. Tell me about the Perskee family. Do they have children?"

Arien watched Charid pitching stones in the river. "They're about your age and have been joined for several sun cycles. One of the reasons they are eager to adopt Charid is their inability to have children of their own. They're good, honest people. Mont has a passion for agriculture and animal husbandry. Their farm is well-kept and well-managed. Catha is a teacher in the village school and a local mystic. You'll meet them soon. Let the questions wait. I don't want to color your perceptions with mine." He stood up and brushed off his pants. "Ready to go, Charid?"

The eager child scrambled up the bank and ran to Arien. "Oh yes. Can I ride in front this time?"

Arien laughed. "You bet." He untied Streek, helped Charid up, and mounted behind him. With a soft click of his tongue, he urged the piebald into an ambling walk.

Esta stroked Patch's neck, put foot in the stirrup, and threw her leg over the horse's back. She listened intently. No one pursued them. Patch lifted her head, gave a soft whinny, and followed Streek along the narrow track to the bridge. When they reached the far side, pine trees gave way to cultivated fields in the midst of which sat a house and outbuildings surrounded by deciduous trees.

Arien led them along a well-used trail. As they drew nearer the house, the door flew open. A woman ran across the porch and down the steps. A man hurried from an out building and joined her. Streek flipped his tail and broke into a trot. Patch nickered and picked up her pace.

Esta smiled at the petite woman who rubbed Patch's nose and then grabbed her reins while Esta dismounted. The man, almost as petite as his mate, helped Charid down and steadied Streek for Arien. At first no one spoke. Catha beamed when Charid offered his hand.

"I'm Charid Darine. I love your horses."

She took his small hand between hers. "I'm Catha Perskee." She grinned "And I love them too." She released his hand drew her mate to her side. "This is Mont."

After introductions, Mont, Arien, and Charid led the horses to the barn to be unsaddled, groomed, and fed. Catha gave Esta a tour of the rambling two-story house. They ended up in the homey kitchen where, she fixed steaming cups of Persowan duckberry tea and sat down at the table opposite Esta.

"I know your true name is Floree. Do I call you that, or would you prefer Esta?"

"For Charid's sake we'd better stick with Esta or Esta Mae. Floree may trigger memories and..." She hesitated.

Catha nodded. "Arien told us parts of his story. He said you would provide us with the details you feel are important." She poured more tea and cradled the cup between her hands. Staring into the steam, she blew. The amorphous cloud shifted to form a wolf, shifted again to a galee, and evaporated. "When Charid's hand touched mine, I sensed the depth of his knowledge. If you choose to leave him with us, I will make sure he is trained in the arts of DiMensionery." She put her mug on the table. "Shall we join the men? They are done grooming the horses."

Esta rose with her. "You're telepathic."

Her hostess smiled. "Persowans use telepathy to communicate with people they know and care about. We are a small but magical planet. You and Charid will fit right in."

The next morning, Arien returned to the jumper with the promise he would return in six moon cycles.

Charid watched him go with a knowing smile. "When he comes back, you will leave me, won't you Momee?"

They walked to the small garden Catha had cultivated near the edge of the fields. Sitting in the midst of blue horns and yellow knots, she clasped his hands, let the rush of emotion rising at the thought of leaving him ebb, and exhaled. "If you and I decide you will be happy here, I want to return to our home planet. I don't want to leave you, Charid, but you cannot go where I must go."

Mobile features expressed his mixed emotions. He withdrew his hands and sketched a pattern in the dirt.

Esta looked closer. "SaHal's mystic insignia…"

He nodded. "I do not remember much of my life before *Meti Chala II*. I do remember a girl telling me, my grandsire's knowledge would reemerge when I was safe." He brushed away all traces of the pattern. "I'm safe here. Mont and Catha will take care of me." He knee-walked to her side and kissed her cheek. "Don't worry, I won't ever forget you." His brow creased and smoothed. "Someday when I remember, I'll know your real name." He hugged her. "I love you, Momee."

The turnings flew by. Esta shared much of Charid's story with Mont and Catha. Some things she left undisclosed…the things that would endanger them or others.

One morning, Catha joined her on the porch swing. "I don't believe the necklace is safe here. We have an ancient mystic who resides in the mountains north of here. I encourage you to entrust it to her care."

An image of a waterfall amidst shimmering rainbows formed in Esta's mind. "Its magnificent. How will I find it?"

"I suggest you shape shift and fly a straight line from here north to the back of Rainbow Gorge. Gloryum will meet you there. She will let me know when Charid is ready, and I'll take him to meet her."

Esta did not question Catha's wisdom. Following midday meal, she shifted and flew to the gorge. Gloryum awaited her arrival, took the necklace and a poem Esta had written, and placed them in a small wooden box. They spoke long into the night of many things. When Esta flew back to the farm at dawn, any doubts she might have had about returning to El Stroma were gone. Charid would be safe with the Perskee. Someday, he would become a VarTerel. She knew he would achieve his destiny. Pursuing her destiny must now become her focus.

Two moon cycles later, Arien arrived at the farm. Supper that night, though merry, contained an undercurrent of anticipation. The next morning Charid bid her good-bye.

He hugged her and whispered, "Remember, I will never forget you, Momee." He shook Arien's hand. "Take good care of her. And thank you for finding Catha and Mont for me."

Arien shook the hand. "You stay safe."

Mont rode with them to the field where the jumper craft waited. He dismounted and hugged Esta. "Thank you for giving Catha and me the gift of parenting. We love Charid. I promise to protect him with my life." He shook Arien's hand, placed his foot in the stirrup, and swung into the saddle. Leading Patch and Streek, he urged his horse into a gallop and headed back to the farm, his wife, and his son.

Arien brushed a tear from her cheek. "What do you think, Floree, should we go home?"

She pulled her gaze from Mont's disappearing form. "Floree..." She inhaled. "It's been a long time since anyone called me by my real name." Thoughts focused on the future, she boarded the jumper craft and began the journey back to El Stroma.

The Persowan moon, a shimmering pearlescent ball, hovered above the Perske's farm. Charid slipped down the stairs and out the front door. Walking to the edge of the fields, he let the stillness seep into his soul. He placed a hand on his heart and gazed up at the celestial beauty overhead. *You are out there somewhere, Momee. I remember my promise.*

A moment of dizziness claimed him. Surging memories from another time flooded his mind. His grandsire spoke, whispered his secrets, urged Charid to embrace the moment. A ball of white light filled his vision and exploded into moonbeams. Forêst sat in the field, his eyes bright, his shadow long behind him. Charid started forward. Four paws carried him to his mentor's side. Lifting his head, he howled his delight.

From the upstairs window, Catha squeezed Mont's hand and smiled.

E. Eleebanna

Part 3
Conflict

Ancestral roots hidden deep in the mind
Began to unravel, emerge, and unwind.
Haunted by anger, Rayn's internal strife,
Threatened to last for the rest of her life.

31

Historians write that a time will arrive
When halves of the whole must rejoin to survive.
Uncovering the secret repairs the forsaking;
Returns to the planet the means of remaking.

"Rayn! Rayn!" The words whispering through her brain woke her. A covert gaze searched the room. Nothing moved. Her dormmates slept. So many female children captured as she had been, but none who carried the secrets she carried. Her gaze crept to the empty desk near the door. The matron had long since gone to bed.

She pulled the sheeting under her chin and pretended to sleep. How many times in the past nine sun cycles had dreams of her previous life awakened her, left her shaking with the fear she had spoken the name out loud...spoken what must stay hidden.

Even after so long, the SorTech came twice a moon cycle to question her, to use The Box in the hopes she might drop her guard. Hatred kept it rock firm. She had seen a Rompeer's Klutarse bury his knife in her maman's womb...in the place where she and her birth-mate had gestated, arms around each other. The shock of her maman's murder had left her numb. Better numb, she had learned, than living the emotions.

Soon after they brought her to the children's compound, the SorTech had told her the Klutarse had found and killed *him*——her birth-mate, the one with whom she was destined to save her people, the Eleo Preda."

She squirmed on the narrow bed. The strangeness resting between her legs propelled her thoughts a new direction. Four turnings ago, she had bled the first bleed of womanhood. Most of her dormmates longed for the time when they would become a woman. She did not. Transfer to the ConSortisanes' Communal Residence meant the unthinkable——she must become a consort to Lusktar Rados, *and* she would never be able to sneak away again.

Remembering hammered the walls she had built around her true self. She squeezed her eyes shut. When the SorTech had told her of her birth-mate's death, she had spent turnings in denial. Certain he lived, she tried to runaway, to find someplace safe to do a mind search. She hid in a merchant's wagon. Unaware he carried the Rompeer's possession, he had taken her beyond the walls. She had found time to search for *him*. The merchant lived only long enough to cross the park.

Captured and returned to the compound, she savored the brief knowledge her escape had provided. *He* lived. Guilt *almost* destroyed her joy. She chose to ignore it, to forget the merchant had lost his life because she snuck into his wagon, only to have the guilt resurface the turning her birth-mate's energy signature ended.

It had been a cold turning in Chunarrie, cold and wet and miserable. The matron sat huddled by the fire. The other girls engaged in silent play. She had, as she so often did, slipped away to a little-used lookout in the high wall surrounding the Rompeerial grounds. During one of her solitary sojourns, she had discovered it and the life existing beyond the walls. From this vantage point, several important things had come to her notice, but on this particular turning, she was unaware of anything but the soul deep loss of part of herself. *He* no longer existed. The merchant had died for nothing. And she was alone——bereft of hope and desirous of death.

In that moment of despair, a fleeting mind touch left her gasping. *His* tukoolo perched in a tree nearby. Aquila guarded her. Stuffing the knowledge into her mental fortress, she stole back to the dormitory, curled up on her bed, and slept the light sleep of one who must always be on guard.

On subsequent sojourns, she discovered another from her previous life. He emerged from the shadows: tall, black, and beautiful. Maman had loved him. He had fought for her the turning of her death——killed her killers. Now he stood garbed in the slave garments of the Rompeer, his amber eyes searching the wall.

The morning bell screamed its wake up message. The matron's assistants prowled between the cots, shaking awake anyone unfortunate enough to still be beneath the sheets.

A nurse strode up to Rayn's cot and yanked the covers away. "It's time to check your bleed, Mari."

Expressionless, Rayn scuffed her feet over the tile floor, kept her mind blank, and stared unseeing at the dormitory wall. Remaining unreadable, she had learned early in her stay, also meant she was often unseen. Since her arrival, she had neither spoken nor let her captors know she could hear, thus allowing her attention to remain fixed on the fortress in her mind. She smiled inwardly. Assuming her deafness to be a reality, others spoke in front of her——shared important information——dropped tidbits she could use to her benefit.

The nurse grabbed her arm. "Stop shuffling." She gave her a shake. "You are the most frustrating girl. How do they expect to train an imbecile to be anything other than a kitchen wench is a mystery." Half dragging her, the woman propelled her into a small room across the hall. The short examination revealed the end of her bleed.

The nurse's grim expression softened. "Tomorrow you will no longer be my responsibility. If you could hear, I would tell you some things to ease your journey." She returned her to the dormitory, regarded her for her a long moment, and sighed. "Poor Mari. I wonder what will become of you?"

Quiet footsteps retreated.

Refusing to think of herself as Mari or poor, Rayn glared at the nurse's back. *Soon I will be no one's responsibility, and no one will call me poor Mari ever again.*

The turning passed like thick honey dripping from the comb. Breakfast, sewing, music, drawing, midday meal, study time, evening meal dragged by. Bells chimed the beginning of each new time circle until at last a reverberating song announced the end of the turning.

Rayn lay on her cot, pulled the pillow over her head, and pretended to sleep. The distant chiming of middle night nudged her to move. A peek informed her the young nursing assistant at Matron's desk slept. Inching the pillow beneath the sheeting, she slid to the floor and molded it's lumpiness into the shape of a body.

Tummy to floor, she slid under one cot, and then the next until she lay a short distance from the door. The nurse straightened and survey the dorm. A wide-mouthed yawn ended in a relaxed slump against the chair. Eyelids drooped. Head nodded. The nurse jerked awake, yawned again and, pillowing her head on folded arms, gave in to sleep.

Beneath the cot, the desire to run for it made Rayn's legs twitch. Forcing herself to remain motionless, she listened for the single chime which tolled on the circle plus half. The nurse snored. The chime sounded.

Crawling to the open door, she crept into the hall and achieved standing in one silent movement. Unheard and unseen, she made her way to the lookout. On the far side of the park, the man from her other life waited, just as he had waited every night since they first made eye contact. In an instant, her mind filled with his message and went blank.

Removing a brick from the floor, she withdrew a pair of dark pants and a shirt, rubber-soled shoes, and a man's close-fitting cap. A grim smile almost made an appearance. She had learned of the loose brick and the hiding place beneath it because the gardeners ignored the deaf, mute girl from the children's residence. The clothing came her way in a similar fashion. A conversation heard by a child who could not hear.

Scrambling out of her night dress, she stuffed it in the recess, pulled on the pants and shirt, and shoved her feet into the shoes. With deft movements, she tucked her long, dark hair under the cap. Mind blanked, she crept from the lookout.

Night stillness hung over the grounds. Guards patrolled. An occasional figure strolled. One shadow skulked from tree to tree, from building to building. A soft whistle stopped her. Her gazed traveled the trees lining the wide drive.

"I'm here." An arm's length away, amber eyes in an ebony face studied her. "Don't speak or think. SorTech close."

He turned and sprinted away from the drive. Using her excitement to overcome her unforeseen trepidation, she followed. The Rompeer's garden opened in front of them. Without a backward glance, the man dodged onto a narrow path, trotted across a stretch of manicured lawn, and circumvented a small building. As she rounded the corner, he shaped a smoky galee and soared over the wall. She stopped. Stifling a startled cry, she accepted Aquila's tether and shifted form. Strong galee wings lifted her domeward, over the wall, away from those she hated. Aquila flanked her to one side; a smoky galee to the other. A fourth galee took the lead. Diving over the lip of the mesa, it glided downward, swooped over a lake, and landed in human form in the midst of trees on the canyon floor.

She perched on a pine bough, immersed in a rush of memories so poignant she ached. Rethdun's imprint in Aquila's mind battered the walls of her fortress until she thought they might explode.

The man stood beneath her, understanding in his gaze, urgency in his stance. His attention wavered, leaving her wallowing in the lack of it, then returned to wrap her in its protective warmth.

"You can change, Rayn. We were not followed. You're safe."

Tilting her head, she observed him from one galee eye, and then the other.

He touched his chest. "I am Kuparak. I promised your mother I would rescue you and give you this." He withdrew a silver locket from beneath his tunic. Moonstone capturing moonlight shimmered iridescent against his dark palm.

She shifted. Soft sobs trembled on her tongue. Too many memories... Fighting for control, she slammed self-imposed doors and shook her mind free of remembering. A shaky breath filled her lungs. Unfamiliar scents assailed her nostrils. She touched the bark of a tree, broke a piece free, memorized its roughness, its smell, its message of life.

When her humanness took root, she sought the man who had called himself Kuparak. His face, his name, his love for her maman washed over her. She sighed. A silent plea for understanding brought a nod.

"I know you have not spoken since you were captured. You need not speak until you're ready, but we must go. The longer we remain close to Chunarrie, the more at risk we are. Nod if you feel ready to make a longer flight."

She licked her lips and whispered, "Rayn." Surprise held her momentarily silent. She shivered and gripped the piece of bark until her palm stung with the bite of it. "I...Am...Rayn."

He smiled and nodded. "You are Rayn." Removing the necklace from around his neck, he offer it.

Her brow creased. She tried to find the words, shook her head, and pointed at him.

"You want me to keep it?"

Internal silence formed an answer, lathered her tongue with sounds, and finally shaped them into words. "You...keep."

He tucked it away. "It's yours when you're ready. We must fly, Rayn. Can you shift?"

Aquila fluttered to the ground beside her. *"Compeer."* It's thought tingled through her mind. Her heart skipped a beat.

Kuparak stepped to her side, touched Aquila's head with one hand, hesitated, and then placed the other on her shoulder. "Rethet Ceerus."

Heat ran the length of her spine, pooled around her heart, and traveled through blood vessels to all parts of her body. A memory jolted to the surface: Kia flying beside her——Kia dead next to her mother's motionless body. Tender threads of love encased the image until it faded into soft nothingness. Rayn knelt beside Aquila, and ran a hand along his glass side. An instant later, she flew beside him with Kuparak leading the way and Toa flying behind.

I am protected. I am free. Relief buoyed her spirits and her galee form. For the first time in nine sun cycles, joy made a brief appearance.

Kuparak felt a touch of surprise at Rayn's level of endurance. Their flight to Cimondeli lasted from well past middle night until mid-morning. When they glided to a landing at the base of the cliff face, he observed her slight stagger as she shifted to Human. Instinct kept him still.

Fatigue shook her slight frame. Her gaze flicked to the cliffs and back to him. Her brow raised.

"We are at the Cliffs of Cimondeli. You were born here. When you are ready, we will enter the safe haven."

"Ready?"

Her telepathic question caught him off guard. *"Do you understand me?"*

Surprise registered in her face. *"Yes. What?"*

"Telepathy. The connection you have with Aquila is a form of it."

An unexpected smile brought her remarkable beauty to life. She touched her lips, traced their curve, and laughed, a soft, self-conscious sound. A serious expression replaced her delight. *"Who here?"*

Kuparak watched her closely. "Daar and Katareen, your mother's brother and sister; Awinta, the Serveero of the safe haven; the families of other Vasrosi who work to save our people."

She seemed to shrink. *"So many."*

"Awinta has arranged a private place for you. You are important to everyone here. They understand you need time to adjust."

She stared at the cliff face, seemed to analyze her choices, and sighed. *"I am ready."* A shaking hand reached out. *"I..."* She shook her head. *"Tell them...not touch..."* The hand pressed against her heart.

"You prefer not to be touched. Correct?"

Shyness shaped her nodded response.

"I understand. I'll tell Awinta to inform everyone." Giving Rayn time to prepare to face new people, he sent a quick telepathic message. "Shift and we'll get you to a safe place where you can rest."

Side by side, they soared upward, circled the top of the cliffs and glided into a well-hidden crevice that carried them to a circular space lit with glow lamps. An older woman rose. He landed and shifted. Aquila alighted on a flattened rock. Rayn fluttered to her tukoolo's side, studied the Serveero of Cliff Haven, and jumped to the ground. Disorientation accompanied her shift. He stepped to her side. She steadied. Confusion morphed to curiosity.

Awinta did not move but observed her guest with quiet respect. "Welcome to Cimondeli, Rayn Jaradee Palmira. I celebrate your rescue. I imagine you're tired. Are you comfortable coming with me on your own or would you prefer to have Kup join us?"

Kuparak recognized the fleeting hesitation of a trapped animal. "I will accompany you. When Rayn is comfortable, I can inform the others of her presence."

A tentative 'thank you' whispered in his mind.

32

Rayn lay on a mat on the floor of an alcove carved in the wall of the haven——an alcove hidden from view by a sturdy screen and occupied by only one person——an alcove from which she could come and go at will. The strangeness of it, both thrilling and unnerving, held her motionless. She tried to keep her mind blank, to stay focused in this new moment in this new place. But memories came unbidden.

Rethdun flying with her the last time they were together; vague impressions of goats, of digging in a garden; giggling when she and her birth-mate destroyed their rock fort on the shores of a river——

New memories crashed against her inner fortress. She rolled on her side and covered her head with her arms.

Cold water drenched her small bird body. Currents sucked her beneath the water. Talons gripped her, carried her, placed her on the ground. Consciousness fled. Rethdun's call to awaken...seeing him from strelke eyes. She trembled and curled into a ball. *Her outburst when her mother refused to go with her to find her birth-mate...*

A torrent of guilt and self blame pounded her. Dragging her body upright, she hugged her knees to her chest. *I killed Maman. I ran away. If I'd stayed with her, she would be alive and Rethdun would be with us. Instead, they are dead.*

Tears splattered her arms. A hand flew to her cheek. She licked the salty wetness from her palm and gripped a handful of hair. *I'm crying.* She scrubbed the tears from her cheeks and lay down, staring at the stone wall. *I do not cry. No one will ever see me cry again. No one will know what I am thinking or feeling. No one will hurt me ever, ever again.*

A shadow darkened the screen. She pretend to sleep. Soft footsteps drifted away, leaving her alone with the private most parts of her psyche, the parts that would remain secret forever.

R ayn awoke sometime later to the sounds of stifled laughter. Tiptoeing toward the sound, she stopped to one side of a roughed-out opening. Four young people gathered around a fire. A girl a few years her senior tossed a ball from hand to hand. A gawky, angular boy kept trying to catch it. Brushing wavy, russet hair back from her face, the girl tossed the ball in the air. The boy lunged forward, made an awkward grab, and knocked it away. It rolled to a stop not far from Rayn's feet. Giggling, they scrambled after it. The girl reached for it, saw the feet, and looked up.

"Who are you?"

Rayn contemplated running but held her ground.

The boy hauled his friend to her feet. "It's *you*, right? The girl everyone is talking about." His curiosity bubbled around him.

The girl nudge him aside. "Don't mind Vygel. He's always rude. I'm Rasiana. Don't be shy. No one here will hurt you. The fire is lovely. Come and get warm."

Grabbing Vygel's arm, she propelled him back toward their friends.

Rayn took a tentative step, contemplated a quick retreat, and took another step.

Rasiana patted a spot next to her. "Join us."

A boy called out. "I'm Drue and this is my sister Dyna, we're fraternal twins...kinda like birth-mates but..."

An elbow in his ribs shut him up. His sister shook her head. "Boys, do say the dumbest things. Please, we were just about to go to dinner."

Panic caught Rayn unawares. She curled trembling fingers into fists and looked away.

Dyna jumped to her feet. "I bet we could bring it in here, so you don't have to meet everyone at once. Shall I ask?"

Rayn let out a soft breath and nodded.

Dyna grabbed Drue by the arm. "Let's go. You can help me carry the trays."

Grumbling about bossy sisters, he scrambled after her.

Rayn sat next to Rasiana, staring into the fire. Vygel sprawled across from her. "Tell us about..."

Rasiana shot him a warning look. "You don't have to tell us anything unless you want to, Rayn. People will ask because they're curious, but we all understand you need time to adjust."

Dyna and Drue entering with two trays created a welcome distraction. While her companions ate, engaged in light-hearted teasing, and burst into spontaneous laughter, Rayn kept her eyes on her plate and nibbled at the food. A stab of envy caught her by surprise. *I wish I had the courage to join...maybe someday.*

Overwhelming shyness propelled her to standing. Conversation ceased. All eyes turned her direction. Heat flooded her face. Stammering a whispered thank you, she fled.

In *her* quiet space, she flopped down on the mat and buried her head in trembling hands. *Will I ever feel safe with other people? At least in the Children's Residence no one expected me to join in. Here——*

The whisper of bare feet on stone stopped at her entryway. Rasiana peeked around the screen. "May I come in?"

Her gentle calm eased Rayn's tumultuous emotions. "Please."

Sitting cross-legged opposite her, Rasiana pressed her palms together. "I know how hard this is for you." A hand fluttered to her throat. "I was kidnapped by the Pheet Adole when I was three. Unlike you, they placed me in the children's sector of the servants' residence to train as a kitchen aid." Memory captured her.

Rayn regarded her with interest...tawny nutmeg skin; dark, wavy hair; eyes reminiscent of Kuparak...She struggled to speak.

Rasiana encouraged her with a small smile.

"You." Rayn looked around. "Here?"

"When I turned six moon cycles, the residential matron took four of us to the market place, where we were to be placed on the auction block. I waited until the auction began and snuck away. A man with a black, curly beard caught me. I was so frightened I couldn't move. I thought he would take me back. Instead, he hid me in a wagon along with Dyna and Drue. We were taken to a safe haven in the foot hills and then brought here. We are the lucky ones...you and I; Vygel and the twins. Many children remain in captivity." Her shoulders drooped. A tear dripped. She sighed and looked at Rayn. "I want to be your friend. Even though I wasn't there as long, I still know how it feels to be free after time in captivity. Let me help."

The alcove, quiet but for their soft breathing, soothed Rayn's agitation. She studied the Eleo Predan girl, did a quick mind touch, and found no sign of deceit.

"She's telling the truth, Rayn."

The voice from the entrance yanked her gaze from Rasiana to a woman waiting just outside. Rayn sought Rasiana and saw only warmth and trust. She shaped a silent word...'Who?'

Rasiana smiled. "This is your mother's sister, Katareen. Can she come in?"

Although the woman remained in the tunnel, Rayn felt her calm and something else she did not recognize. Curiosity canceled her angst. She nodded.

Katareen sat next to Rasiana. Rayn studied the porcelain skin, large, honey-gold eyes, and raven-black hair of the Thornlandian Eleo Preda. She recognized the gentleness so like her mother's in her aunt's expression but not the stronger emotion flowing out to her.

"Love." The beautiful features brightened. "What you are feeling from me is my love for you; my gratitude that you are at last here among us; my delight that we will get to know each other."

Rayn searched her fortress. She found a faint memory, reached for its source, and lost it in the chaos of overwhelming loss. The walls slamming into place left her panting. She glanced at the woman. A tender tingling invaded her mind.

"Use telepathy."

Rayn drew in a breath. *"What...love?"*

Her mother's sister folded pale hands in her lap and smiled. "Love is the deep tenderness and affection we feel for someone else: a sister, a friend, a parent, one's tukoolo..."

"Birth-mate?"

She nodded. "Yes. Birth-mates."

"Rasiana?"

Katareen put an arm around Rasiana. "I love Rasiana. She is gentle and caring. If you decide to let her be your friend, she will never abandon or betray you."

Rayn thought hard. Since her capture, no one had befriended her. Solitary and alone, she had navigated her life in the Residence. She licked her lips and wrapped her tongue around the letters R-a-s-i-a-n-a. Taking a breath, she whispered, "Rasiana...friend."

Tears slipped down Rasiana's cheeks. "Rayn...friend."

A rush of emotion left Rayn smiling. She looked at her mother's sister. *"You friend?"*

Katareen nodded. "You are my niece. You are my older sister's child. I was with your maman at your birth. I held you after you took your first breath. You are part of me, and I am part of you. Yes, I am your friend, but I am also your family."

Rayn hugged herself. *"So much..."*

Katareen rose. "You're tired. Rest. Rasiana and I will visit tomorrow."

Rayn reached out and touched her new friend's knee. Surprise made her blink, then smile. "Rasiana, stay?"

"Of course, I'll stay, but I'll need to get my sleeping mat."

"Katareen moved to the entrance. "I'll have Drue or Vygel bring it. Do you need anything else?"

"Not for now. Thank you."

Whenever Rayn woke on her first restless night in Cimondeli, Rasiana sat by her side. She whispered assurances of Rayn's safety, and then sang Eleo Predan lullabies to soothe her back to sleep. The next few turnings, much like the first, allowed her to get her bearings. Rasiana and Katareen helped her to speak with more confidence and introduced her one by one to other residents of the haven.

Several turnings after her arrival, Vygel, Drue, and Dyna offered to show her around Cliff Haven while Rasiana fulfilled her time commitment in the nursery. A winding passage worn smooth by many feet took them to the bottom of a stairway. Soon they stood on a catwalk surrounding the upper most level of the cliff dwellings.

Rayn viewed the large area with interest. Although the turning had only begun,Vasrosi practiced combat maneuvers in groups and one on one. At the opposite end of the space, swords and knives flashed as men and women worked to perfect their skills.

Transfixed, Rayn watched the flash of metal against metal. The world blurred. The training grounds faded.

Run, Rayn! Run! Her mother's scream chased her into the trees, away from the bad men, away…She slammed into a hard body. Rough hands seized her; lifted her. A soldier's leering features mocked her. Attempts to squirm free only increased the strength of his hold. She went slack. He relaxed. She bit his arm, fell from his loosened grip, and dropped to the ground.

Scrambling to recover her footing, she tried to run. He snatched her up, flung her over his shoulder, and marched back toward his comrades.

Her mother's scream pierced the air. A Tukoolo's screech ended abruptly. Rayn pounded her captors back with small, frantic fists. "Maman. Maman!" She wiggled and kicked until he set her down. His iron grip on her arm sent pain thrumming through her. A slap in the face knocked her to sitting, her head spinning. He jerked her to her feet and dragged her into the clearing.

A man dressed in black and purple knelt over her mother. Blood dripped from her mouth. A dagger protruded from her stomach. Screams of terrified rage burst from the deepest part of Rayn's soul. Again and again, they cut through the night. Again and again——

A hand clapped over her mouth suffocated the sound, shoved it down her throat, kept breath at bay until she sagged to her knees and collapsed. The last thing she saw… Kia, her beautiful Tukoolo, deflated of life, shards of crystalline glass scattered around it.

A distant voice called her name. She blinked and swallowed a sob. Rasiana knelt beside her prone body. Vygel, Dyna, and Drue huddled further along the catwalk.

Rasiana's fingers brushing her cheek sent relief rushing through her. The memory faded. Numbed sorrow fled beyond her inner wall.

"Can you sit?"

Rayn stared up at her friend and reached for her hand.

A short time later, Rayn and Rasiana reclined on their sleeping mats in Rayn's special alcove. The walk from the top level had given her time to sort through what had occurred. She regarded her friend.

"How did you..."

"I felt you. I came as fast as I could." Rasiana sat up. "Can you tell me what happened?"

Rayn slumped against the wall. Tracing the pattern on the woven coverlet, she gathered the words to describe her experience. "The knives reminded me..." She rubbed a palm against her forehead, dropped her hand in her lap, and stared at the screen above her friend's head. "Mamam was killed by a Rompeerial Klutarse. I was only four, but I remember it as though it happened yesterday." A desire to cry, to release the pain, almost overwhelmed her.

"It's alright to cry, Rayn." Rasiana's calm voice held no hint of criticism. "I won't tell anyone. And it might help."

Rayn straightened her spine and growled through clenched teeth. "No one will ever see me cry again. No one. Not even you. Please go."

Rasiana made no protest. She simply rose and rolled up her mat. "If you need me, use telepathy. I'll be here."

The alcove, empty of her presence for the first time, set Rayn's nerves jingling. Anger pushed away the unexpected vulnerability. Sprawling on her back, she scrunched the coverlet into fisted hands. "I will *not* let knives or soldiers or the Klutarse frighten me." Something deep inside her stirred. "I *will* become the toughest and best Vasrosi warrior in all of El Stroma."

—

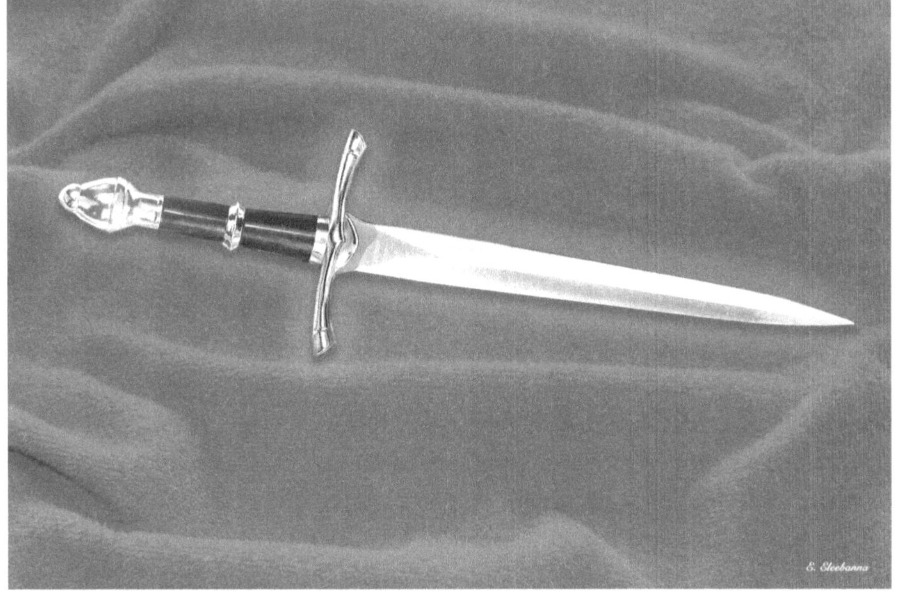

33

Three sun cycles passed quickly. Rayn studied hard and trained even harder. The knife became her weapon of choice although she liked the Pheet Adolan crossbow almost as much. Classes in mapmaking provided her with an understanding of El Stroma's two main continents. She took classes in the language of her birth, learned about the customs of Thornland and Charnland, and grew to love and understand the Eleo Preda and their diverse cultures.

The knowledge that the Rompeer had sent soldiers to El QuilTran to murder her people stoked a fire in her belly, which grew hotter with each passing moon cycle.

One turning following her lesson on Thornlandian Dialects, Awinta waited for her in the passageway. They strolled toward the Serveero's personal enclosure, chatting about happenings in Cliff Haven. Outside her quarters, Awinta paused.

"Last night visitors arrived from Chunarrie. They are here to see you."

Dread weighted Rayn's legs. Her lungs emptied. She forced herself to breathe...to calm the fear. "Who are they?"

The Serveero's smile broadened. "They are people who were important to you in your early cycles. Shall we go in?"

Rayn bit her lip. "You go first."

Awinta preceded her.

Taking a moment to rein in her nervousness, Rayn stepped into the welcoming enclosure.

A blonde woman reclined in a chair. Beside her, a tall man with a curly, black beard peppered with gray rested a protective hand on her shoulder.

Rayn's heart skipped a beat.

The woman rose, blue eyes glistening with tears.

A hornet's nest of remembering buzzed around Rayn's brain. She took a tentative step, looked at the man, and tried to speak. Took another step. A hand reached out. Two names escaped in a husky whisper. "Uncle My. Aunt Floree."

The woman gave a hiccuped sob and hurried to take her hand. "Rayn, I never thought I would see you again. I..."

Mylos walked to Floree's side and put an arm around her. His scarred brow arched. "You are as beautiful as your mother, Rayn."

"I am?" She sighed. "I miss her. I missed you when you left, and I miss my birth-mate." Sudden hope made her stammer. "They t-t-told me he's d-d-dead."

Tears welled up in her aunt's eyes. The hope died.

Floree opened her arms. Rayn moved into them, felt them close around her, let her head rest on Floree's shoulder, and sobbed.

Awinta and Mylos stepped into the passageway. Floree drew Rayn down beside her on a hand-made bench. When the sobs abated, Rayn brushed a hand across her cheek. "I promised myself I would never let anyone see me cry." She sniffed.

Floree dried her cheeks on a sleeve. "Crying is not a weakness. For women it is the gift. It keeps us strong. Tears wash away the things that hurt us."

Picking at a loose thread on the cushion, Rayn shivered. "They make me feel vulnerable."

"I understand, but how do you feel now? Are you as sad?"

"No. But I think it is because you're here. Why did you not come sooner?"

Mylos appeared in the entryway. "May I come in?"

Rayn nodded.

He moved a chair next to Floree. "For your safety and the safety of all those at Cimondeli, we could not come sooner. All Vasrosi who have come to the notice of Lusktar Rados are watched. Kuparak let us know you were safe with Awinta, so we maintained a self-imposed distance."

Floree touched her knee. "Can you forgive us?"

Rayn savored the warmth of her aunt's hand. "You are here now, that's what matters." She grew pensive. "I have so many questions."

Soon they were sharing memories and stories. Floree described the house where the birth-mates were raised. Mylos talked about her mother and how much she loved her children. She answered questions about the Children's Residence and asked them about their lives. When they talked, she listened and watched. Something in the way Mylos looked at Floree caught her attention.

"Uncle My, you love Aunt Floree."

He laughed. "I do."

Floree squeezed his hand. "Awinta did a ceremony of joining for us about the time you were rescued." She touched her belly. "Soon we will have a child."

Mylos cleared his throat. "Which brings us to why we made the journey to see you."

Rayn looked from one to the other. "You're leaving El Stroma." The words sounded flat and lifeless.

Floree glanced at Mylos. He took the lead.

"We don't want our child to grow up in a war zone. As much as we love, El QuilTran and the lives we lived there..." His jaw tightened. "Our home no longer exists. The Rompeer's soldiers have destroyed almost every town and village. Farms are decimated and live stock slaughtered. Those few areas still undamaged are home to the Pheet Adole. Eleo Predans hide in the mountains with no hope of their lives returning to normal. Many are leaving."

"What about Kuparak? Will he go, too?"

"No. He remains on El Stroma." Mylos tugged at his beard. "He has assumed the position of Vasrosi leader."

Floree inhaled an audible breath. "We are here to ask you to come with us. Our plan is to cross the DéCussate and make our way to Tao Spirian in the

Clenaba Rolas solar system. You would be a sister to our child. You would be safe. What do you think?"

Rayn stared at the stone floor. Desire and logic jostled in her mind. Her heart screamed to go; her brain yelled stay. Panted breaths brought her thoughts to a standstill. Interlacing her fingers, she pressed her palms together and slowed her breathing.

"I cannot leave El Stroma. The Eleo Preda are being massacred. I am almost ready to join the fight." She licked her lips. "Momee died to save me. Rethdun is gone. It is up to me to help save our people."

Floree sagged against her partner. "Mylos felt certain that would be your decision, but I wanted to ask. I wanted you to have the opportunity to come if it felt right to you."

"Thank you for making the journey, Aunt Floree. Seeing you means a lot."

Mylos looked curious. "Awinta tells me you are one of the best fighters in the haven. What's your favorite weapon?"

"I am good with a knife, but I love the Pheet Adolan crossbow, the one they developed for the Klutarse."

He whistled. "I've seen 'em, but never had the chance to use one? You have one here?"

Awinta stood in the entry with Vygel. "We have managed to acquire a couple. Vygel, why don't you and Mylos go and have a look at the crossbow, while I speak with Floree and Rayn."

The boy's face lit up. Mylos winked at Awinta and followed him into the passageway.

Awinta pulled Mylos' chair closer. "Since you cannot shape shift, Floree, I have arranged for horses to take you to VenTra——"

Rayn let her thoughts drift their own direction. Memories, washed out and tattered by time, came and went. *Do we truly remember distant events or do we make up stories to match our needs in the moment? I had vague memories of the house.* She hugged herself. *Aunt Floree helped me to remember it better. I remember being happy there with Floree and Momee and Rethdun. Then it ended...the happiness and life as I knew it.* A flood of fragmented images crowded her mind. *Too many——* She shoved them away and opened her eyes to find Floree and Awinta watching her.

The next two turnings flew by. Rayn and Mylos fought practice matches with knives and swords and shot the crossbow. Rasiana played the drums and Rayn performed the choreographed patterns of EriaCapo with her martial arts instructor. For the first time since her rescue, she relaxed her guard and enjoyed the company of others.

Too soon, the time of parting arrived. Floree embraced her and made her promise to take care of herself. Mylos touched his heart in salute to a fellow warrior and gave her a cloth-wrapped package. "This is from Kuparak. He asked me to deliver it. He will be visiting Cimondeli soon, but wanted you to have this now."

"What is it?"

He laughed. "Open it, Rayn, or you will never know."

She unwrapped the fabric covering and held up a long knife in a leather scabbard with a plain metal throat and tip. Withdrawing the blade, she caught her breath. "I've never owned my own weapon. Thank you, Mylos. Please tell Kuparak I am honored."

"You can tell him yourself when he comes. Use it well, daughter of Jaradee." He bowed.

She followed suit, strapped on the scabbard, and slipped the blade into place.

Floree, her expression solemn, also touched her heart and bowed. "Savior of the Eleo Preda live long and with honor."

Awinta entered the common area. "Kuparak sent word. You must leave now. Rompeerial soldiers are headed for Ven'Tra. It's vital you reach the space port before they arrive."

Vygel strode into the enclosure. "The horses are waiting at the cliff top."

Everyone filed after him up the well-worn passage and emerged into the coolness of early morning. Another round of goodbyes and Floree and Mylos mounted, wheeled their horses in the direction of Ven'Tra, and galloped away in a cloud of rust-colored dust.

Heart aching, Rayn watched them go. She turned to her companions. "I need some time with Aquila. I'll meet you in the dining area in awhile."

Awinta gave her a quick hug. "Take your time." She herded Vygel and Rasiana ahead of her into the narrow crevice that served as an opening to the cliff top.

Rayn scanned the dome. Like all Tukoolo, Aquila remained outside on constant guard duty. Even after so long, she yearned to have her compeer with her.

The rustle of wings brought a wave of delight. Aquila landed beside her. Their tether formed. They flew upward, made a wide circle, and soared in the direction Mylos and Floree had taken. The temptation to fly after them, to tell them she had changed her mind flared and fizzled. Instead, she flew beside her compeer until the sunlight began to fade, and then landed on the cliff top and watched the sun set over the mountains.

Time outside acted like salve in a wound. The ache in her heart lessened. She stood and brushed the dust from her pants. *At least I got to spend time with you.* She touched the knife at her side. *And I received a special gift.*

Rayn unsheathed the knife and gripped the handle. A tear leaked. She touched it with a finger, then touched the blade. "No more tears until the Pheet Adole have been defeated." Resheathing it, she hurried to join Rasiana in the dining area.

When at last the turning waned and the sleep cycle arrived, Rayn slipped the knife in its scabbard under her pillow and stretched out on her mat. The visit of Mylos and Floree had changed her. The ceiling blurred. Rasiana and Vygel cared about her. Katareen loved her as family. Others in the haven respected her for who she was and for her skills as a fighter. Awinta regarded her with affection. But Mylos and Floree were her heart family. They had helped to raise her. They had protected her and Rethdun with their lives. Whether they stayed on El Stroma or traveled to the Inner Universe, they would always love her and she them.

She reached under her pillow and fingered the belt buckle. A surge of emotion carried her to sitting, the scabbard in hand. Hugging it to her chest, she sat in the tomb-like silence of night in the haven and made a decision, one she had been dancing around for sometime. Rightness flowed through her. With the knife beside her, she slept.

—

34

Morning dawned outside the haven with wind in the trees and the threat of rain. Inside, members of Vasrosi stirred, preparing to begin their turning. Torches sprang to light. The smells of breakfast cooking wafted through the warren of passages.

Rayn woke, dressed, and headed for the dining area. Some time later, she walked into a makeshift classroom and counted heads. Twelve Vasrosi, a mix of adults and older children, awaited her arrival. She stopped in front of them and in the language of the Pheet Adole welcomed them to class. The next time circle passed quickly. By the end, everyone could speak several short sentences, sentences designed to keep them safe were they caught by soldiers of the Rompeer.

"Please practice until you can speak the enemies words without thinking. In our next class, we will learn to express more complex ideas. Be prepare to share any questions you may have when we next meet."

After they left, she stood in the quiet of the empty space, and thought back to those first difficult moon cycles. She couldn't help but compare the girl of thirteen who had arrived at the haven trapped in a cloak of self imposed silence to the young woman of sixteen who comfortably entered a room full of students and took charge.

Heading back to her alcove, she pulled the scabbard from under her pillow and sank cross-legged onto the mat. Withdrawing the knife, she balanced it on her palm and reviewed her decision of the night before, felt the correctness of it, and buckled on her weapon. *It is time.*

She arrived at the entry to Awinta's quarters to find the elder Vasrosi waiting to usher her inside.

Awinta sank on to a chair. "I believe you have something important to say?"

Rayn rubbed her palm along the length of the sheathed knife. "It is time for me to join the fight against the Rompeer. I can stay hidden no longer."

Awinta pursed her lips. "What do you intend to do? Where do you intend to go?"

"I will go to Chunarrie and fight for our people."

The Serveero's demeanor steeled. "I believe we must be circumspect, Rayn. Lusktar Rados continues to offer a sizable reward for your capture. Your anonymity must be preserved as long as possible."

"But I want to fight. I am ready, Awinta."

The Haven Serveero glanced toward the door. Kuparak walked into the space.

Awinta hurried forward. "It is good to see you, Vasrosi leader. It has been far too long since you graced the haven with your presence."

Kuparak took her offered hand, lifted it to his lips, and smiled his radiant smile. "You look wonderful. It is good to see you as well." He released the hand. "Would it be possible to have a bite to eat?"

"I'll see what I can find. How long will you be here?"

"Not long."

As soon as the Haven Serveero had gone, Rayn jumped to her feet. "I will not be held captive here, Kup. You can't make me stay." She squared her shoulders and lifted her chin.

Kuparak straddled a chair. "Sit down, Rayn. I did not say you had to stay at Cimondeli. However, we cannot allow you to jump into the thick of battle with no experience but the practice ring. You will not be going to Chunarrie."

Muttering under her breath, she slouched on her chair. "You can't tell me what to do." Arms folded across her chest, she glare beneath half-closed lids.

Twinkling amber eyes met hers. "You remind me of your Uncle Daar at your age...Stubborn...quick tempered..." He folded his arms and stuck out his bottom lip. "And pouty."

Unable to help herself, Rayn laughed. "Alright, Chunarrie is out, at least for now." She stroked the scabbard at her hip. "Thank you for the knife, Kuparak."

"Mylos tells me you fight with a knife better than most older warriors. What made you select it?"

She drew the blade from the sheath and examined it with focused attention. "I remember Momee with a knife buried in her belly." She sucked in a breath. "You were there! You killed the soldiers! You———" She shook her head in disbelief.

"I sent you to the Rompeer. Why do you think I did so?"

Rayn braked an angry retort and swallowed. Her quick mind checked off several reasons for his decision. One kept leap frogging to the head of the line.

"You knew I would be safest there."

"I knew an attempt to hide you would have brought the Klutarse and the Rompeerial guard down Vasrosi throats quicker than a lightening strike. I wanted you safe; and I wanted the Vasrosi to have the ability to continue its work."

"I understand. But how could you trust a Klutarse to take me to the Rompeer?"

Kuparak's features hardened into a sculpted ebony mask. "*He* had killed your mother. A source inside the Rompeerial guard had informed me their orders were to find and bring you, Rethdun, and your mother back alive. Lusktar Rados is an unforgiving man. The Klutarse knew my training as an Animilero. When I told him if you were hurt in any way he would slit his own throat, he did not question the truth of it."

"What did you do to him?"

"When I rendered him unconscious so I could free your mother, I placed an hypnotic suggestion in his subconscious."

Rayn rubbed the metal tip of the scabbard. "You told me never to speak a word, didn't you?"

"By the time I had taken care of the other soldiers, you were numb with shock and terror. I knew your safety depended on your silence, so I placed the suggestion in your mind before I sent you with the Klutarse."

"I want to be an Animilero. Teach me."

"You do not know what you ask. It is not an easy journey or a short one; and we have little time."

"If you cannot teach me, who can?"

"How old are you?'

"Almost seventeen sun cycles."

Kuparak rose, repositioned the chair to face her, and sat down. "We'll talk more later."

Awinta hurried into the enclosure, carrying a laden tray. "You are anxious to leave, Kup, but you must eat before you go." She placed the tray on a low table next to him.

After several mouthfuls, he looked from the Serveero to Rayn. "I am taking Rayn with me. I doubt she'll be back."

A gasp from the passageway preceded the shuffling of feet and a muffled expletive.

"Rasiana and Vygel, come in here now." Kuparak's command gave no room for disobedience.

The two eavesdroppers entered. Vygel hesitated by the entry. Rasiana walked straight to Kuparak. "If Rayn is going with you, so am I."

Implacable and forbidding, the full force of his personality created a barrier between them. She didn't blink or flinch.

Rayn squirmed on her chair. "Kuparak, please let her come. She is my first friend and…"

Awinat shook her head. Rayn shut her mouth and waited.

"How much of our *private* conversation did you hear?"

Rasiana answered. "We heard you tell Awinta, Rayn is going with you and might not be back."

Kuparak looked at Vygel. "How old are you?"

The angular face reddened; the bulgy eyes widened. "Twelve sun cycles, sir."

"And you, Rasiana?"

"I'm twenty-one."

"Hmmmm."

Kuparak washed down the last of his meal with a mug of water, which he continued to cup in his hands. "Vygel, you will stay here. You *will* work hard in all your classes. You will be Awinta's helper. When *she* decides you are ready, I will come back for you. You *will* forget the conversation you heard. Tell no one Rayn..." He paused, took a sip from the mug, and placed it carefully on the table. "...and Rasiana have gone with me. Do I make myself clear?"

"You do sir, but I want to go with you."

Kuparak stood. "Sometimes life does not give us what we want." He turned to Rasiana. "You have a Tukoolo."

She grinned. "Yes, it is an El Stroman whak. I call her Oha for friend. Thank you, Kuparak, for taking me."

"Don't thank me. The journey will be difficult. The place I am taking you won't be easy either. I understand you have a gift for healing. Is that correct?"

"It is."

"Good. We will be traveling light. Wear layers. I'll meet you here in one half a circle."

Rayn clasped Rasiana's hand and pulled her into the passageway. "Where do you think he's taking us?"

"I guess we'll find out when we get there. I'm hungry. You?"

"Yep. Better eat while we can."

Rasiana hurried toward the kitchen. Rayn followed, her thoughts in a whirlwind. *I'm to be trained as an Animilero...I know it.*

Rayn met Rasiana at Awinta's enclosure a half circle later. When they entered, the Serveero knelt in front of a small fire pit feeding twigs to the dancing flames. Rasiana moved to her side and assisted her to standing.

"Thank you, Rasiana. I will miss your instinctive understanding." She held out a hand to Rayn. "And you my dear...I will miss your eagerness to learn and your quickness." She released her hand as Kuparak entered.

He gave the Serveero a quick hug. "Thank you for all you do and will do. I'll check in when I can. Daar is in charge of the Vasrosi while I am away."

Awinta nodded. "You will be gone how long?"

"I'll be back when I'm back. Come girls, we have a long way to go."

Awinta led them through a short passage and across a wide, dim expanse. Behind a natural barrier, a narrow opening the height of the average man looked over the rugged cliff face to the trees beyond. She hugged Rasiana. "Take care of our girl."

Rasiana kissed her cheek. "I promise."

Awinta's attention focused on Rayn. "You have not yet seen the carnage of warfare. When you do, don't allow it to taint your spirit."

Rayn accepted her words and her embrace with a strained smile. "Thank you for all you have done for me. Please tell Katareen good-bye. Tell her I will never forget her."

Vygel dashed around the barrier and ran straight to Rayn. "I wanted to say good-bye. I'll work hard. When Awinta says I'm ready, I promise to find you and to fight at your side."

Rayn touch her heart with a fisted hand and bowed. "It will be an honor to fight at your side, Vygel Vintrusie."

Vygel grinned, hugged Rasiana, and bowed to Kuparak.

The Vasrosi leader placed hands on the boy's shoulders. "Help Awinta keep Cimondeli safe." He stepped away, shifted, and shot through the opening, his black and silver feathers gleaming.

Rasiana and Oha soared after him. Rayn embraced her galee form and flew into the filtered light of mid-turning.

Clouds scattered across the dome intermittently obscured the sun and her companions. Pinning her attention on Kuparak's smoky galee, she abandoned herself to the joy of flight. Although she had flown often since her rescue, she had only traveled short distances. Kup had said little about their destination accept that it was a long distance away. *Where are you taking us?*

Aquila sailed higher, disappeared through a dragonesque cloud formation, and tugged at her mentally to hurry. Fog-white dampness closed in around her. Catching a sudden updraft, she shot from lambent gloom into bright sunlight. A glance to the side gave her a glimpse of Rasiana and her tukoolo. Above her, two smoky galee circled higher and higher, reached an apex, and dove. Black and silver bodies gleamed in the sunlight one moment and disappeared beyond a misty curtain the next.

Aquila soared upward. Two red-tailed whaks flanked Rayn. Leaving the bright sun behind, they broke through the clouds. A grass-bordered beach stretched in both directions below them. Two smoky galee landed. Kuparak searched the dome then scanned the shoreline.

Rayn came to rest beside him, caught her breath, and bent to touch the foaming edge of a breaking wave.

Rasiana materialized beside her. "Oh my."

"It is the Dirredaca Seâ." Kuparak looked grim. "Catch your breath. We must cross it before Alkina reaches perigee. Six birds together in flight inspire curiosity in the light of the turning, but six at night will bring the brotico." He searched the wide stretch of knee-high beach grass. "We need water. I saw a stream from the air. Spread out. Let's see if we can find it."

The sound of the water against the shore, the dampness of the sea breeze, and a nagging disquiet accompanied Rayn through the grass. Wet earth gripped her boots then let go with a soft sucking sound. A sea bird shot upward, the warning of a nest nearby in its squawk and whistle. Rayn altered course, cutting a diagonal toward the splashing song of water over rocks.

"Found the stream!"

She knelt and cupped her hands. Cold water dripped between her fingers, washed the dryness from her tongue and throat, and left her revitalized and refreshed. Straightening, her eyes level with the top of the grass, she froze. Kuparak and Rasiana had disappeared. An unfamiliar sound overhead flattened her to the ground.

Three brotico flew wide circles over the beach. She inched away from the stream and into the taller grass. *"SorTech,"* her compeer warned. A tether eased into place. Rayn became grass and mud.

Grateful for the dusky dimness creeping over the landscape, she pressed her ear to the ground. Two human heart beats intermingled with the many life forms inhabiting the beach.

The winged men swooped overhead. Two landed a short distance upstream. The third brotico shot further along the beach.

The rhythmic pounding of horses at a full gallop vibrated the ground and sent tremors through Rayn's body. Suppressing the urge to run, she sank deeper into her connection with Aquila.

A scream washed the beach in terror. A second, cut short, left the unuttered sound strangling in the turning's end.

Two horsemen slowed opposite the spot where Rayn had knelt and forded the stream. Luck obscured her presence but not Rasiana's. A fourth brotico dropped from the dome. The soldiers dismounted. The temptation to rise and fight died a quick death. Rayn smothered her fear in earth and matted sea grass and observed the action playing out through the images Aquila placed in her mind.

Whispered orders sent two brotico into flight. The riders remounted. One settled Rasiana's limp body in front of him, and, at a signal from his comrade, trotted after him into the pre-moon duskiness.

35

The rising moon had crested the distant mountain tops by the time the two brotico took flight, their black wings melting into the gloom of early evening.

Rayn's tether to Aquila released. One limb at a time, full consciousness returned from mud and grass to awareness of her human body. Tiny pin prickles raced over her skin. She started to rise. A hand on her shoulder kept her prone.

Kuparak leaned close to her ear. "Crawl upstream. Shallow ravine ahead." He crept by her.

She wiggled forward on her belly until her fingertips found water. On hands and knees, she made her way upstream.

Dyad's cool light soaked the landscape by the time the flatness of grass and sand transitioned to the ravine where Kuparak sat, ebony skin shining and amber eyes soaked with moonlight. Rayn almost smiled.

He beckoned.

Scrabbling up the bank, she sat next to him. "We have to rescue Rasiana." The quiver in her soft words made her angry."

Kuparak's intense stare turned her direction. "Toa is in touch with Rasiana's tukoolo. The Pheet Adole have hidden her near the outskirts of Port Saticch. Do you think you're ready for what might be a tough encounter? The Rompeer's men are well-trained and much more experienced than you."

Rayn fingered the handle of her knife. "It's past time to test my skills. What better cause to fight for?"

Kuparak's chosen route to Port Saticch carried them along the water's edge. The incoming tide chased the waves higher up the beach to soak the tidelands and return in a repeated pattern...a large wave, four smaller ones, and a large one again. Near the outskirts of the the seaside town, he landed in a junkyard filled with old farm equipment, ancient cars, and wrecked boats.

Aquila descended and perched on the metal roof of what might once have been an office. Toa remained airborne, a solitary silhouette against the blue moon.

Stooped low, Kuparak led the way between rubbish heaps to an opening in the fence and dropped to a knee. Rayn squatted beside him.

"Oha senses her in the house on the far side of the vineyard. Keep your wits about you, and do exactly what I tell you. Toa says two brotico patrol the area. If we get separated, hide in the junkyard. I'll find you."

Quieting the accelerated beat of her heart, she nodded.

A zigzagged path brought them to the fence bordering the vineyard. Kuparak clipped three wires closest to the ground and pushed them aside. On his belly, he shimmied through the gap, climbed to his feet, and motioned her to stay. Umbra-like, he slinked between trellised-rows of vines heavy with fruit. He flashed from sight.

Rayn smothered the desire to disobey, inhaled a quiet breath, and bit down on her lip. The next instant, he knelt at the end of the first row of trellises motioning her to follow. Throat tightened against unexpected fear, she shimmied under the fence and dodged after him.

The large farmhouse, shadowed by the trees surrounding it, stood at the center of a wide, overgrown yard. A rutted driveway wiggled a circuitous path through calf-high grass and ended to one side of the house. A single light cast an eerie glow over the back porch. Blank windows stared, dark and ominous, across the moonlit expanse.

A stocky, balding man in the uniform of a ranking officer stepped onto the porch and whistled. Kuparak gripped Rayn's arm and pulled her lower. Two soldiers jogged around the corner of the house. One remained by the steps. The other joined his commander on the porch.

The officer's quiet words floated across the clearing. "SorTech in place?"

"All secure."

Waving both soldiers inside, he scanned the clearing one final time. After a moment of intense listening, he pivoted and followed. The small light blinked out.

Kuparak's grip continued to bite into her arm. The message——*be still*. At last, his hand relaxed. He pointed at her, and then around the house to the left. He pointed at himself and to the right. A whisper rustled her hair. "Look around. Meet me on the opposite side. Questions?" The spot where he had been emptied before she could utter a response.

Wishing she had already trained as an Animilero, Rayn slipped from bush to bush along the front of the yard and them dodged to a rough-trunked sycama. Aquila's quiet presence in her mind helped to calm her anxiety. She wiped her hands on the seat of her pants and gripped the handle of her knife. A cloud shrouded the moon and blacked out the clearing. Dashing to the house, she pressed against the rough planking and sidestepped her way to the corner. Nothing stirred. Pitch-black camouflaged her presence. She searched the area for a good place to hide. A tree at the edge of the drive caught her eye. Hunching low, she ran. Midway to the tree, the clouds parted. Dyad's blue light illuminated the night.

A soldier stepped from the bushes, his unsheathed knife glinting in the moonlight. A slow smile, made all the more frightening by its lack of warmth, exposed uneven white teeth then vanished into a threatening sneer.

Rayn held herself steady, her gaze fixed on his face. Her mind clicked into defense mode. Her fighter's instincts heightened.

He closed the gap between them. She danced from side to side. His fist shot out and met only air as she pivoted toward the shadow of the trees. He dropped to a predatory crouched. Dominant hand free, she spun around. He lunged. The palm of her hand connected with his nose. His head snapped back. A yelp...A stumble...Kuparak darted from the trees behind him. A black hand found the man's mouth. The gleam of silver flashed across his throat. A soft sucking sound and he slumped against Kuparak's chest.

The Vasrosi leader dragged the man into the trees and lowered him to the ground. Rayn looked at him. "He's dead?"

"He is." Kuparak put a finger to his lips. He pulled her behind a tree. "Oha and Toa head this way. Where's Aquila?"

"Near." She shivered. "SorTechory—— Wait." The tingling faded. She dropped to her knees and peered toward the house.

Rasiana wiggled through a basement window on the near side and scrambled to her feet. Aquila whistled. She started to run. A soldier yanked the front door wide, bound down the steps, and sprinted after her.

A whak streaked from the trees, extended talons aiming for his face. Rayn started to rise. Kuparak shoved her lower. "Hide." They mustn't know you're here."

Two long, loping strides brought him to the soldier's side as the whak's talon's raked his cheek. The man yelped and flung up a protective arm. Kuparak moved in.

Rasiana reached the trees. Rayn grabbed her hand and pulled her in the direction of the junkyard. With a hunter's stealth, they circumvented the vineyard and came to a stop in the dark shadow of the office hut. High overhead a brotico circled.

Rayn shot a look at her friend. Rasiana, doubled over and gulping in air, raised her head. "I'm fine." She scanned the dome. "Better hide."

Rayn sought her tuckoloo. It flew from a tree, circled over the yard, and landed. A quick image shot through her mind. "Aquila found a hiding place."

Rasiana gulped in another breathe. "You go first, Rayn."

"Not leaving you."

The older girl straightened. "Then follow me."

Dodging from one junk pile to the next, they reached a narrow opening between a wagon bed and a mangled piece of farm equipment, where the tukoolo perched. Rasiana paused, listening.

Crawling beneath a broken wagon wheel, Rayn peered past the crushed cab of the tractor. A soft scraping sound made her pause.

"No one followed."

Rayn's head flipped around. Rasiana knelt next to her. "Da'am, you're quiet, Rasi."

"I pulled a broken barrel in front of the opening. Better move. Oha signaled trouble."

Rayn scrambled under jagged metal and splintered boards to a hollow under the wagon seat.

A moment later, Rasiana touched her arm. "I'm here."

Huddled next to each other, they strained to locate their stalkers. When only night sounds penetrated to their hideout, Rasiana rested her head on bent knees. Rayn tethered to Aquila and searched for Kuparak. He and Toa seemed to have vanished.

Rasiana stirred. "Can't find Kup. Do you think they have him?"

"No. I think he led them away from us. When it's safe, he'll be in touch."

"What if he doesn't come back?"

Rayn tried to see your friend's face in the dimness. "He will. Our tuckoloo will warn us of danger. Tell me how you got away."

Once again, Rasiana rested her head on her knees. When she finally looked up, she tucked her hair behind her ears, stared straight ahead. "Are you sure you want to know?"

Rayn merely waited.

"They brought me to the farmhouse and dumped me on the floor in the basement. I feigned unconsciousness and waited. After they went upstairs, I explored and discovered barrels piled beneath the window. I had just jimmied the lock when I heard footsteps overhead. Since they found the knife in my boot, I grabbed a brick, and lay back down.

A soldier clumped down the stairs and rolled me onto my back. He straddled my hips, smoothed my hair back, and licked my face." Her nostrils flared. "I did not move. He got up and peered up the stairs. When no one appeared, he unfastened his britches and let them drop. I came to my feet with the brick in hand and hit him as hard as I could on the back of the head." She hugged herself. "He staggered, tripped on his pants, and fell. The side of his face slammed into a step."

A shudder jolted her shoulders. "He thought I was still unconscious and he could do with me what he pleased." Another shudder. "I grabbed his knife. I thought I could kill him but..." She grew silent and then continued. "Instead, I made a quick exit through the window."

Staring ahead, she said, "I have never killed another Human. I couldn't do it, Rayn." She shuddered. "We aren't in the safe haven anymore. I hope you're ready to kill." Soundless sobs shook her.

Anger rose in Rayn's throat, anger so all-encompassing she thought she would strangle. Her world blurred. A rush of rage stunned her. Grappling to regain her composure, she put an arm around her friend. *I will make them pay...for my mother, for Rasiana, and for our people. Clutching the handle of her weapon, she glared into the darkening face of her fury.*

When Rasiana at last fell into an exhausted sleep, Rayn tethered to Aquila. Her compeer showed her two brotico flying away and the junkyard quiet but for the occasional rat scurrying from one heap to the other.

She rested her head against the rough boards of the wagon and analyzed what had just happened. Never had she experienced that depth of anger. To exhausted to think, she dozed.

Cold night air whispering through the cracks and crannies of the junk pile roused her. A smothered sound close by left her wide awake and alert. *Animal or Human?* Aquila hadn't warned her. *Where are you?* A tingle of SorTechory racing up her neck answered the question.

"Rasi."

The urgent whisper woke her friend. "Wh..."

Subdued voices penetrated the night silence. "I'm telling you she's in this yard."

"We've looked everywhere. If she were here, we'd o' found 'er." The words dripped with sarcasm. "You really know how to work that——"

A muffled thud vibrated the wagon and then the ground. "Ya, I know how to work it."

The careful tread of one pair of feet moved away. The tingle of SorTechory intensified. Rayn blanked her mind.

A moan, the scrape of movement against the wagon bed, and a muttered curse reverberated through the confined space. The wagon creaked. Feet shuffling against littered ground ended abruptly. An uneasy hush settled over the junkyard. Moments later the tingling ended.

A wha wha wha of wings passed overhead. Rayn clutched Rasiana's arm. A whak whistled. Aquila's presence filled Rayn's mind. She relaxed.

"We're safe. Time to go."

Rasiana moved. "I'll make sure we're clear. Only come out if Aquila confirms I'm alright." She didn't wait for a reply but crawled into the debris-constructed tunnel.

Rayn edged nearer the opening, anxiety making her fidget. Aquila's *all clear* sent her creeping into the monotoned hues of early morning.

From the circle of Kuparak's arm, Rasiana gave her a wan smile. "We are safe."

Rayn rose from all fours. "Are they all dead?" The question lacked any emotion.

Her hard tone raised Kuparak's brows. He released Rasiana. "If you truly wish to train as an Animilero, Rayn, you must learn the value of all life. We only kill when there is no other way."

His words as gentle as the hand resting on her shoulder brought a rush of heat to her face.

He moved away. "We must go. The flight across the Dirredaca Seâ will be a long one."

Toa flew into view. Kuparak shifted and shot domeward. Rasiana changed to whak and joined Oha on the rusted cab.

Rayn stared after the smoky galee. "I'm glad they're dead." Shaking herself, she frowned. *Now where did that come from?*

Aquila's tether tingled in her mind. Sighing, she shifted and soared upward with two whaks in her wake.

36

From a great height, Rayn absorbed the immensity of the open sea; from skimming above the rolling surface, its tremendous power. Galee, whak, and sea birds soared together. Gigantic fish launched from the water, sailed through air, and splashed back into their home amidst spray and mist and sparkling water droplets.

The sun painting clouds, horizon, and water vivid shades of teal, fuchsia, and middle-night blue ushered them to a landing on a small, tree-covered island at the center of an archipelago.

Rasiana's feet touched down and her knees gave way. Kuparak's hand on her elbow helped her to stabilize. Rayn landed next to them, conquered her touch of dizziness, and absorbed her humanness. She savored the smell of the sea, the touch of a breeze in her hair, and the sound of waves on the shore. The sight of the surrounding islands silhouetted against the brilliance of the setting sun left her breathless.

"I have never seen anything quite this stunning. The water…the dome…the colors…" She smiled up at Kuparak.

Sadness tinged his irises sooty gold. "El Stroma is a planet of much diversity and beauty. I hope Lusktar Rados and his lust for power do not destroy it."

Leading them beneath low-hung, leaf-laden branches, he stopped beside a spring trickling over a weather-worn outcropping of beige and orange rock into a shallow pool. "Drink up, and then we sleep. In the morning, we'll forage for food."

Thirst quenched and tired beyond measure, Rayn sat with her back against a tree and stared up at the stars sprinkling the night dome. "How far did we travel today, Kup?"

"We're about halfway to our destination."

"You gonna tell where we're going?"

White teeth gleamed in the fading light. "To the Isle of Osullini."

Rasiana flicked a bug off her pants. "I've heard it said Osullini is a desolate place…flat and barren as a sandbar. Why there?"

"I believe you will find it far from barren, but we shall see." He rolled onto his side. "Rest. Tomorrow will be another long turning."

T he sun had not yet shed its welcoming light on the archipelago when Kuparak shook Rayn awake. She groaned, sat up, and glared at the first hint of morning hues accenting the distant horizon line. "Hard ground doesn't make for restful sleep." Stiff legs made her grumble. "Feel like an old lady."

Kuparak laughed. "Stop complaining. It's going be a beautiful day."

She shot him a dirty look and knelt by the spring. Muttering under her breath, she washed her face, swished the dryness from her mouth, and moved aside to let Rasiana do the same.

Kuparak offered her a handful of small hard buds. "Eat these and then we'll see if we can find some shellfish on the beach."

Popping a bud in her mouth, she sank to the ground and bit down. Sour puckered her mouth even as sweetness washed her tongue with flavor. "What are these? They taste great."

"The natives of Thornland call them bay buds. They're from a tree with wide, leathery leaves which can be found bordering the beaches of northern El Quil'Tran. It grows well in sandy soil and can handle the heavy winds and seas of winter." He finished his handful. "Time to move."

Rayn and Rasiana trailed after him to the water's edge. A gentle wave broke and receded. He dug his fingers into the sand. When he pulled them free, he held up a thumb-sized shellfish. "This is a beach cockle. It's edible raw and has lots of nutrients. Watch for bubbles on the sand when the water flows out. Dig directly under the bubble. Gather enough for breakfast and meet me over by those rocks."

Rayn found the first one. Rasiana found two in quick succession. The hunt became a game. They giggled and laughed; chased each other along the beach; and when they couldn't hold one more cockle, they joined Kuparak on rocks worn smooth by water and time and added the wealth of their gathering to his pile.

"Now what?" Rayn held up a cockle.

Amusement smoothed the wrinkles between his brows. Picking one up, he inserted the tip of a knife between the ridged, pale gray shells, pried them apart, and tipped the contents into his mouth.

"I can do that." Rayn withdrew her knife and popped the shell open. She grimaced. "Are you sure we can eat this?"

Kuparak shrugged. "Eat it or go hungry." He tipped another into his mouth, swallowed, and licked his lips.

Rasiana ate her first one and grinned.

"Alright. I'll give it a try." Rayn tipped up the shell. A cockle slid onto her tongue. She gagged.

Rasiana slapped her on the back. "Bite it and swallow."

"Oh!" A second one and then a third followed. She grinned. "Alright, Kup I love 'em."

More merriment accompanied the meal. When they had eaten the last cockle, Rayn smiled at the shells littering the sand. "I had no idea raw shellfish tasted so good."

Kuparak's smile matched hers. "Glad you like them. Get a drink and take care of your personal needs. We leave in one quart time circle."

The girls headed for the trees, went their separate ways, and met up at the spring. Aquila and Oha perched close by. When Kuparak had rinsed his breakfast down with cool water, he reminded them to stay in close proximity to each other and to him. Shaping his smoky galee, he soared up to meet his tukoolo. Rayn and Rasiana shifted and shot domeward. The long flight to Osullini had begun.

Wing stroke by wing stroke galee and whak covered the long miles. The monotony of blue water meeting the blue dome had begun to wear on Rayn's nerves. Her excitement of yesterday's discoveries faded into the unchanging rhythm of flight, the bright clarity of the turning, and the need for sleep. The sun, the only sign of progress, chased them across the dome, caught them at middle-turning, and outpaced them as it descended to the horizon. Once again, the dome glowed with the atmospheric optics of the turning's demise.

"Descending soon. Stay alert." Kuparak's message jerked her attention into focus.

Far ahead, a phantom-like island stretched its featureless length over the sun-tinted sea. Heady with relief, Rayn flew with renewed vigor. Each wing stroke took on new meaning, carried her closer, enlivened her with the knowledge their destination loomed in range.

Kuparak gave Rayn and Rasiana the order to remain in flight and alighted on the glowing lapis blue sand. Rayn squelched a desire to rebel, to shed her raptor form, to feel her feet on solid ground. *I have to trust him. He knows what we face. I do not.* She repeated the words over and over until calm prevailed. Soaring in yet another circle in the fast dimming light, she studied the size and shape of the Isle of Osullini. Three bays, one on the northwestern side and two on the southeastern coast provide safe harbors for sea going vessels, though she saw none. The island itself did not invite interest. It appeared to be a deserted island with nothing but lapis blue sand streaked with gold.

Aquila flew to her side and hovered. *"Land."*

Banking to bring herself in line with Kuparak's position, she swooped lower. Talons extended, she prepared her mind for the shift to Human. The atmosphere shimmered around her. Sand and sea vanished. Her boot-shod feet touched down on a carpeted floor in a room flickering with candle light. Struggling with the shock of her unforeseen surroundings coupled her shift to Human, she fought to slow her racing heart and to prepare herself for battle.

"Take your time, Rayn Jaradee Palmira. No one will harm you here." The feminine voice held no threat.

Rayn pivoted. Light blue, hazel-speckled eyes regarded her with open interest. The ageless face framed by a riot of graying curls seemed vaguely familiar; the slight smile tantalizing. Prepared for the unexpected, Rayn kept her face and mind blank. "Who are you? Where am I?"

"I am your paternal grandmameen, Keelyn Nashota Viho Palmira. You are on the Isle of Osullini."

"I saw the island from the dome...blue sand...gold beaches...nothing else." She kept her voice soft and steady, even as her emotions scrambled around the word grandmameen.

The woman smiled. "We see what we expect to see, Rayn. Those of us who live here simply reflect the expectation back." She moved with fluid grace to a bench seat beneath a tall, divided window. "Please join me."

Caution held Rayn still. "Where are my companions and my tukoolo?"

Keelyn unlatched the window, pushed it wide, and stepped to one side. Aquila swooped into the room and alighted on the back of a chair. The galee lowered its head, beak to chest, then whistled a long, soft note.

The woman touched her heart. "I honor you, Aquila. Thank you for taking care of the offspring of my son."

Rayn crossed to her tukoolo and ran a hand over its back. "You little traitor."

Aquila made a purring sound and resettled its wings. Rayn scratched its chest and sat down on the window seat.

"Is my father alive?"

Keelyn joined her. "He is not." She sighed. "Like so many of our relations, he was mortally wounded in a battle with the Pheet Adole. When asked by the Vasrosi to donate sperm, he agreed in the hopes that his death would not be in vain. He would be happy and proud to know you, Rayn. You are his legacy and ours. We are grateful to Kuparak for bring you to Osullini."

"We?"

Her grandmameen looked beyond her and smiled.

Rayn swiveled and came to her feet.

A broad-shouldered man of medium height and indiscernible age walked into the room and moved a chair closer. Skin tanned by the sun gleamed in the warm glow of candles and oil lamps placed around the room. Lowering onto the chair, he tilted his head to regard her. "Please sit." Burnished copper eyes filled with the smile curving his generous mouth. "You have a look of your grandmameen. Jacy would be pleased."

"Jacy?" She perched on the edge of the bench.

He rubbed his close cut beard. "Dohata Jacy Palmira. Your father. He preferred to be called Jacy." He lowered his hand to his knee. "Kup says you've asked to train as an Animilero. Why?"

Forcing her rising animosity to subside, she said, "I assume you are my granddah?"

"Arden Dohata Palmira, companion of Keelyn and father of Jacy. I am indeed your granddah." His exaggerated calm flustered her more. "I require an answer to my question, Rayn. Keelyn and I will give you some time to think about it."

Her grandparents left the room. Rayn rubbed trembling fingers through her hair and sworn under her breath. *Maybe Kup's right...I have inherited Daar's bad temper.* She made an agitated circle of the room. It's decor, unassuming yet elegant, gave her the feeling of understated opulence. Gold and burgundy formed a background for splashes of cream and rose. Pausing at the window, she peered at the garden. To one side, the first light of the rising moon illuminated an apple orchard planted in straight, even rows. In the opposite direction, a roiling mist obscured whatever lay beyond.

Rayn sank onto the bench and rested her arms on the window sill. *Why do I want to be an Animilero? More to the point, why does Arden make me so angry?* An image of her granddah formed in her mind...the close cropped gray hair and beard, the eyes with their strange coppery cast...She bit her lip. *If I want to study with him and Keelyn, I'd better get control of my anger.*

A wink of light caught her eye. A quartz crystal glistened on a table at the end of the bench. Sliding nearer, she picked it up. Prismed rainbows shot in all directions, danced on the creamy walls, and vanished when she lowered it. Tracing each side with an index finger, she counted. *Six sides with a centered point. Awinta would call this a generator crystal.*

Fatigue, held at bay by the adrenaline rush of arriving in an unanticipated place and meeting her grandparents, raised its sleepy head. The crystal pulsed in her hand. Warmth spread through her body. She yawned and stretched out on the bench. Holding the crystal next to her heart, she peered at the cool, blue moon hovering outside the window. "Why do I want to be an Animilero?"

37

The smell of smoke and decay woke Rayn to gray mist swirling in serpentine loops over a muted landscape. The screech of scavengers fighting, the only discernible noise, sounded dissident and unreal. She sought the edge of the window seat, found rough ground instead, and lunged to her feet, mist cycloning around her. A quick wave of her hand dispersed it into hazy, drifting wisps.

Vomit rumbled up her esophagus and spewed from her mouth. Dry heaves bent her double. Gasping and coughing, she straighten and wiped her mouth. The stench of death flared her nostrils. A bloodbath of bodies, Human and animal, lay scattered over the ground.

Sidestepping around rotting carcasses, she made her way to the still smoking foundation of what had once been a home. Scorched stones, ember-edged boards, and blackened steps marked a family's grave. A child's broken toy lay on the ground, entangled with a sooty pink ribbon. She bent to pick them up. Her fingers met nothing but air.

Mist boiled into dense smoke, concealed the carnage, and stung her throat. A gradual thinning exposed specter-like forms which wafted in the dissipating haze and solidified. Burnt structures lined two sides of a rubble-strewn street.

Reticent to see more but unable to stop herself, she walked past a blistered post bearing a charred apothecary's sign, a dry goods store where burnt bolts of fabric still smoldered, a market with blackened baskets spilling carbonized food into the street.

A young boy, his head wrapped in a tattered, filthy bandage peered around the corner of a collapsed building. His searching gaze hesitated where she stood. Squinting, he shrugged and skulked back the way he had come. He reappeared supporting an older man, whose battered appearance told a clear tale. A woman with a small child strapped to her chest pulled the man's uninjured arm over her shoulder with one hand and supported him around the back with the other. The rumble of an approaching vehicle prompted a panicked retreat into smoke and haze and what remained of the village.

Rayn jogged across the road and dodge into the shadows. She scowled. *They can't see you, silly. Why are you afraid?*

Two Rompeerial military trucks passing within an arm's length of her hiding place sparked a wave of aversion so powerful it left her shaking. She glared after them. *I hate you.*

Enmity propelled her along the road for a better view. They braked to a stop in front of the sacred hall, the only building left standing. The front doors flew open. Soldiers herded frightened women and children into the street, marched them to the back of a truck, and loaded them into the bed. Huddled together, they peered between boards and the canvas roof.

A soldier closed the hall doors and jogged down the steps. "All clear."

An order was given. The building exploded into flames.

A woman screamed. "You are nothing but murders. How can you roast men alive? Is your god so heinous..."

A soldier caught her by the hair, yanked her around, and slapped her so hard she crumpled and lay unmoving. He jumped from the truck bed, slammed the gate shut, and threw the bolts.

Amidst the crackle and hiss of the raging inferno, the soldiers climbed aboard the second truck. Engines growled to life. The trucks roared out of sight.

Rayn ran toward the hall. The aroma of roasting flesh tainting the air made her gag. A bell's dissonant clang rose above the audible groan of blazing walls. The bell tower trembled in the murky light and collapsed in a flaming heap. A miasma of death rose from the ruins. Wavering specters of men floated over the hall. Their whispered moans escalated into a tortured keening.

Outrage rumbled in her gut, outrage fueled by so much force her knees buckled. Gulping air into lungs squeezed empty, Rayn calmed her pounding heart. Shaking loosened hair back from her face, she rubbed her hands in the burnt grass and with a finger marked her forehead, cheeks, chin, and nose with black.

Thunder crashed and lightening flashed. She came to her feet, threw her head back. Arms raised to the heavens, she yelled above the approaching tempest.

"With the storm gods as my witness, I swear to avenge the deaths of our people and the destruction of our homelands." She lowered her arms and bowed her head as rain pelted down.

Rayn bolted upright. The quartz in her hand throbbed. Alkina's topaz warmth pooled on the windowsill and spilled onto the bench. Uncurling her fingers, she set the crystal in the moonlight and rested her face in her hands.

The tranquility of night on Osullini diluted the horror of her dream, but not the ached in her heart. *I will not forget you or the promise I have made.*

A soft knock preceded her grandparents into the room. Arden held a chair for his companion and pulled his next to her.

Observing them from a new place of understanding, Rayn realized they, too, had experienced the dream. Keelyn's tear-damp eyes reflected her sorrow in their moonlit depths. Her granddah's, gleaming with Alkina's warmth, did not hide the ache in his soul.

He cleared his throat. "Why do wish to become an Animilero?"

"To avenge our people." She picked up the crystal and pressed it between her palms. "I realize, Granddah, that I must release my personal need for revenge if I am to accomplish this as an Animilero."

"Are you able to do that, Rayn Jaradee Palmira? Can you leave revenge behind and allow love for all life to guide you?"

She held the crystal up in the golden light and watched the prisms dance. Cradling it next to her heart, she gave him her answer. "I cannot promise that I will succeed, but promise to do my best."

A smile changed his serious expression to satisfaction. "That is all I can ask of any student, Rayn. If you wish to be an Animilero, we will be proud to teach you."

A smiling Keelyn indicated a door at the end of the room. "I think you might want to clean your face before we invite your friend to join us."

Rayn touched her cheek and stared at the black soot on her finger tips. "This is from the village in the dream. I don't understand."

Her grandmameen hugged her. "Not all questions have an answer. Go, wash your face. Rasiana is anxious to see you."

Rayn's throat tightened. "And Kuparak."

Impenetrability cloaked her granddah. "He's gone, Rayn. He received a message soon after you landed, one important enough for him to depart without seeing you."

"Do you know where..."

Arden stood. "Go wash your face. Your friend waits."

Rayn scowled at her reflection, glimpsed a resemblance to her granddah, and frowned. "Why does he make me so cross?" Pushing the unanswerable question to the back of her mind, she pondered her refection and thought back to her lessons about the indigenous tribes of El QuilTran.

"Charnlandian's paint their faces on feast days and for birth celebrations and spiritual ceremonies and to alert the gods to protect them in battle."

She touched the surface of the mirror, traced the soot black lines, and raised a quizzical brow. "Why did you paint your face, Rayn Jaradee?" Understanding flashed back at her. She squared her shoulders. "I painted my face to show I am willing to fight for my people. I *am* ready."

When Rayn returned to the main room, Rasiana sat alone by the open window. "Where are my grandparents?"

"They have gone to prepare food and to allow us to catch up." She patted the seat beside her. "What happened to you? One moment you were beside me, the next your were gone."

Rayn withdrew the crystal from her pocket and placed it on the sill. Focusing on its glowing iridescence, she shared her story, reliving it one word at a time. With the sound of the bell tower's final moments ringing in her ears, she released a long breath and looked at her friend.

"Oh, Rayn, it must have been awful." Rasiana hugged herself and shuddered.

"It was horrible, but also good. Kuparak told me I wasn't ready to jump into the height of battle in Chunarrie. Of course, I thought I knew better." The young boy's image formed in her mind. Resentment seeped into her tone. "I know nothing about the agony of our people."

Rasiana responded in her gentle unhurried way. "But you do, dear Rayn. You have lost your mother, your birth-mate, and your tuckloo. What you lack is the knowledge to and experience to understand others. That is why we are here, is it not?"

Alkina's light had gradually diminished until the garden and the room were dark, but for one candle. In its flickering light, she observed her friend's beautiful nutmeg skin and long, russet hair. She soaked in her gentleness, even as she recognized the will of steel beneath it.

"That is why I am here. Why are you?"

A laugh filled the room. "Oh, Rayn, do you have to ask? I'm here because I have sworn to fight by your side and to protect you." She grew serious." But most of all, I'm here because I love you as a sister...like the one I lost so long ago."

Rayn clasped Rasiana's hand between hers. "Rasi, I had no idea...I am sorry."

Rasiana looked from their sandwiched hands to Rayn's face. "You have never touch me of your own accord. Thank you."

Releasing her hand, Rayn sat for a time in silence. Calming a rush of emotion, she drew her knees to her chest and wrapped her arms around them. "Tell me what happened to you after I disappeared."

After a long look at the night dome, Rasiana released a soft breath. "I landed next to Kuparak, panicked because you had vanished. When he smiled that knowing smile of his, I knew you must be safe. Abruptly his demeanor changed. Quiescent energy as sharp as the blade of your knife cloaked him. Toa swept over the beach. The next instant two smoky galees streaked across the dome headed toward El SyrTundi. You can imagine my chagrin. The sunset had melted into the soft hues of early evening. A few stars already twinkled over my head."

"What did you do, Rasi. Where you scared?"

She leaned an elbow on the window sill and wrinkled her brow in concentration. "Not really scared. Oha landed close by. You were safe...At least I assumed you were. Kup would not have left me on a deserted island to die. I chose not to panic. Instead, I accepted I was safe also. The moment I released the need to control the situation, the air around me began to undulate and glow. Blue sand and ocean vanished. I stood in a glass house. Long tables covered with planting boxes lined the space.

At one of them, a woman not much older than I placed a handful of herbs in her basket and faced me. "Come, Rasiana, we have much to do. I'm so glad you've arrived." She hurried through a doorway.

"Collecting my scatter wits, I hastened after her along sterile white hallway and into a room lined on both sides with beds——beds full of injured men, women, and children. The woman handed the basket to a girl of perhaps twelve sun cycles and instructed her take them to Granni Aloe. Over her shoulder she instructed me to follow."

Rayn nodded. "Kup did say Osullini was more than it seemed. You were in an infirmary, right?"

"Yes. The woman turned out to be the head healer. Your grandmameen had told her to watch for me. Her name is Ceri. A family had just arrived from the mainland. The boy and the granddah were both wounded. The mother was in a state of shock. Her baby daughter's arm was badly burned. Ceri had been informed of my training as a healer, so we worked on the family together."

"I saw a similar family in my dream." Rayn mused. "They couldn't be the same, could they? After all, it was a dream...not real, right?"

Rasiana stood up. "There's one way to find out."

—

38

Ayoung woman with the blonde hair and fair skin of the full-blooded Thornlandian met them at the infirmary entrance, acknowledged Rayn with a harried smile, and brief and crisp 'welcome to Osullini', and addressed Rasiana.

"I so glad you're here. We have more wounded arriving and our little family is having difficulties. The granddah passed. I could use your help."

Rasiana drew Rayn forward. "We can both help, Ceri. Rayn is not a fully trained healer, but she acquired some excellent care giving skills during her time in Cimondeli."

Ceri led the way along a corridor defined by rows of beds on both sides. At the far end she beckoned Rayn to follow and made her way to a curtained cubicle, where a tearful woman clung to a fussy baby, and a boy snoozed on an infirmary cot.

Rayn gulped down an exclamation of disbelief and tried not to stare.

Ceri checked the boys pulse and turned to his mother. "This is Rayn, Nolee. She'll watch Mati, while you and I take care of the baby's burns."

Nolee sniffed. "I can't leave him. I won't loose him, too."

Rayn controlled a wave of astonishment and knelt in front of the woman she had seen in her dream. "Your little one needs help, and she needs you to be with her. I promise I won't let anything happen to Mati."

The woman pulled a dirty piece of paper from her pocket. "I didn't think you were real. The Rompeer's soldiers have hunted everywhere for you. Every village in El QuilTran has been searched, and when you weren't found, torched and the woman and children taken away."

Rayn accepted the poster, unfolded it, and gasped. Her likeness and the amount of the reward stunned her. "I had no idea people were dying and loosing their homes because of me. I am so——"

The woman shook her head. "Don't be sorry. We know you're going to save our people and barring that you'll find a way to save El QuilTran. Even had you been hiding in our village, no one would have turned you over to the soldiers." She stood up. "I trust you with the life of my son."

The cubicle curtain whispered shut behind them. Rayn sank onto her chair and studied the drawing on the flyer. The exactness of it left her shivering.

"What's your name?"

She looked up to find Mati observing her with interest. "I'm Rayn."

"I'm Mati, and I'm ten." He rubbed his eyes with fists and peered at her again. "I saw you."

"Where?" She scooted the chair nearer the cot.

"You were in the village after it burnt down. But you were hard to see... kinda blurry around the edges. You saw me, too, didn't you?"

"I did. I wanted to help but couldn't."

He pushed up on an elbow. "Were you a ghost?"

"I think we were in a dream."

Sitting up, he fingered the bandage on his head. "It wasn't a dream, Rayn. Dreams don't hurt."

The curtain whished open. Arden walked to the side of the cot. "Hello, Mati. I'm Rayn's granddah. May I sit?"

The boy's chin quivered. "*My* granddah died. I tried to help, but I'm not big enough."

Arden sat at the end of the cot. "But you saved your mother and sister. I'm certain your granddah would be proud of you." He cupped his hands and held them out. "Perhaps if you put your sorrow in my hands, you would feel better."

Mati pressed his hands to his heart, placed them over Arden's, brushed them together, and gave him a tremulous smile. "That feels better." He cocked his head to one side. "What will you do with my sadness?"

Arden closed his hands and raised them to his lips, then pressed them to his heart. "I will keep it safe until it is no longer needed."

Relief steadied Mati's smile. "Thank you, Arden."

"It is my honor. Now, I believe you're tired. Perhaps a nap?"

Mati yawned, winced, and touched his head. "Will a nap help my head, Rayn?"

"I am sure it will." Rayn tucked him in and planted a kiss on his cheek.

He smothered another yawn. "Will I see you again?"

"I'll come by tomorrow."

"You, too, Arden?"

"Of course." Arden touched Mati's temple. "Sleep and dream your healing."

Soft, relaxed breathing floated through the cubicle.

Ceri peeked around the curtain. "Good. He's resting. Best thing for him." She motioned them into the ward. "Keelyn picked up Rasiana. She asked me to tell you your meal is ready. Thanks for helping."

Preceding Arden through the ward to the hall, Rayn paused. "After we eat, I need to know how my dream and Mati's reality blended together."

Good food and good conversation left Rayn relaxed. A torrent of fatigue hit the moment she let down. Keelyn gave her a draught to keep her dreams at bay and sent her to bed. She wondered as she drifted into sleep if she would ever catch up.

When she finally woke, the light of mid-turning poured through her open window. Padding across the carpeted floor, she inhaled the sweet smells of grass and flowers. A dog's elated bark and a child's laugh floated up from the garden. Rayn leaned out. Mati sat in a wheel chair in the midst of a litter of yipping puppies. He glanced up and waved, then held one up. She waved and withdrew, smiling. *What a nice way to begin the day.*

Sinking onto a chair next to the window, she contemplate how Mati had come into her life and Arden's explanation of why her dream and Mati's reality had intersected.

"I t's all about perception," he said. "We all perceive our world from our own perspective, which in itself is dependent upon our personal knowledge and understanding of where we are and how things work. I see Osullini differently than you. You see the island from a fresh perspective. I, on the other hand, have lived here the majority of my long life. It is my home and I perceive it from my connection to it.

"When your grandmameen and I left you to consider your reasons for wishing to be a Animilero, we went to our room."

Keelyn picked up the thread of the conversation and continued to weave the explanation. "We knew you would sleep. When you did, we were ready. Arden took us on a seeker's journey. He felt it was important for you to understand events on El QuilTran so you could make an informed decision."

Arden reclaimed the thread. "We traveled through a time-fold, which paralleled Mati's world. His youth allowed him to suspend disbelief and to see you. The subconscious of the soldiers perceived your presence; their conscious minds dismissed it. It is all a matter of perception." He paused to let his explanation sink in.

R ayn watched a healer push Mati back toward the infirmary. *I think I understand.*

She sank onto the edge of the bed. A mental image made her smile: Awinta at her loom, her foot pumping the treadle; the shuttle fly back and forth. The whole conversation had resembled the weaving of one of her tapestries. Arden represented the warp and Keelyn the weft. *I was the shuttled caring the yarn of weft through the shed to weave it with the warp in an effort to make sense of the whole.*

Her thoughts returned to the conversation.

S he asked. "What is a time-fold?"

Arden shook out his napkin and folded it in half. "In order for you to see what was occurring without being seen, I used my shameen's skills to create a distortion or fold in the continuum of space and time. This allowed you to walk in Mati's reality, but slightly behind the flow of it." He placed the napkin on the table and smoothed it with his palm.

Rayn frowned. "I thought you said *we* went on the seekers' journey. Why didn't I see you there?"

Keelyn explained. "Because we remained in this dimension and Arden transported you via a parallel dimension. We wanted you to have the autonomy to perceive and react to happenings without our influence."

Arden pushed back his chair. "Let's adjourn to a more comfortable place. We have a few more things to discuss."

On the veranda off Arden's office, a tray with a decanter and glasses awaited them. Settling in comfortable chairs, they sat for a time sipping light berry port and enjoying the quiet of dusk.

Arden placed his glass on the tray. "Tomorrow you will both begin your training in the skills of the Animilero."

Rasiana gasped. "But Arden, I cannot kill. I don't want——"

He dismissed her unwillingness with a wave of his hand. "If you are to accompany Rayn and protect her, than you must know how to fight. I understand your reticence to kill. Animilero honor life. They do not take one unless there is not other choice. You will be studying with both Keelyn and me. Keelyn's classes with cover spirituality, general survival skills, and the anatomy of the kill. I will teach physical conditioning, weaponry, and one on one combat. In addition, Rasiana will continue to help in the infirmary and, you, Rayn, will work in the greenhouse and gardens." He stood up. "I suggest you get some rest. You are about to work harder than you have ever worked in your lives."

Keelyn hugged them goodnight. "Don't worry, Rasiana, you'll do fine. There will come a time when you'll be grateful for your training. Sleep well."

Rasiana stared after her with self-doubt written all over her face. "Oh, Rayn, I'm not prepared for this? What is Arden thinking?"

Rayn pulled her to her feet. "You are one of the strongest women I know,

Rasi. You'll be fine. Besides, I won't have to worry about you as much." Linking arms, she escorted her friend from the room. "We'd better get some sleep. I have a feeling my granddah is a task master."

Alone in her room, Rayn almost whooped with excitement. Kuparak was her idol. Now, she would train to be just like him. "I will help to save our people and defeat Lusktar Rados and his Pheet Adolan army," she announced to Alkina's glowing orb.

Several moon cycles later, Rayn arrived for a session with Arden to find the practice ring empty and a note on the board: *Please review what you have learned.*

Walking to the middle of the ring, she ran through the list of things her practice sessions with Arden had taught her.

Make eye contact and keep it. Protect from your collar bone up. Keep your chin down. Do *not* expose your neck to the enemy. Keep your hands up, wrists inward. You have large blood vessels on the inside of your thighs. Protect them. Keep your legs close to the body. Remember the palm is stronger than the fist. If you are unarmed, use it.

She flexed her hand and stared at her palm, remembering the soldier at the farmhouse when she slammed her palm into his chin.

Most important...If there is no choice, do not hesitate. It is your life or your enemies.

The list was endless. Arden had taught her to kill with quiet efficiency. Keelyn had taught her to do so with utmost respect for the life she took and for all life. She felt more ready than ever to fight for her people.

The eerie hush in the practice area chaffed on her nerves. "Where are you, Granddah." Pacing a restless circuit, she attempted to ignore her growing disquiet. "I have come a long way since my first day in the ring with you." She paused, then continue to contemplate her Animilero training.

Arden had pushed her to the brink of quitting. His demand for perfection outstripped anyone she had ever know, even Kuparak. At times she hated him, but her respect for his skills and his knowledge only grew. She ran her hand along the rope defining the ring. *I was so spoiled when I arrived here. At Cimondeli everyone treated me as though I'm special.* She curled her fingers around the rope. *Arden and Keelyn drive me hard, and I've learned to love it.*

Running footsteps amplified her escalating apprehension. Rasiana dodged into the ring. "Arden sent me. Trouble just landed on Osullini. We're to create a time-fold and hide until…"

Rayn folded her arms. "If there's trouble, I'm staying."

"He said to tell you an order is an order. If you disobey, you won't like the consequences."

"Is this a test?" Rayn put her hands on her hips and glared. "Or is there a real threat?"

Rasiana returned the glare. "If it's a test, do you want to fail it?"

"No, but if its real…"

"Then Arden has a good reason for telling us to hide." Making an about face, she walked to the outside door, pulled it open, and glanced back. "Are you coming or not?"

An angry retort caught in Rayn's throat. *Why am I reacting this way?* She scowled. *I'm afraid for us and for my grandparents.* Running from the ring, she grabbed the door as it swung shut, yanked it open, and raced after her friend.

They reached the center of the orchard and climbed an apple tree, where Aquila and Oha perched in the upper most branches. When their breathing normalized, they clasped hands and focused the way Keelyn had taught them. A mist roiled around them and faded.

Rayn examined the reality through which she wandered with momentary awe, then tensed. The apple orchard waved. Undulating light dispersed into blue and gold sand. Rasiana squeezed her hand and pointed.

Several rowing boats skimmed the water between a large steam ship anchored in the bay and the golden beach. Two had been dragged onto the sand. Uniform men helped unload three large black boxes and place them equidistant along the shoreline. A third boat crunched to a stop. A soldier jumped out, waded ashore, and with the help of a comrade pulled it higher.

The remaining passengers disembarked. Three men in the purple and black uniforms of the SorTech hurried to individual boxes and began to prepare them for use. More boats landed. Round containers were unloaded, hauled over the sand on canvas skates, and positioned in a line. The soldier in charge checked with each SorTech in turn and signaled them to begin.

The tingling surge of SorTechory at work flooded the island. Rayn squeezed Rasiana's hand. Holding the time-fold steady, they merged into blue sand, their minds blank. Waves of energy washed over them. Again and again, it rolled over the sand, seeking to find the presence of life. The leader shouted an order. The barrage of SorTechory ceased.

Rayn rippled into Human form, felt the roughness of bark beneath her, glanced at Rasiana, then back toward the men on the beach.

An argument ensued. Voices rose and fell, some angry, some calmer. At last, the boxes and SorTechs were loaded into boats and pushed away from the shore. Three soldiers worked with the round containers. The rest ran to the rowing boats, climbed aboard, and began the trip back to the ship. A shouted command and the three soldiers sprint toward the last boat and scrambled aboard.

"Hold the time fold steady. Fly, now!" Keelyn's cry rang in Rayn's head. Her tether to Aquila snapped into place. Rasiana's hand pulled free as she shifted and soared after her tukoolo. Clinging to the time-fold's illusion, Rayn shot after her.

An explosive blast rocked the world. Concussed currents quaked through the atmosphere. Rayn tumbled head over tail. Galee wings snatched at the air, pressed against it, fought for balanced flight. A second blast flung her upright. The third catapulted her away from Osullini as the time-fold floundered and she shot into real time.

"Calm." Aquila's mind touch diffused her panic. His appearance in front of her reestablished her equilibrium. A red-tailed whak soaring in the smoky light close to her side brought a wave of relief with it. Rasiana flew beside her. Banking after Aquila, Rayn circled back toward the island.

Where the ship rolled in heaving waves, blinding white light pooled under it, closed up around it like a draw stringed-bag, and lift it domeward. Rocketing higher, the ball of light and its contents exploded into glinting sprinkles of white, which rained down on Osullini's obsidian sand. Where it touched, veins of burnished gold criss-crossed the land and bled into the sea.

As the ocean calmed and the smell of acid smoke faded, Rayn flew a wide curve above the island. Aquila landed and whistled an all clear. She swooped toward the beach and descended to the sand beside her compeer.

Rasiana touched down beside her. "What just happened?"

Rayn knelt and scooped up a handful of black sand. "I think Arden and Keelyn worked their magic." The sand funneled between her fingers. She stood and brushed the remaining particles from her palms. "Anyone looking at Osullini will think the explosions destroyed whatever might have been here."

"And you, Rayn, what do you think?" Arden's bodiless voice floated on ocean scented air.

She rotated, seeking her granddah and mentor. "I think you should show yourself, so we can stop worrying."

Garden and house replaced the sand and sea. Keelyn greeted them with a tremulous smile.

Rayn exhaled. "I thought we had lost you." Her grandmameen's expression made her heart sink."

Arden's image blurred and refocused. "You almost did. It was close, Rayn. In fact, it was too close. The island is safe. Everyone survived the explosion." He took Keelyn's hand. "When I dispatched the Rompeer's ship and passengers to another dimension, I trapped your grandmameen and me in a time-fold from which we cannot return."

Keelyn blinked back tears. "We wanted to say good-bye." She began to fade and steadied. "The battle to save the Eleo Preda is coming to an end."

Arden's features hardened. "You must not be killed, Rayn. You must find a way to save our ancient bloodlines and preserve the diversity and beauty of El Stroma." Their image blurred. "Our home is your inheritance."

Keelyn's cry penetrated the dimensional barrier, "We love you, Rayn."

—

39

Sorrow blanketed the house and yard. Rasiana had gone to check in with Ceri and to see Mati and his maman and sister. Rayn wandered the house absorbing the loss of her grandparents and considering what to do next. She unlatched the window in the main salon, pushed it wide, and breathed in apple blossom scented air. "I can't stay on Osullini and accomplish the goals Arden laid for me. *Preserve ancestral bloodlines and the diversity of El Stroma...*"How do I——"

A harrier hawk swooped through the window and landed at the center of the room. A tall, muscular man materialized. Short, dark hair bristled on one side of his head. Tattoos covered the other. His resemblance to her mother and Aunt Katareen made it hard not to stare. The jagged scar running from chin to brow and into the tattoos on his scalp didn't help, nor did the feelings she observed beneath his self-disciplined calm.

Astonishment cocooned her in an emotion-filled stillness.

After a protracted silence, he sank onto the window seat. "I'm your Uncle

Daar, Rayn. You look so much like Jaradee." Gentleness softened the metallic glint in his blue-gray eyes. "The last time I saw you, you were only a few turnings old. I have wanted to come to you for a long time, but Vasrosi business has kept me in El SyrTundi." A flicker of amusement softened his wounded visage. He patted the seat. "Perhaps you should sit."

Her paralysis melted. "I have always wondered about you." A memory made her smile. "I'm told I have your temper."

A laugh changed his warrior's unyielding countenance, making him seem younger, more Human. "I expect that mean's you're stubborn, too?"

Loneliness almost choked her. "Arden would definitely agree."

Keen interest took the place of levity. "And where is your esteemed granddah? I have news for him."

Rayn let her gaze wander the garden. Sunlight on apple blossoms soothed the ache in her heart. She considered the man opposite her, ordered her thoughts, and described the events of the last two turnings. When she completed the tale, a predatory prowl carried Daar in a circuit of the room. He ended looking down at her. "Kup told me you and Rasi have been training as Animilero's. Is that true?"

"That's correct. Why?"

"I think Rasiana should be part of this conversation. Please get her."

Rayn looked toward the door. "She's on her way."

Daar's brows arced. "Telepathy. I can still only use it when I'm tethered to Rangi."

Rasiana jogged into the room and slid onto the window seat. "Good to see you, Daar. Rayn said you have news."

Returning to his seat, Daar massaged the scar bisecting his hairline. "I've been staying close to VenTra. Just before I left to come here, I witnessed a conversation between two Pheet Adolan workers. One, a messenger newly arrived from Chunarrie, shared the latest gossip with his comrade. A Rompeerial ship, last seen making for Mer â Chi Strait, and its crew and three SorTechs had vanished. I knew when I saw the changes in Osullini it must have been headed for here. I'm sorry about your grandparents, Rayn. I will miss their counsel." He pursed his lips. "I'm just glad it wasn't worse."

"Worse." Rayn lathered her reply with disbelief.

"They could be dead, but they're not. From what you've said, they're somewhere alive and well. And knowing them as I do, I predict they will make wherever they are work for them."

Rayn lowered her gaze. "You're right, Daar." She looked up. "I miss them."

Rasiana sighed. "They'll be missed by many. I understand few shameenu remain on El Stroma."

Daar rubbed the coarse, bristly hair on the side of his head. "We have managed to smuggle a few off planet. The rest have been massacred. We believe Arden and Keelyn were two of the last. The Pheet Adole are winning. We press them back, and they return with double the strength. El QuilTran will soon be theirs. To make things worse, the Vasrosi are divided. One side is focused on helping people escape. The Vasro rebels have declared that if the Eleo Preda cannot live on El Stroma neither can the Pheet Adole."

A jolt of understanding shook Rayn. "They want to destroy El Stroma?"

"They do. Kuparak sent me to seek Arden's advice. Since he is beyond reach, I'm not sure what to do."

"Arden told Rasiana and me the Eleo Preda were loosing and to preserve the ancient bloodlines and the diversity of El Stroma's ecological systems."

Daar's expression animated with interest. "Kuparak is procuring a ship, one that can be fitted with a cryogenics lab and storage. I'm to meet him in Chunarrie to help arrange for the selection and transport of all Eleo Predan specimens."

Rayn recalled a conversation with her grandmameen. "Keelyn had a vision, one that prompted her to prepare for the worst. She has been collecting and preserving seeds and cuttings from El Stroman flora as well as micro organisms from dirt, the ocean, rivers, and streams for the past two sun cycles. A group on El QuilTran adapted the technology developed at the Protariflee Center and has collected samples from as many animal species as they could. Looks like we have a good start."

Rasiana curl her legs under her. "Now, we have to find a way to move everything to the ship without alerting the Rompeer and his followers."

Daar whistled. His tukoolo swooped to the windowsill. "Rangi and I had better go. Kup should be in Chunarrie by mid-turning tomorrow. I'll know then if he found a ship." He scratched Rangi's chest. "I'll be back when I can."

Rayn launched to her feet. "I'm going with you, Daar." Excitement made her feel giddy. "It's time I did more than while away my time on Osullini."

Her uncle folded his arms. "Kuparak wants you here and safe."

"And how do I help our people if I'm stuck here? If I were a man, I would already be in the fight. I trained to be a warrior. After my last, workout in the practice ring, Arden told me I was ready." She planted her feet and glared. "You can't stop me."

Profound quiet cloaked him. "Don't test my resolve, Rayn. Stay here. Help prepare——"

Anger shot up the back of Rayn's neck. Daar's voice faded. Memories of her mother's final moments, Kia dead in a pool of blood, cycles of confinement, the loss of her grandparents, Mati's village burned to the ground, and men burned alive in a sacred hall gushed through her body. The geyser of emotions whipped her head back. A howl rose in her throat. Baritone deep, it burst forth. Her head jerked up. She glowered at Daar. Saw the disbelief in Rasiana's upturned face. Neither spoke.

Unfamiliar strength rippled from muscle to muscle. She clenched a fist, raised it, and uncurled large, battle-scarred fingers. Pivoting, she strode to a mirror at the end of the room.

Dark, haughty eyes in a masculine face locked onto her startled gaze. Thick black hair brushed broad shoulders above a broad, muscular chest. Clarity hit with such force she doubled over. *I shaped a man.* She straightened. Her nostrils flare. She marched back to her uncle.

"I am going with you, Daar Palmira."

"Rayn, shift back." Rasiana's voice held a note of panic.

A devious laugh snapped to a growl. "Why should I. I like the feel of this male body of this masculine mind. I may never…"

The cry of a smoky galee heralded Kuparak's shift to Human. Calmness poured from him. Cool, cleansing calm squelched the flames of her rage.

Suspicion snaked through her mind. She stepped back. Her fists came up.

He did not change his stance. White teeth flashed. Warmth and charm strangled her dubiety. "You make a handsome man, Rayn. Does your male form have a name?"

Arrogant pride welled up inside her. "*I* am The MasTer. I will conquer the Pheet Adole and give the Eleo Preda back their homeland."

"Ahhhhh. I see." His knowing nod almost retriggered the snake in her head.

"Come back to me, Rayn." The gentleness of the feminine voice touched a cord. "I miss you, my sis...ter." Emotion cracked the word in two.

A memory swam the currents of The MasTer's pride. "Rasiana..." The world dipped. Haughtiness ripped recall to shreds. Disdain coated his laugher, stabilizing the world...the room...the place...

A forest galee swooped to a landing on Kuparak's arm.

The MasTer wrinkled his brow. "I distrust your pet, Charnlandian."

Sweetness caressed Rayn's mind. Partnership, sharing, and love warmed her heart.

The MasTer guffawed. "I do not need this scavenger of lies...this eater of garbage——"

Rayn surged into being. The MasTer thwarted her attempt to gain control. Using her love of Aquila as a foothold, she fought to return. War between masculine and feminine, lion and lioness, tore her confidence to shreds and devoured her dignity. Dropping to one knee, she cradled her breasts in her hands. Her shoulders quaked from the depths of the battle to remain in her own body, to hold to her femininity and her power as a woman. She lunged to her feet, knife in hand. "Leave me or I will end your existence and mine." A shudder ran through her. A breath hissed between her lips. She sheathed the knife and collapsed as Kuparak's arms closed around her.

Rayn traipsed the terrace of her subconscious in a hunt for self, her ego riveted to the maleness of The MasTer. In her sleep induced trance, she luxuriated in the power of his presence. *He* walked with her...tempted her to change again. Seduced her with promises of successes beyond her wildest dreams. *He* would win the war, recover El QuilTran from Rompeerial troops, and save the Eleo Preda and El Stroma. Buried in the background of this land of dreams, an undercurrent of truth shredded his façade and exposed him for the peddler of power he was.

She woke in a cold sweat. A warm hand touched on her brow and withdrew.

Rasiana's strained smile spoke volumes. "How do you feel?"

"Tired. What happened? Did I shape a man?"

Kuparak moved from the shadows and sat beside her. "You provided a malignant personality with the opportunity to manifest itself through you. It granted you what you wanted most."

She drew in a breath. "All I want is to fight for our people."

"And so you shall. First tell me what it felt like to be The MasTer."

"I have never experienced such overwhelming power, mentally or physically. How can I not aspire to be all he is in order to save our people?"

"He has no desire to save the Eleo Preda. All The MasTer cares about is the adoration of those who are less than he. Beware the allure of his self-aggrandizement. It is the cry of an insecure personality scrambling for recognition."

Shutting her eyes, she recalled the experience of his manifestation, his take over of her being. She sought Kuparak. "I did not ask him to manifest. I had no intention of shape shifting a man. This MasTer can induce the shift at will."

"Only if you give him an opening. Promise never to shape him again, Rayn. If you succumb to the temptation, you will loose yourself in The MasTer's overblown ego."

She swung her legs over the side of the settee and perched on the edge. "How did I open the door for him this time?"

Rasiana handed her a glass of water. "What were you thinking when he appeared?"

Fluid coolness cleansed the bitter taste of sleep from her mouth. She reviewed her conversation with Daar. "I was so angry at the injustice of being trapped here while others died simply because I am a woman." She surveyed the room. "Where is Daar?"

"I've sent him to finish a project I left undone to be here." Kuparak studied her. "Have you discovered the trigger?"

She placed the empty glass on the end table. "Anger. My anger..." Her brow furrowed. "Wait. I have never felt discriminated against as a woman. I have fought in the ring with male and female opponents. Arden never eased up on either Rasiana or me because we are girls." Fighting to control the fury threatening to overtake her, she walked to the window and looked at the garden. Aquila flew to the sill. Composure drenched her inner inferno. She turned. "I remember watching women demeaned at the Children's Residence in Chunarrie and wondering why they were considered inferior. The MasTer is a part of me, true?"

Kuparak nodded. "An alter ego of sorts but stronger. For nine rotations you were forced to bury the true you inside an internal fortress. Your anger festered. Your need to be recognized became a boil beneath your psychic skin. Unbeknownst to you, The MasTer's personality began to evolve."

"How do you know all this, and why didn't you warn me?"

"Nioka feared this might occur. Because of who you are and the genetic history you carry, she surmised the possibility of multiple personalities. I considered telling you. She warned that if you were told too soon, it might invoke a takeover before you were strong enough to fight."

Rayn flopped down next to Rasiana. "So what now?"

"You are armed with information to help you keep the reins of self in your own hands. Rasiana and Aquila will help. You are strong-willed, Rayn. Remaining alert and aware of your emotions is vital. You maintained a disciplined silence for nine sun cycles. I have confidence you will be fine. As for now...While you slept, Rasiana and I arranged for Arden and Keelyn's home to be taken care of and the samples and specimens your grandmameen collected to be prepared for transporting. As soon as we've eaten, we must leave for VenTra."

A prickle of excitement prompted Rayn to smile. "You have a ship."

"Indeed. There is much to do before she is ready, and we have things we must accomplish on El Stroma but..."

Rayn hugged him. "Thank you, Kup."

"For what?"

"For leaving everything to come here and help me. Rasiana and Daar might have pulled me back to myself but..." She shivered.

He returned the hug and released her. "We leave early in the morning Get some rest. I'll be back for you then." His smoky galee soared out the window.

For a time, they sat in the tranquility of Osullini's transition to night, each wrapped in their own thoughts. Rasiana, the first to stir, rose.

"Let's go see Mati and his mother. I think we should say good-bye."

The visit was a tearful one. Mati clung to Rayn until she promised to return when she could. At Ceri's suggestion they ate with the family, hugged them one last time, and bid them a second farewell.

Rasiana slept the moment her head touched the pillow. The soft sounds of her breathing helped to soothe Rayn's over-stretched nerves. For a time she stared up at the ceiling. Determination ignited. *I am Rayn Jaradee Palmira. The MasTer does not control me.* The silent mantra gave her the confidence to sleep.

40

Kuparak collected them as pennants of pale pink and teal announced the sun's imminent arrival. He broke the long trip to Chunarrie into two parts. The flight across the Dirredaca Seâ took the better part of the turning. They landed by the light of Dyad's solo rising and spent the night at a safe haven on the outskirts of Tahellive. Exhausted by the long journey, Rayn chose not to take a tour of the town where her mother and siblings had spent time. Instead, she curled up on a cot in a small, dark room and slept. When Kuparak nudged her awake in the gloom of pre sunrise, she dragged her tired body to the kitchen table, wondering if she had slept at all.

After a quick breakfast, they tethered to their tukoolos and flew inland toward Chunarrie. Mid afternoon, Toa, followed by Aquila and Oha, swooped between two bronze-tinted mesas and alighted in the trees by the banks of a slow moving river. Kuparak flew further into the trees landed in late afternoon duskiness beneath a secoe pine.

At his signal, Rayn and Rasiana landed, released the tethers to their compeers, and shuffled after him along a little used track. Rayn squinted beyond him, sighed, and ordered her tired legs to keep moving. Cold night air teased her lassitude into wakefulness. Total darkness had taken over the forest when Kuparak halted.

The sting of SorTechory froze Rayn midway to speaking. Rasiana grabbed her hand. Kuparak urged them off the track. Animilero training clicked into play. Minds blanked, they moved through the close-packed trees. Long after the SorTech's intrusive search had faded, they arrived at the river bank a short distance from the Rompeerial Mesa.

Too tired to think, Rayn sank to the ground and leaned against a smooth barrow trunk. In the glow of Dyad's singular light, Aquila came to rest on a branch above her head; Oha perched nearby; and Toa flew to his compeer's outstretched arm. A harrier hawk dropped through the trees, and Daar appeared. A quick exchange of information and Rasiana hurried to her side, kissed her cheek, and whispered, "I'll see you soon." She shifted and flew after Daar away from the river.

Kuparak, captured in the cool blue of the full moon, reminded Rayn of a carved obsidian statue, polished to a satiny sheen. Luminous amber eyes scanned the night dome and came to rest on her face. "I know you're exhausted, but we can't stay here. Too many soldiers in this valley. I wanted to take you to Chunarrie." He squinted up at the mesa and seemed to come to a decision. "The Vasrosi have a safe haven near Lake Scarla. It's on the other side of the Plains of Los Ateed, a goodly distant but not unmanageable. Daar and Rasiana will meet us there."

She allowed him to assist her to her feet. "What about the project in Chunarrie? Do you need to stay for that?"

"Daar took care of the final arrangements. The cryogenics canisters are on their way to VenTra. The next step is to be there to receive and load them." His hand rested on her shoulder. "How do you feel? Can you fly?"

Aquila fluttered to a lower branch. She tethered to her tukoolo. "I'm stronger than I look. Let's go."

The Plains of Los Ateed el Rida, a barren and impoverished landscape, spread below them in the light of the moon. Cracks careening in all directions presented an abstract of geometrical shapes in stained varying shades of blue. Plants pushing up through the crevices in search of moisture shriveled in despair. Nothing stirred but an occasional night bird and tundi sage, quivering in the erratic currents of flurry fiends whining over the plains.

Grateful for Dyad's stable presence in the night dome, Rayn contemplated El Stroma's two moons. Dyad, cool, blue, and consistent, circuited the planet with no deviations. Alkina, in all its radiant topaz and rose glory on the other hand, created minor havoc with its biannual retrograde orbit and its shifts from barren to resplendent. In two days time, it would go direct. Slack tide would still the seas and then, rising too high and falling too low, lash out against the shoreline. Cyclonic winds would whip the planet, rain would fall where it rarely fell, and harsh sunlight would beat down on wetlands and rain forests. Fortunately, the results of its return to a prograde loop lasted only a couple of turnings.

As the warm light of the rising sun chased Dyad's coolness from the plain and behind the Chaporicas Mountains, Kuparak touched down in Human form on a rugged trail through a high mountain pass.

Rayn hovered and at his signal glided a lazy line to his side. Their tukoolos perched on the upper branches of a dead tree, telie-eyes searching.

Kuparak scanned the distant plains. "We'll rest soon." He began to climb.

She trudged after him. "How much further?"

The broad shoulders shrugged. He kept climbing. She groaned and pushed to keep up. When they had almost reached the peak, he flashed her a smile and rounded a hairpin-sharp corner. Her brow wrinkled. The trail continued along a narrow ridge. Kuparak was nowhere to be seen.

"In here." The muffled voice came from her right. A narrow shaft of sunlight picked out an upwelling of rock and earth. To one side, the light exposed a waist high opening though which Kuparak peered.

"In here. Scooch in on your fanny. The entrance is steep and the ceiling is low."

Using the rock ledge above the opening, she lowered and, feet first, inched ahead. A hand torch sketch a path. She soon found herself in an underground expanse twice as wide as it was tall. Black and burnt orange sand covered the ground. No boulders or protrusions marred the unbroken regularity of the rounded ceiling and walls. Kup smiled at her obvious surprise.

"Interesting, isn't it? Arden directed me here several sun cycles ago. I haven't been back since. Wasn't sure I could find it, or if it would still be here. These mountains are prone to slides." While he talked, he scooped out a shallow hollow in the sand. "Suggest you sleep while you can. We'll fly to the safe haven tomorrow as the sunsets." He stretched out in the pit, wiggled around to mold the sand to his body, and slept.

Rayn scooped out a sleeping hollow. Try as she might, she could not get comfortable. Muscles twitching from fatigue didn't help. Rambling thoughts pulled her one direction and then another until she sat up and rested her head on her knees. A series of yawns brought tears to her eyes. Curling up, her head on her arm, she drifted at last into dreamless slumber.

Afternoon coolness woke her to an empty cave and a moment of panic. Footsteps on the trail and Kuparak's hand light washing over her, cancelled it.

"Good, you're awake. Come on. I found water."

Scrambling up the incline, she crawled into a mountain landscape awash with a recent shower. The air felt damp on her skin and smelled fresh and invigorating. Kuparak led her to water puddled in a rock formed basin. It tasted of minerals and sunshine, quenched her thirst, and left her revitalized and ready to fly.

The trip took them over mountains drenched in the sun's farewell light. Above them, fleecy clouds soaked up teal, fuchsia, and rich royal blue. A lake up ahead reflected their soft-hued colors.

Kuparak flew along the western edge of Lake Scarla, circled above the northern most shore, caught an air current, and skated to a landing in a grouping of sgàile aspen.

Rayn touched down a short distance from him. "You look like a god surrounded by angels."

A soft laugh accompanied the dip of his head. He motioned her to follow and made his way to a rustic white-washed cabin, well-hidden amongst the white-trunked, white-leafed trees.

The door opened a crack. A dark face peeked out. Rasiana pulled the door wide, jumped from the low porch, and hugged Rayn. "Oha told me you were here. I am so relieved to see you. Daar has gone to VenTra, Kup, to find out what's happened since you were last there." She stepped back. "I bet you are hungry. I've a meal ready."

The inside of the cabin proved to be less rustic than the outside suggested. The aroma of stew cooking on an oil stove made Rayn's mouth water. After relieving herself in the lean-to out back, she sprawled on a patched sofa and sipped hot, fragrant tea from a large mug, while Rasiana set the table.

Restless for no reason she could put her finger on, she finished her tea and wandered to the door. Kuparak stood in the clearing watching the stars wink their way across the dome. Rangi glided to a landing on the steps. Daar landed at the edge of the clearing, shifted, and jogged to Kuparak's side.

"Ship's here and hidden. Vasrosi are beginning to gather. Supplies and "secrets" will start arriving in a couple of turnings."

"Good work. How many Eleo Preda are left to transport?"

"Of those willing to leave their homes, one more large load for the cargo ship."

Kuparak motioned him ahead. "Food's ready. We can talk more as we eat."

Daar shot her an easy smile. "Saw Katareen in VenTra. She sends her love."

Rayn walked beside him to the table. "What's she doing there?"

Kuparak pulled out a chair. "She's in charge assembling what we need for the cryogenics lab. You'll be seeing her soon."

Rasiana placed a loaf of fresh bread on the table. Bowls of steaming stew followed. Daar and Kuparak were on their second bowl when their conversation turned to events in VenTra. Cimondeli was no longer safe. Awinta was already aboard the cargo ship. Drue and Dyna would be there tomorrow with a group of younger Vasrosi to finish loading and preparing for the final lift off from El Stroma.

Daar wiped his bowl clean with a crust of bread and followed it with long drink of water. "The Vasrosi who remain are making their way here. We're only a handful, Kup. We need to leave soon."

Rayn's secret hope that the tides would turn in the Eleo Predan's favor, dissolved. *Winning is truly no longer an option. Escape has become the goal.*

Her vision blurred. *Where have I been? Protected and pampered when I might have made a difference.* A seed of anger sprout. *He* stirred. *Set me free.* The words lurked in her mind like a forbidden caress. His restlessness chaffed against her self-will. Every moment of the turning, his power prodded her self-discipline toward submission.

She looked up to find her companions observing her: Rasiana with dreaded anticipation, her hand clutching something hanging on a chain around her neck; Daar with the inscrutability of a warrior; Kuparak with absolute calm. Gripping the table, she brought her chin up, soaked in the Vasrosi leader's tranquility, remembered his love for her maman...his love for her as Jaradee's daughter. Love for him, for Rasiana, for Daar and Katareen pushed The MasTer away, removed the finger from the trigger. Air gushed into her lungs.

Kup smiled. "Well, done daughter of Jaradee. Use your mother's strength coupled with your own. Let love be your savior."

She swallowed. "You were in my mind?"

He did not falter. "Only close by...in case you had need of me. The longer you can keep him in check, the less potent will be his hold on you." He lifted his mug. "A toast. To Rayn and the power of love."

Later that night she and Rasiana curled up on their small cots and discussed the happenings of the turning. Rayn propped her head on her hand. "What are you wearing around your neck?"

Rasiana touched a spot between her breasts. "Kup told me not to tell you...well you, Rayn, are not the problem, but The MasTer must not know."

Rayn rolled onto her back and focused. "He is not present."

Rasiana cleared her throat. "It is a gift from Nioka. That's all I'm willing to share. If you want more detail, please speak with Kuparak." She pulled the blanket up to her chin and pretended sleep.

"Can you tell me how you got it?"

A soft expletive and sound of fists plumping a pillow preceded a short silence. "We stopped into see her when Kuparak and I took a quick tour of the Tahellive. Go to sleep."

Swaddled in the night's quiet, Rayn pondered what Nioka might have given to her friend that The MasTer could not know about. She thought about him, his power, and the actions that provoked his appearance. *You do not get to control me.* She yawned and gave into her fatigue.

The next morning Kuparak accompanied Rayn and Rasiana to a deserted factory center at the edge of the Dirredaca Seâ to meet the captain of the

Capese, the old battered cargo ship procured by the Vasrosi. Captain Cammoll, a man in his medial cycles with intelligent brown eyes greeted them with an appraising look. His no nonsense manner suggested to Rayn that he knew his job. The obvious respect shown him by his small crew...the second in command/communications officer, the engineer, and the science officer/med tech...confirmed it. The solid bond existing between them suggested they worked together well.

For the next moon cycle, Rayn and Rasiana received, catalogued, and packed samples and specimens of the flora, fauna, and microbial life into *Capese*. Cryogenics canisters arrived in small, smuggled batches along with the equipment required to create a fully functioning lab at their final port of call. Katareen had done a thorough job of collecting what they would need.

One turning Rayn and Rasiana had just completed reviewing the list of stowed items when the image of three whaks and their compeers flashed through her mind. Aquila's images faded. A message from Kuparak followed: *Intercept guests. Keep them away from the ship. Be careful.*

Rayn pursed her lips in thought. Vygel Vintrusie was one of the guests. Yet, Kuparak's message had been clear. She ducked out the back of the warehouse and jogged to a long, low building housing several offices and sleeping quarters for the Vasrosi. Once inside, she hurried to the front door, ordered her thoughts, and gripped the knob.

41

Rayn stepped into the overgrown parking lot. Vygel Vintrusie and two men jogged toward her.

"Hey, Rayn!" Vygel waved, picked up speed, and stopped beside her. Self-importance bristled around him. He scanned the area and flashed her a toothy smile. "Where's Kup? And…" He lowered his voice to a conspiratorial whisper. "Where's the ship?"

"Nice to see you, too, Vygel." She led them into an office. "Who're your friends?"

Vygel scowled. "Taze and Styn…Rayn."

"You the one everyone says is going to save us?" A bulky guy with a defiant attitude, looked her up and down and smacked his lips.

Rayn returned his lecherous gaze with disinterest. "I'll see if I can find Kup."

Vygel grabbed her arm. "I'll come with ya."

Kuparak walked into the office. "I understand you wish to speak with me, Vygel. Please sit. Rayn, join us."

Defiance radiating around him, Vygel pulled out a chair. His companions flanked him and though less overt about their feelings, glared at Kuparak with a touch of rebellion.

Keeping his attention on Vygel, Kuparak stated casually, "I understand you are the leader of the VasRo rebels, Vintrusie. What brings you here?"

"I have discovered a way to destroy El SyrTundi and end this war. We're here 'cause you have a ship, and we require the use of it."

Kuparak remained quiet.

Vygel pushed ahead. His eye twitched. He pulled his gaze from Kuparak to his hands and then, contempt blazing, raised it. "I'm aware of your *principles*, Kup." The word, dripping with sarcasm, hung in the air between them. "But if the Eleo Preda must give up their homes and flee, we do not intend to let the Pheet Adole live here either. I brought my men with me. If you won't give us the ship, we'll take it."

Daar rushed into the room. "We've got trouble." He scowled. "And not just this riffraff."

Vygel came to his feet. "We aren't riff——"

"A Rompeerial corps truck and a jeep drive this way. My tukoolo picked up the presence of a SorTech and several soldiers."

Kuparak pushed his chair back. "I don't expect the Rompeer's men will care which rebels they kill. Call your men and join the fight or turn tail and run. It's up to you." He motioned Rayn and Daar to follow and hurried from the room.

When they were out of hearing, he gave quick orders. "Rayn, get Rasiana and tether up. I need you on a roof top keeping watch. Daar, warn Cammoll. Tell him to hide the ship."

Vygel and his comrades strode from the office. "We'll help, but only because we don't want to loose the ship. I'll ready my fighters." Without waiting for a response, he motioned his two men to follow and disappeared behind the office building.

Rayn jogged down the field in Daar's wake. She found Rasiana in the ship. A quick explanation and they tethered, shifted, and flew to the caved-in roof of a nearby building to keep watch. Aquila lifted off and flew a wide circle. Two distinct images formed in Rayn's mind: two military vehicles closing in;

Vasrosi and the Vasro rebels creeping through the prairie grass surrounding the warehouse.

The MasTer stirred. His presence intensified. She clung to her galee form.

Vehicles racing down the deserted parking lot screeched to a halt, dust and dead grass flying. A SorTech jumped from the jeep and began to assemble his equipment. Placing the patch on his temple, he scanned the dome and pointed. "tukoolo!"

The tailgate of the truck flew open. Boots hit the ground. A soldier shouldered his rifle. A shot rang out. Aquila's body jerked and floundered. Strong wings fought, righted it, and carried it over the sea. Rayn's tether to her compeer broke as the forest galee vanished behind a rocky headland.

Unprotected and terrified for her compeer, she swooped into the dingy interior of the building and changed form. Rasiana materialized beside her. "Oh, Rayn——"

Rayn raised a hand. Holding back tears of rage, she whispered, "Hide." A sharp pain shot through her head. She gripped her temples and flinched.

Rasiana steadied her. "What?"

"SorTech. Much stronger. Keep your tether secure." A shudder left her gasping. "The MasTer. Help me focus."

Rasiana held her and whispered the names of the people she loved. The MasTer withdrew.

Shouts, shots, and the roar of engines shook the building. Creeping to a jagged break in the wall, Rayn pulled her knife. "Time to use our training." She hugged her friend. "Thanks for helping me."

Battled raged around them. A dozen soldiers met as many rebels. Knives flashed and rang out. Fists hit their target with a dull crunch or thud or the recipient's grunt of pain. Rayn ignored her regret at taking a life. Need dictated each thrust of the knife. Rasiana fought at her side. Staying out of firearm range, they downed a soldier with the quiet efficiency of their Animilero training.

He crumpled to the ground. Rayn withdrew the blade and wiped her brow as she sought her next target. A hand jerked her around. She dropped her arm, knife hidden behind her back. Two men sized her up. Rasiana lay unmoving behind them. One of them whipped out a worn piece of paper and compared the picture with her face.

"She's the one. We got her! We got the reward."

The second man began to undo his pants. "Let's make sure she remembers us."

His comrade stopped him. "Rompeer wants her for hisself. Better not mess up the merchandise. But you can help yourself to the other one."

Kuparak stepped from behind a truck. White teeth gleamed in a black face beaded with sweat. Blood oozed from a gash in his side. He crouched lower. "Come play with me instead."

The soldier fastened his pants, whistled, and leapt forward. The dull thud of bodies hitting, the groan as they slammed to the ground, the smash of a fist against a jaw...Rayn kicked her captor in the knee, slashed the hand holding her wrist and spun around. Eye to eye, they circled. Keeping her chin down to protect her neck, she analyzed his movement patterns. He lunged, hit her arm as she dodged clear, and sent her knife flying. Hands up, wrists inward, she danced one way and then darted forward. His hesitation gave her the advantage. Grabbing his knife arm with both hands and using his natural reflexes and her forward motion to help, she rammed his knife toward his throat.

A slight sucking sound accompanied his collapse. Another soldier leapt her direction. A hand pulled her out of range and shoved her toward Rasiana. Retrieving her weapon, Rayn slid it into it scabbard, scrambled to her friend's side, and pulled her behind a row of rumble. Gasping for breath, she regarded the pandemonium on the other side of the rubbish heap.

The fierce momentum of the Vasrosi's fight littered the area with uniformed bodies. A double blast of the truck's horn's mingled with the chaos of battle and pain. A soldier on the running board of the truck fired over head. The loud report scattered his comrades. Vasrosi dove for cover, bullets whizzing past too close for comfort.

Engines revved. The SorTech climbed into the back of the jeep beside The Box. Those soldiers left standing clambered aboard the truck. The vehicles roared along the service road bordering the lot.

At first, nothing moved on the field of battle. An occasional groan drifted over blood-drenched bodies. Vasro and Vasrosi crept from the shelter of trash piles and old buildings.

Rasiana stirred and pushed herself to sitting. She touched her bruised face and grimaced. "I'm alright. You?"

Rayn scowled. "Bruised shoulder, a couple of cuts——"

"You Rayn?" A man she did not know peered down at them.

She nodded.

"Daar says you'd better come."

They made their way though the carnage to where Rayn had last seen Kuparak. The Vasrosi leader lay on his back, his head resting in her uncle's lap. His black skin had lost its luster. Scarlet covered his side and chest. A blood-covered hand clutched the silver moonstone locket.

She fell to her knees beside him. "Kup. It's Rayn. Kup, please don't leave me."

His eyes fluttered open. A pink tongue licked his full lips. "Closer." The whisper ended in a gurgle of pain. With a shaking hand, he offered the locket. "Take this. Find Rethdun. He's——" He coughed. Dark red fluid dribbled from the corner of his mouth. Daar wiped it away. The hand gripped hers. "Don't let *Him* gain control. Don't give in——" Another cough quaked through him. The hand went slack.

Death came so quickly Rayn fought to comprehend what had happened. She stared from the locket to the man who had been in her life longer than anyone else...the man who had rescued her, mentored her, and loved her like a daughter. Desolation ripped through her. Looping the silver chain around her neck, she pressed the catch. The locket clicked opened. Rethdun's miniature face smiling at her fanned the embers of her despair. She gripped the front of Kuparak's shirt. "You told me he was dead. You, the man I trusted more than any other, lied to me." Betrayal burned her throat. Anguish and loss twisted her gut. *Rethdun's alive, but where?*

She snapped the locket shut and hid it under her clothing. Wiping her hands on her pants, she came to her feet. The blood-smudged reward poster laying in a pool of Kuparak's blood infuriated her. Spasms of emotion doubled her over, roiled so hot they exploded in a long, drawn out moan. She grabbed the paper; crumpled it into a tight ball. Her head flew back. Her arms flew wide. The MasTer's emerging presence ripped her female essence to shreds. He glared at Kuparak's body.

A gasp of astonishment went through the crowd.

Rasiana reached for his arm. "Rayn, don't let him——"

"Stay out of my sight woman, or I will make certain no one ever looks upon your person again." A venomous glare devoured her.

When she did not move, he took a threatening step. Immobile and blank-faced, she stood her ground. A slap sent her reeling.

Daar eased Kuparak's head to the ground, came to his feet, and strode forward. "Leave her alone."

The MasTer smirked. "You think you can best me? Do not put your desire to the test, Daar Palmira. I care less for you then a flea on a dog."

Fear for her friend and her uncle hit Rayn's subconscious with the force of cold water thrown from a bucket. She exploded into being, fought to keep The MasTer at bay.

Huddled Vasrosi, gasped.

The MasTer heaved her essence deeper. Strangling her in his hatred, he rose like a tsunami. Floundering in the cesspit of his loathing, Rayn experienced her conscious awareness flooding away. Masculine submerged the feminine. Brutalizing power trapped her in the total darkness of not being.

Rasiana slipped behind Tealin. *I will help you, Rayn. I promise.*

The MasTer's head came up. He scanned the crowd. She masked her mind and hid her essence in the restless, uncertain energy roiling around her.

"Kuparak is dead." Rayn's masculine voice boomed. "I am The MasTer. *I* am now the leader of the Vasrosi. The Pheet Adole have destroyed our home, killed those we love. Today we return the favor, beginning with the man who killed Kuparak."

A soldier held between two Vasro struggled. His captors shoved him forward. The MasTer caught him up by the front of his uniform and lifted him off the ground. "Unlike Kuparak, I kill to avenge and for revenge. I kill for the thrill of it. But you..." He set him down, forced him to his knees, and pulled Rayn's knife. Holding the soldier by the hair, he placed the blade on his cheek. "You will be my messenger to the Rompeer. You will tell him the Vasrosi now follow *The MasTer*. Every Pheet Adole we encounter will die. But before they do...man, woman, or child...we will mark their face as I mark yours."

The blade gleamed and split the cheek from the top of the ear to the jaw on both sides of the man's face. Quaking with pain, he choked back a scream and fell forward on his hands. The MasTer's grip on his neck kept him from standing. "You will crawl from my sight. Then you will to go to the Rompeer, delivery boy, and give him my message." He wiped the knife clean on the man's back and sheathed it. "Do you understand?"

The soldier's feeble nod inspired an answering kick in the ribs.

"I did not hear your answer, cur of El SyrTundi. Do you understand?"

"I understand."

"I cannot hear you. Speak Eleo Predan, the true language of El Stroma."

A pain wracked answer brought a sardonic smile to The MasTer's vulturine features. "You two." He motioned the Vasro captors forward." Escort this vermin to the end of the service road, then get back here."

A steel-hard gaze scrutinized the gathered crowd. Broad shoulders squared. He clutched the locket and yanked it from around his neck. A baritone voice rumbled, "I, The MasTer, am now your leader. You will never see Rayn again." The silver locket and chain sailed through the air and hit the ground some distance away. A savage scowl distorted his features. "Forget her! Follow me or leave and never return."

No one moved; no one spoke.

"Where is the man named Vygel?"

The leader of the Vasro raised a hand. "Here! My men and I are at your disposal."

The MasTer's charming smile made a fleeting appearance; then morphed into a stern, thin line. "You have no men, Vygel. They are now *my* men. *You* are *my* man. Agree, or leave."

Vygel pushed his way through the small crowd. "We are yours to command."

"VasRo, make sure that truck never makes it to VenTra. I want The Box and the SorTech brought back here. Vasrosi set up a perimeter around the center."

Men and women scattered. The MasTer glared down at Daar. "Are you with me or against me?"

"I will fight with you."

Rasiana heard the flatness in the answer and held her breath.

"Good. Arrange for the cremation of the dead. And make sure the area looks deserted. Come, Vygel. I would learn more of your thoughts on how to destroy El SyrTundi."

They strode toward the office building.

Rasiana joined Daar. "Will we ever see Rayn again?"

Daar pulled his attention from the retreating figures. "I don't know. I need Rangi to spy for us. I know you made a complete tour of the area when you arrived. Suggestions?"

She made a quick mental review of the low building. "There's an air vent in the office wall. Your tukoolo will fit. If we remove the outside grid, he can get in."

"Give me a minute. Umbba and Watuli despatch tukoolos to keep watch. Don't get caught. Tealin supervise the building of funeral fires on the beach."

While they conversed, Rasiana sprinted to the place the locket had landed. She found it lying open in a clump of weeds. The faces of Rethdun and Rayn looked up at her. Cradling it in her hands, she pressed it to her heart and looped the chain around her neck. "I will keep it safe, Rayn. I promise."

"Rasiana, let's go." Daar ran toward the office.

At the back of the building, they removed the metal grid and sent Rangi into the ventilation system. Daar tipped his head. "Good. We're tethered. Now I have a surprise for you."

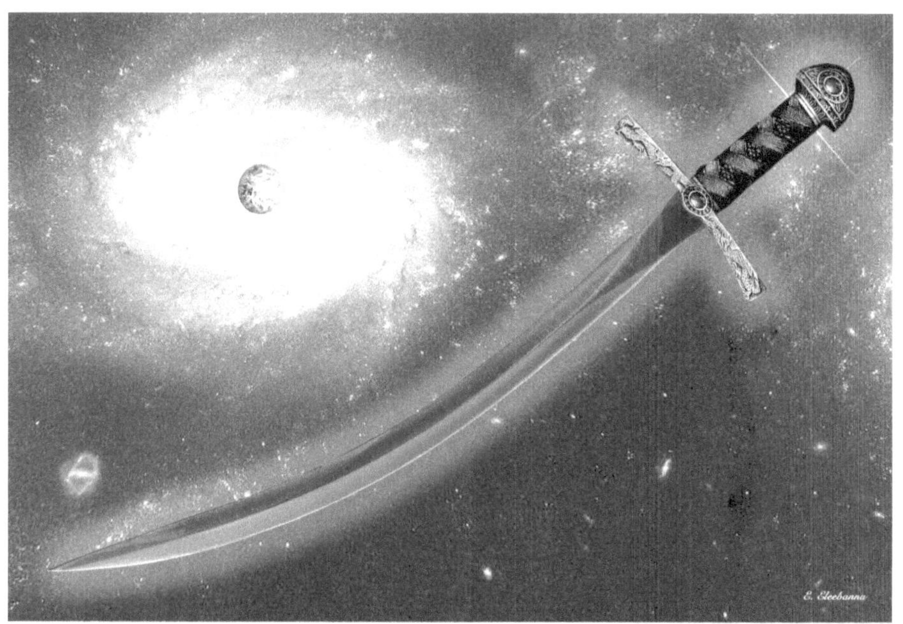

42

Hurrying to keep up with Daar, Rasiana double-timed his long stride across the tarmac and into the blistered warehouse. *Capese* undulated into view. The cargo bay doors gapped open. Daar climbed the ramp, led the way to a small cabin, and knocked.

A gravelly voice answered. "Come in, Daar Palmira."

Daar ushered her in ahead of him. Her heart leapt. Aquila perched on a cot in front of a thin, stoop-shouldered man whom Rayn knew and admired. White hair framed fading brown eyes narrowed in concentration. Gnarled fingers worked with meticulous care on the tuckoloo's mechanical wing.

Tazio glanced up. A wide smile formed beneath a nose much too big for his narrow Pheet Adolan face. "Good to see you, Rasiana." His attention return to the galee. With slow precise movements, he made several minute adjustments and sat back. "Wing's almost as good as new. Nioka is working with the ship's engineer. She'll finish the job when she comes back."

Rasiana glanced at Daar and back at the royal jewelry maker. "Does Rayn know you're here?"

Tazio made careful notes in a small black notebook before running a hand over Aquila's mechanical wing. "No. We arrived just ahead of the Rompeer's men. Kuparak hid us here. We'll miss him." Careful fingers stretched the wing open and folded it back into place. "Now, Aquila, show me how it works."

Rasiana moved nearer. "How do you know its name?"

"It shared it. After all, Nioka and I saved its life and rebuilt its injured side."

Aquila's wings opened wide and fanned the air. A soft whistle accompanied their return to place.

"Good. I've done what I can do. Nioka should be here soon. She'll fine tune the new attachment. You're a lucky bird."

Rasiana sat on the cot. "Thank you, Tazio, for saving Aquila. You know about The MasTer?"

"Kuparak informed us. He was hoping we'd be able to remove the personality from Rayn's psyche. Now that it has taken over again..." The old man shook his head.

A slender woman a bit shorter than Tazio stepped into the cabin. Long, white hair framed an angelic, fine-lined face. Specks of gold glinted in jade green eyes. Her smile warmed the room. She offered her hand. "It's good to see you, Rasiana."

Rasiana clasped the hand. A rush of images left her breathless. "You're Keelyn's sister."

A solemn nod. She released the hand. "Daar and Tazio, I know you have things to do. Let me see to Aquila, and then Rasiana and I must talk."

Nioka explained as she worked. "With The MasTer holding Rayn's personality at bay, Tazio and I decided it would be best if I inserted a new silica chip at the base of Aquila's brain stem to amplify its telepathic abilities. It will help us to monitor her alter ego."

"Kup told us there were no more shameenu on El Stroma?"

"I may be the last. Tazio has worked for the Rompeer's Courtesan's for many sun cycles. One of them warned him I was being watched. He let it be known I'd been killed, and we disappeared. We hid at Cimondeli for a short time. You know the soldiers discovered it?"

"I do. You told Kup Rayn might have trouble with a renegade personality. How did you know?"

She ran a hand over the coverlet on the cot. Her expression grew distant. "She carries the ancient memories of two families. Jacy's family had a couple of unsavory souls who created drama for everyone around them. It is not unheard of for these unsettled personalities to reappear in future generations. Fisaco, The MasTer's personality, caused decades of unrest between the Thornlandian and Charnlandian cultures. A lust for power, a desire to be adored, a need to control manifested in his dysfunctional personality."

"How can we help Rayn control him?" A wave of hopelessness washed over her.

Nioka patted her knee. "Do you have the gift I gave you when you visited in Tahellive?"

Rasiana withdrew a small disc on its on a flesh-colored chain. "You didn't tell me much about it when you gave it to me."

"All things in their correct time, Rasiana. When Tazio and I made the birth-mates' lockets, we added magnetite to act as a magnetic compass, a point of contact. Your disc is also magnetite. It will help you to awaken Rayn." She touched a spot behind Rasiana's left ear. "When The MasTer is asleep or unaware, press it here. It will stimulate a psychic switch and bring Rayn to the surface. Make sure The MasTer doesn't learn you have it."

Rasiana tucked the disc under her shirt. "I promise to keep it well hidden. Thank you, Nioka."

Umbba appeared in the doorway. "The tukoolos have reported in. The Pheet Adole have been taken care of. It's time to honor our dead."

Vygel's plans to destroy El SyrTundi made Rasiana sick to her stomach. Fascinated by Pheet Adolan technology, he had made good use of his time at Cimondeli and studied everything he could get his hands on. As a result, he had concocted a blend of chemicals to poison the planet's water systems. An additional chemical added to the mix would ignite everything it touched. His calculations indicated that the most damage could be rendered when Alkina went direct after its next retrograde cycle. In addition to seeding the clouds, canisters equipped with humidity and pressure sensitive detonators were hidden in strategic positions throughout El SyrTundi. When the climate reacted to Alkina's return to a prograde orbit, the canisters would dump chemicals over the entire continent.

Rasiana observed the preparations with an aching heart. The MasTer and Vygel chose to disregard the wind and the potential it would carry the chemicals over El QuilTran. Life on the planet of El Stroma would be obliterated.

Keelyn had stressed the importance of knowing one's enemy. Rasiana, therefore, observed The MasTer whenever circumstances provide an opportunity. It wasn't long before she realized Fisaco's personality lacked Rayn's shameenu gifts.

Hurrying to Nioka's small cabin, she shared her discovery and asked why this was so.

The shameenu explained, "If Rayn had shape shifted to a form of her choosing, her abilities would have transitioned with her. The MasTer, a separated and distinct personality who rose by overpowering Rayn, can only access his own talents."

Unable to tether to a tukoolo for protection, Fisaco shaped an ossifrage, one of the largest and most dangerous birds on El Stroma and led small groups in forays against the Pheet Adole living between VenTra and Chunarrie. Word soon spread. Much to his delight, he became know as the Nightmare from El QuilTran.

For two moon cycles, Rasiana bided her time as he luxuriated in his power and wallowed in his menacing reputation. He studied SorTechory and practiced its tenets with a fervor frightening to behold. When he slept, a rare occurrence, he slept behind a locked door in a cabin aboard *Capese*. Vygel prepared and served meals which were tasted in Fisaco's presence before he picked up a fork. The MasTer was quick to punish and slow to compliment. With the exception of Vygel, his followers learned to keep their distance.

Rasiana's hope of releasing Rayn weakened by the turning. She lost interest in food and could not sleep. One turning, Daar took over *the watch* and sent her to see Nioka.

The shameena observed her with a mother's concern. "How can you hope to help Rayn if you are worn out and starving?" She set a plate in front of her. "Eat every bite. Alkina goes retrograde in seven turnings. With luck, Fisaco will burn himself out and need to sleep soon. You are Rayn's hope. You have to be ready."

"And what of Aquila. Can't it help its compeer?" She chewed a tasteless bite and considered spitting it out. One look at Nioka, and she swallowed.

The shameena's gentled features hardened. "Aquila cannot help, Rasiana. Until The MasTer sleeps, like you, Rayn's compeer can do nothing."

From that turning forth, Rasiana reported to Nioka at mealtimes. At night, she drank a sleeping draught. The return of her physical and mental energies revitalized her hope.

Excitement on the ship escalated as Alkina neared the end of her retrograde cycle. Arrangements were checked and double checked. Captain Cammoll and his crew were put on alert.

Then the unthinkable occurred. Vygel discovered Nioka, Tazio, and Aquila and informed The MasTer. Fisaco's fury sent everyone scurrying for cover. Tazio, Nioka, and Daar were thrown off the ship. Clothed in a shield of invisibility, Rasiana watched Taze and Styn drag them to the bottom of the ramp and shove them to their knees. Vygel carried Aquila, masked and trussed, and flung the tukoolo after them.

With the echo of the doors clanging shut, Rasiana's hope fizzled. She slipped away and gathered her things from Nioka's cabin. A brief mind touch brought her up short. Oha fluttered from its hiding place and landed on her shoulder. Their tether formed. *"Don't worry. Headed to VenTra to join Katareen."* The tether withdrew. Determination blossomed.

The door sliding open sent Oha back into hiding. Moora, the *Capese*'s Roahymnian science officer entered and put a finger to her lips. Gesturing for Rasiana to follow, she jogged down the companionway. Rasiana hastened after her with Oha clinging to her shoulder. When they reached the engine room, they descended to a level of the ship Rasiana had not visited before.

Moora slid a panel in the wall aside and handed her a battery pack and a hand lantern. "He's on the war path and wants your head. Stay put. I'll let you know when it's safe to come out."

Rasiana crawled into a cubby hole barely big enough to sit and lie down in and whistled for her tukoolo. Oha fluttered to the mat beside her. The panel closed. Footsteps retreated. A distant hatch clicked shut.

Switching on the lantern, she looked around. In a box to one side, she found packages of snacks and a water pouch; on the other side, a bucket and wipes. "Well, Oha, it looks like we're not the first ones who have needed a hidey hole." She stretched out, tethered to her tuckoloo for protection and slept.

Rayn haunted her dreams. Together they wandered the dusk of not being, the place where soul and heart waited to connect. Emptiness stretched in all directions——no sound...no color...nothing tactile...nothing aromatic. Formless and unformed, Rayn's essence floated beside her, her vitality and life force trapped by The MasTer and The Box.

Rasiana awoke with a jolt. *The Box! What if I can get it to work against him?*Nibbling on a cracker, she considered her moment of inspiration. *I can't get near it.* She snapped a second cracker in two. *I bet Moora can help.*

What seemed like sun cycles later, the panel moved aside and Moora's face appeared in the opening. "Pass me the bucket. I'll empty it. You'd better get out and stretch while you can. We lift off in the morning."

Rasiana pushed her chamber bucket out, crawled onto the deck, and stood up. "How long have I been in there?"

"Almost two turnings. The MasTer and Vygel are off the ship so you can relax. I'll be right back." She picked up the bucket and made her way down the narrow walkway.

Rasiana stretched and paced, glad to be moving. When Moora returned, she hurriedly joined her. "Where does Fisaco keep The Box?"

"In his quarter's. Why?" She set the bucket next to the panel

"Since you're helping me, I'm assuming you are not in his camp."

Moora nodded. "Correct."

"Do you know anything about The Box?" Rasiana rubbed her chin." How it works?"

"No but Danza, our engineer might. He's always been curious about SorTechory. He befriended the SorTech, poor man."

Rasiana swallowed. "Poor man?"

"After The MasTer learned everything he could from him, he slit his throat and left his body on a nearby beach for the animals. Fisaco is a nasty piece of work. Sure wish we could free Rayn. Let me see what I can discover." Her com-button hummed. "They're back. In you go."

The panel had barely closed when the sting of SorTechory rocketing through her mind curled Rasiana into a fetal ball, hands clutching her head. Oha landed on her shoulder. Their tether connected in slow motion. Its completion brought tears of relief. She could only hope The MasTer had not sensed her initial reaction. If he did, she hoped he couldn't track it.

The tingling current continued its search. Rasiana imagine Rayn's alter ego in wading boots standing in the center of a river, the graceful casting of the line a rhythmic hunt for his prey. Out and back and out and back…She pressed her hands against her ears. Oha nibbled her fingers and crooned. Her body relaxed. She sat up and rubbed her compeer's breast. The searching energetic fingers withdrew. Tears leaked down her cheeks. Oha drank them like nectar, its beak and tongue as gentle as a kiss.

The ship trembling propelled Rasiana from a light sleep to wide awake. The electrical power source whined. Repeated shuddering shook *Capese.* Weightlessness hit her ears with a thrumming throb and equalized. Oha jumped to her knee, its frightened squawked drowned in a rhythmic clamor of metal on metal. The shuddering ceased.

They had only been underway a short time when the panel slid open. Moora waved her out. "Hurry. Danz managed to adjust a couple things in The Box. The MasTer is out cold in his quarters. Vygel is busy in hold preparing to dump chemicals on El SyrTundi."

They left the engine room at a run. When they reached, the companionway to The MasTer's cabin, Umbba waved them forward. "Better not waste a moment. Vygel and his buddies could be back at any time."

Rasiana shut the hatch and withdrew both the locket and the disc from beneath her shirt. Kneeling, she slip the locket around The MasTer's neck. A shudder shook the inert body. When the disc touched the spot behind his left ear, he twitched and moaned. His eyes popped open. A hand reach for her, caught her by the elbow, and squeezed. Energy rocketing through him arched his back.

Rasiana held her breath.

Awareness hit Rayn like a shower of sparks blistering her skin. The hum of the moonstone locket vibrated the vast emptiness. She grasped at her consciousness, clung to it with the tenacity of a dog to a bone, fought The MasTer with all her strength. The power of the shift propelling her into her true form left her gasping for air. Her hand gripped an arm——Rasiana's. Relief turned her world into a spinning top.

Rasiana's voice reached out to her somersaulting mind. "Rayn. I'm here. You're back. Focus on my face. Breathe...in and out, in and out. That's right. Slow your breathing."

Tears spilled in a torrent down her cheeks. She reached up and touched Rasiana's face with trembling fingers.

Rasiana gathered her up in her arms. "I've got you, Rayn Jardee Palmira."

"Don't let me go, Rasi." Rayn gulped one panting breath after the other.

When the shaking stopped and her breathing calmed, Rasiana eased her to sitting. "How do you feel?"

Rayn clenched and relaxed her hands, stood up, paced to the hatch, and turned. "How long, Rasi?" She sank cross-legged onto the bunk.

"Over two moon cycles."

"How much damage has The MasTer done?"

Rasiana grimaced. "With Vygel's help, he's done quite a bit."

"Sounds like I have a lot to catch up on." Her brow furrowed. "I don't feel Aquila."

Rasiana sat facing her. "The MasTer threw him off the ship with Nioka, Tazio, and Daar. They managed to reach the cargo craft, the last one to leave El Stroma." Her face grew grim. "The MasTer was furious that they got away safely. Luckily, I wasn't within reach."

Rayn curled the fingers of one hand into a fist and stared at it.

Rasiana touched her knee.

"Don't worry, Rasi." She squeezed her friends hand. "I refuse to let anger bring him——"

The hatch door flew open. Vygel stepped into the cabin and gaped. "Where is he?" He rounded on Rasiana. "What have you done?"

Umbba filled the open hatch. "Tealin and I are here if you need us, Rayn."

She smiled. "Thanks. Give us a minute. Then I'll need to see the captain and be brought up to date." Rising from the bunk, she challenged Vygel. "There was a time, Vygel Vintrusie, when you made a promise to fight by my side. It appears, however, The MasTer has claimed your loyalty. What would you have me do? We have a long journey to make. I could use your support." All traces of the smile disappeared. Her eyes hardened.

Vygel squirmed, then lifted his chin in defiance. "You don't scare me, Rayn."

"I'm not *him*, Vygel. I don't use fear tactics to control those who work with me. What I can't have is you and your gang causing problems. You have a choice. You can join me, or you will be restricted to a specific area of the ship." She moved to the hatch. "Think about it and let me know. I'm sure The MasTer won't mind if you stay in his quarters for a time. Rasiana and I need to see the captain."

Anger clamped Vygel's mouth shut.

Rayn followed Rasiana into the companionway and closed the door. "Tealin, keep him contained until I get back. Umbba, take Watuli and round up Vygel's followers for a meeting after I talk to Cammoll."

At the entry to the bridge, Rasiana chose to remain outside. Rayn step through. "Permission to enter the bridge, sir." Cheers of surprise and delight, escorted her to the captain's side. He clapped her on the back. "Am I delighted to see you!" He then grew serious. "Vygel dumped the chemicals to seed the clouds. Chemical rain falls on El Stroma. We can't go back."

Standing at his side, she watched her home planet growing smaller. "Where will we go?"

"Kuparak intended us to make for TreBlaya, a small planet in the Inner Universe. It's close to the DéCussate and has a small humanoid population. He felt it would be a good place to rest and regroup. Sound alright to you?"

Rayn sighed. "It sounds just fine. How long will it take?"

"This is an older craft, but Danza is a great engineer. He's given us jumper capability, so I'd estimated four to six moon cycles at the most with a couple of stops for supplies."

He drew her across the bridge to a small office and faced her. "I need to know if you can keep *him* contain?"

Rayn met his candid gaze. "I *will* keep him contained. If he even begins to raise his head, I'll inform you. Promise me you will lock me in the brig."

"It's a promise. And Vygel?"

She continue to meet his eye. "You are the captain and this is *your* ship. Do what must be done."

"Good." He crossed the office. Withdrawing a red bundle from a storage locker, he placed it on the desk. "Kuparak asked me to give this to you if anything happened to him." He handed her a small rectangular box. "This is a recorder. It will explain. Just push the green tab." He moved to the hatch. "I'll give you a little privacy. Join me on the bridge when you're ready."

A quiet thud left her alone. Emotion left her shaking. "Oh, Kup, I'm sorry. I know you never intended to betray me." She folded back the red satiny cloth. A trembling hand went to her heart, then hovered above a curved black sword with a ruby gleaming in the hilt. She pushed the recorder's tab.

"Rayn, if you are listening to this, it means I am not there to present the sword to you in person. It is the Thornlandian Sword of Truth. Keep it close to you. It will help you to ascertain the honesty of those with whom you must do business. Tell Rasiana to hide it if The MasTer takes over. When you make the return journey to El Stroma, take it to El QuilTran. It will help you bring our homeland back to life."

S he listened a second time and place the recorder on the desk. "I miss you, Kuparak. I wish you were alive and here to help me resist The MasTer." She touched the locket." I wish you'd had time to tell me where Rethdun is. I promise to find him and all the Eleo Preda who are related to us, so I can take them back to El Stroma."

Her fingers wrapped around the sword's hilt, she heft its weight and tested its balance. Holding it up in the light, she gazed at its elegant shape. *Someday, I'll take you home to the land of my ancestors. Someday I will walk again on the continent of El QuilTran. Someday...*

D eep in Rayn's subconscious, The MasTer waited. When Rayn's anger once again overwhelmed her, *he* would be ready...

—

E. Eleebanna

And the story continues . . .

GLOSSARY LINK

A searchable glossary for the
VarTerels' Universe™ is available online at:

www.skrandolph.com/glossary

ACKNOWLEDGMENTS

It takes a village to write and illustrate a book.

I learned early that the more eyes on my manuscripts the better.

As a writer, my brain sees what it expects to see on the page, automatically filling in missed words, grammar mistakes, spelling issues... The list goes on. Those who spend the time proofreading my drafts are vital!

As a digital artist a critical eye on my chapter headings, book covers, and maps helps me to correct the things my artist's eye misses.

I acknowledge the following people with gratitude:

A special thank you to Linda Lane, my editor and mentor, who over the years has stood by my side. Her in-depth critique of my work always raises it to the next level. I can't imagine doing what I do without her.

Ann McEntire, my beta and proofreader, finds the little stuff better than anyone I know. Thank you for sticking by me and always being honest.

A huge thank you to Tom Krantz, the Captain of our boat, whose range of experience and talents make him a multitask master. He not only formats my books for paperback, hardback, and eBooks, manages my website and my newsletter, publishes my novels, and critiques my work, both written and graphic, but he also is my personal support person.

To Madison Stocker, Courtney Krantz, Jared Olmsted, Sean Krantz, Charles Lawrence, Guy Molnar, and Lela Paultre: A very special thank you for allowing me to use your images to represent characters in my illustrations.

Although I prefer to use my own photography to create my digital art, I don't always have the breadth of material and visuals required. I thank all the talented artist who contribute the original images to www.pixabay.com, www.stock.adobe.com, and nasa.gov for the supplemental photos that allow me to create detailed illustrations for my novels.

ABOUT THE AUTHOR

FROM DANCE STAGE TO WRITTEN PAGE

STORYTELLER

Dance, humanity's most ancient narrative art, captivated S.K. Randolph as a child living and dancing in the British Crown Colony of Bermuda. After graduating from the University of Utah with a BFA in Ballet, her dance career spanned four decades of performing, mentoring, teaching, choreographing, and directing. Over sixty of her original choreographic works were brought to life for theatre audiences around the globe, establishing her deep foundation in pacing, movement, and narrative structure. She was the Ballet Mistress of the Colorado Ballet and the Alberta Ballet as well as cofounder of the Bermuda Dance Theatre. For the last two decades of her dance career, she educated the next generation of creatives, as Director of Dance at Interlochen Center for the Arts, named the "#1 Best High School for the Arts in America", and at St. Paul's School.

S.K. at the helm of her forty-foot boat leaving Seattle, Washington on a transformative seventy-five day voyage up the Inside Passage to Sitka, Alaska. Then a decade writing while living afloat swinging on the anchor rode in one remote Alaskan cove or another. 2010

DIGITAL ARTIST

S.K., a pioneer in the digital art sphere, has been creating original digital art since 1997. Utilizing a unique, self-taught technique, she transforms photographs into vibrant, otherworldly masterpieces using Adobe Photoshop. Today, her VarTerels' Universe™ series features nearly 500 of these hand-crafted digital illustrations.

VOYAGE TO WRITING

In 2010, S.K. retired from the dance world to live with her partner on their boat in the world's largest temperate rainforest along the remote and rugged coast of Alaska. Isolated in nature, she spent a "gap decade" afloat honing her writing, refining her digital art style, and mastering shipboard skills (including catching dinner). It was during this creative voyage that she transitioned her storytelling from the dance stage to the written and illustrated page, self-publishing her first novel, *DiMensioner's Revenge*, in 2011.

TODAY

Now, in 2026, S.K. is currently writing the twenty-first installment of her saga. She and her partner reside in the lower-48 states, living on the side of the largest flat-top mountain in the world. From her mountain studio, she continues to cultivate her "Illustrated by the Author" Science Fantasy series, VarTerels' Universe™, dedicating her life to the timeless journey of a true storyteller.

S.K.'s website
www.skrandolph.com

Facebook
facebook.com/skrandolph11

Substack
skrandolph.substack.com

An epic science fantasy saga told through art and words
in companion shorts and illustrated novels,
available as paperbacks and eBooks.

Illustrated by the author, color in eBooks
and black and white in paperbacks.

Presented in suggested reading order.

DiMensioner's Revenge

Illustrated by the Author
VarTerels' Universe™ Book 1
Part I - UnFolding
Novel
642 pages, 73 illustrations

Four young people from a regimented city discover their destiny when they journey to Myrrh—the hidden remnant of Old Earth—only to find themselves hunted by a vengeful DiMensioner, his death shadow, and alien mercenaries determined to destroy everything they've come to cherish.

Available as a paperback with black & white illustrations and eBook with color illustrations.

Gifts

VarTerels' Universe™ Book 2
Part I - UnFolding
Novella
34 pages

A pregnant art student must deceive a ruthless surveillance state about her twin daughters' true father, the brother of a powerful Guardian, or become the perfect hostage in a deadly political game.

Available in the paperback *Agothany 1* and as an individual eBook.

Discovery

VarTerels' Universe™ Book 3
Part I - UnFolding
Novelette
32 pages

Fourteen-year-old Torgin must choose between protecting his passion for music and spying on the only friends who understand him in a dystopian city where the government controls every aspect of life.

Available in the paperback *Agothany 1* and as an individual eBook.

Rescue

VarTerels' Universe™ Book 4
Part I - UnFolding
Novella
31 pages

In a dystopian city where surveillance is constant and conformity is mandatory, twin sisters Ari and Brie must navigate secret portals and evade ruthless patrollers to rescue a lost boy and return him home before their forbidden act lands them all in the dreaded Five Towers.

Available in the paperback *Agothany 1* and as an individual eBook.

ConDra's Fire

Illustrated by the Author
VarTerels' Universe™ Book 5
Part I - UnFolding
Novel
504 pages, 59 illustrations

Kidnapped to a hostile desert planet, Esán must survive while his friends race to rescue him, unaware that their rescue mission will unleash ancient powers and reveal family secrets that could destroy three worlds.

Available as a paperback with black & white illustrations and eBook with color illustrations.

Encounters

VarTerels' Universe™ Book 6
Part I - UnFolding
Novella
29 pages

When a vengeful DiMensioner forms an unholy alliance with a death shadow to steal a legendary crystal and destroy the Guardian who banished him, he discovers that the children he saves along the way may hold the key to his own redemption—or his ultimate damnation.

Available in the paperback *Agothany 1* and as an individual eBook.

Metamorphosis

VarTerels' Universe™ Book 7
Part I - UnFolding
Novella
31 pages

Wrongfully banished from his home planet and left disfigured by a catastrophic magical accident, Laurent must shed his arrogance and accept his broken reflection before he can master the ancient art of dimensional magic and discover his true purpose.

Available in the paperback *Agothany 1* and as an individual eBook.

MasTer's Reach

Illustrated by the Author
VarTerels' Universe™ Book 8
Part I - UnFolding
Novel
686 pages, 60 illustrations

As the UnFolding reaches its climax, teenagers wielding legendary artifacts must evade deadly hunters across multiple worlds while uncovering shocking truths about The MasTer's identity and a centuries-old conflict that threatens to destroy the Eleo Preda people forever.

Available as a paperback with black & white illustrations and eBook with color illustrations.

Wanted

VarTerels' Universe™ Book 9
Part I - UnFolding
Novella
33 pages

A fugitive with a dark past escapes prison only to discover he's being hunted by a powerful mystical league that wants to control his untapped ability to bend reality itself.

Available in the paperback *Agothany 1* and as an individual eBook.

Jaradee's Legacy

Illustrated by the Author
VarTerels' Universe™ Book 10
Part I - UnFolding
Novel
336 pages, 51 illustrations

Separated as children during a brutal genocide, birth-mate twins Rayn and Rethdun must survive across galaxies while carrying the genetic legacy that could save their dying civilization or destroy them both.

Available as a paperback with black & white illustrations and eBook with color illustrations.

Agothany 1

An anthology of
the Companion Shorts
*Gifts, Discovery, Rescue Encounters,
Metamorphosis,* and *Collision*
in VarTerels' Universe™
Part I - UnFolding
256 pages

Available as a paperback.
Each Companion Short also
available as an individual eBook.

Incirrata Secret

Illustrated by the Author
VarTerels' Universe™ Book 11
Part II- CoaleScence
Novel
428 pages, 45 illustrations

Racing against ruthless enemies across mystical dimensions, the Universe's youngest VarTerel and a prophesied leader with legendary eyes must rescue kidnapped mentors from a cloud-shrouded island where a phantom octopus guards secrets that could reshape their world—or destroy it.

Available as a paperback with black & white illustrations and eBook with color illustrations.

Lessons

VarTerels' Universe™ Book 12
Part II- CoaleScence
Novella
26 pages

On the desert planet of DerTah, blind oracle WoNadahem Mardree must overcome devastating loss and her deepest fears when a mysterious shape-shifting DiMensioner arrives seeking knowledge, challenging everything she believes about fate, power, and love.

Available in the paperback *Agothany 2* and as an individual eBook.

Corps Stones

Illustrated by the Author
VarTerels' Universe™ Book 13
Part II- CoaleScence
Novel
438 pages, 52 illustrations

A young VarTerel and her friends journey to 1969 New York City to recover three stolen Corps Stones before their entire solar system collapses into chaos.

Available as a paperback with black & white illustrations and eBook with color illustrations.

Fishing

VarTerels' Universe™ Book 14
Part II- CoaleScence
Novella
30 pages

A twelve-year-old boy with extraordinary powers must survive slavery, betrayal, and the relentless pursuit of a deadly league that murdered his parents and will stop at nothing to control him.

Available in the paperback *Agothany 2* and as an individual eBook.

Duplicity

VarTerels' Universe™ Book 15
Part II- CoaleScence
Novella
30 pages

A sworn protector with shapeshifting abilities and a future Guardian destined to unite worlds must outwit a ruthless League of sorcerers determined to claim her before she can fulfill her destiny.

Available in the paperback *Agothany 2* and as an individual eBook.

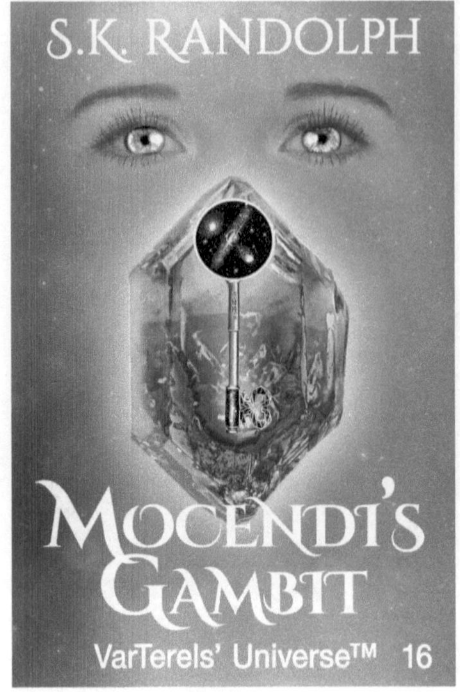

Mocendi's Gambit

Illustrated by the Author
VarTerels' Universe™ Book 16
Part II- CoaleScence
Novel
328 page, 35 illustrations

Stripped of her protective Star of Truth and held captive aboard an enemy ship young VarTerel Brielle AsTar must trust an unlikely ally—a former enemy seeking redemption—and escape through folded time before The MasTer's followers destroy everything she loves.

Available as a paperback with black & white illustrations and eBook with color illustrations.

Destiny

VarTerels' Universe™ Book 17
Part II- CoaleScence
Novella
32 pages

Brielle AsTar, the youngest VarTerel in the Inner Universe, must hide her genetically engineered babies and their surrogate mother from ruthless spies while battling a dangerous gene threatening to resurrect an ancient evil.

Available in the paperback *Agothany 2* and as an individual eBook.

Cimondeli

VarTerels' Universe™ Book 18
Part II- CoaleScence
Short Story
12 pages

Sixteen-year-old Desty has never seen the sky, but when she ventures beyond her underground refuge for the first time, she discovers her telepathic gifts, befriends a majestic flying lizard, and learns that healing a poisoned world may begin with bridging the divide between enemy tribes.

Available in the paperback *Agothany 2* and as an individual eBook.

Queen's Quest

Illustrated by the Author
VarTerels' Universe™ Book 19
Part II- CoaleScence
Novel
420 pages, 44 illustrations

A young VarTerel, a bearer of cosmic seeds, a musical genius, and a street-smart boy with magical spectacles must unite their extraordinary powers to shatter an impenetrable dome, defeat a rogue demi-god, and complete a universal cycle before time runs out.

Available as a paperback with black & white illustrations and eBook with color illustrations.

Collision

Prequel to VarTerels' Universe™
VarTerels' Universe™ Book 20
Part II- CoaleScence
Novella
64 pages, 14 illustrations

A genius physicist barely out of university must lead a team of Galactic Guardians wielding ancient instruments of power to rescue Earth from total annihilation, even as enemies from his past conspire to ensure the planet's destruction.

Available in the paperback *Agothany 2* with black & white illustrations and as an individual eBook with color illustrations.

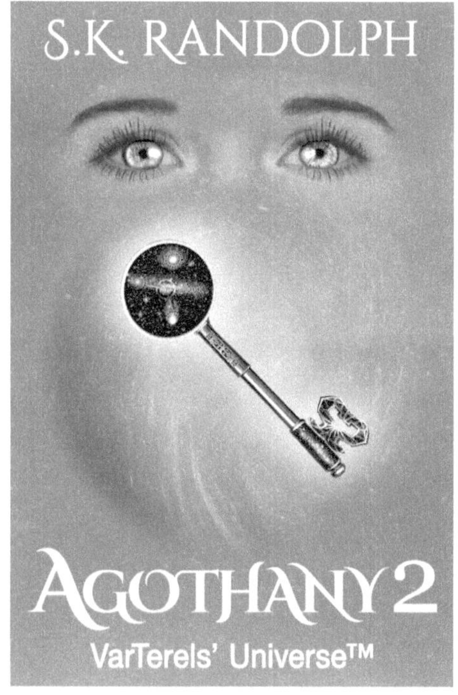

Agothany 2

An anthology of
the Companion Shorts
*Lessons, Fishing, Duplicity
Destiny, Cimondeli,* and *Collision*
in VarTerels' Universe™
Part II - CoaleScence
284 pages

Available as a paperback.
Each Companion Short also
available as an individual eBook.

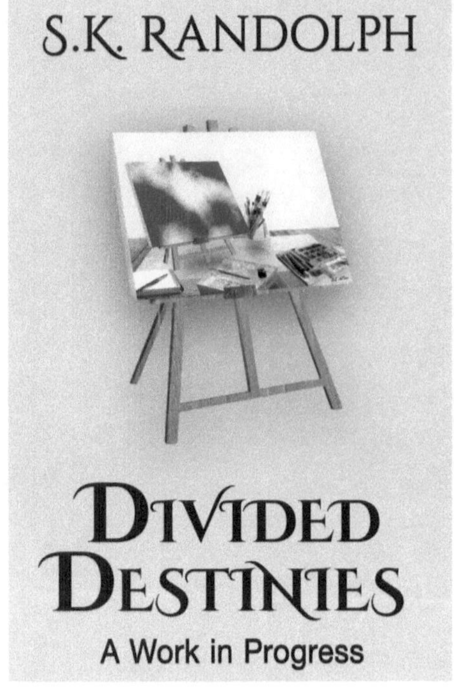

Divided Destinies

Illustrated by the Author
VarTerels' Universe™ Book 21
Part III- QuicKening
Novel
a Work In Progress

Divided Destinies is a work in progress with a targeted release date of late 2026. An illustrated novel, it starts QuicKening, Part III of the VarTerels' Universe™.

See www.SKRandolph.com for current status and subscribe to S.K.'s newsletter to receive progress updates.

www.ingramcontent.com/pod-product-compliance
Lightning Source LLC
Chambersburg PA
CBHW061114310726
48974CB00002B/526